# FAREWELL TO THE
# WHITE COCKADE

*by*

## JANE LANE

FREDERICK MULLER LIMITED
LONDON

FIRST PUBLISHED IN GREAT BRITAIN IN 1961 BY FREDERICK MULLER LIMITED
PRINTED AND BOUND BY
HAZELL WATSON AND VINEY LTD.
AYLESBURY AND SLOUGH

TO
DOUGLAS A. SCOTT
*who has never abandoned*
*a good cause*

*Farewell to the White Cockade* is a brilliant and authentic reconstruction of the life of Bonnie Prince Charlie from the time of his escape from Scotland, in 1746, until his death forty-two years later, when the adored young hero who, with seven men, had set out to recover his father's throne, had become a sick and lonely old man.

With deep compassion Miss Lane traces his fortunes as he roamed the courts of Europe, ever seeking to accomplish his life's purpose. Used as a pawn by kings and politicians, dogged by assassins, spies and duns, he grows reckless to the point of outraging his conscience by apostatising from his religion; but always, through hope deferred and bitter disappointment, clings desperately to the one driving aim to which he had devoted himself in youth.

Against the background of eighteenth-century Europe, drawn with the consummate craftsmanship with which Miss Lane's readers are so familiar, are living portraits of Charles Edward's contemporaries, the men and women who played their part in shaping his tragic destiny. Dominating this crowded canvas are the four characters who had the greatest influence during his latter years: his difficult brother, his emotional mistress, his hard-headed baggage of a wife and his devoted natural daughter.

Here is a very human and superbly-written tragedy of a prince who, for all his faults and failings, remains to this day "King of the Highland hearts". The title is taken from a Gaelic lament which expresses the undying love he inspired in the men who shared with him the epic

desire
the L
in the

ura
al

As I walked across the hill
On Sunday, and a friend with me,
We read together a letter's news—
No joyful tale we gathered there.

Many a hero, mighty, brave,
Today in Scotland mourns for thee,
In secret are they shedding tears
Who keenly would have followed thee.

Each hill-slope and mountainside
On which we ever saw thee move,
Now has lost its form and hue
Since thou ne'er shalt come again.

Farewell to the White Cockade,
Till Doomsday he in death is laid,
The grave has ta'en the White Cockade,
The cold tombstone is now his shade.

From *An Suaithneas Ban*, a contemporary Gaelic lament for
Charles Edward Stuart, 1788.

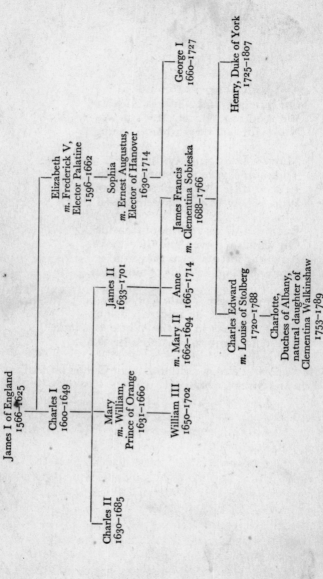

James I of England
1566–1625

Charles I
1600–1649

Charles II
1630–1685

Mary
m. William,
Prince of Orange
1631–1660

James II
1633–1701

Elizabeth
m. Frederick V,
Elector Palatine
1596–1662

Sophia
m. Ernest Augustus,
Elector of Hanover
1630–1714

William III
1650–1702

m. Mary II
1662–1694

Anne
1665–1714

m. James Francis
1688–1766

Clementina Sobieska

George I
1660–1727

Charles Edward
m. Louise of Stolberg
1720–1788

Henry, Duke of York
1725–1807

Charlotte,
Duchess of Albany,
natural daughter of
Clementina Walkinshaw
1753–1789

With the descendants of Henriette Anne, youngest daughter of Charles I, and with those of two elder children of his sister Elizabeth (not shown), there were fifty-seven persons with a better claim to the throne of Great Britain than George of Hanover in 1714.

# PART ONE

## 1746 – 1750

## HENRY

## ONE

### I

HENRY, Duke of York, was the first to receive the news. It was October 11th. He was returning from a concert of sacred music at the Opera House in the Palais Royal, to the Hôtel de Sens, a gloomy old mansion rented to him cheap, in the Place de l'Ave Maria. As he stepped down from his carriage in the courtyard, an officer, in a stained French uniform bespattered with mud, approached.

"Colonel Warren!" exclaimed Henry, apprehension in his voice.

The last time they had met, six months previously, Warren had brought him the news that all their hopes had been destroyed on the fatal field of Culloden.

He took the Colonel by the arm, hurried him into his private apartments, and closed the door. But before he could stammer out a question, Warren cried joyfully:

"I bring your Royal Highness news of a miracle—no less! I landed the Prince, your brother, safe and sound at Roscoff, near Morlaix, yesterday afternoon. He sent me express with this letter to your Royal Highness."

Henry took the letter in an unsteady hand, and gazed at

it for a moment as though doubting its reality. Since Culloden there had been nothing but rumours, horrible rumours. It had seemed impossible that Charles could escape capture, with half the British Army and Navy hunting him through the mountains and round the coasts of Scotland. But he had. Here was the familiar dashing scrawl, so different from Henry's own neat handwriting.

'Dear Brother, as I am certain of your great concern for me, I cannot express the joy I have, on your account, of my safe arrival in this country. . . .'

He sat down by the fire, forgetting the presence of Warren. He felt as weak as when he had caught a fever at Avignon last autumn. The untidy scribble swam before his eyes, so that he had to dash his hand across them before he could read on.

'I enclose here two lines to his Majesty, just to show him I am alive and safe, being fatigued not a little, as you may imagine. You must write immediately to the F.K., giving him notice of my safe arrival, excusing my not writing myself on account of fatigue. *It is absolutely necessary*'—these words were heavily underlined—'I must see the F.K. as soon as possible, for to bring matters to a right head, and you must arrange it, consulting only Colonel O'Bryen. I embrace you with all my heart, and remain your most loving brother, Charles P.R.'

The shock was so great that it was not until he was alone late that night that Henry could analyse his emotions. It was the hour he devoted to his private prayers; he was as pious as a monk, was the young Duke of York, sneered Paris, which had little use for piety. But tonight, instead of kneeling at his *prie-Dieu*, he paced up and down his bedchamber, this short, rather heavily-built young man, whose long upper lip deprived his mouth of humour, and whose habitually sweet and gentle expression concealed a passionate temper and an obstinacy inherited from his Sobieski mother.

Under his genuine joy and thankfulness at the news that Charles was safe, he was uneasily aware of the flickering up of an old jealousy. It dated from the year 1734, when he was only nine, and he had been refused permission to accompany his elder brother to the siege of Gaeta. He had flung his little sword away in a rage, and his father had punished him by removing his Garter ribbon; Henry could not wear one without the other, quietly remarked King James. Charles had returned from the siege covered in glory, everyone praising his rash courage, his coolness under fire.

Yes, seeds of jealousy had been sown then; and the melancholy exiled Court in the Palazzo Muti in Rome had been an all too fertile ground for their cultivation, a Court of petty little cliques. And sometimes the saintly King, who passed more and more of his time in his religious devotions, resigned to exile though punctilious in his efforts to retrieve his rights, would talk to his younger son, lamenting that his dearest Carluccio, as he always called Charles, should be encouraged to an independence of his father, should entertain such rash ideas for winning back the lost throne.

But jealousy had deepened into a sense of injury when, on a January night of 1744, Charles had vanished from Rome. For he had deceived his brother; he had arranged with Henry to go on a boar-hunt at Cisterna; when Henry arrived for the appointment he had been met with the story that Charles had sprained his ankle, but would join him presently. It was a lie.

Disguised as a groom, Charles had galloped through the Gate of St John at midnight, doubled, found post-horses provided by the Spanish Ambassador, Cardinal Acquaviva, ridden breakneck for Massa and Genoa, slipped through the English fleet at Antibes, and only when he had landed safe in France, having neither slept nor taken off his clothes for five days, was Henry told. A tempest had destroyed the great French invasion fleet that year, but it had not shaken Charles's resolution. Refusing to return to Rome, or to tell father or brother his plans, he had skulked in a wretched lodging in Montmartre; until like a thunderclap had come

9

the news that with only seven companions he had sailed for Scotland.

King James had received the news with a groan, but Europe had applauded the young hero, and so, quite genuinely, had Henry. Henry had pawned his jewels to help his brother, had badgered his father for permission to follow Charles, and when the King refused unless he went with a strong French force, the young Duke had come to France to implore Louis XV to keep his solemn promises. But the news from across the Channel, news which at first had been of a succession of brilliant *coups*, of the deeds and victories of a fairytale hero, had turned suddenly to a tale of retreat, followed in due time by the death-blow of Culloden. Louis would do nothing.

Sick with disappointment and anxiety, Henry had lingered in France. He could not go home to Rome, not until he knew for certain his brother's fate. Captured or dead, it must be one or the other. . . . But it was neither; a miracle had happened; Charles was alive and free and safely landed in France.

Henry knelt down to say his prayers, his conscience at ease. Of course he was devoted to his brother, and had outgrown all foolish childish jealousies. If there remained a faint shadow on his joy, it was only that he shrank from the sordid business of plot and counter-plot, of trying to enlist reluctant aid, of whispered plans, of treacherous hopes which always ended in nothing. Charles had made a glorious bid for their father's lost throne; let it end there—in romance. One must grow up and accept hard facts. One must seem (only seem, Henry told himself) to reject principle for expediency; or rather one must accept outward events, however apparently unjust, as the finger of God. . . .

'*It is absolutely necessary* I must see the F.K. as soon as possible, for to bring matters to a right head, and you must arrange it. . . .'

Henry sighed sharply. It was clear that Charles refused to accept hard facts. Charles had every intention of renewing his humiliating petitions for aid from King Louis, careless of snubs and slights. To Charles the wrong of yesterday could never become the right of today.

### 2

From two o'clock until half-past four in the afternoon, the streets of Paris were ordinarily deserted by all save the lower people, the quality being at dinner. But on the afternoon of October 17th, 1746, there was such a block of coaches and chaises and sedans, besides pedestrians, that the whole of Paris seemed to be abroad. The *bourgeoisie*—doctors, lawyers, merchants, bankers, the better sort of tradesmen—for once were united with the *canaille* in their determination to welcome the most popular young man in Europe.

Only the nobles and their ladies were absent. There was to be no official welcome; King Louis had made that plain; and therefore one could not, however eager and curious and admiring one was, witness Charles Edward's entry into Paris. Not if one wished to remain in a perpetual house-party at Versailles, the shudderingly horrible alternative to which was being banished to one's country estates.

Henry had driven out a few miles along the road to Morlaix to meet his brother, and he was astonished by the crowds. The stock-jobbers and the brokers had deserted the Bourse, the old-clothes vendors their pitches under the colonnade of the Louvre, writers and artists their cafés, the women who sold coffee and cordials their street corners. Flourishing hats, fluttering handkerchiefs, they jostled for a sight of the hero, besieging his carriage, begging for bits of the rags in which he had landed for relics, their lively voices yelling continually:

"*Vive le Prince Edouard!*"

"That was indeed a royal welcome!" exclaimed Henry, when after a final appearance on the balcony of the Hôtel de Sens, his brother closed the window and flung himself down in a chair.

Henry talked on nervously; he felt oddly shy of this stranger who was his only brother. He had scarcely known Charles when they had met on the road, he laughed; he had grown not only taller but fatter—

"All the good food I've been having these past six months, and the idle life I've been leading," Charles interrupted dryly. "By the way, Harry, you'll have to speak up a trifle; I have a slight deafness due to a fever."

He waved aside, with a touch of impatience, Henry's exclamations of distress; he had always hated talking about his health. Henry had been touched by the warmth of his greeting when they met, and every now and again Charles would jump up from his chair to embrace his brother. But for all his affection, he remained a stranger. The youth of his face gave to his expression of fixed and desperate resolution a deep pathos, and it seemed suddenly to Henry that that expression was both fated and fatal.

And even in his outward appearance and habits Charles had altered. He had always been hardy and active, sleeping on a chair in his riding-coat so that he might be up at two in the morning to hunt or shoot. But now he seemed to the fastidious Henry to have lost all sense of refinement. One must make allowances; he had been living very rough these last six months; but surely it was not necessary either to smoke so foul a cutty-pipe or to sit down to supper in a disreputable tartan plaid which had an ill smell hanging about it.

"I have an Indian nightgown you would find more comfortable," suggested Henry. "They are all the rage now for undress."

"It's free from lice if that's what you fear," replied his brother, referring to the plaid, and causing Henry to wince. And then, his voice vibrating with passion: "I hope in God to walk the streets of London in it yet, this good plaid that was my only covering many and many a night in the

12

heather. Don't you think, Harry," he went on with unconscious wistfulness, "that God Almighty has made this body of mine for doing some good? In Italy very often the sweat would come through my coat with the heat; and yet in Scotland, in piercing cold and drenching rain, and exposed to every hardship, I found I agreed equally with both."

"You don't *look* very well," observed Henry, "and I have noticed that you limp."

"Oh, dysentery, and my feet cut to bits in my wanderings, and my legs ulcerated, but it's nothing at all," Charles replied airily.

Something of an epicure himself, Henry had been at great pains to provide a supper worthy of the returned warrior, including the champagne which King Louis had made the fashion; and he was rather hurt to observe that Charles did not seem to know what he was eating, gulped down the champagne as though it were *vin ordinaire*, and seemed to have forgotten not only his table manners but the observance of his religion.

"I hope you find this eel and gudgeon stew to your liking. I am sorry I cannot offer you any of this roast; since my fever last year, my physician has forbidden me to abstain on maigre days, and today is unfortunately a Friday."

"A Friday?" echoed Charles, looking blank.

"I suppose you were not able to observe abstinence and fast days during your travels?" enquired Henry, bent on making allowances.

His brother stared at him for a moment, then burst into a hearty laugh.

"I observed as many abstinence and fast days these past six months as will suffice me for the remainder of my life, Harry," he chuckled, reaching over his brother for a slice of the roast.

It seemed the moment to ask to hear the tale of his romantic adventures, and Henry settled down eagerly to listen. But to his astonishment and chagrin Charles absolutely refused to name persons or places.

"But don't you trust me?"

"When it comes to shielding those who are still in peril for aiding me, I will trust no one, not even you. I will not even name their names in my own thoughts, lest inadvertently one should slip from my tongue. Harry," he said, abruptly changing the subject, "what fortune have you had in arranging an audience with the French King?"

Henry's voice took on a defensive note as he answered. He had done his best. He had applied to Colonel O'Bryen, King James's accredited representative in Paris, and he himself had written personally to Louis; but his Most Christian Majesty had replied that a period of Court mourning for the death of the young Dauphine prevented him from giving audiences at present. Chattering on because he was nervous, Henry embarked upon a description of an audience Louis had granted the Duke himself last year.

"You will scarcely credit it, but he forgot all about it until half-past six in the evening of the appointed day. Then in a violent hurry he sent for the Duc de Gesvres, and bade him summon 'the Prince'; but de Gesvres did not know which prince, nor where to find me, and it was against Court etiquette to ask for further information. At last he found me where I had been waiting a full hour in a small closet below stairs."

He grew pink with mortification as he went on to describe the audience, the appalling moment when Louis had hesitated to kiss him, Louis's obvious boredom, his silence while Henry stressed his brother's brilliant prospects, the zeal of his Scottish adherents, the vital need for the promised French support.

"It was the longest half-hour in my life," groaned Henry, "and at the end of it his Most Christian Majesty forgot to send someone to show me out, so that I nearly lost myself in that vast palace. He has always been completely ruled by his women, first those three sisters, and now this daughter of a common prostitute, she whom he has created the Marquise

14

de Pompadour. France is losing all respect for the Monarchy——"

"The Marquise de Pompadour," interrupted Charles, meditatively puffing at his pipe. "She's still the reigning mistress, is she? Then she'll be the one to court."

Henry was stricken dumb with horror. His brother, obviously unaware of his feelings, went on with desperate urgency:

"I'll get an audience somehow, and a private one, Harry, don't you fear. I must. All through my wanderings I kept myself sane and cheerful only by holding on to my resolve to get back to France and force Louis to honour his solemn promises. And I have you to stand by me, God bless you; I knew you'd be here, I knew you'd never go back to Rome while I needed you."

He rose, and with hands blackened from exposure gripped his brother's shoulders, smiling down on Henry from his superior height. Henry, troubled anew by his air of concentration on a single driving purpose, murmured feebly:

"You must be greatly looking forward to sleeping in a comfortable bed."

Charles smiled absently, thinking of the only comfortable bed he had slept in during six months' skulking in the heather. Kingsburgh House; dear Mrs Macdonald carefully folding the sheets next morning; they were to be laid away in a kist, she told him, until they served as grave-clothes for herself and Flora.

## 3

Showing his brother to the bedchamber so carefully prepared for him, making sure he had all he required, Henry's bewilderment and faint uneasiness increased. He had offered Charles the services of some of his own gentlemen for his undressing, but Charles had brushed aside the offer with a laugh.

"I have Iain Beag. He knows my ways. No ceremony at present, Harry; I'm too damned tired to put on the prince again for a day or two."

The man he referred to as Iain Beag did not commend himself to Henry. His real name was John Stewart; he was a very little man, as his by-name implied, and while following Charles about like a dog, he treated him with what Henry considered a very improper familiarity. He seemed half savage, with his matted hair, his frequent lapsing into the Gaelic, and a way he had of diving his hand under his coat as though to snatch out a dirk when any stranger came near his master.

"You really seem to love these poor Highlanders," murmured Henry, remembering how one of the first things his brother had asked him when they met that day was whether Henry had provided lodgings for the ragged companions who had shared in the escape.

Charles rounded on him almost fiercely.

"Love them! When they left home and country at my bare word, when they followed me into a land they hated and where they are despised as barbarians, when for six months any starving homeless man among them could have earned thirty thousand pounds for betraying my hiding-place. Love them, by God!"

Even more disconcerting was Charles's manner as he prepared to go to bed. Snatching up a candle he searched the room, pulling aside hangings, throwing open the doors of cupboards. Seeing Henry's astonished look, he laughed and said gruffly:

"The habit of the hunted. I think I shall never be able to lay it aside."

He had asked if there were certain herbs in the house, and now with his own hands began to stir a brew over the fire.

"I learnt to be my own doctor. Indeed my quackery was much admired." And then, abruptly: "Can you let me have a bottle of *eau de vie*, Harry? I take a dram sometimes when I can't—when I wake in the night."

16

Henry selected a bottle with care, handling it reverently, reciting its pedigree. He was puzzled by the enigmatic smile with which his brother listened; but then all his bewilderment and uneasiness vanished as Charles embraced him, hugging him like a boy.

"Dearest brother," murmured Henry, "all my prayers are answered. Every day I have committed you to the care of Our Blessed Lady and your Guardian Angel; I cannot tell you how many Masses I have had said for you, how many *novenas* I have made for your safe return. It is indeed a miracle, as even Colonel Warren admitted, and he a Protestant."

Sitting on by the fire, smoking a last pipe, Charles thought about his brother.

He must, he thought, be very patient. He must remember that Harry was only twenty-one, something of a hot-house plant, delicate in childhood, their father's darling, and, until her early death, the victim of their mother's hysteria. Queen Clementina had carried her nerves into the nursery, as Charles, five years Harry's senior, remembered only too well. For months together she had refused to speak to her husband in revenge for his wise refusal to let her meddle in politics, and Harry had been much under her influence.

But he was a good lad. How eager he had been to follow his elder to Scotland . . . yet not so eager as to slip over from Dunkirk one dark night last year. He, Charles, had been in exile again only a few days, and already the Duc de Richelieu had hastened to tell him about Henry's refusal of Richelieu's suggestion that the Duke should try to slip past the English fleet.

No, he must not think of that. Save for some of their womenfolk, the Stuarts, unlike the usurping Guelphs, had always been a united family. It was unwise, as well as unfair, to criticise Harry. They truly loved one another; and he must remember that Harry had never come up against the stark realities of life. He had never starved or frozen, never been hunted like a fox. He had never (monstrous thought!) crawled with lice.

And never, thought Charles, his hand going out to seek the bottle of brandy, has he endured the kind of nightmares, waking and sleeping, which make a man find his only relief in drink.

He slept at last the deep sleep of exhaustion, while Iain Beag, rolled in his plaid, lay like a watch-dog across the door.

But even in that heavy sleep he heard the crackle of flames from burning villages, the shrieks of fugitives roasted alive in a barn, the groans of wounded packed into a gaol without food or water, the thud of whips on human flesh, the laughter of soldiers relieving themselves into a ship's hold where dead and dying were lashed together, the voice of Butcher Cumberland bawling:

"Laws, by God! I'll make a brigade give laws!"

He woke sweating and moaning and sprang from bed, calling to dead comrades, listening for the feet of the hunters closing in upon his latest hiding-place.

# TWO

## *I*

HIS Most Christian Majesty, King Louis XV, descended the stair from his Petits Cabinets, with his Persian cat draped like a shawl around his shoulders and the silken skirts of his nightgown rustling on the polished wood. He administered a slight kick to the recumbent form of the First Valet in Waiting to inform him that he was about to get into the State Bed in which he never slept; and there lay listening in comfort to the preparations for the Lever.

It being a fiction that King Louis had lain here all night

instead of in the arms of the Pompadour, and was still soundly asleep, the First Valet tiptoed into the anteroom and dressed himself, summoned pages who noiselessly opened the shutters, removed the Night Cupboard and replenished the fire, and presently, with three genuflections, approached the bed and announced:

"Sire, the hour has struck."

Holding a gilt basin under his Majesty's hands, the First Valet poured over them a ewer of perfume, while the Lord Chamberlain stood ready to hand him a prayer-book from which he would recite the Office of the Holy Ghost, and the First Lord of the Bedchamber ushered in the barber with a selection of wigs from which his Majesty would choose the one he would wear that day. As he recited the prayers to himself, it suddenly occurred to Louis that today he had honoured Prince Charles Edward with an invitation to the Petit Lever.

Louis's rosebud mouth pursed with disquiet. Cardinal de Tencin had persuaded him to this because Paris championed the cause of the Prince. Though Paris, four miles distant from Versailles, was almost a foreign town to Louis, who never went near it if it could be avoided, he feared its weapon of ridicule expressed in its popular songs, its salons, theatres, and cafés. "What are the frogs saying?" he would ask; and he had been known to dismiss a Minister if 'the frogs' expressed too marked a displeasure of him.

So he had consented to receive this awkward young relative of his. He was always inclined to the course which promised the least amount of trouble, and here in his State Bedchamber he would be barricaded by etiquette. Formal compliments would be exchanged, and that was all. Firm orders to Charles had accompanied the invitation; he must come strictly incognito and on no account must he wear his Orders.

Louis closed the prayer-book, thrust his feet out of bed for the First Valet to put on his slippers, and leaving the rail which surrounded the great bed, walked to his armchair before the fire, where the Chief Cellarer presented him with a cup of sage-water. A relay of ushers, stretching to the door, repeated in a whisper to one another and at length to the First Gentleman of the Bedchamber the names of those who had been accorded the supreme privilege of assisting at the Petit Lever, and who were waiting in the anteroom.

Charles was cheerful as he mounted the Marble Staircase at Versailles, accompanied by a somewhat nervous Henry and an officer of the Maison du Roi.

He had come incognito because he knew he would not be received unless he did, but he had come in full splendour, in a rose-coloured velvet coat and black satin breeches, hired for the occasion, and with the Garter and Thistle blazing on his breast. Paris had lined the road to applaud him, as it did whenever he showed himself out of doors, and as he passed through the long series of apartments all opening out of one another, he was conscious of admiring eyes upon him. He was fully aware of his vivid personal charm, and used it like a weapon.

Through the Salon of Diana, filled with orange-trees perpetually in bloom; through the War Salon, where in the painted ceiling Louis the Sun King trampled his foes beneath his charger's hooves, while Victory, Valour, and Renown walked meekly at his bridle-rein. Through the Salle, where his Majesty dined in public, and where the officer escorting the two Princes made a profound obeisance to a silver dish in the shape of a dismasted ship in which, upon a perfumed cushion, reposed Louis's napkin, guarded by two colonels.

Through the Galerie des Glaces, where their reflections paced beside them in the three hundred and six great mirrors. A lady passed them in a flying-armchair borne by liveried footmen.

"Madame la Marquise de Pompadour," discreetly whispered the officer.

Through the Oeil de Boeuf, thronged with petitioners,

with great nobles who stood about here from morning till night waiting to get a word or even a nod from the King whose personal servants they had become. And so to the anteroom of the State Bedchamber, that sacred ground on which only the Princes of the Blood, Ambassadors, and distinguished visitors might tread. An usher whispered to one of his fellows inside the door:

"Monsieur le Baron Renfrew and Monsieur le Comte d'Albanie," and performing a reverence which brought his periwig an exact number of inches from the floor, passed Charles and Henry on into the Bedchamber.

Louis had reached an intricate stage in his dressing. The Page of the Wardrobe had handed to the First Valet of the Wardrobe his Majesty's stockings; the Master of the Wardrobe and the First Valet of the Bedchamber had taken hold of the right and left arms respectively of his Majesty's nightshirt and pulled it off. The dayshirt, already warmed at the fire, had been handed by the Second Valet to the Lord Chamberlain, who had passed it on to the Dauphin, who had presented it to his Majesty on his knees; and now, while the First Valet of the Bedchamber held the right sleeve, and the First Gentleman of the Bedchamber the left, the Master of the Wardrobe pulled his Majesty's breeches over his shirt and tucked it in.

Charles had a sudden almost irresistible desire to laugh. Controlling himself, he walked straight up to his royal kinsman, bowed low, and before Louis was aware of what was happening had given him the embrace sacred to Royalty. There was an instant's frozen silence; then, very naturally and cheerfully, Charles said:

"Monsieur mon oncle, I render your Most Christian Majesty my most hearty thanks for your courtesy in putting at my disposal your Castle of St Antoine. I shall do myself the honour of accepting your Majesty's kind hospitality until such time as I may lead another expedition to Great Britain."

There was another silence, broken only by the Clockmaker who at this stage of the Lever went round winding up all the clocks and his Majesty's watch. Then the stout, short young Dauphin stepped forward, and regarding in great admiration the tall manly figure in the rose velvet, embraced Charles. His Majesty murmured something, looking at himself in the mirror a page was holding while the Grand Master of the Wardrobe put on his sword, his blue riband studded with pearls worth a million livres, and the diamond cross of St Esprit.

An atmosphere of acute embarrassment settled down on the Bedchamber. Louis never knew what to say to anyone who was not his intimate, and it was his habit to become absolutely dumb, to the agitation of his courtiers who knew that such dumbness often heralded one of his malicious tricks. Charles, however, seemed quite at his ease, standing there in front of the King's armchair, upright and soldierly, his well-built frame hardened by war, his fair hair, combed over the toupee of his wig, emphasising the deep tan of his face.

He spoke of Louis's war against the usurping King George, "your Most Christian Majesty's foe and mine." He again congratulated his Majesty upon the great French victory of Fontenoy, and after a graceful compliment upon his Majesty's generalship, went on in that direct, forthright way of his:

"Under God, and your Majesty, those who turned what threatened to be a defeat into so brilliant a victory were the Irish soldiers in French service. My father's subjects, exiled for their devotion to his cause. I rejoice that they served you so well, Sire, but now I beg you most earnestly that you will release them to fight under me. I implore your Majesty to consider that by upholding the justice of my claims, you will be putting yourself into a position to achieve a stable and lasting peace, the sole object of the war in which you are now engaged."

Louis made no reply, but with his toe stroked the cat to

whom the Third Valet of the Bedchamber had just presented (on his knee) a silver dish of cream.

"Your Most Christian Majesty cannot fail to remember that immediately after my victory at Prestonpans last year, the Elector withdrew regiment after regiment from his army in Flanders, thereby enabling your Majesty to overrun the Austrian Netherlands with the greatest of ease. One good turn, Sire, surely deserves another; and I cannot fail, with the greatest respect, to remind your Most Christian Majesty that according to the treaty of alliance signed between your Majesty and my royal father's envoys before I left for Scotland, you undertook to aid me."

" 'As far as is practicable,' " quoted Louis, breaking his long silence. He shot Charles a covert glance from his big black eyes. He had always been exceedingly childish, and took extreme delight in scoring a point. He added graciously: "Monsieur le Baron, when I go to hunt at Fontainebleau, you must give me the pleasure of your company at the chase."

"I beseech your Majesty from my heart," cried Charles, clenching his hands, "to grant me a private audience. I have that to say to your Majesty which can be said only in your private ear."

"Alas," sighed Louis, "a King of France must never be alone for one single instant of the day or night. It is a species of slavery, I assure you, Monseigneur; but we are all God's slaves," he added piously, taking his place in the little processsion which waited to conduct him to the privy, before those who had only the privilege of the *entrée de la chambre* were admitted for the conclusion of the Lever.

## 2

Henry could scarcely believe his eyes when, only a week later, his brother showed him a note, written by Louis's own hand, inviting Charles to a *petit souper* at Versailles.

"I feel sure you owe this to the influence of the Queen,"

23

he decided. "It is not only that she is our cousin, but she is goodness incarnate, a shining light of virtue in this pagan Court. The King merely fulfils his Easter duties, and though matters are not quite so bad as in the late Regent's time when, I'm told, the Regent actually read Rabelais between the covers of a prayer-book during Mass, yet that old lecher, the Duc de Richelieu, made fun of me because he noticed how I never pass an altar without genuflecting—like a sacristan, as he termed it."

Henry, poor innocent, fervently believed in the influence of a good woman: but it was certainly not Marie Leczinski who was responsible for this invitation to Charles. Louis had tired of her very soon after their marriage, and in 1738 had broken off marital relations; she had no influence at all. No, it was the Pompadour who had persuaded Louis to invite Charles to this *petit souper*.

Like Charles himself, Jeanne-Antoinette Poisson had one driving purpose in life; in her case to keep her royal and difficult lover from being for one instant bored. One after the other he had become bored by her three aristocratic predecessors, and for a year now, she, the first bourgeoise mistress of a King of France, had fought might and main to stabilise the position they had forfeited.

She had enemies in plenty. In the streets of Paris the hungry populace called down curses on this 'blood-sucking upstart from the gutter', and sang the virulent songs called *poissonades*. At Versailles even great men like Maurepas, Minister of Marine, and the Marquis d'Argenson, Minister for Foreign Affairs, did not disdain to bribe some of her sixty attendants to listen at keyholes, to fumble in drawers, to bore little peep-holes in her bedchamber door, ears pricked for some indiscretion that could be used against her, spiteful tongues whispering of the number of aphrodisiacs the Pompadour took to overcome her naturally cold temperament.

But the enemy the Pompadour feared more than these was Louis's terrifying habit of discarding Ministers and

24

mistresses simply because they bored him. She gave herself no respite in her war against this boredom; she changed her gown a dozen times a day, learnt whole scenes from the latest comedies to recite to Louis in some pause in his sexual ardours, invented new dishes, new games, anything to amuse him. Thus always desperately on the look-out for a fresh diversion which could ward off for an hour the thing she dreaded most in life, the sight of Louis's rosebud mouth opening in a yawn, she had seized on the romantic escape of Prince Charles Edward.

"It would be quite diverting, Sire, to hear at the first-hand of some of his adventures, which I'm told surpass those of a classical hero." And she added slyly: "I hear that these savage people among whom he has been have certain burial customs which will amaze your Majesty."

Knowing her Louis, she had struck the right note. His Most Christian Majesty had a morbid obsession with death and could never hear of a funeral without demanding exact details of the sickness, decease, and burial of the departed. And there would be no question of his being pinned down to honour past promises made to this awkward, but possibly useful, young Prince. The Pompadour excelled in never prolonging a conversation beyond the point when conceivably it might pall on her lover, and she had acquired the habit of herself indicating when distinguished visitors were to take their leave.

Of all this was Charles ignorant. His astonishing campaign in the previous year had misled him into believing that his refusal to take no for an answer could win over the most evasive and the most lukewarm of friends. He believed, too, that though Louis seemed unfit by temperament to shoulder responsibility, and was always at the mercy of any Minister who would relieve him of it, he could be brought to the point of being shamed into honouring his sworn word. Moreover, Charles supposed that if there were a third person present at this *petit souper* it would be Cardinal de Tencin, the real director of French policy, who, while he owed his political ascendancy to his notorious sister who had been the late Regent's mistress, owed his Hat to the patronage of King James.

Once again in a hired suit, the rent of which had cost him 1,500 livres he could ill afford, he set forth in high spirits to Versailles, and from one official to another at last was handed over to Le Bel, the King's confidential valet, the keeper of all his sordid secrets. They passed through the State Bedchamber, where the valet bowed to the ground before the empty bed, up a private stair, and into those apartments known as the Petits Cabinets, but to Parisians as 'the rats' nests'. Here not even the King's children were ever seen, and the most privileged courtiers entered by invitation only. Here the ushers and the pages must be blind and deaf and dumb if they hoped to retain their offices.

But Le Bel led him up an even more secret stair, and as they ascended, Charles became conscious of the heavy scent of flowers and *pot-pourri*, and of the sound of many singing-birds. He realised with distaste that the third person present at this vital interview would not be Tencin but the Pompadour. He had said airily to Henry that it would be necessary to cultivate the Pompadour, but, essentially the outdoor man and the soldier, already he found the intensely feminine atmosphere oppressive. Sisterless, his childhood overshadowed by his mother's faintings and hysteria, he had always been shy of women, only the more so because they had a habit of falling instantly and intensely in love with him.

Well, he must do his best, he thought, wrinkling his nose at that overpowering perfume, pulling his flared coat-skirts away from tables overloaded with Sèvres elephants and porcelain monkeys, speaking a word to an indifferent Persian cat in a jewelled collar lying in a chair wide enough to accommodate a lady's huge panniers, wondering how any man could feel at ease in these intimate little rooms all painted in baby blues and pinks, with pictures of masked ladies crooking their fingers at silly youths disguised as shepherds prostrate at their feet.

He had a sudden vivid wounding vision of grape-coloured hills against an ivory sky, smelt the heather, and heard the barking of seals and the lost cry of gulls wheeling over a Highland loch.

Louis greeted him graciously, and, safe here from prying eyes, gave him a royal embrace. He liked this young kinsman so far as he was capable of liking anyone, and Charles remained potentially useful since he could always be used as a bugbear in Louis's quarrel with England. The Pompadour sank into a graceful curtsy, experting kicking her little train out of the way; and while compliments were exchanged, Charles observed her, wondering if she were friend or foe.

She was certainly decorative, with her dazzlingly fair complexion set off by one large black patch, her beautifully rounded figure, her captivating smile which revealed perfect teeth. But she betrayed her origins in her affected speech, and above all by her thinking of everything in terms of money.

In the intimate dining-room, from the windows of which could be seen one of the wonders of the world, Le Nôtre's gardens, the Pompadour hoped that their guest was enjoying a certain omelette.

"I invented the recipe myself. Partridges' and pheasants' eggs preserved in snow are its principal ingredients, and its cost is twenty-five gold louis."

Six hundred francs, thought Charles, outwardly making the right response. He could have done with them for his starving followers. And then he thought of the butter with cows' hairs in it, the oatmeal mixed with sea-water, the flounders caught with bare hands and half cooked over a smoky fire, which he had eaten during his wanderings. They had tasted better than this expensive omelette, for they had been seasoned with comradeship and devotion.

"We are going to Fontainebleau next week," the Pom-

27

padour prattled, while Louis ate in silence. "The move will cost us one hundred thousand livres. I am always telling his Majesty that we live too dear. If you can credit it, Monseigneur, her Majesty's Keeper of the Wardrobe receives nearly three thousand livres a year, his sole duty being to transport her Majesty's trunks when she travels—which she never does."

"I rejoice that his Majesty has been so blessed with material goods," Charles replied dryly. "It was very largely through lack of financial resources that my late expedition failed."

Louis appeared absorbed in the delicate operation of peeling a grape, and made no comment. The servants had withdrawn, and, his long sunburnt fingers stroking the stem of his champagne glass, Charles resolved to put his cards on the table.

"What I have to say to your Majesty in particular is this," he began abruptly. "That the brutalities of the Duke of Cumberland and the punitive measures of the usurping Government against my father's faithful subjects, will be the ruin of Scotland unless I can return immediately with twenty thousand regulars. As for any measures for my own personal benefit, I want none, and if suggestions have been made for them they have not come from me. All I ask is military aid against a foe who has outraged every rule of civilised war, and who is France's enemy as well as mine. Most of the Highlands joined me when I landed with but seven men. Throughout my campaign, I met with only one defeat in battle——"

"But that, alas, a fatal one," murmured Louis, speaking for the first time in ten minutes.

"It would not have been fatal, it would not have been a defeat, if France had sent me the aid she promised me. Such few of my father's subjects in French service who were sent to me under Lord John Drummond were sent too late, and when they came they had positive orders not to cross the Border into England."

Louis said nothing, but reached for another bunch of grapes.

"I implore your Majesty to believe me that it is not only the winning back of my father's throne that concerns me now. It is the fate of my comrades-in-arms. Cumberland's temper was ferocious enough while I was still victorious. Not daring to put to death the prisoners he took, because I had so many of his, he encouraged the country people to murder them. But since Culloden he has turned the Highlands into one vast shambles."

For the first time Louis betrayed some interest. He pressed for details. Charles gave them to him straight between the eyes.

"Actual orders have been issued to destroy the country. The little pitiful crops are burnt, cattle driven off, the very shell-fish on the shore destroyed so that the people might have no food of any kind. It is the Massacre of Glencoe on a national scale. The innocent suffer with the guilty; peaceful men have been shot in the back while they worked in the field, pregnant women have had their homes burnt over them, girls have flung themselves into the flames to escape the lust of a savage soldiery. A wounded Highlander imprisoned in a cellar escaped by the aid of a poor woman and her son. The son was lashed to death, the mother incarcerated in a dungeon in such a position that she could neither lie nor sit. Cumberland kicked downstairs a provost who protested against the cruelty with which his fellow countrymen were being treated. After Culloden, the Butcher, as even his own party call him, amused himself by compelling local women to strip naked and ride races for his diversion . . . do you want me to go on?" he cried; and the wine-glass snapped in his clenched hand.

"Come, come, Monseigneur!" protested the Pompadour, with a quick glance at Louis. "You are making the King look quite bilious."

"You are newly escaped from death," remarked Louis,

29

"and such a horrid one." He shuddered elaborately. "I cannot understand why you are so eager to court it again."

"Death!" Charles cried with passion. "Would it not be better to die at the head of such brave men as I found in the Highlands, than drag out my life in exile and dependence? For what use was I born but this? Since I was a boy I have hardened my body, learnt to live rough and to bear fatigue, for *this*—only and always for *this*! I had, as I knew without vanity that I had, the gift of leadership, the soul of a military commander. I proved it. In every strategy and tactic in which I was not hampered by a Council, I was right, and I was victorious. All I lacked was military and financial support, the support, Sire, I was most definitely and solemnly promised."

"The promises of kings," remarked Louis, giving a tremendous yawn, "are, alas, dependent upon international circumstances for their fulfilment. You are, if I may say so, my dear cousin, very young, and unversed in the sordid ways of diplomacy. A reigning monarch is in the hands of his Ministers by whom he must be guided and advised unless he would rule as a tyrant, and must needs put aside his personal feelings and affections."

This was sheer bluff, and they both knew it. Charles made an impatient gesture.

"Sire, shall we fence without the masks? It is known to all Europe what solemn promises were made me, not once but many times, before I sailed to Scotland——"

"I beg Monseigneur's pardon," the Pompadour interrupted hurriedly as Louis gave another yawn, "but I fear his Majesty is somewhat fatigued. If you would care to see the little distillery and the jam-making room his Majesty has fitted up here for my diversion——"

She broke off, suddenly frightened by that set white young face across the table.

"My great-grandmother was a Daughter of France," Charles said thinly. "In my veins runs the blood of Henri le Grand. Though my father is an exile and I a fugitive, I

have a claim to the aid of France in regaining my just rights
—aid, I repeat, promised me on the word of a king. Your
Majesty mentioned just now what you were pleased to term
the sordid ways of diplomacy. Does diplomacy look only to
the present? When I have regained my father's throne——"

"Ah, when!"

Charles winced as though struck across the face by a whip.

"His Majesty and I," said the Pompadour, giving a nervous flutter with her fan, "would be so charmed to hear of
the romantic adventures experienced by you, Monseigneur,
before a French ship most happily rescued you from death,
adventures, we are told, almost as surprising as those which
befell your great-uncle, King Charles II."

He looked at the pair of them lounging there, she, the
daughter of a petty official who had been obliged to flee to
escape arrest for embezzlement, with four rows of pearls
worth the price of an army round her white neck, and he,
the spoilt little boy who had never grown up. In an interval
of love-making and jam-making and changing their clothes,
they wanted to hear for their diversion the tale of 'romantic
adventures'. Charles seldom hated; but in that moment he
hated women, and he hated France.

"My great-uncle, King Charles II, madame, regained his
throne after eleven years of exile—and, so I remember,
without the aid of France. I shall regain my father's for him,
if I have to league with the Devil to do it."

This time Louis's yawn was so loud that Le Bel, who had
been listening at the keyhole, slipped in to announce that it
was time for his Majesty's official Coucher.

## 3

In his brother's cabinet in the Hôtel de Sens, a room
cluttered with statues of saints and holy pictures, Charles
waited impatiently for Henry next morning. He had to
wait an hour before the young Duke arrived home, and pacing restlessly about he noticed a letter addressed in Henry's

neat hand to their father in Rome. He thought nothing of it, and he was too much preoccupied to notice how Henry, directly he entered, swooped on the letter with a guilty air and whisked it out of sight.

"I am sorry to have kept you waiting, but it being All Saints I have attended High Mass at Notre Dame. Did you sup with his Most Christian Majesty? Did he———?"

"No, he did not," Charles interrupted shortly. "And to-day I have had a visit from another inhabitant of Versailles —that rogue and rascal, Tencin."

"Rogue and rascal!" gasped the horrified Henry. "He is a cardinal, Charles, a Prince of the Church."

"He could be the Pope and still a rogue. D'you know what he dared to suggest to me? After a lot of soft talk about France having her hands full and being encompassed by enemies on all sides, he hinted that she might yet be induced to lend me aid, on one condition. That as a compensation for the expense she would be put to, I would promise to cede Ireland to her if by her help I won back my rights."

He drove his fist into the palm of his other hand.

"I did not mince my words. I would rather see my country whole and intact under the rule of the Usurper, said I, than recover my own by dividing her. I want generous help, not a vile bargain. As though I didn't see his game! He would expect to be made Primate of Ireland, and get I know not how many new ecclesiastical benefices."

"I don't think you should speak in that way about a Prince of the Church."

Charles was silent a moment. Then he came up to his brother, and laid an affectionate hand on his shoulder.

"Look, Harry, I'm a Catholic as well as you, but there is no need to be such a fierce one. All this church-going of yours —it gives offence to his Majesty's subjects who are not of our faith. I realised well on my late expedition the handicap our religion is to us. In all my proclamations I took care to promise complete religious toleration, but that did not move the Lowland Scots nor the English. Anything—the National Debt, the hated Union, cruel taxation, a foreign usurper, the crew of jobbers who rule him, the German favourites—anything is better to them than a Papist on the throne."

"It was in this very quarrel that our grandfather sacrificed his crown," Henry retorted stubbornly. "With his dying breath he bade our father keep his faith against all things and all men."

"I know, I know. All I'm saying is that one can be a good Catholic without being fanatical about it. It is not a sin to be tactful; on the contrary."

"I can't help remembering how it grieved Mama (God rest her soul) when his Majesty made my Lord Dunbar, a Protestant, your Governor, and how he taught you to laugh at the custom of baring one's head at the sound of the Angelus."

"Well, don't let's quarrel about it," said Charles good-humouredly. "But by God, Harry, Tencin put me in a rage! When I had told him what I thought of the ceding of Ireland, he offered me as an alternative a French pension of 12,000 livres a month and a royal residence."

"And you refused it?"

"Do you think I would consent to become a pensioner of France? What effect would *that* have on my English adherents?"

"It is clear that France is all shifts and evasions, and will not honour her promises. Did I tell you about my audience last year when——"

"Yes, Harry, you did."

"Well, then, would it not be better to return home to Rome? You need a good rest after all your exertions."

"God damn it, you make it sound as though I've fought a wrestling match or something. Exertions! Rest! There will be no rest for me, nor for you, Harry, until we have conquered or died. And you must never speak of Rome as 'home'. We have but one rightful home, one only vocation . . . Harry, why do you look at me like that?"

Henry turned quickly aside, and began fiddling with the coloured markers in his missal which lay upon the table.

"It seems to me," he mumbled, "that it is far better to accept the situation. Clearly it is the will of God."

His brother sighed, half humorously, half in exasperation.

"You seem to be very intimate with the Almighty, Harry. But when you say the will of God, are you quite sure you don't mean your own comfort?"

"That is most unjust!" cried Henry, his swarthy face flaming.

"Yes, it was. I'm sorry. But mark well what I say about Rome. It is precisely what the Usurper's Government desires, to make us like our father pensioners of the Pope. Nothing could do our cause more harm—nothing! You are good, loyal, and loving, Harry, I know that well; but you are also very young and inexperienced. You have never been in England or Scotland. Those who were with me there, Lochiel, his brother, Dr Archie Cameron, old Gordon of Glenbucket, Colonel Sullivan, all agree with me that to accept a French pension or to return to Rome would be fatal to the prospects of another rising."

"Lord Elcho does not think so. When he escaped soon after Culloden he came to see me, and he told me you were deceived in thinking there would ever be the chance of another rising."

Charles frowned.

"Listen, Harry, you must be extremely circumspect in any dealings with Elcho. I curse the day I ever accepted him as a recruit; I think he joined me only as an investment. He is a man of fashion, which is to say he is a man of vice; he has a bad reputation for cruelty, for which I had to rebuke him on more than one occasion, for which reason he has taken a violent dislike to me. Above all, he is a mischief-maker."

"There are those you trust who are as bad or worse,"

34

grumbled Henry. For some reason he seemed determined to pick a quarrel. "This Father Kelly whom you chose as your confessor when you were hiding in Montmartre; everyone knows he is too fond of wine. And then there's the other Kelly, the old heretic parson; oh I know he spent thirteen years in the Tower for his loyalty, but they say he is given to swearing, and——"

He stopped. His brother had sat down beside him at the table and put an arm about his shoulders.

"If there are any among my people who have offended you, Harry, tell me what they have done and I will reprimand them, if necessary even dismiss them. But to accuse men on hearsay is unworthy of you."

He got up again and began to roam about the room, pausing once to open the door sharply and glance up and down the corridor. During his boyhood in Rome he had gained a lasting impression of the way in which Jacobite secrets were continually thwarted by spies, informers, and the indiscreet, and it had become second-nature to him to expect to surprise someone listening outside the door.

"I have been thinking," he said, returning to his chair and speaking low, "that this offer of a French pension might be transferred to you, when it would not be in the nature of a bribe. And that would enable you to marry. For while I concentrate on plans for another expedition, your duty is to provide for the Succession."

The Duke had started at the word 'marry', and now murmured significantly that he was not a marrying man. Either Charles did not hear or decided to ignore it, for he went on:

"I know our father has often said that while we are in exile it would be a jest to think we could have either a Daughter of France or an Infanta of Spain. Had I been victorious, I was determined to press for the hand of Madame Henriette, Louis's twin daughter, and since I do not agree with our father that we must look lower, I would have made over my suit to you now. But I hear she is dying, literally dying, poor lass, with love for the Duc de Chartres who, for political reasons, her father won't allow her to marry. Well, we shall see. He's been blessed with a large family of girls, thank God. Be often at Versailles, Harry; if you can't find it in you to court the Pompadour (and after last night I could not blame you), make your addresses to the Queen and the young Dauphin. They are both most kindly disposed towards us, and pious enough to please you," he added with a smile.

When he had gone, Henry took from beneath the cushion where he had hidden it his letter to his father, and stood weighing it in his hand. His conscience pricked him. He ought to have confided in Charles; now if ever had been the time to do it when Charles had been talking of marriage for him.

But no, he was being scrupulous. His confessor had often warned him about scruples. Charles had set the example of their having secrets from each other, sneaking out of Rome like that two years ago, and now not telling him anything of his own plans. And being so dictatorial. 'Our' duty, 'our' vocation; it was not for him to decide the vocation of another soul. Since their father had given him a commission to act as Prince Regent, he seemed to imagine that he was the head of the family and could issue orders, say and do whatever he pleased.

But King James would understand, thought Henry, smiling down at the letter. So wise, so little weighing crowns and thrones in the balance with eternal things, he would understand and help his younger son who, for a long while now, had felt he had a clerical vocation.

# THREE

*I*

ALL day long and every day throughout that winter, visitors and messengers called at the Castle of St Antoine. Now that Charles had been received at Versailles, both the old nobility and the mushroom millionaires who had made their fortunes in Law's Mississippi scheme in the twenties, plied him with invitations to hunt or dine. Their ladies sent him little scented billets begging for the honour of his presence at their salons, conversaziones, and masked balls.

Among all these fine ladies none was so persistent as Marie Jablonowski, Princesse de Talmond, cousin both of the Queen of France and of Charles himself, extremely rich, of very great influence, one of the very few ladies who enjoyed the privilege of being seated in the Queen's presence and embraced by the King.

But the Princesse de Talmond had no better success than her lower rivals. Charles refused all invitations, would not go into society, and excused himself to all visitors save his adherents and agents. A number of old servants and gentlemen had joined him, content to live hard and be owed their wages so long as they might be with their adored master. And also, of course, the spies. The spies of the English Government had never recovered from the fright Charles had given them when, while they were writing confidently that he was in Rome, he had been setting up his Standard in Scotland. Now they cursed his iron discretion; it was useless to bribe his gentlemen for they were ignorant of their master's plans.

Charles had acquired many things, some good, some bad, during his campaign and his wanderings after Culloden. An indifference to comfort and refinement, a rough skill in doctoring, a slightly childish love of disguise, an utter confidence in the loyalty of humble men and women, particularly Highlanders, a contempt for the vacillation and self-interest of the great, a conviction of his own natural genius as the leader of a forlorn hope, varicose veins in his legs, and appalling and recurring nightmares which sometimes drove him to find refuge in drink.

But above all the need to keep his own counsel; even from his father, since nothing was said or done in the Muti Palace but the Elector's spies sent it over by the next post; even from his brother, because, though he never for one instant doubted Henry's loyalty and affection, Henry was apt to be indiscreet and was easily prevailed upon, especially by clerics, to babble out secrets.

And never was there more need for absolute secrecy. For by the beginning of the new year, 1747, Charles had decided on a daring venture. For the moment at any rate he had failed to move France; while keeping that door open, he would turn to her great rival, Spain.

His hopes of help from across the Pyrenees had a perfectly solid basis. When his father was a young man, Philip V had received James at Madrid with royal honours, had housed him in the Buen Retiro, had fitted out a great expeditionary force for the invasion of England, and had put at his disposal a million livres. The scheme had come to nothing only because, so Charles believed, the spies had got hold of it through indiscreet talk. Again, when he himself was in Scotland, Spain had sent a ship with arms and money and had been full of vague promises; that these were not fulfilled was due to the jealousy of the Spanish Court at his having entered into an alliance with France. Or so Sir Charles Wogan, that staunch Jacobite now in Spanish service, assured him.

He had yet to learn the bitter lesson that to Spain, as to France, he was merely a pawn upon the political chessboard.

In mid-February, while Versailles, and Paris, and the spies, and the Duke of York all believed him to be living his life of chosen seclusion in the Castle of St Antoine, a tall young man in a black periwig, with his face painted in a manner which simulated smallpox scars, arrived with one servant at Seville, and giving his name as Mr Douglas, put up unostentatiously at an inn. Next day there called on him Sir Thomas Geraldine, King James's agent at the Court of Spain, very agitated and flustered.

"I do assure you, Sir," he said to 'Mr Douglas', "that nothing here is to be done in a hurry. Delay is the original sin of Spain. When you sent Mr Stafford here from Scotland he was obliged to wait fifty days before he could get a word with his Most Catholic Majesty. And this new King, Ferdinand, is even more dilatory. Oh I know what promises have been made to you, but they have their own way of excusing their non-fulfilment. King Philip would not act on the news that you had arrived in Scotland because he had not yet received the official tidings from his Ambassadors, and I really believe the news was in Persia before it came from them. If your Royal Highness——"

" 'Mr Douglas'," corrected Charles sharply. "The chief Minister, Caravajal, has always been a warm supporter of my father, and traces his own ancestry back to the Royal House of Lancaster. You will carry this letter to him, if you please, Sir Thomas, and you will see that I shall obtain an audience."

The days went by and there was no answer. He roamed the town impatiently, indifferent to the cold, hard beauty of Spain, fixing his gaze upon the Moorish palace of the Alcazar within its embattled wall, and the flag above the Patio de las Banderas which told him that Ferdinand VI was in residence. He was in bed and asleep one night when he was awakened with the news that Caravajal had called at the inn for the purpose of driving him to an audience at the Alcazar.

"It is our habit to transact all important business at night, Monseigneur," the Spaniard told him gravely.

Ferdinand, most polite and most cautious of monarchs, received him with an excessive formality which he soon found more baffling than Louis XV's silence. His Most Catholic Majesty insisted on pretending that Charles had come to Spain merely to see the sights, and begging for the honour of being allowed to show his guest over the palace, he became a walking guide-book. Here were the baths of the ladies of the harem in Moorish times; here in this patio Pedro the Cruel had administered justice in Oriental fashion, ordering a noble lady who had refused his advances to be burnt at the stake, and his niece to be thrown to the lions.

"But the generous animals refused to touch this holy virgin. These wall paintings are by Granelio; here we have John II triumphing over the Arabs at Higueruela, and here Granada surrenders to the Catholic Kings. This door is opened only for Royalty, alive or dead. There are one hundred and twenty miles of corridor, and eighty-six staircases. . . ."

And so on. When Charles tried to make him talk business, it became clear that Ferdinand had been primed beforehand by his Ministers, and was just a weak man put in motion like clockwork. Unluckily the state of his affairs prevented him from doing anything practical at present; and at last, wrapping it up in a thousand flowery compliments, he begged Charles to leave Spain as soon as he conveniently could. To sweeten the pill he made him a present of the expenses of his journey; but, though Charles had watched the wealth of the Indies being unloaded beneath the Golden Tower on the quayside of Seville, his Most Catholic Majesty could not be prevailed on to contribute one peseta towards a military expedition.

Giving the spies and the would-be assassins the slip, Charles returned to the Castle of St Antoine. The first thing he found there was a long letter from his father.

King James began by saying that his dearest Carluccio would need to acquire great fortitude and complete submission to the will of God. He then went on to warn his son against bad companions; old Sir Thomas Sheridan, once Charles's Sub-Governor and one of the beloved seven men who had accompanied him to Scotland, had died of apoplexy in Rome, and Providence had removed also Sir Francis Strickland, his former tutor. Both these gentlemen, asserted King James, had had a very bad influence over his dearest Carluccio, and unfortunately others remained alive. He listed Charles's particular friends, the non-Juring parson, George Kelly, young Sheridan, Colonel O'Sullivan, and Henry Stafford, his equerry, referring to them as 'a gang'.

The King then complained that Charles kept both his father and his brother in the dark as to his plans, and rebuked him for causing Henry 'uneasiness', though he did not specify in what way. He concluded by saying that in his opinion Charles should come and settle in Rome, and added touchingly: 'I shall always love you, and I will always believe you love me.'

Tormented by his recent failure in Spain, and cut to the heart that at such a time he should fail to find trust and sympathy where it should be readiest and warmest, Charles sat down to reply to his father that he had no intention of throwing up the sponge, nor of dismissing faithful followers, and that he simply did not understand in what way he had caused Henry uneasiness; when he noticed a postscript which in his impatience he had overlooked.

'I had near forgot to tell you,' wrote the King, 'that my Lord George Murray has been to see me here on his way to Cleves, where he intends to settle with his family. But he is so troubled in his mind because, during your late expedi-

tion, he was unlucky enough to cause you some offence,
that he begged me most earnestly to give him a recommen-
dation to call on you and offer you his explanations and
apologies before he goes to Germany. You know, my dearest
Carluccio, that I have bred you up in the Christian virtue
of forgiveness. . . .'

Charles stared at that name, Lord George Murray, as
though it had been a poisonous snake. He was by nature the
most forgiving of men; during his campaign he had been
criticised again and again for his clemency towards his
enemies. But there was one man he could never forgive,
could never bear to meet again—Lord George Murray.

That night he had the recurring nightmare he dreaded
most of all.


It was dusk on December 4th, 1745.

He had marched twenty-five miles that day, cheerfully
foot-slogging through snow and slush at the head of his
Highlanders who marched six abreast, the pipes playing
round the Royal Standard he had set up that glorious day in
August in a Scottish glen, that had been carried to victory
at Prestonpans, waved in triumph over captured Edinburgh
and Carlisle. A clamour of church bells ringing joyfully
greeted him as he entered Derby this evening—Derby, but
a hundred and twenty-five miles from London, his goal.
Lord Elcho rode up to him, very smart in his blue uniform
faced with red, and the motto, *A Grave or a Throne*, in his
hat, Elcho with his pop-eyes and his perpetual air of veiled
insolence and his overfed young body.

"My Lord George and I arrived at eleven this morning,
your Royal Highness. We have drawn up the cavalry in the
market-square for your inspection."

"They need their beds, and so do I. We are all too tired to
bother about reviews, my lord," said Charles.

He threw himself on the bed provided for him in the Earl
of Exeter's house, mud-caked brogues and all. I won't take

42

'em off, he vowed happily, until I reach St James's. The sound of joy-bells lulled him to sleep.

As he dressed next morning he could see from his window a party of his Highlanders arguing with a clergyman on the steps of a church; they were demanding to be given Holy Communion before setting off on the final stretch of their uninterrupted advance. The Derby townsfolk stared at them in round-eyed amazement, at these dreaded 'savages' who, instead of looting last night, had been quite content with bread and cheese (and lifting their bonnets had said a Gaelic grace over it), and with straw for their beds.

Whistling a tune, Charles clapped on his bonnet with its bedraggled white cockade, and went bounding down the stairs to go the rounds of his men. In the hall he found Lord George Murray hovering, obviously wanting a word with him. Charles did not like this middle-aged, overbearing man, who from the time when he had joined at Perth (after having at least flirted with the other side) had wished to have the exclusive disposal of everything, and who, worse still, had always been a defeatist. But this morning Charles was in love with all the world, and gave my lord a comradely greeting.

"In the opinion of your Royal Highness's Council," said Lord George, "it is high time to think what we are going to do."

"To do?" repeated the Prince, very puzzled. "Oh, you mean which is the best route to take to London. Yes, I agree. Ask my officers to come to me, if you please."

As they came into the room he called for a map, and began eagerly speculating.

"I myself am inclined to think we should go by way of Oxford. That would give Sir Watkyn Williams-Wynn and his Welsh levies a chance to join us, and Oxford has an old record of loyalty. Dr King, the Principal of St Mary Hall, is one of the most forward of my English adherents——"

He broke off, suddenly aware of an atmosphere he did not like. What was it? he wondered, looking round the faces. There was an air of unanimity about this usually quarrelsome Council of his, and he could not for the life of him understand why it should be a gloomy air.

Lord George Murray rose to ask if he might express an opinion, which he believed was the opinion of them all. Of course, replied Charles, still supposing it was merely a question of the best route to take to London.

"I have, Sir, as is my duty as your Royal Highness's sole second-in-command, thoroughly reviewed our situation," began Murray. He cast a quick, defiant glance at the young Duke of Perth. At the beginning they had been joint Lieutenant-Generals, but so jealous had been Murray that in order to prevent an open breach, Perth, after the capture of Carlisle, had begged the Prince to let him serve as a simple volunteer. "First, in regard to England. Except for a handful at Manchester, not a single Englishman has joined us, and though we marched by the West for that purpose, the Welsh also have failed to keep their promises."

A tense, uneasy silence had settled down upon the group. Eyes avoided those of a comrade, above all of the Prince.

"Next, it will be impossible to reach London without having to fight in turn two vast armies of regulars, Cumberland's twelve thousand at Lichfield, and Wade's eighteen thousand, last heard of at Wetherby, but undoubtedly much nearer to us by this time. Suppose we manage to elude both Cumberland and Wade? There are thirty thousand militia encamped at Finchley to defend London. Again, even supposing we could succeed in entering London, what response may we look for from the citizens? What response have we received from those of the other towns through which we have passed? Here at Derby it is true they rang the bells, but the civic authorities took care to send away their robes and chains of office as an excuse for not giving your Royal Highness a civic reception. If the mob is against us, four thousand five hundred men will not make a great figure in London, and once bottled up there, we shall have thirty thousand regular troops, Flanders veterans, converging on us from all directions. . . ."

His voice droned on and on, painting a picture as black as he could make it. As a background Charles could hear from the street other voices, high-pitched, chattering in Gaelic about the wonders of London, roaring out their clan slogans and their gathering-rants as they queued up at the cutlers' to have broadswords and claymores sharpened.

". . . The opinion of your Royal Highness's Council is, therefore, that we ought to march back and join our friends in Scotland, and live and die with them."

A kind of humming silence, deep as a well, succeeded. Then as though he dropped a stone into that well, Charles whispered:

"*Retreat?*"

No one answered him. Lochiel's chin was sunk on his breast, young Perth's face was haggard, ancient Glenbucket who had fought at Killiecrankie was swaying himself gently backwards and forwards within the folds of his plaid as the women of his race swayed when they keened for the dead. Charles looked at the coldly defiant face of Lord George Murray, and once again, as so often before, the dread of treachery leapt up in his mind. Murray's past was suspect; he had obtained his pardon after being out in the Fifteen, though he was a deserter from the Elector's army, and throughout the first weeks after Charles's landing he had been in constant touch both with his Whig brother and Sir John Cope.

The Prince half rose in his chair. He had an impulse to rush to the window, fling it open, and appeal to the men who were prepared to follow him to the ends of the earth. But no; he must win over his Council; he must keep his head. This scene must have been prepared in advance; Murray must have been at them in secret for days, dropping his defeatism into their ears, he whom they all looked up to as the experienced professional, a man of fifty who as a youth had served in Marlborough's armies.

45

"For your objections, my Lord George," he said, and he was surprised by the calmness of his own voice, "I will answer them one by one. First, few of the English have joined us. Now from all I hear, the English have always been inclined to wait for the loup of the cat; let us once achieve our goal and reach London, and you will find a different story. Then, we cannot, you say, reach London without having to fight in turn two formidable armies, and therefore must retreat. But retreat from whom? Thanks to your excellent tactics, my Lord George, our enemy is behind us; we have given both these armies the slip."

He paused for comments, but none came. He had a strange and painful sensation of wading through water that grew deeper with every step.

"But suppose we have to meet and fight these regulars? We have information that the allegiance of many of them is doubtful; in October we heard how a man of Sinclair's Regiment received a thousand lashes for drinking my health and boasting that half his comrades desired to desert to me. And again, are we to be frightened by the idea of encountering regulars? Have you so soon forgotten Johnnie Cope and his brave dragoons fleeing in panic from the field of Prestonpans? Next, this army of militiamen at Finchley. For shame, my Lord George, would you fright us with such a bogy! You know as well as I the tale of how it is in fact a drunken rabble, that the City is in a panic, its walls plastered with Jacobite slogans, that there's a run on the Bank, that the Elector has packed up his goods preparatory to flight, and that the Government is so desperate that it is offering a bonus of six pounds a day to any man who will enlist as a volunteer."

"Rumours," grunted Lord George. "Are we to base our hopes on idle talk?"

"We may well base our hopes on the old adage that nothing succeeds like success. Our success so far has been due to audacity and lightning movements, such as won Montrose and Dundee their battles. Look what we have

46

achieved so far! It is not six months since I landed with seven men, and now we have an army of nearly five thousand. Remember our capture of Edinburgh, remember how Carlisle surrendered without a blow." He crashed his fist on the table. "Can't I make you see that a retreat *now* would mean the failure of the whole enterprise, that we are but a hundred and twenty-five miles from London, that we have a chance——"

"A gambler's chance."

"It has been a gamble ever since I landed. So far we have achieved the impossible, because we believed we could. We would have been in London by this time had not you, my Lord George, refused my suggestion of attacking Wade when his newly landed transports were still tired—no, I won't speak of that. The road to London is clear if we march *now*; my friends, will you hesitate when a final victory is in sight? Keppoch, will a Macdonald turn his back? Lochiel, will a Cameron run away from the foe?"

He felt so passionately in every fibre of his being what he had said that he moved them. Keppoch's hand instinctively sought the hilt of his broadsword, Lochiel leaned forward to give his assent. But then the cold voice of Lord George quenched the flame.

"Your Royal Highness has little regard for the lives of your faithful clansmen who will be massacred if we attempt to advance further. The Scots have now done all that can be expected of them."

"Have they? Listen to those pipes! *Listen* to them, I tell you! My Highlanders are in the most magnificent heart and fettle ever army was in; they are prepared to take on the greatest force of regulars in Britain, and to go on even if they risk being cut to pieces in the end."

"My Lord George is right," broke in Lord Elcho. He disliked Lord George, but he was even more violently jealous of Charles. "The Scots have done all that can be expected of them, and now it is the turn of the English. And why have not the English come in? I'll tell you. It is because your

47

Royal Highness has neglected to frighten them. You refused to hang that spy, Weir, and it has been the same all along. When we marched out to meet Cope at Prestonpans, you compelled the Edinburgh doctors to come along with us to tend the enemy wounded as well as our own, and afterwards you forbade public rejoicings because victory had been obtained by the effusion of your father's subjects' blood. Again, when you were urged to send to London a cartel as to the exchange of prisoners, threatening that if it were not accepted to give no quarter (a most necessary measure, as many were waiting to see which side the hangman would take), you refused, saying it was beneath you to make empty threats."

Charles made an aimless gesture. He had fallen from the bright wavetop of all his life's hopes, and was suffocating in the trough of the sea.

"I will never in cold blood take away lives which, in the heat of action, I have spared at the peril of my own."

"Then your Royal Highness knows little of the English character. I know it, having been bred at an English public school. Believe me, Sir, they are not to be won over by such squeamishness."

Again Charles made that strange gesture, brushing the air in front of him as though sweeping away a cloud of insects.

"What is all this to the purpose? When I came to Scotland I knew well enough what I was to expect from my enemies, but I little foresaw what I meet with from my friends. I have never been beaten yet in battle or skirmish— until today. The Battle of Derby; it has been won against me by my friends." He flung his arms on the table and beat his head against them. He felt deadly sick and so weak that he feared he could never rise from that table, he who only yesterday had marched twenty-five miles at the head of his nimble clansmen. "Rather than go back, I would wish myself six feet underground!"

He heard voices muttering excuses. They had agreed with Lord George, they whispered, only because they foresaw that an advance could not succeed while the second-in-command was in that frame of mind. But to retreat at present would be only a temporary set-back; give my lord his way in this, and when we have joined our reinforcements in Scotland, we will return.

"We have thrown away our fortune at the flood," he answered fatefully. "There can be no second chance."

## 3

Charles was not without the weakness of superstition, and when the nightmare of Derby revisited him he feared it as an omen. During these days when, having failed in Spain, he must tap new sources, make fresh plans, his one comfort was the thought of his brother. So convinced was he that Henry was working with him, that they were a team, that he did not notice a certain atmosphere of whispering and intrigue when he visited the Hôtel de Sens.

"I met Cardinal de Tencin leaving as I arrived," he said one day when he called there. "Is he prepared to help you in our marriage schemes?"

"He—I—we did not discuss the subject today," stammered Henry.

"I've had another letter from the King. I can't understand why he keeps saying I am causing you uneasiness. Am I, Harry?"

"Naturally you caused me uneasiness when you slipped off to Spain without telling me."

"But I have explained that. I have decided on a system; by a secret and secluded life, by a constant change of disguise, I intend to come and go at will through Europe to plead in person with the Powers without the spies getting on my track. And you haven't learnt yet to keep your own counsel, Harry. It's only because you're so young and inexperienced; you will learn in time."

"Did the King say in his letter that I would be more use in Rome?" Henry asked, not looking at his brother.

"Yes, he did. On the grounds of expense. You would be less expense to him there, he said, and he would be better able to supply me at a pinch. But we'll starve together, eh? Until we've got you a rich wife."

Henry mumbled something, and flushed.

"I believe you are nearer success at Versailles than you have told me, you sly dog!" laughed Charles. "Is it Madame Victoire, who has just returned from her education at Fonterrault? I thought she was going to be a nun."

In the middle of April Charles received a note from his brother begging him to come to supper at the Hôtel de Sens on the 29th.

Charles arrived in good time on the appointed evening, and noticing that his brother's house was lit with more than usual brilliance, thought to himself: he's celebrating something. Can't be his twenty-second birthday, that was last month; but any good news will be a welcome change. Perhaps he really has persuaded Louis to entertain the idea of his marriage with one of the Mesdames.

Henry's hard-drinking Master of the Household, Sir John Graeme, received him in the hall, where there were rich smells of supper; through an open door Charles could see the servants laying the table. But where was the host?

"His Royal Highness, my master, has been called out unexpectedly, Sir," said Sir John. "He bade me make his excuses, and if your Royal Highness would please to take a whet in the withdrawing-room, I am sure he will not be long."

A very faint stab of uneasiness pricked Charles. Unlike himself, Henry had never paid sufficient attention to the peril of assassins. It was night, and a dark one. What errand could have called Henry forth into the ill-lit streets of Paris so suddenly? Then he was filled with renewed hope. Nothing could have prevented Henry from being here to greet his brother except a summons from Versailles.

In the withdrawing-room, Charles found a fellow guest, and in his secret exultation at the thought that Henry had been sent for by King Louis, he was indifferent to the distrust he had always felt for this man, Lord Sempill, whose own cousin Hugh had commanded the Elector's left wing at Culloden, and though he himself was a trusted agent of King James, had always worked in opposition to Charles whom he chose to blame for his youth.

Sempill greeted the Prince with elaborate deference, but with a side glance at Graeme which revived Charles's uneasiness. Sempill and Sir John had the air of men who were in the possession of some exciting but dangerous secret. They pressed Charles to drink. They would not talk about Henry. Sempill launched forth on a pet and novel idea of his own which had become a standing joke among the Jacobites.

"If only we could persuade his Majesty, our master, to come to Paris and direct his affairs in person, we should soon see some happy change. There indeed is a great king! — brave without rashness, prudent without timidity, trusting of his friends and charitable towards his enemies. I hear he received my Lord George Murray with every possible kindness."

Charles was not listening to these remarks so obviously aimed at himself.

"Did my brother receive a letter that called him out?" he demanded of Graeme. "Or did some messenger call?"

Graeme did not know; or said he did not. Charles summoned the rest of his brother's household; no, none of them had any idea what had caused their master to go out so suddenly. Charles's uneasiness became increasing apprehension as an hour went by and still there was no Henry. He would not eat; he dispatched messengers to Versailles, to Cardinal de Tencin, to various friends of his brother; all returned without any news of the missing Duke. At midnight Charles went home to St Antoine, leaving instructions that he was to be informed directly there was news.

Three days passed; three years they seemed to Charles. He tormented himself by imagining his brother kidnapped

51

or perhaps lying dead somewhere, the victim of an assassin's knife. He cursed himself for not having taken better care of Henry. He could scarcely bear to look at Henry's portrait, painted when the Duke was a child, the face so sweet and open under the powdered wig, the big black eyes so innocent and unworldly. On the fourth day his torment was ended by a letter from Henry himself, but though it relieved him from the worst of his fears, it bewildered him. It had been written on the very day Henry had invited his brother to sup with him, but had not been delivered, by Henry's express orders, until now.

'I have had for a great while a longing to see his Majesty, and have just received permission to visit him in Rome, be it only for a fortnight. Besides my natural desire to see the King, a change of air, my physician tells me, is necessary to my health. I departed secretly only because I feared you would not let me go, and I will return at once if I can be of any service to you. . . .'

Well, that was that. Charles was hurt and irritated, but clearly there was nothing to be done at the moment. Confident of the somewhat difficult Henry's deep affection and loyalty, Charles was sure he would return as he promised when his brother sent for him. Meanwhile the season of the year was approaching when another expeditionary force could be fitted out; and, still steadily refusing all social invitations, Charles immersed himself in correspondence with his agents.

To a man of action it was heart-breaking work, this trying to infuse warmth into the tepid and resolution into the timid. Versailles still echoed with the festivities of the Dauphin's second marriage, and everyone there was too gay and too busy to listen to the pleadings of a prince who, for the moment, had ceased to be politically useful. The English Jacobites, who had been so large in their promises before the rising, and had sat still during it, were buzzing like angry wasps because Murray of Broughton, Charles's secretary captured after Culloden, had turned king's evidence to save his life, and seemed resolved to take revenge on half-hearted Jacobites, who in fact meant the English. Old Earl Marischal, the doyen of King James's supporters, who had made a muddle of every Jacobite enterprise in which he had engaged and who had taken a dislike to Charles when the latter was a child, had gone off to seek his old friend the sun in Venice. Lochiel, Colonel Warren, Jack Sullivan, and several other warm adherents, on Charles's advice had obtained commands in French service because he could not maintain them. From Scotland came nothing but tales of attainder, forfeiture, and men shipped as slaves to the Plantations.

June was far advanced when Charles received a letter from his father, breaking a silence of many weeks. Plagued by his own worries, lonely and depressed, he broke the seal with the Royal Arms impressed on the wax, and almost indifferently began to read.

It was an extremely long letter, but Charles did not get farther than the first paragraph. He sat there reading it over and over, for a long while his mind refusing to take in what he read.

'I know not whether you will be surprised, by dearest Carluccio, when I tell you that your brother will be made a cardinal the third of next month. Naturally speaking, you should have been consulted about a resolution of that kind; but as the Duke and I foresaw you might probably not approve of it, we thought it would be showing you more regard that the thing should be done before your answer could come here, and so have it in your power to say it was done without your knowledge and approbation. As I am fully convinced of the sincerity of his vocation, I should think it a resisting of the will of God, and acting directly against my conscience, if I should pretend to constrain him in a matter which so nearly concerns him. . . .'

He did not know how long he sat there, stupidly reading and re-reading those incredible words. The shock was too great for anger, too cruel for tears. In his flaccid mind words rose up, as though another spoke to him:

'This is a worse blow than Derby or Culloden. Your sacred purple, Harry, is the pall of the Cause; your Red Hat is the seal on the coffin of all our hopes and enterprises.'

## 4

Far away in Rome, Henry was entering upon the reward of the sensible and realistic.

On June 30th he had received the tonsure from the Pope's own hands in His Holiness's private chapel, in the presence of his father and the Cardinal Protectors of England, Scotland, and Ireland. And now, on July 3rd, with specially splendid ceremonial, the royal postulant was being presented in St Peter's by Benedict XIV to the assembled Sacred College. Sweating under his robes on which, as a particular privilege, he was allowed to wear ermine, he listened to the Pope recalling the Stuarts' services and sacrifices in the cause of the Holy Catholic Faith, a eulogy upon the piety of his parents and grandparents, and a recital of his own worthiness to take his place among the Princes of the Church.

"His Royal Highness is not yet twenty-three, but St Charles Borromeo was no older when exalted to the same dignity, Peter of Luxemburg was but sixteen and Robert de Nobilibus only twelve, yet We need not remind your Eminences how these sustained the dignity to the love and admiration of the Christian world. So do We confidently expect that his Royal Highness, who has ever taken piety as his guide, will, in like manner, be an ornament to the Sacred College. . . ."

The words fell gratefully upon Henry's ear. If the Father of all Christians applauded his decision and was convinced of the sincerity of his vocation, why should he fear the malice or ignorance of those who whispered that he liked Rome and an easy life, that to him the secure position, with the fixed precedence (and income) of a Prince of the Church, was infinitely more desirable than the position of a proscribed and disowned royal outcast?

He had had some qualms about the matter when, during Charles's absence in Spain, Cardinal de Tencin and Lord Sempill had called upon him in Paris, and had told him that the Pope, advised by the French Ambassador, and desiring to do something for the exiled James III, had offered to create his second son a cardinal.

"But my brother would never consent to it," Henry had cried.

There was no need for his brother's consent, they had told him. But absolute secrecy must be maintained in case Charles opposed.

"There are the interests of your Royal Highness's rightful country to consider. You can repay her ingratitude in a Christian spirit by removing yourself for ever from busy plotters and thus enable her to become peaceful and prosperous under the rulers she herself has chosen."

How Christian indeed was such a sentiment! How odious the mind of the Marquis d'Argenson, just dismissed by Louis through the Pompadour's intrigues, d'Argenson who was saying that Tencin had been bribed by England to persuade the Pope to make this offer, and thus to reduce her fears of the House of Stuart to the person of Charles alone. And how foolish he himself had been, how scrupulous, in wondering whether he was taking revenge on Charles by slipping out of Paris and keeping his brother in the dark, thus parodying Charles's slipping out of Rome and keeping him in the dark in '44.

He had felt from boyhood a desire to devote himself to religion; he had always shrunk from the idea of marriage; he had always been afraid of the temptations of earthly purple. No further harm could be done an already ruined cause; and he had been impressed by the fact that his father, even in the days of Charles's brilliant successes during the rising, had never hoped for an ultimate restoration. How futile were poor Charles's dreams and ambitions! How mature and sensible his own acceptance of hard facts!

*"Quid vobis videtur?"* the Pope's voice solemnly enquired.

Without one dissentient, Henry, Duke of York, was elected a cardinal-deacon of the Holy Roman Church, of the title of Santa Maria in Campitelli; and as a Prince of the Blood Royal was granted precedence over all the other cardinals except the Dean of the Sacred College.

# FOUR

## I

THE midday Angelus rang out from the churches of Paris, as Charles emerged from the office of his banker, Mr Waters, near the equestrian statue of his ancestor, Henri IV, on the Pont Neuf. His companion, George Innes, Principal of the Scots College, who had encountered him at the banker's, raised his hat in salutation to the Mother of God, noticing that Charles, in company with most of the folk on this busy highway, remained covered.

Like all true friends of the Stuart cause, Innes had been shocked and disgusted by the Duke of York's acceptance of the cardinalate. But while sympathising with Charles's feelings in the matter, he was at the same time uneasily puzzled by the mood that had fallen on the elder prince since the news. That air of gaiety was obviously affected, that neglect of the ordinary observances of his religion was unworthy.

"Did I show you this?" Charles enquired abruptly, as they walked along the bridge.

He thrust into his companion's hand a newly minted little medal. On the obverse was Charles's profile, and on the reverse some ships of war with the motto, '*Amor et spes Britanniae*'.

"Since his Most Christian Majesty's defeats by Britain have been caused chiefly by the British fleet," Innes remarked dryly, "I am afraid he may see in these medals a deliberate insult, Sir."

Charles gave a careless laugh, but made no other reply.

"And, Sir, is this so happy a device, since the past has shown that the British Navy has been your enemy rather than your friend?"

"That will never prevent me from defending it against a foreign foe," cried the Prince, his fair skin flushing. "The glory of England I shall ever regard as my own, and the glory of England rests on her Navy, originally created by my House."

It was impossible to doubt the sincerity of his patriotism, and Innes was touched. But it was impossible also to doubt his indifference to the giving of offence to Louis, and Innes feared whither that might lead.

They parted at the end of the bridge, Charles remarking that he was going to the Café Anglais on the corner of the Quai Conti to have a free look at the English papers always available there.

It was winter, and the cafés wedged between the booksellers on the *quais* were crowded. Around the stove in the Café Anglais, each in a chair sacred to him, were seated two of the reigning *philosophes* (a term which had come to have a meaningless laxity), young Denis Diderot, and his contemporary, Jean-Jacques Rousseau, who had not yet made his mark as a writer. Surrounded by their admirers, Rousseau sipped an appalling blend of coffee and chocolate, the speciality of the prince of the *philosophes*, the absent Voltaire, while Diderot, daring, pungent, a professed atheist, pursued the favourite pastime of his kind, that of attacking and ridiculing religion.

"If matter produces life by spontaneous generation, and if man has no alternative but to obey the compulsion of nature, what becomes of the conception of God? What remains for Him to do?"

"A conception of *a* god is part of the compulsion of his nature," objected Rousseau, the essence of whose creed was sentimentalism.

Diderot ignored this, and swept on:

"But of all the religions that ever were, the Catholic is the most absurd and atrocious in its dogmas, the most unintelligible, the most mischievous for the public tranquillity, the most dangerous to Sovereigns by its hierarchic order, the most dreary and Gothic in its ceremonies, the most puerile in its morality."

"Oh hush!" a voice implored in an audible undertone. "The Cardinal's brother has just come in."

There was a half-suppressed titter and eyes glanced furtively at the tall young man who had halted as he went to fetch the London *Evening Post*. Charles turned on his heel, marched straight up to the group about the stove, and said politely to the last speaker:

"I have not the honour of your name, sir, but I would take it as a favour if you would not mention my brother in my hearing. You may not have heard that since his recent action I have made this a rule."

He bowed and went to a table in the corner. His hands were not quite steady as he opened the newspaper, and he could not concentrate on what he read. 'The Cardinal's brother'; that was what Paris was calling him. But he did not blame Paris; he did not feel he would ever again have room in his heart to blame anyone, to feel bitterly and mortally hurt by anyone—except the brother who had so meanly deceived him, whose name he would not have mentioned in his presence, whose portrait he had ground under his heel.

Half unconsciously he listened to the talk around the stove. While never pious like Henry, he had always been a sincere Catholic. Sitting here alone, a little memory came to him. He was in the cave of Coiraghoth in the braes of

Glenmoriston, teaching the rudiments of Christianity to the little band of savage outlaws who were sheltering him, and who regarded him with wonder when every morning he knelt down in the heather, made the sign of the Cross, and said his prayers.

And yet, was it not at least partly true what Diderot had said just now—that the Catholic religion was the most dangerous to Sovereigns? Indeed it had proved fatal to his own family. Naturally it had occurred to him often enough that in recent generations the only successful man of his House had been Charles II, a realist, a libertine, indifferent to religion until he was on his death-bed. Charles II had been restored and had kept his throne; James II had lost it again only because of his religion, and his son, Charles's father, chaste, good all through, had never been able to recover it.

They were dangerous thoughts, but he gave way to them, deliberately. Henry's defection had hardened him, made him reckless. Was it not a fact that the English Jacobites had failed to rise chiefly because he was a Papist? All his promises of toleration had fallen on deaf ears; never again would England stomach a Catholic king. Then was not England worth the renouncing of the Mass, as Paris had been worth accepting it to his ancestor, Henri le Grand, whose statue he had looked down on when he had been trying in vain to induce his banker to lend him some money just now?

2

The Princesse de Talmond was tired, and a trifle waspish. This was no unusual state when, around eleven o'clock in the morning, the hours devoted to her toilette were nearly over. She was past forty and extremely vain. Her beautifying, which resembled the preparations of some careful general for a major campaign, began when she went to bed with a forehead cloth soaked in malt vinegar tied tightly round her brow to erase wrinkles, and the remainder of her face spread with frog-spawn.

Now by mid-morning all but the final touches had been accomplished. She had been encased in the cane and whalebone hoop which, enormous at the sides, was flat back and front and gave her, said the unkindly, the appearance of a hobby-horse parading sideways. She had been hooked and buttoned and tied into her quilted petticoat and her sac-backed gown with its low décolletage and pasteboard stomacher. Her hair had been twisted by hot tongs into the tight little curls known as *tête de mouton*. A black velvet ribbon enhanced the artificial whiteness of her neck, while cork 'plumpers' inside her cheeks restored their lost roundness though slightly affecting her speech.

She had already received her early callers, dressmakers, milliners, a palmist, a sailor who had tried to sell her a parrot, a fisherman who had succeeded in selling her an exotic fish for her aquarium because in her opinion it much resembled her enemy, the Pompadour. Now, with a mask held in front of her face, she sat in her powder-closet, and viciously slapped one of the pretty little soubrettes who was puffing powder on to her hair from the bellows.

Her feelings somewhat relieved, she returned to her vast bedchamber in which were prominently placed the dias and chair of estate due to her rank. Reclining on a chaise-longue with her feet up, she took a glass of champagne from the tray her black-boy was holding, and greeted the first of her aristocratic visitors, this Scottish lord with the pop-eyes, Lord Elcho. Practising the negligent smile, the click of the fan to express various emotions, rapidly blinking her eyelids and biting her lips to make them red (they were so moist that salve would never stay on them), she observed him, murmuring meaningless nothings in response to his awkward compliments.

The product of an English public school, he was always impressing on everyone. Well, whatever this Winchester had taught him, it certainly had not given him *le bel air*.

She did not like Elcho, but she received him because sometimes he gave her news of a certain person whose favours she had been courting ever since he returned to Paris.

"Has your Highness heard the latest from Rome?" enquired Elcho. "His Royal Eminence, the Duke of York, has decided to enter the priesthood, and the Pope wept on hearing the noble resolution of this holy youth who, I hear, is doing very well for himself. King Louis, delighted by this reduction of his embarrassments, has promised him the wealthy Abbey of Anchin *in commendam*, and the Bailli de Tencin, who is returning to Malta, has put at his disposal a great many of his servants, carriages, and horses, so that his Royal Eminence may not be burdened all at once with the cost of his new dignity."

"Astonishing!" murmured the Princesse, delicately using her back-scratcher.

"I am in hopes, therefore, that I shall be able to persuade his Royal Eminence to repay me the fifteen hundred pounds I lent his brother during the late unfortunate rising, and for which I have been devilishly embarrasssd."

"How divinely fortunate! Especially if your lordship is able to persuade King George to grant you your pardon at the same time."

Elcho's full lips fell open. He had imagined it a dead secret that he was suing for his pardon. Then he remembered that among all the silly women in Paris who had fallen madly in love with Prince Charles, this woman, old enough to be his mother, was the most infatuated. It maddened him. He had been furiously jealous of Charles's popularity among the ladies when the Prince had held his Court at Holyroodhouse.

"I encountered the Cardinal's brother last evening," he drawled, "at the Comédie Française. I thought he had decided to live the life of a hermit, but I suppose time hangs heavy on his hands now that his brother has administered the *coup de grâce* to the Cause. I was disgusted by the behaviour of the audience; not a word of the play could I hear

61

for their acclamations of the Cardinal's brother in his box, and a poor Roman matron who was trying to commit suicide upon the stage was quite unable to do so because of the silly mob of gentlemen who left their seats at the side of the stage to go and gape at him."

"Incredible! Extraordinary!" cooed the Princesse, pressing down her false eyebrows made of mouseskin, to make sure they were secure.

"But not a smile had he for any of the ladies who did everything possible to attract his attention, the Duchesse d'Aiguillon being the most forward. It was the same when he was in Edinburgh. So awkward and shy that the Whig papers sneered at him, 'Charles is chaste but Cumberland is brave'. And when he was blamed for neglecting the ladies, he pointed to the Highland sentries with their matted beards and lousy plaids, exclaiming, 'There are my beauties!' I sometimes wonder whether the story about his father being smuggled into the palace in a warming-pan as an infant might not be true after all. The Cardinal's brother must have inherited his taste for low company. He actually preferred to consort with these barbarous Highlanders than with a man like myself who was bred at an English public school."

She was not listening. Her mind had fastened upon two pieces of information. For the first time since his return from Scotland, Charles had appeared at the theatre; and her bosom friend and deadly rival, that crooked-nosed, thick-waisted, huge-breasted d'Aiguillon had seen him there. Undoubtedly d'Aiguillon would lose no time in renewing her invitations to him.

As soon as her callers had left her that midday, the Princesse de Talmond wrote a note to Charles on paper heavily impregnated with perfume. No longer could his Royal Highness make the excuse that he never went into society, she wrote; he had been seen at the Comédie Française. She was having an amateur performance of *Tartuffe* in her private theatre on Wednesday evening, and she would be prostrated, suffocated to the pitch of not being able to breathe, if his Royal Highness denied her the honour of his presence.

Charles accepted, for a variety of reasons. *Tartuffe* had been banned in the days of Louis XIV because it ridiculed the clergy, and even now could only be performed in private theatres which were free from the royal censor. Since Henry's defection it had seemed to him vital to take away the impression that he, like his father and brother, was a bigoted Papist. But apart from this he needed distraction, the alternative to which were long, lonely evenings when he tended to drink too much to blunt his sensibilities. And again, it was pleasant to find people who desired his company, who offered him their friendship, even though in his heart he knew it was a very superficial one.

During the performance of *Tartuffe*, he found himself accepting an invitation to one of the Princesse's salons. In the sober light of next morning he regretted it, for he despised what he had heard of the rage for this New Thought, the intellectual game played in the salons. Essentially a man's man, always shy with women and now bitterly biased against the sex since his *petit souper* in the Pompadour's apartments, the drawing-room was a territory he regarded with distaste.

But he was pleasantly surprised. It was an aspect of contemporary life of which he knew very little, though his friend and cousin, the Duc de Bouillon, was its patron, and had established in his household an ex-priest. Charles was astonished to find in the salon of the Princesse de Talmond, the Comte de Vaudreuil, very much of the old nobility, meeting penniless artists and unknown men of letters upon an equal footing. Here, as at Versailles, there was a rigid etiquette, but this stilted politeness was really rather charming, and as a mere spectator (and a very much honoured and courted one) he could find plenty to amuse him.

The Princesse sat in her armchair before the fire; this

63

chair had to be of a particular kind so that no one else would dream of using it, and yet not so ornate as to give the impression that she had changed her usual occupations for the salon. She had a fire-screen before her, which she used as an excuse for breaking up a group by calling someone to move it up or down; and in her lap was a piece of embroidery at which she stitched with apparent industry, thus exempting herself from rising every time a guest entered or left. It must, thought Charles, have taken serious study for her to have acquired the nice mixture of assurance and grace with which she greeted each guest, and the charming way in which she put in his place one whose position was yet unsure and who mistook her kindness for permission to show off.

No one was allowed to monopolise the conversation; a gay dialogue, in which each spoke and replied in rapid, prompt, and vivacious fashion, aiming at a felicitous phrase, even a mere exclamation uttered at the right moment—this was the rule. The subject-matter was deadly serious: Reason and Facts were their twin gods; they worshipped dictionaries and almanacks. But they expressed themselves in witty and flippant ways, *l'esprit* being the first essential of any who aspired to be a *philosophe*. It was all very silly but rather fun; it resembled the sparkling champagne and the ices served in cups of spun sugar. At least it was a drug; and Charles did not realise that in his present mood it could be a very insidious one.

He found himself presently talking with Diderot, whose wild and daring sallies amused him. Diderot had been having an argument with a famous blue-stocking, Madame du Deffand. That which distinguishes man from the beast is Reason; but could one believe that the *canaille*, who carried out all tasks imposed on them as unquestioningly and as patiently as the ox and the ass, were in possession of Reason? They have the virtue of patience, she argued. But is patience a virtue? retorted Diderot. The priests have made it so for convenience' sake.

64

Now, always the proselytiser, sensing Charles's mingled attraction and faint revulsion, Diderot became the man of the world.

"These ladies!" he whispered, as Madame du Deffand began to hold forth on the need for reforming female education. "The sexes are transposed nowadays; Monsieur tatts or does tapestry work, has the vapours, breaks off a conversation to speak sweet nothings to his poodle, while Madame discourses on monads and predestination, with a sphere in one hand and a compass in the other. I assure you, Sir, these she-scientists flock to lectures on anatomy and physics, and there is one I know who travels with a corpse in the boot of her coach, that she may lose no time in her practice of the art of dissection."

He lowered his voice.

"Yet the rich ones are very necessary as patronesses to any man of genius, if he is poor. It was thus Voltaire became wealthy and famous, first under the patronage of old Ninon de l'Enclos, then taken up by the Pompadour, and now, having offended so many people that he has been obliged to sell for a good round sum his post of Historiographer Royal, he has retired to Luneville where he shares with her husband and another lover the munificence and favours of the Marquise du Châtelet."

Turning to address the company in general, he asked:

"Have you heard the latest? Voltaire has decided that God exists. One wonders whether this could have anything to do with his determination to enter the Academy at Luneville, to accomplish which he must needs make his peace with the Church."

"Voltaire!" exclaimed someone. "Oh, he is supreme. I have never known a man cultivate to so high a degree the art of making enemies and keeping them."

Amid the general laughter Charles approached his hostess and took his leave. She was suffocated, wailed the Princesse, by his leaving so early. Positively she would not let him go unless he promised to come to her fireworks display next Monday.

"The Dauphin will be there," she added meaningly. "He is such a fervent admirer of your Royal Highness, and both he and his mother, our royal cousin, often express the wish that they could make a party for your interests."

What Diderot had said about the necessity for cultivating wealthy women as patronesses recurred to Charles as he drove home. Money and influence were the two things he lacked for the accomplishment of the purpose to which his whole life was dedicated. Had he not been somewhat stupid and unrealistic in refusing to go out into society or to cultivate the influential?

He was no fool, yet it simply did not occur to him that the Princesse de Talmond, twenty years his senior, would expect anything from him in return for her patronage except gratitude and friendship.

## 3

During the next few weeks, Charles was often invited to the apartments of the Queen of France, supping at her table, taking part in her everlasting *cavagnole*, a new game from Italy, and listening while she very inexpertly played the viol.

It was a dull little Court; Louis scarcely ever visited her, and both she and her only son, the Dauphin, were rigidly devout. But they were also good and kind and simple; and Marie Leczinski had a natural sympathy with exiles. Her own father was the dethroned King of Poland, and her girlhood had been one of genteel poverty at Luneville where ex-King Stanislaus lived in exile. Moreover, all who hated the Pompadour had attached themselves to her, so that her Drawing-rooms were attended by men who had had, or who hoped to have, some influence.

"The Duc de Luynes was asking me if I thought there was any service he might perform for your Royal Highness," de Talmond whispered to Charles. "He is a great friend of the Minister of Marine, and I told him that if he could arrange a little private supper. . . ."

And so on. Charles was very grateful to the Princesse, feeling for her the affection a young man might have for a kindly, generous aunt. She was rather absurd, with her posing and her vanity, but under it all she had a shrewd head and, he believed, was capable of courage and sincerity. Always anxious to avoid hurting the feelings of others, he did his best to please the Princesse, sitting with her for as long as she chose in her over-heated, over-perfumed rooms while, in language brimming over with affected verbiage, she advised him about his affairs.

Thus things continued until the end of June, 1748, when Charles's kinsman on the wrong side of the blanket, the Duke of Richmond, descendant of King Charles II, came over to France as King George's Ambassador Extraordinary to negotiate with Louis XV a treaty of peace. At the same time there called at the Château of St Antoine, Cardinal de Tencin.

"You cannot be unaware, Monseigneur," began this smooth old prelate, "that after so many losses both on land and sea, his Most Christian Majesty is anxious to relieve the hardships of his subjects by concluding as soon as possible the treaty now being negotiated at Aix la Chapelle. Nor can you be unaware that England will insist upon the insertion of an article whereby his Most Christian Majesty pledges himself to refuse any further aid or harbourage to any member of your family."

"I cannot believe that his Most Christian Majesty would ever consent to such an article," Charles replied coldly, "seeing that I have his pledged word to harbour and protect me."

"Your trust in his Most Christian Majesty's honour does you credit, if I may say so, Monseigneur, and is well justified. He has empowered me to offer you a very fine house at Fribourg in Switzerland, a guard of honour, and a most

67

handsome pension. And that you may know how greatly he admires you and compassionates your distresses, he has made me the bearer of a gift."

Reverently he laid upon the table a document. It was a draft upon the Royal Treasury for 25,000 livres, with a promise of 70,000 more as soon as Charles had quitted French soil.

"You do not take up this magnificent gift, Monseigneur,' the Cardinal observed after a short silence.

"I have never soiled my hands by accepting bribes," Charles said in a low, deep voice. And then, his face flaming with indignation: "I would rather cut my throat than quit France! I have letters in which his Most Christian Majesty has promised never to desert me."

Both the Queen and de Talmond encouraged him in his resolution which, when it became known, made him more than ever a hero in the eyes of the Parisians. The peace was exceedingly unpopular; it was shameful to France, it was generally believed to have been engineered by the Pompadour, and it would bring no relief from crippling taxation. Since Louis refused to allow him to continue to reside at the royal Château of St Antoine, Charles rented a small house in the Faubourg St Honoré, where he was courted by all the malcontents, high and low.

The Treaty of Aix la Chapelle was duly signed. When, after reading it in the streets of Paris, the heralds cried as usual, "Vive le Roi!", the crowds were ominously silent, and there were several serious riots. A new phrase was coined—"You are as silly as the Peace".

That evening Charles had promised the Princesse de Talmond to be present in her box at the Comédie Italienne to see a burletta, but he could not face it. He sent his patroness a brief note excusing himself on the plea of indisposition, and began to write a furious Protest against the article in the treaty whereby he and his family were forbidden French soil. His contempt for Louis and his hatred of the upstart Pompadour carried his pen along at a furious rate.

'No one is ignorant of the hereditary right of our Royal House to the throne of Great Britain. All Europe is acquainted with the wrongs we have suffered. She knows that length of time cannot alter the constitution of a State, nor ground a prescription against the fundamental laws. She would not expect us to remain silent while the Powers in war make a treaty for a peace which, without regarding the justice of our cause (in which all Sovereigns are concerned), stipulates articles prejudicial to our interests and to those of the subjects of our most honoured Lord and Father. . . .'

He tugged impatiently at the bell-rope, and when a servant appeared called for brandy. Stimulated by drink, his pen continued to race across the paper. But now he was more concerned for the loyal ones at home than with the perfidy of France. Ever since he was born, and more particularly since the defection of his brother, they had pinned their hopes on him alone amid all the wrongs and cruelties to which they were subjected.

'We declare to all the subjects of our most honoured Lord and Father, that nothing shall alter the warm and sincere love which our birth inspires in us for them, and that the just sense we have of their fidelity, zeal, and courage will never be effaced from our heart——'

"What is it?" he cried impatiently, in response to a tap on the door.

Old George Kelly entered with a letter from Rome.

It could not have arrived at a worse moment, for it was precisely calculated to increase Charles's mood of complete recklessness. King James had learned that one of the articles in the treaty stipulated the expulsion of his elder son from France, and wrote: 'The maxims I have bred you up in, and have always followed, of submitting oneself to the will of God, will not a little, I am assured, enable you to receive this fresh misfortune with true Christian resignation. However that may be, I command you, as your King and father,

to obey his Most Christian Majesty, and to come to me forthwith, who for a long time have yearned to see my dearest
Carluccio. . . .'

He crushed the letter in his hand.

"Rather than go to Rome I will be content to hide in
some hole in the rock!" he cried fiercely. (It was strange
how often the memories of his six months' skulking in the
heather still coloured his speech.) "Doesn't my father see
that that's precisely what the Elector's Government is aiming at—to drive me to become the Pope's pensioner?"

He flapped his hand in dismissal to Kelly, and without
troubling to read over what he had written, concluded his
Protest.

'And that far from listening to any proposal that may
tend to weaken those indissoluble bonds which unite us, we
look upon ourselves, and shall always look upon ourselves,
under the most intimate and indispensable obligation, to be
constantly attentive to everything that may contribute to
their happiness, and that we shall be ever ready to spill the
last drop of our blood to deliver them from a foreign yoke.'

But his mood changed as he threw down the pen. How
futile were protests when what was needed was action! The
old sense of urgency tormented him. It was sixty years since
his grandfather had been driven from the throne; men grow
used to anything, he thought, even to slavery; men will
accept anything in time, even the most bitter injustice.

But France would do nothing, Spain would do nothing.
"I am going back if I have to league with the Devil to do it,"
he had cried at Louis. But how did one league with the
Devil? It had been a silly, childish outburst, an empty
threat, unlike him too, for though always for the desperate
throw, the gambler's chance, he had never been unrealistic.
Yet such was his mood of desperation that night that he was
prepared to enter into any alliance, however unworthy.

He glanced at the clock. It was only a quarter to nine.
The play would be over, but of course there would be a
party afterwards at the Princesse de Talmond's. A party of

people who thought things out for themselves, who shared his own contempt for the faithless Louis, who believed that phrases like 'true Christian resignation' and 'the will of God' were insinuated into men's minds by wily priests avid for power.

Something within him cried urgently in warning—It is dangerous; do not go in your present mood. But he crushed it down.

There was not the usual string of coaches and sedans drawn up outside the Princesse's house, but a footman hastened to assure Charles that her Highness was at home. By the alacrity with which he was conducted to her, it almost seemed as though he were expected. She was in her boudoir, all alone, and at first he thought she must be ill.

She reclined upon a downy *bergere* before a fire which burned despite the summer warmth. It perfumed the room from the spices sprinkled on it. It seemed to him, unacquainted as he was with feminine wiles, that her hair and nightgown were in unconscious disorder; little did he guess the hours which had been devoted to producing such pretty dishevelment. Seen thus by the light of a solitary taper she looked young; she was slight and fragile without the huge panniers and the high-piled coiffure. A muslin mob with kissing-strings tied under her chin, a face as pale as cosmetics could make it, and a complete absence of jewellery and patches, combined to produce almost a little-girl effect.

As he bent over her hand, asking in real anxiety if she were ill, a crystal drop spilled over from each eye, while others quickly formed to take their place.

"How could you be so cruel, Charles? How *could* you?"

Her voice was different too. She had removed the cork 'plumpers' from inside her cheeks.

"Cruel, Madame la Princesse?" He was simply bewildered.

"When I have done everything I could do to champion your cause. And tonight of all nights, when I desired to show

71

Paris I was willing to risk banishment to my country estates by your presence in my box at the theatre, you send me an excuse at the eleventh hour. Have I offended you? Is there anything I could have done to show my love for you which I have neglected to do? Tell me, and I will beg your pardon on my knees."

He was silent, a prey to conflicting emotions. Recently he had begun to suspect that this middle-aged woman's affection for him was not platonic, but he had shied away from the implications of that suspicion. On the other hand he was moved, not only by her kindness towards him and the very real risk she was willing to run on his behalf, but by this new aspect of her. Gone the silly posing and the affected speech; she who wept unashamedly, who looked at him with such hungry passion, was pitiful and flattering and strangely exciting.

Unconsciously his hand went out to find a wine-glass, and it was there ready set for him with some strong cordial in it. He burst out abruptly, almost wildly:

"I could not go to the theatre—not tonight! I sat down and wrote a Protest stating the reasons why I refused to leave France——"

"I knew you would not submit!" she interrupted, seizing his hand and passionately fondling it. "They were laying wagers that you would, but I knew better. That silly fool d'Aiguillon, who wears a miniature with the head of Christ upon the one side and your profile on the other, was saying that your kingdom, like His, was not of this world. It is very much of this world, I told her, and if I, my powerful friends, my influence, my fortune, can establish it, you will see him crowned yet."

Oh, it was sweet to him, that championship, a salve to his bitter humiliation. She wanted him to read his Protest, and when he said he had not brought it with him, pressed him to rehearse the arguments he had used, vowed she would finance its publication throughout Europe.

He was her hero, she cried. She and all her friends would stand by him in defiance of Louis and the Pompadour.

"There's the woman who has persuaded the King to abandon you, because you did not court her, this pretty bourgeoise whose mother was a common prostitute. But the King will never dare to expel you while you have so strong a party both at Versailles and here in Paris."

"I shall not leave Paris," he said between his teeth, "unless I am carried out of it bound hand and foot."

She leaned forward and kissed him full upon the mouth.

He was a man of twenty-seven, but through all his youth he had been wedded to an idea, consumed with passion for one driving purpose; there had been no room in him for the love of women. Now for the first time he was no longer shy in the presence of a woman, no longer faintly nauseated by the intensely feminine atmosphere of this boudoir, so intimate and seductive.

He had thought of Marie Jablonowski, Princesse de Talmond, as a sort of generous and affectionate aunt. In a mist of alcohol and nervous exhaustion and gratitude to someone who believed in him, stood by him in a crisis, someone who had warm lips and smooth white flesh, Marie Jablonowski became merely a woman in whose arms he could find a sort of relief.

# 4

Charles was still young, decent and simple, and next morning he was ashamed of the liaison into which he had been seduced. In memory he shrank in distaste from the love-making of this sophisticated middle-aged woman, and in normal circumstances would have broken away from her.

But the circumstances were far from normal. She had caught him at a crisis in his career. She had worked very cleverly upon his *idée fixe*, and had succeeded in making him believe that it was only with the backing of her set, which included not only the displaced Minister, the Marquis d'Argenson, but Maurepas, Minister of Marine, whom the Pompadour was trying to oust, that he would be able to defy Louis XV and the Treaty of Aix la Chapelle.

He was weakened at the very time when he had most need to be his innately realistic self. He had forgotten for the moment his 'system', his deliberate policy of making it possible to slip hither and thither throughout Europe without the knowledge of the spies. He stayed on in Paris, living in style in the house in the Faubourg St Honoré, temporarily rich with the presents lavished upon him by his mistress and her rivals and friends, cheered to the echo by the Parisians every time he appeared on the streets, desperately pinning his faith to those two most fickle allies, the passion of a spoilt woman and the enthusiasm of a mob.

Catching him at such an age, and in such a crisis, de Talmond's influence could not have been worse. Before she had become his mistress, he had been secretly disgusted by some of the modernistic talk in her salons, wherein were attacked not only what Voltaire and his fellow *philosophes* chose to call the superstitions of the Church in which he had been bred, but all rational morality. But now his clear thinking had been blunted, his native fastidiousness which despised the fashionable amours had been taken by storm; and to stifle his uneasy conscience he lapped up the cynical, shallow arguments of the *philosophes*.

There had always been in Charles's nature a certain childishness, a neutral quality which could have been fostered into strength. Now it had been given a fatal twist; and with a silly little exhibition of insolence he would have despised a few weeks previously, he insisted that in order to make him a set of plate by the date arranged, a goldsmith should neglect one ordered by King Louis.

Not once but several times, Louis sent to him the Duc de Gesvres, Governor of Paris, urging Charles to depart, offering him a *carte blanche* to be filled in with any annual pension he chose to name. He tore the paper up in contempt. De Maurepas, who had always been his admirer, now began to warn him that the English Ambassador was bringing pressure to bear on Louis to honour the newly signed treaty, and that his Most Christian Majesty might be compelled to use force.

Charles merely laughed. He despised bribes, he said, and surely his conduct had demonstrated that he was equally indifferent to threats.

Louis was watching a performance of *Tancrède* in the newly enlarged private theatre at Versailles when, on December 9th, the Comte de Vaudreuil, Captain of the Maison du Roi, approached him with a paper. The King glanced at it, pouted his rosebud mouth, made the cat upon his knee serve for a desk, and taking the jewelled pen handed to him, signed his name.

"Poor Prince!" he murmured to the Pompadour who sat beside him. "How hard it is for a king to be a true friend."

Then he forgot all about the matter in wondering how he was going to replace the Pompadour, whose beauty was faded and whose broken health prevented her from keeping up with his sexual ardour.

On the following evening Charles entered his carriage, accompanied by two of his gentlemen, to drive to the opera. He observed at once that a formidable force of the Maison du Roi lined the streets; and as he drove along the Rue St Honoré a friendly voice called out to him from the crowds:

"Prince, they intend to arrest you! The Palais Royal is surrounded!"

"It may be true, Sir," one of his gentlemen, Henry Goring, said in great agitation. "You remember the anonymous letter you received warning you of this."

"I hardly think his Most Christian Majesty would venture to draw such odium on himself," the Prince replied calmly. "He has always feared the displeasure of the 'frogs' whom he affects to despise."

They reached the Palais Royal, where the opera was still houses, and Charles alighted. He had just time to notice that a host of uniformed men, with their bayonets screwed into the muzzles of their muskets, guarded every entrance and every avenue of approach, before he was roughly seized, and with his arms gripped behind him was confronted with the Comte de Vaudreuil, who only a few evenings previously had been chatting with him at a salon.

"Sir, I arrest you in the name of his Most Christian Majesty," the Comte said in a voice that quivered like a harpstring.

Charles had turned deathly pale, but he answered without emotion:

"The manner is a little too violent for a Christian king."

While the guards kept back at the point of the bayonet the crowds who were trying to get into the theatre, Charles was hurried down a passage which led into the kitchen-court of the Palais Royal. That most extraordinary precautions had been taken against a popular riot in his favour was evident here; the place was prepared as though for a siege, with cannon covering every entrance and even scaling-ladders propped against the walls. Also it was plain that they expected their solitary prisoner to attempt to fight; he was hustled into a room where he found a physician and three surgeons ready with salves and bandages.

"I must request you, Sir, to yield me your sword," quavered de Vaudreuil.

"I shall not yield it to you, Monsieur le Comte, but seeing I am in your power you may take it if you please."

They did more. They searched his person, and took from him a pair of pistols and even his pocket-knife.

"You must not be surprised," Charles remarked, still in that flat, dead tone, "at seeing me with pistols. I have carried them with me ever since I returned from Scotland, being constantly in danger of assassination by my enemies. I did not imagine I was in the like peril among my friends."

"You mistake, Sir. Your weapons must be removed lest you make an attempt upon your own life."

"You do not know me if you think I would."

76

The Duc de Biron now entered, carrying some black silk cords.

"I must crave your pardon, Monseigneur, for the indignity I am about to put upon you, but I only carry out my orders, and such precautions are taken solely out of his Most Christian Majesty's regard for your person and to prevent you from endeavouring to injure yourself."

Charles's pallor increased to chalk-white as he was bound hand and foot with the cords, and he observed with bitter contempt:

"Such work must be very mortifying for one of your rank, Monsieur le Duc. I assure you these proceedings will affect your master more than they do myself."

He asked after the welfare of his attendants. In spirit he was back in Scotland, always more anxious for the safety of his friends than for his own. They told him his gentlemen had been taken to the Bastille.

"France promised me asylum," he said between his teeth. "If I had only a morsel of bread I would share it with a friend."

Bound like some dangerous felon, he was carried to a coach and almost thrown into it. The blinds were drawn, de Vaudreuil sat opposite him with cocked pistols, and a strong military escort formed up round the vehicle.

"Are you taking me to Hanover?" he asked in bitter jest.

"To the Château of Vincennes, Sir," replied the Comte.

This castle, a half-hour's drive from Paris, had long ceased to be a royal residence and had become part prison, part military academy. The trees of the Bois de Vincennes which surrounded it dripped melancholy rain-drops upon the roof of the coach, and through the winter darkness the vast donjon of five stories, turreted at each angle, loomed grimly from across the moat. As the coach rumbled over the drawbridge into the great courtyard, the Governor of Vincennes, the Marquis du Châtelet, came forward to receive the illustrious prisoner, and exclaimed in horror at seeing him bound.

77

"I would be glad to embrace you, Monsieur le Marquis," said Charles, who knew and liked him, "but you see I am trussed like a fowl."

"You have your orders, Monsieur le Marquis," said Vaudreuil, and hurriedly took his leave. For a fleeting instant Charles saw his face plainly in the torchlight, and a foolish little thought came to him that he would remember that rather commonplace countenance to his dying day.

Muttering condolences, with his own hand cutting Charles's bonds, the Marquis ushered his prisoner through the covered galleries which united the Pavilions du Roi and de la Reine, and brought him at length into a narrow white-washed room which contained only a chair without arms and a camp-bed.

"It is not very magnificent," Charles observed dryly, "but I have slept harder than this. You need not trouble yourself, Monsieur le Marquis, to order any jailers to wait on me. I long learned to be my own valet."

The Marquis fell on his knees and burst into tears.

"This is the most unfortunate day of my life!" he sobbed.

Charles gave the old man his hand, raising him, and saying kindly:

"I know your friendship for me, and shall never confound the man with the jailer." He looked round the narrow cell; his lip trembled uncontrollably, and he seized it between his teeth. "After Culloden I was hunted like a wild beast, but like a wild beast at least I had ground to range over."

The arrest of 'Prince Edouard' appalled all France.

The Dauphin remonstrated publicly with his father; the whole of Europe, he raged, would despise a Court which showed no regard for its pledged word. In the salons the *philosophes* used this as but another instance of the way 'the infamous one', as they called the Church, duped her followers; the King could do any dirty act he pleased because his priests had taught him that the virtues of his ancestor, St Louis, ensured the salvation of all that saint's descendants.

78

At the theatre the wits called across to each other new epigrams they had invented on the Pompadour (undoubtedly behind the whole deplorable business). The Press bristled with invectives against the Duc de Biron and the Comte de Vaudreuil. An official order was issued prohibiting any mention of 'Prince Edouard' in the cafés, 'because people have taken the liberty of blaming the King for what has occurred'. The poets hymned the praises of *Edouard captif et sans couronne*; and several great ladies, including the Princesse de Talmond, for their outspokenness regarding 'Edouard's' treatment were banished from Versailles.

So threatening became the situation that after a week of near revolution, Charles was smuggled out of France to the borders of Savoy, a lie being circulated that he had gone of his own free will.

# FIVE

## *I*

IN the spring of 1749 the spies and ambassadors of the British Government were thrown into a sudden flutter. 'The Boy', as Horace Mann, English Resident at the Court of Florence, had always called Charles, had vanished completely. Mann and his colleagues had never recovered from the thunderclap of Charles's landing in Scotland when they had firmly believed he was still in Rome; and now, when they as firmly believed he was living quietly in the old Papal city of Avignon, scandalising the clergy there by inaugurating boxing-matches, the news leaked out that he had disappeared.

'When his Majesty's Government threatened the Pope with the bombardment of Civita Vecchia unless he commanded the Boy to withdraw from Avignon,' Horace Mann wrote to his bosom friend, Horace Walpole, 'I rejoiced, seeing that not an inch of European soil except the Papal States would then be open to him. But now it gives me the greatest concern that notwithstanding the utmost diligence I have taken to discover where the Boy conceals himself, I have not been able to discover the smallest information about him.'

'He is dead,' the optimistic Baron Stosch, a German Jew who called himself Walton, wrote home to the British Government from Rome. 'The Pretender his father and his brother the Cardinal, under pretence of making a pilgrimage to Loreto, have gone to bury him.'

He was in Poland, wrote someone else, negotiating for the hand of a Polish princess; he was in Russia, wooing the Czarina. He had been invited to Oxford for the opening of the Radcliffe; he had met the partisans of King George's hated son, Frederick, Prince of Wales, at a tavern in Pall Mall; he had actually been present when the coalminers of Newcastle had struck and had proclaimed him King. He was as infuriatingly elusive as when he had skulked in the mountains and glens of Scotland, under the special protection of God, said his friends, of Satan, said his enemies.

Actually he was in Paris, secreted in the rooms of the Princesse de Talmond in the guest-house of the Convent of St Joseph in the Rue St Dominique.

But only for the moment. It was a *pied à terre*. He had left his household at Avignon, and once more he would go freely about Europe, disguised now as a lackey, now as a Capuchin friar, trusting only to his own wits, keeping his own counsel. The double shock of Henry's defection and of his own arrest had bitten deep, and if he had been reckless before, he was now a man who would stop at nothing to gain his goal, would consider neither his own safety nor that of his friends, would trust nobody. He was completely without illusions; or so he thought.

While, secreted in an alcove in the Princesse's salon, he listened unseen to the talk of the *philosophes*, while he paid a visit to Venice to see if he could persuade the Doge to do something for him, and went on to Poland to appeal to his mother's relations, more and more the eyes of his mind were turned upon England. For his arrest by Louis had stirred the English Jacobites; several among them who for years had been silent had suddenly come alive again, and wrote congratulating him on his defiance of perfidious France, and his refusal to do that which would ruin his cause for ever— to become like his father and brother a pensioner of the Pope. In these letters was a constant refrain; his English adherents would be prepared to rise for him if he would take off the terrible impression made by his brother when the Duke had accepted the Red Hat.

Charles knew very well what they meant. They were asking him to apostatise. He evaded a direct answer, but in his mind he played with the idea, a mind already affected by the talk of the *philosophes*, and further hardened by what he heard from Rome.

Henry was now a cardinal-priest. He had his beautiful villa at Albano and running-footmen so well trained that they could keep up with the fast horses he loved to drive when he went to Rome. He was fervently collecting depositions concerning a new miracle said to be performed at Macerata by a relic of his mother; he was taking his ecclesiastical duties very seriously, reprimanding his canons for coming into choir with their hair powdered, and at the same time he was touchy about his titles. It was only after much intriguing, and to the furious jealousy of the other cardinals, that he had got his way in having 'Royal Highness' precede 'Eminence'. Every single thing he said and did was reported by the spies, to be lampooned in the English papers.

In Paris Charles had found a new friend and agent, Mlle Ferrand, who occupied other rooms at the convent in the Rue St Dominique, Mlle Luci as he soon came to call her. She was a blue-stocking, but young, brave, kindly, and full of common sense. She had just written an account of a famous outlaw, Cartouche, which had taken Paris by storm,

81

and as another outlaw Charles appealed to her tender heart. It was she who now undertook to collect from his banker, Waters, all letters addressed to him under the alias of Mr John Douglas, the letters of his English supporters.

But Mlle Luci did more than that. She gave him the kind of practical, undemanding, understanding friendship such as he had known only when he was in the heather. It was Mlle Luci who noticed if he had a button off his coat, needed a new shaving-glass, a pocket-book with a strong lock. It was Mlle Luci who procured for him English novels, *Tom Jones* and *Joseph Andrewes*, to while away the hours when he could not sleep.

In her gentle company he went back in his thoughts to that night which had been the crisis in his wanderings after Culloden, hemmed in on all sides by the hunters, with the vast Atlantic below him dotted with the dim silhouettes of the ships of war and the gunboats searching for him. And then the chance meeting with a Highland girl, tending cattle in a shieling, a girl with a steadfast face and honest eyes full of unsentimental compassion. Instead of the voice of Mlle Luci earnestly explaining to him that virtue consists only in a constant fidelity in fulfilling the obligations dictated to us by our reason, he heard the voice of Flora Macdonald, small and tuneful, singing a Highland song during that appalling voyage in an open boat to Skye, shyly asking him for a lock of his hair for a keepsake, briskly bidding him hold his breath as, with the efficiency of a sister, she had hooked him into his female disguise.

The Princesse de Talmond, who had been staying at her country estates and vainly entreating Charles to join her there, descended upon him at the convent, and automatically suspecting the worst, violently upbraided him for his relationship with Mlle Luci.

"This is your return for all I have done for you! This your gratitude for all the gifts I have showered upon you, all the risks I have braved on your behalf."

She was the more infuriated when Charles refused to resume their liaison. He had always found his relations with her distasteful, and now her practised love-making had become intolerable. In his thoughts of her she was '*la tante*', sometimes even '*la vielle tante*'; and if only she would behave like an elderly aunt he could be affectionate and grateful. There were violent scenes during which the Princesse kept reiterating that she had done her best for him. She was honestly unaware that she had also done her worst.

What Henry had begun, she and her set had continued; a process of coarsening, of making him reckless and cynical. Diderot had given him a copy of his *Pensées Philosophiques* which pressed the stock rationalistic objections to the supernatural. It was poor stuff, but in Charles's present mood he found it unanswerable; or rather he did not seek an answer. How could he ever have believed in such puerile superstitions? Mlle Luci had a hand in the process; though she detested Diderot's grossness and Voltaire's insane vanity, she was at one with them in believing that the only hope for mankind lay in natural virtue. Henry now had come to represent the tyranny and superstition of the Catholic Church; and the thought of him made his brother more ready to play with an idea which in his heart of hearts he knew was despicable.

He had vowed he was ready to league with the Devil; and the Devil was putting such an alliance in his way.

2

It was November of that year, 1749. Like his great-uncle, King Charles II, before him, he had vowed he would get back his own before he was thirty, and in December he would be twenty-nine. He was desperate, plagued by de Talmond, maddened by the necessity to live on the presents of the women who fought over him, stifled by the feminine atmosphere in the convent, exhausted by the soul-destroying business of writing letters which remained unanswered.

Into the prim convent room, with its beeswaxed floor and

holy pictures, came Mlle Luci in her black Capuchin hood and cloak, her cheeks rosy with the cold. She smiled at him with a sort of mischief, and he had a strangely clear vision of dear Lady Clanranald, smiling at him in just the same way that night the pair of them, with Flora, had been eating kidneys he had roasted over the fire in the wretched bothy where they were sheltering, and a messenger had come rushing in to tell my lady that the notorious red-coat, Captain Ferguson, had arrived at her house to search it.

"Och," said Lady Clanranald, rising without haste, "I'll just keep the mannie well plied with the bottle, so that he'll not be after wanting to leave in a hurry."

"A letter for Mr John Douglas," said Mlle Luci, drawing a fat package from her swansdown muff.

He felt the familiar quickening of the heart. A letter from England. But when he opened it, and something fell out, and he found that the something was a money-bill for fifteen hundred pounds, he simply sat and stared, incredulous. Fifteen hundred pounds! It could have only one significance: the English Jacobites meant business at last.

"Don't go!" he said to Mlle Luci, putting out a hand to detain her, this woman friend with her delicate manners, her natural, unaffected sympathy. "Did I ever tell you about dear Mrs Macdonald of Kingsburgh, who got such a fright when, disguised as a lassie, I kissed her, and she felt the bristles of my beard, and how on parting she gave me a snuff-mull with two clasped hands on it which signified what she called 'Rob Gib's contract', stark love and friendship . . . how ridiculous I am! I don't know really what I'm talking about; I want to dance, sing, shout . . . Mlle Luci! fifteen hundred pounds!"

He turned to the letter, glancing first at the signature. There were, in fact, quite a number of signatories, the Duke of Beaufort, the Earl of Westmorland, Lord Barrymore, Sir John Hinde-Cotton, Dr William King—familiar names. The English Jacobite leaders, not one of whom had raised a finger for him in '45—but it was ungrateful to think of that now. For they had had, it seemed, a change of heart.

They began by regretting they must tell him the sad news that their great Welsh confederate, Sir Watkyn Williams-Wynn, who should have added his signature, was lately dead. They went on to give a list of his Royal Highness's attendants who, for one reason or another, were obnoxious to them, and whom they hoped he would dismiss. Then, and not till then, they got down to business. They had plans it would be indiscreet to commit to paper, but for which it was absolutely necessary they should have a personal discussion with his R.H. Would his R.H. give them a time and place for an accredited agent of theirs, Colonel Brett, secretary to the late Duchess of Buckingham, to come over for a meeting with him?

They added two postscripts. One informed him that 'the majority of the Church of England' would be willing to espouse his cause 'under a certain condition it is needless to specify'. The other explained that the enclosed money-bill was merely a token of their undying loyalty and affection, and was sent for his 'present necessities'.

"I shall go over myself, of course," he said, doing a few steps of a Highland fling.

"Go over, Sir? You cannot mean—to England?"

"Of course I mean to England, Mlle Luci," he chanted, catching her round the waist, drawing her into the dance, looking at her with star-bright eyes, making her realise, instantaneously, how he had bewitched the most cautious among his adherents in '45. "I must find out for myself what these gentry intend, how far they mean what they say, what sort of allies they are. If I wait for them to send somebody over—Colonel Brett, secretary to the late Duchess of Buckingham; I think she was my aunt on the wrong side of the blanket; I get so confused with all my worthy grandfather's and my wicked old great-uncle's bastards . . . what on earth was I saying? Yes; if I wait for them to send some agent over, they are sure to change their minds."

He plunged into his preparations. A good slice of the £1,500 went to his starving household at Avignon; a small sum was invested in little silver medals, with the motto, '*Laetamini Cives*', for distribution among the English Jacobites. Half the remainder would be needed for the expenses of the trip; the other half went into a certain strongbox he kept beneath his bed. Ever since he had returned from Scotland he had continued to add little sums to this hoard; it was a fund, never to be touched, however poor he might be, until he received the call for which he could never give up hope, the call to lead another expedition.

Of course there was delay. It was necessary for him to obtain from his father a renewal of his commission as Prince Regent; he must have full authority during the forthcoming negotiations. His father demurred, wanting to know Charles's plans. Charles was not going to disclose them to his father or anyone else, and there were months of struggle before James gave in and sent the required commission. Then a ship had to be found. It was not until September, 1750, that word reached him from his agent in Antwerp that a small brig had been chartered to land him somewhere on a lonely part of the English coast.

By a circuitous route, with frequent changes of disguise, with no attendants, he travelled to Antwerp. On the 12th he sailed; on the 16th he, a man with thirty thousand pounds on his head, walked boldly into the lions' den of London.

## 3

The widowed Lady Primrose, that popular hostess, was giving a faro-party in her house at Grosvenor Gate.

As usual the High Tories were there in force. The Earl of Westmorland, just come up from his country seat of Mereworth in Kent, was engaged in an animated discussion on the growing of melons with the fourth Duke of Beaufort, who was on the point of returning to *his* country seat, the splendid Badminton. Lord Barrymore, the Irish peer, was present with his handsome son, Lord Barry; the new Sir Watkyn Williams-Wynn, in deep mourning for his father; and of course the leading Tory in the House, Sir John Hinde-Cotton, famous for his knowledge of all parliamentary arts and tricks. He was famous also for being able to consume more wine than any other man of his day, which was saying something.

Upon this select gathering, which included several ladies, there walked in a young man with the bearing of a soldier, announced by the footman as 'Mr Douglas'.

Lady Primrose took one look at him, turned pale beneath her paint, and dropped her cards. But she instantly recovered herself, gave the newcomer her finger-tips, told Mr Douglas how charmed she was to see him, and asked him what he would please to drink. He stood chatting with her, perfectly at his ease, immediately under a portrait of Prince Charles Edward which hung above the chimney-shelf.

The company broke up at last, only the High Tory leaders lingering. When the servants were safely out of the room, Lady Primrose reached for her smelling-bottle, agitatedly fluttered her fan, and gasped:

"How could your Royal Highness choose to stand there under your own picture! All my guests must have remarked the likeness."

"I have not so remarkable a face as that," Charles replied airily. "But I beg your ladyship will use no titles, even when we are private."

The gentlemen pressed round him, as agitated as her ladyship. Surely he had not come alone? He was running the most devilish risk in coming to London at all. If only they had had notice, they would have advised him to a more prudent course. . . .

"I am quite alone, gentlemen. I have always had a preference for the audacious, and London is the last place on earth where my enemies will look for me. You wrote that it was vital to have a personal conference with me, and here I am."

But where was he to lodge? A public inn was unthinkable; and then they all began to regret that their own town houses would be equally unsafe. At last Hinde-Cotton had a happy thought.

"Dr William King is in town, Sir, and has a most secluded lodging. We will give him the honour of being your host. Such a forward, brave gentleman! At the opening of the Radcliffe Library last year he gave a Latin oration in the Sheldonian Theatre in which he most adroitly contrived to express his principles, introducing the word *'redeat'* no less than six times in his peroration, to the applause of the distinguished audience."

Charles had decided to stay in London for a week. That should be long enough for him to discover just what these gentlemen were prepared to do for him, and it would be foolhardly to stay longer. But he found that what they disliked above all things was being pinned down, and when it came to committing themselves to a course of action they were almost as fond of delay as the Spaniards. A meeting of the Oak Society which he attended on his second day in London ought to have warned him of the real nature of English Jacobitism.

The Oak Society called itself a dining-club, and a lavish dinner was eaten every Wednesday in a private room of the Crown and Anchor tavern opposite St Mary-le-Strand. The members brought their own servants to wait on them, one of whom kept the door and allowed no one to enter without the whispered password, *'Fiat'*. When all the members had arrived the door was locked, and the dining-club threw off the mask and became a treasonable society.

That is to say, it drank out of special glasses engraved with a white rose and two buds; it passed these glasses over a water-jug when 'The Health' was drunk from a vast silver punchbowl inscribed with the names of all the men who had died for the Cause in '46. It proffered snuff-mulls with *'O Charlie you've been long a-coming'* engraved upon them, and it wore upon its legs garters in which were cunningly embroidered the words, *'Come let us with one heart agree to pray that God will bless P.C.'*

"I wish you could have been present, Sir," Sir Watkyn Williams-Wynn confided to Charles, "at my father's White Rose Cycle at Wynnstay, which he instituted as long ago as 1710. 'The Great Sir Watkyn' they called him in the Principality; none of your namby-pamby London fops, but a country squire in the good old tradition. So much did he detest Methodists that he imprisoned one of their preachers for twenty-four hours in his dog-kennel. But I digress."

He took a sip of wine and looked disparagingly at the glass.

"*Our* special glasses, Sir, I mean the Cycle's, were exchanged for new ones directly we heard the lamentable news about—er—your brother. We had a whole new set made, removing one of the buds. And we have a special council-room at Wynnstay, in the moulded ceiling of which is a white rose, seeded, with the motto, *Under the rose be it spoken. . . .*"

Someone mentioned the name of Murray of Broughton, and there was a chorus of execration. This traitor had betrayed their names, while concealing those of several prominent Highland chiefs, when he had turned king's evidence. How very unwise of Charles to have trusted him. *They* had not. When he had sent Lord Traquair to them in '42 to discover their intentions, they had absolutely refused to disclose them. A Judas! And Charles's own secretary all through the rising!

"I supppose if it were not blasphemous," Charles said slowly, "one might say it was unwise of Christ to have trusted Judas Iscariot. But Murray was a man who never wavered in his faith in me, never quarrelled or complained, and when he was captured was a very sick man. Under what kind of pressure he succumbed we don't know, but I who knew him well can assure you that he was a man of honour, and that his betrayal must have outraged his every instinct and tradition."

"I hear his wife has just left him," Lord Barrymore remarked with satisfaction.

"And they say he is losing his reason as well," tittered Barrymore's son.

Charles bit his lip. He wanted to denounce them for their judging of Murray, they who had always been in a mortal fright for their skins and their estates, they whose precious Oak Society and White Rose Cycle had shown no sign of activity either in '15 or in '45, they whose 'Great Sir Watkyn' had thought himself exceedingly brave and daring when he had declared in the House that England had become a mere province of Hanover. So far as action was concerned, that was the most Sir Watkyn had ever done. He could not prevent himself from saying:

"Though it is true that Murray, I repeat under what sort of pressure we don't know, disclosed some of your names, gentlemen, I have not heard that you have suffered by it."

Hinde-Cotton, who had begun on his third bottle and had reached the truculent stage, burst out thickly:

"Not suffered, Sir, not suffered! Damme, I was dismissed from the Treasurership of the Elector's Chamber in '46. Both I and my Lord Barrymore here were under house-arrest for several months; and there is not a gentleman present but was obliged to retire to his country estates in the middle of the London season."

Again Charles bit back a furious retort. He thought of Butcher Cumberland and his 'little blood-letting'. He thought of the ships packed with prisoners like negroes in a slaver, which, when they came into the Thames and the hatchways were taken off, gave out a stench sufficient, it was said, to poison all London. He thought of old Lord Balmerino brought to Westminster Hall for his farce of a trial, the dispute as to where the axe should be carried on the journey, my lord crying cheerily, "Come, come, put it in with me!", his last words on the scaffold, "If I had a thousand lives, I would lay them all down here in the same cause". He thought of the prayer that had risen from the lips of man after man, great and humble, young and old, seventy-seven of them, on the scaffolds of Kennington Common, York, Carlisle, Brampton, and Penrith:

"Long live King James III!"

The great moment of the Oak Society dinner had arrived. Rubicund with food and drink, a trifle unsteady on their feet, the members rose, and passing their glasses over the water, reverently and softly (for in spite of one's footman keeping the door one must be cautious) murmured:

"Long live King James III!"

Charles was not to be put off with evasions. They had written him that they had plans which could not be entrusted to paper; they had asked for a personal discussion, and he had risked life and freedom in coming over to London for the purpose.

Infected by his resolution, they found themselves assembled in the lodging of Dr King.

"I think I should mention to you, Sir," said Dr King, before Charles could bring them down to business, "that while I much appreciate the honour, I run a considerable risk in harbouring you. My servant remarked to me this morning that he thought my guest very like Prince Charles. Why, says I, have you ever seen Prince Charles? No, says he, but this gentleman, whoever he may be, exactly resembles the busts sold in Red Lion Street, and they are said to be busts of the Prince."

"Then the common people have some devotion to me?" Charles asked eagerly.

Dr King looked pained.

"The rabble, Sir? Why, one would have to fall very low indeed to care for the devotion of such wretches. As for the ordinary people, those of England are not by nature revolutionaries. They are lazy and inert and inclined to make the best of things; while many of their betters have learnt the advantage of having a king who is a mere salaried official. The Elector is disliked, and his morals are a byword; but a few whores at Court, even German ones, are better than a horde of Popish priests."

Charles was silent. He understood that hint. But he was not going to promise anything on his side until he had learnt what they were prepared to do on theirs. Driven to it at last, they laid their plans before him; and although those plans were somewhat nebulous, he saw at once that they could be shaped into a formidable *coup* which might have a better chance of success even than the Forty-Five.

"First of all, Sir," began Hinde-Cotton, "we are all agreed that though there must be some support from Scotland, the Scots are not to cross the Border. It was because we English have always regarded the Scots as thieving savages that your English adherents did not join you in '45."

"But they did not thieve on our march into England. Even our enemies were obliged to acknowledge that."

"Perhaps not, and it was very creditable to you, Sir, that they maintained such good discipline, but the fact remains that they are thieves by nature. Moreover, so many of the loyal clans are dead or transported or broken, that England must needs be the chief scene of activity. You agree to that?"

He agreed heartily. Certainly it was England's turn.

"Next, there must be foreign aid. Though nothing is to be expected from France, she might be persuaded to countenance underhand the sending of an invasion force by King Frederick of Prussia, for he is her ally and detests his uncle, the Elector."

"Frederick," Charles repeated thoughtfully. "Yes, the Earl Marischal's brother, Marshal Keith, is in his service, and Marischal himself is at Berlin with a pension from Frederick of two thousand crowns."

He would not allow himself to remember how cold was this old friend, Marischal, how much Marischal had always disliked him personally. He would not permit even a drop of cold water to be spilled on this new growing hope.

"For our plans at home," continued Hinde-Cotton, "they are not yet by any means complete, but roughly, Sir, they are of this nature. It must be a *coup de main*, somewhat on the lines of the conspiracy of the unfortunate Sir John Fenwick in your grandfather's interests. That is to say, an attack on certain public buildings to be made simultaneously, and for this we count upon a number of officers and men of the Elector's own army."

"It is true, Sir," broke in Colonel Brett, leaning forward, "that there is great dissatisfaction in the Army. This is partly due to the intense unpopularity of the Duke of Cumberland, who is most heartily hated, not only on account of his brutalities but because of his humiliating defeats by the French during the late war."

Hinde-Cotton nodded sagely, and went on:

"An Alderman Heath, a very worthy person, has undertaken to command an assault upon the Tower, and for the providing of a mortar for blowing up the outer gate. Meanwhile, in the preceding weeks, the placing of the sentries at St James's and elsewhere will be minutely studied; men must be picked (good Dr King here has sworn he can contribute at least three hundred), for the assault on St James's——"

He stopped, as Charles made a sharp movement.

"I must interrupt you, Sir John. From the beginning I must make it clear that I cannot, under any circumstances whatsoever, agree to any plans which include an attack upon the Elector's person or on those of any of his family."

They hastened to assure him that no such thing was in their minds. On the night appointed, fifteen hundred Irish chairmen were to extinguish the lights of London at a given hour; the sentries at St James's would be rushed and overpowered, and the Elector and his family hurried to the waterside where a vessel would be waiting to transport them back to their own native land.

There was a short silence. They looked furtively at one another; and presently the clerical member of the company, Dr King, cleared his throat in a significant manner.

"Sir," said he, "under your favour, we must now put to

you some questions. First, would his Majesty, your father, consent to abdicate in your favour if our plans were blessed with success?"

"He would. I can answer for that. He is elderly and sick; he would be content to continue to live his quiet life in Rome."

"Just so. But now there comes an even more delicate question. Sir, there is not one of us, not a lover of your cause among our friends, could ever give his heartfelt allegiance to a Popish king. I speak plainly, for I must. It is not enough that such a king gives assurances of religious toleration; so did your royal grandsire, Sir. No; he must renounce Popery in his own person, and become a member of the Church of England established by law."

The silence this time was very pregnant. This was it. Charles had known it would come, and he was astonished that he hesitated. For he was convinced that these men really meant business, and in any case were his only allies in achieving his life's purpose and in healing the wounds of stricken Scotland, the well-beloved. This was going to cancel out Derby, Culloden, and Henry's defection. This was his last chance. Once again it was now or never; was *he* to hesitate this time?

And for what reason? He hated the Catholic Church for its seduction of Henry. He had no longer any real belief in any form of religion. And these men were holding a pistol to his head. Not even the cleric, Dr King, had thought of asking him whether he was, or could be, honestly converted to the Church of England; to please *them*, to make *them* feel easy, he was required to become a member of her. It was as sordid and as simple as that. And yet. . . .

"I must have—a little time," he heard himself stammer. "It is not—decent—to take such a decision without thought and—and prayer."

He was conscious that the sweat had broken out on his forehead; and wondered why.

On the eve of his leaving London, Charles was received into the Church of England in St Mary-le-Strand.

It was a new church, and the vicar, determined that its beautiful clean interior should not be used as a resting place by beggars and porters, kept it locked except during divine service. But he was a friend of Dr King, and was easily persuaded to lend him the key for a certain very private little ceremony of an unspecified nature. The party consisted of Charles, Hinde-Cotton, Lord Barry, who was deputising for his cautious father, and Dr King himself. Since there was no official rite in the Prayer Book for receiving a convert from Popery, Dr King had drawn one up with his own hand, taking infinite pains and great delight therein.

Charles knelt upon a velvet cushion before the Communion Table, with his right hand resting upon a copy of the New Testament. The mild sunlight streaming through the stained-glass windows tinged with yellow the paper in his hand, and his voice sounded strangely hollow in the empty church.

'The Roman Catholic religion has been the ruin of the Royal Family, the subversion of the English Monarchy and Constitution. In the last century it did, like an earthquake, raise up that fatal rock on which both Monarchy and Constitution split. In that religion was I brought up and educated, with a firm attachment to Rome. Had motives of interest been able to make me disguise my sentiments upon the material point of religion, I should certainly in my first undertaking in the year 1745 have declared myself a Protestant. . . .'

His attention wandered as he went on reading aloud. Yesterday he had paid a visit to the Tower with Colonel Brett and had decided that the outer gate could indeed be blown up with a mortar. The day before that he had strolled past St James's, looking with painful interest at the old palace where so many of his ancestors had been born. He had seen the Banqueting House at Whitehall outside which his great-grandfather had lost his head, had rowed on the busy river into which his grandfather had dropped the Great Seal, had walked the crowded streets where he was jostled by those who were his father's own subjects, might be his subjects if Hinde-Cotton and the others kept their promises, and he was willing to pay their price. . . .

And here he was paying it, in the cold, elegant, empty, echoing St Mary-le-Strand.

'. . . The adversity I have suffered since that time has made me reflect, has furnished me with opportunities of being informed, and God has been pleased so far to smile upon my honest endeavour as to enlighten my understanding and point out to me the hidden path by which the finger of man has been introduced to form the artful system of Roman infallibility. . . .'

(How could anyone write such pompous stuff!)

'. . . I, therefore, Charles Edward Louis Philip Casimir Stuart, the lawful Heir to the Crown of these realms, solemnly and from my heart renounce and abjure the Romish religion, and embrace that of the Church of England as by law established in the Thirty-Nine Articles, in which I hope to live and die. So help me, God, and these His Holy Gospels which I touch with my hand.'

Dr King gave a short homily, and said a long prayer. There were discreet congratulations from the witnesses. All then adjourned to the Crown and Anchor opposite, where there was a special dinner of the Oak Society. New glasses had been rushed through for the occasion. From the roots of a dead oak there sprang a vigorous sapling, with the single word, '*Revirescit*', and the date. The President, the Earl of Westmorland, made a speech. At last, said his lordship, after more than sixty years, they had a Protestant Prince again, who, in God's good time, surely would be rewarded for his renouncing of the errors of his family. The wine flowed free, and tongues were loosened. They vowed and they swore, every man among them, that they were ready to risk their estates, their families, their offices, their very lives, in the service of their true Protestant Prince; that they would never rest until they had restored to England her lawful Sovereign and to the Church of England her rightful Head.

He drank as deep as any of them, even as the redoubtable Hinde-Cotton. He drank to drown the voice crying within him that he had sold his soul.

# PART TWO

## 1751 – 1760

## CLEMENTINA

## ONE

### I

THE Paris Opera House, always in low water finan-
cially, had obtained for itself the privilege of holding
masked balls, to which anyone could gain admission
if sufficiently well costumed. On a night in the summer of
1751 one of these popular entertainments was in full swing,
when Mlle Ferrand, who had become separated for the
moment from the rest of her party, was startled to hear a
familiar voice whisper:

"Mlle Luci."

She turned sharply. A tall man dressed as a harlequin was
standing close to her. For a second he raised his mask, and
she saw the face of Charles Stuart. Clutching his arm, guid-
ing him through the throng of Indians, Turks, columbines,
scaramouches, goddesses, and men wearing great animal
masks, she took him through a door into the gardens of the
Palais Royal, where lovers dallied and famous artistes of the
Opera sang.

"You are most unwise to venture into Paris, Sir," she
whispered, as they strolled down an avenue roofed with
enormous trees. "An acquaintance of mine was telling

Diderot that the spies had got on to your track again. It is known that you have been in Spain——"

Charles interrupted with a short laugh.

"Then the spies are very much *off* the track. Dear Mlle Luci, I had to see you. I am on my way to Luneville, where the former King of Poland has offered me asylum. I shall arrange to have my letters sent there in future, but will you, for the last time, go to Waters and bring me what letters may be lying there for me?"

She promised readily, and when he had thanked her, he went on:

"I have been in Germany, seeing the King of Prussia. I have never met anyone I admire more than he, not as a king but as a very clever young man."

"*Admire? You* admire King Frederick? I can imagine no more dissimilar characters."

"Indeed yes. I am a failure; he is a resounding success."

"You know I did not mean——"

He took her hand and tucked it under his arm. Anyone seeing them would have sworn that they were lovers.

"Dear Mlle Luci, let me entertain you with an account of my visit. I went to Potsdam first, for old Earl Marischal is living there and could get me an audience. A most peculiar household, Marischal's; his valet is a Tibetan supposed to be related to the Grand Lama, and he has a little Turkish mistress, and servants who are all Tartars or Buddhists or Moslems. When I arrived he was indoctrinating New Thought into his True Believers, who sat cross-legged at his feet and did not, I swear, understand a word."

She was only half listening. Under his flippant tone her quick ear had caught a hardness that disturbed her.

"I was not able to see Frederick himself until March. All through the winter he commands in person his army's manoeuvres; so many mock battles and attacks on forts and villages that a stranger would think there was a civil war in progress. When he returned to Berlin I got my audience. What a town! Every householder of whatever degree is obliged to have soldiers quartered on him, and it's droll to see hanging from the most genteel mansions buff belts, military breeches and waistcoats, put up to dry. And what a palace! Even the window frames are solid silver, and yet somehow it instantly suggests a barracks, and even the Three Graces on the roof look military."

"He is a man who, for all he pretends to the New Thought, is a brute and a boor," said Mlle Luci, refusing to be amused. "How can you have wished to make an alliance with one who is own cousin to—to Butcher Cumberland?"

"Set a thief to catch a thief," Charles replied with a shrug. "The point is, he has a standing army of one hundred and sixty thousand men; think of it! And such an army! I was permitted to be present at the great moment of Frederick's day, the parade. They were more like machines than men; one poor fellow was caned unmercifully only because he chanced to sneeze. And down by the Spree he has the best-stocked arsenal I've ever seen. It is no wonder that Prussia has become the third greatest military Power in Europe."

"He is a brute and a boor," she repeated coldly. "A mere brutal despot as his father was before him, and indeed they say the old King was mad. There was a horrible story that when his son rebelled in youth against his iron discipline, he beheaded the lad's greatest friend underneath Frederick's own window."

"And Frederick has lived to thank him for it, so he told me. 'A man's spirit must be broken, Sir, ere he can be made into a hardy soldier,' " mimicked Charles. The mimicry was clever, but still she did not smile. "As for brutality, he was certainly brutally frank with me."

She caught her breath. She was deeply devoted to Charles, and it was horrible to imagine the kind of frankness he must have received from this German boor.

"He had begun by saying that he wished the conversation to be perfectly free, but I very soon discovered that this meant only on his side. Since his principal rival is Austria, whose ally is Great Britain, he is aware, he told me, that it is in his interests to encourage my cause underhand, even to the extent of lending me some of his precious soldiers. But at a price. He keeps a very strict hand on public expenditure, his chief trust being in his Army and Treasury."

He laughed shortly.

"The devil of a price, which somehow or other I must find, for my English adherents insist on a foreign force."

"Then will they not raise the money, Sir?"

"Good God, no! They have already sent me fifteen hundred pounds."

Next day she met him by arrangement in a café. He was dressed as a wig-maker, his clothes covered in powder, and his tongs and combs carried in a bag over his shoulder. The previous evening he had only for a second raised his mask, and now when she saw his face for the first time after so many months, she knew that her uneasiness was justified.

He was not yet thirty-two, but though he was still extremely handsome there was no longer anything of youth in his face. It was hard now where before it had been resolute; it was cynical where it had been pitifully desperate. Mlle Ferrand was perceptive; and though she knew nothing of what had passed during his visit to England last year, she was convinced that here was a man at war with his own better self, tormented by his own conscience.

Yet when, having received from her the letters she had collected at the banker's, he said good-bye to her, he became for a moment the vital, vivid person, the sweet-natured, affectionate friend she had grown to love. He took her hand and laid his lips upon her fingertips below her black silk mitten. And though she did not know it, he repeated almost the self-same words in which he had taken farewell of another true woman friend, of Flora Macdonald in a wretched Highland inn.

"For all you have done for me, Mlle Luci, I hope I shall yet have the honour of welcoming you at St James's."

There was only one letter from England, but it cheered him, for it came from a new adherent.

This Lord Elibank was an exceedingly eccentric character, dividing his time between amorous adventures and learned discussions with Dr Carlyle and David Hume. All during the rising of 1745 he had stood aloof, cannily watching the course of events from his castle on the Tweed. Just recently his younger brother, Alexander Murray, had been charged with violence and intimidation at the famous Westminster Election, and refusing to beg the pardon of the House upon his knees had been imprisoned until the close of the Session, when an enthusiastic mob had escorted him to his brother's house in Henrietta Street. For some strange reason, this incident had turned Lord Elibank into an enthusiastic Jacobite.

Unlike Dr King and his friends, Elibank had great faith in the London mob, and with the London mob the Government had never been more unpopular. Cabinet Ministers were hanged in effigy outside their own houses, their windows smashed, their carriages pelted with stones and filth as they drove to Parliament, and the feeble Government dared not order the reading of the Riot Act. Five hundred men could be raised in the City of Westminster alone, wrote Elibank, good stout fellows who were burning to put on the white cockade and proclaim a Restoration. He added that the recent Act forbidding the wearing of the tartan had so infuriated the Highland clans that they were ready to rise, with or without the consent of their chiefs.

Charles's obvious course was to put Lord Elibank in touch with the English Jacobite leaders, so that they might pool their resources, while he sent to Scotland Dr Archie Cameron, brother of Lochiel who had died in '48, to discover the truth about the eagerness of the clans. For the first mission he needed an agent who was not only trustworthy but tactful; and here he had what he considered a piece of luck. Almost immediately after he reached his new retreat at Luneville, there called upon him a man he had not seen for many years, but whom he had known when they were both boys in Rome.

Alastair Ruadh Macdonnell, commonly known as Young Glengarry since his father, the old Chief, was still alive, had been educated at the Scots College in Rome at King James's expense. Soon after Charles's sailing for Scotland in 1745, Young Glengarry had set out to join him, but had been arrested on the voyage and lodged in the Tower. Since then Charles had had no news of him; but here he was now in Luneville, this red-haired young man, lapsing into the Gaelic in his rapture at seeing his dear Prince again, begging to be allowed to serve him.

"You have come at the very moment I needed you, Alastair," said the Prince; and told him of his need for a confidential agent who must carry messages too dangerous to be committed to paper.

Young Glengarry's joy was touching to witness. He swore upon the Holy Iron, the most sacred form of oath among the Gaels, that he would accomplish his mission or be ready to hang for it. He seemed almost beside himself with joy and fervour; and indeed he was.

For when Young Glengarry had been released from the Tower, he had offered his services in any shape or form to the British Government. Since then he had been hunting around for Jacobite secrets which he could sell for a good price to his new masters, to whom he was known as Pickle the Spy.

### 3

The new year, 1752, found Charles at Ghent in a mood of black depression. His English adherents were far too busy quarrelling among themselves to put their plans into action, and Frederick of Prussia refused to lend his precious soldiers unless and until the English Jacobites appeared in arms. Meantime Charles had never known such stark poverty. During the past year, pathetic letters had reached him from his household in Avignon about the straits they were in; according to his orders they had sold whatever they could, but what were they to do with a postchaise so anti-quated that no one would buy it, a coach-horse that had the staggers, a wine that had spoiled, and a trunkful of his clothes which most unfortunately had got the moth?

Write them off as a dead loss, he replied, and beg, borrow, or steal the money to go to Rome where the King will make shift to maintain you. The King sent them back to Avignon, and wrote his dearest Carluccio a reproachful letter on the subject of discarding faithful servants. He gave Charles the news. Dear Henry had just been appointed Archpriest of the Vatican, which lucrative dignity carried with it a mag-nificent house outside the tribune wall of St Peter's. During the Jubilee Year dear Henry had given Rome a special treat by having Vespers sung by two hundred voices to the accom-paniment of twenty-eight hand-organs. And dear Henry's income had just been further increased by the death of Cardinal Alberoni, which brought him the reversion of three thousand scudi a year upon the bishopric of Malaga.

Charles crushed the letter into a ball and flung it into the empty grate. A smell of soup issued from the bowels of the house in which he was lodging; always soup in Flanders, greasy and nauseating, if you were poor. But even soup needed bones, and bones meant a butcher, and a butcher meant money. He owed his butcher twenty francs, and the man was dunning him for it.

Across from his window on the north side of the Place St Pharailde he could see the massive donjon of the castle rising sheer from the waters of the Lys, reminding him of the most bitter humiliation of his life, of being bound with black silk cords and flung into the donjon of Vincennes. It was May, and tomorrow the fair called the kermesse was beginning; wandering merchants from Turkey and the Orient were setting up their stalls of rugs and embroidery, a gorgeous matador picked his way among the flower-sellers, a peasant girl, come up from the country, picturesque in her huge coif and velvet breast-plate, hugged the arm of her swain who was buying her oranges.

Something about the girl reminded Charles of Mlle Luci. Until he had heard of the sudden death of Mlle Luci last year he had not realised how much he had depended on her quiet, undemanding friendship. The very thought of her, so kind and so true, had been a comfort to him in his black moods, moods increased by a tormented conscience since his English visit. Now she was gone; and perversely, though he had known her for so short a time, had never been in love with her, and had seen her so seldom, he felt a terrible void in his life.

Through Charles's open window came the stink of the two great canals, and the mighty voice of the bell Roland which had acclaimed the birth of his ancestor, John of Gaunt. So loud was that voice that he did not hear a tap on the door, and turned with a start to find he had a visitor.

Colonel Jack Sullivan was puffing and panting from the stairs, for he was stout. After the rising of '45 he had returned to his regiment in French service, but every now and then he would take what he called 'a jaunt' to see his old master. A rough-spoken, good-natured man, he had been an immense comfort to Charles when the Prince was wearied and discouraged by contradictory counsels in 1744, and he had served with distinction as Quartermaster General all through the campaign.

"My leave ends this evening, Sir," said Sullivan, "so you'll honour me, I hope, by taking a hearty dram for old times' sake." He set two bottles of Rhenish upon the table. "I wish it were brandy, but that rich widow I married keeps me devilish short, the bitch, and my pay was ever wont to run through my pockets, you remember."

As he pulled the corks, he glanced compassionately at his master. Charles was wearing an old 'frock' which lacked two buttons; his neckcloth was dirty, his shoes unbrushed, and his bob-wig uncurled. He limped a little as he came to the table; his ulcerated legs must be troubling him again.

"What a devil ails that Iain Beag of yours that he is such a slattern?" grumbled Sullivan, flapping his handkerchief at the dust on the table. "Has he so much to do that he cannot clean a room or sew on a button? I think——"

"You think what?" enquired Charles, after a considerable pause.

Sullivan appeared absorbed in removing a minute particle of cork from the glass of wine he had poured, but actually he was trying to decide a problem. Is it fair? he wondered. Shall I tell him? Damn it, he needs a woman. someone to look after him, someone to come home to, someone from the old days. And after all, she's not a silly young wench, but his own age, as loyal as they come, and so adoring. . . .

"I met one of your Scottish admirers today, Sir," said Sullivan, taking the plunge. "Miss Clementina Walkinshaw."

"Walkinshaw?" Charles repeated blankly. It was plain the name meant nothing to him.

"Fie, Sir! She was the foremost among the ladies who entertained you in Glasgow in defiance of their Whiggish fathers and husbands, in this case of her mother, for her father was dead. Come now, you must remember her; when you fell sick of a fever after our fight at Falkirk, she nursed you at Bannockburn House which belonged to her uncle, Sir Hugh Paterson."

Charles drank his wine, but made no comment.

"I remember her well, a pretty lass, ravishing black eyes, and a fair skin with freckles. I had a mind to court her myself, but what chance had I, when she went round vowing to all and sundry that she would follow you whithersoever Providence might lead you, so mad in love was she."

He talked on in his usual animated fashion, but Charles was not listening. Bannockburn House; the name evoked a

107

memory that had nothing to do with love-sick lassies. It was a name almost as bitter to him as that of Derby.

The bitter winter of 1746. Ever since they had turned back from Derby he had ridden in the van instead of marching with his Highlanders, for he could not bear to meet their hurt, bewildered eyes, to hear their feet dragging through the slush. Both he and they maintained the silence of men stunned. But at Glasgow, the most Whiggish town in Scotland, he put on French silks and gave balls, trying to charm the dour Glaswegians; and in that bitter weather he caught a chill.

He refused to pay attention to it, for suddenly there was the promise of pitched battle. General Hawley, a veteran, almost as distinguished for brutality as Cumberland himself, was marching out from Edinburgh against him with nine thousand regulars. On January 17th the two forces encountered one another near Falkirk; and despite Lord George Murray, who made almost every possible tactical mistake, Charles at the head of his Highlanders won as complete a victory as that of Prestonpans.

When he marched back to Bannockburn House where he was lodging, he was in better spirits than at any time since the fatal Council meeting at Derby. As for his fever, he believed himself cured, despite the band of pain clamped about his forehead.

"Hawley has lost all his cannon, tents, and baggage, and has fled as ignominiously as Johnnie Cope," he exulted to his officers. "He has seven hundred dead, whereas our losses are not more than fifty. And now, gentlemen, to follow up our advantage. Cumberland is marching to relieve Hawley, so our scouts inform us; in my opinion the only question now to be decided is whether to await him on the field of Bannockburn or to advance against him. I have drawn up my own suggestions concerning this imminent battle, and I ask your approval of them."

They debated; with certain slight modifications, they

approved. It was decided to advance against Cumberland; and when the news was given to the clansmen, Gaelic voices roared out songs, the pipes skirled defiance round the camp-fires, for the first time since the beginning of the fatal retreat.

Charles was setting out to inspect his army next morning. It was January 30th, ominous date, the ninety-seventh anniversary of his great-grandfather's execution. A deputation was announced; and at its head was Lord George Murray.

"It is desired that your Royal Highness accept this Memorial, drawn up by your superior officers."

It was long, but the gist of it was plain. It urged an immediate retreat to the north, 'because of the number of desertions, and the risk of your Royal Highness's capture by Cumberland'.

Already light-headed with fever, for a brief space he lost his reason. He struck his head against the wall until he staggered, gasping:

"Good God! Have I lived to see this!"

Recovering himself, he tried to reason with them, living over again the nightmare of that Council at Derby. His arguments made as little impression on Murray, their ruling spirit, as his head had made on the panelling just now.

"I can see nothing but ruin and destruction to us all in case we think of retreat. Has the loss of so many of the enemy killed and captured, and the shame of their flight still hanging on them, made them more formidable than when we routed them?"

"The inequality of our numbers, and the great fatigue of our men," inexorably replied Lord George, "would make a meeting with Cumberland fatal. We are resolved that only instant retreat can preserve the flower of your army, and prevent the capture of your Royal Highness's person."

The futility, the patent insincerity of this, coming on top of Lord George's approval of an advance only the night before! The dreadful, fatal spirit of defeatism Lord George had shown from the beginning! Another brilliant victory to be thrown away!

"Can you imagine that where we go the enemy will not follow and at last oblige us to the battle we now decline?" The room swam round him so that he was fain to clutch at a chair. "If you are resolved upon it, I must yield. But I take God to witness that I wash my hands of the fatal consequences which I foresee but cannot prevent."

By retreating from Derby they had lost England. By retreating from Falkirk they had lost Scotland as well.

He came slowly back to the present, blinking as he stared round the sordid room in this cheap lodging in Ghent.

Sullivan, his stout legs sprawled, his neckcloth slewed round under one ear, was sleeping noisily, an empty wine bottle clasped to his stomach. Charles gulped down the contents of his own glass, and refilled it with a sort of defiance. He was perfectly aware that wine was a most deceptive friend; it promised temporary relief, the numbing of sensibilities; instead, as now, it released thoughts and fears which his will ordinarily kept at bay. Eighteen months had passed since he had paid the price of English aid; and still their fine plans remained plans only, Hinde-Cotton and his friends quarrelled with Lord Elibank, Frederick of Prussia raised the price of his soldiers, and the Oak Society confined its activity to eating dinners and drinking healths.

He got up from his chair, staggering a little, for the Rhenish was potent and he had nothing but Flanders soup in his stomach. Today for the first time in his life he felt tempted to despair. A morbid self-pity, utterly uncharacteristic, preyed on him as he saw himself as Europe saw him, the 'Young Pretender' (and not so young now), a figure of embarrassment to friend and foe, at most a potentially useful pawn, writing appeals and begging letters which went unanswered, told with varying degrees of politeness by evasive Frenchmen and formal Spaniards and power-mad Germans and suave Venetians to get off their soil.

Gazing out of the window at the bustling, industrious folk of Ghent, he suddenly envied them, suddenly yearned to be an ordinary man with a home and a business and a normal existence, and children—he adored children. Envied the country lad buying oranges for his sweetheart, the man driving a wine-cart who, when his work was done, would go home to his wife, to someone who shared his hopes and fears. . . .

What was the name of that Scots girl of whom Sullivan had been speaking? He could not for the life of him remember, but one thing Sullivan had said about her had stuck in his mind : that she had nursed him when he had succumbed to his fever at Bannockburn House. It was shameful to be so ungrateful as to have forgotten her name; even his worst enemy had never accused him of ingratitude.

But then the wine overcame him, and he slumped down on the window-seat with his head against the mullion. In his dreams he was imploring Lord George Murray to give battle to Cumberland; and when he woke exhausted, and with a vile mouth, he had forgotten to ask Sullivan the name of the Scots girl with the ravishing black eyes and freckled face.

## TWO

### I

HE was standing on a bridge over one of the canals a few mornings later, looking down at the barges carrying wine and iron ore, immersed in his own thoughts. No one took any notice of him; he was just a very shabby man who appeared to be wondering where his next meal was coming from.

But presently he became aware that beside his own reflection in the water was another, and that this other was as stationary as his own. The old instinct of the hunted immediately awoke. A spy who had managed to get on his track? An assassin? Last year he had been warned just in time that one of the latter gentry was dogging him.

He looked hard at the second reflection, wavering as the water rippled, and saw that it was that of a woman, whether young or old he could not tell. She was wrapped in a hooded cloak, though the day was warm, and she held a handkerchief to her face, perhaps to conceal her features. Slipping his hand into his pocket where he carried a pistol, he whipped round to confront her. He found himself looking into a pair of large black eyes, shining with tears.

"Madame?"

"I—I beg your pardon." She spoke in English, with the hint of an accent he recognised immediately as Lowland Scots. "I've been trying to pluck up my courage to speak to you, Mr—Mr——"

"Johnson," he said deliberately, still very much on his guard.

"Mr Johnson. I'll remember. I'm truly discreet. Don't you know me? I'm Clementina Walkinshaw."

He stared at her a moment longer, then suddenly burst into a boyish laugh.

"But how very strange! A mutual friend was speaking of you only the other day. Jack Sullivan."

"I know. I asked him to. I begged him to bring me to your lodging but he would not—oh!" she cried, the tears spilling over, "you looked so worn and sad when I was watching you just now—and you have a tear in your coat."

Her naïvety touched him as much as her compassion. Leaning against the balustrade of the bridge, he observed her, and now he did faintly remember her, though when last they had met she had been merely one of the many ladies who had fallen so embarrassingly in love with him, while he had been a man obsessed by the ruin of his great enterprise.

He supposed now that she was several years younger than himself, misled by a certain child-like air she had. Her figure was sturdy, but not unshapely, and her face was more attractive than beautiful, somewhat piquant and faun-like. Her eyes were startlingly black in her fair face which was, as Sullivan had said, freckled, and for some reason he found this touching.

"You knew me," he said in wonder, "though it is so long since we met. They tell me I am greatly changed."

"Knew you, Sir! There is no disguise you could put on but I would know you instantly. And you have not forgotten me. They told me how you toasted 'the Black Eye' when you were in—in danger."

He almost spoke, then refrained. It was true he had toasted 'the Black Eye' during his wanderings after Culloden, but the lady of the toast was Madame Henriette, Louis XV's daughter. How could he disillusion this charming, faithful girl? Often and bitterly in the years to come was he to curse himself for that cruel-kind impulse which forbade him to shatter her illusion that 'the Black Eye' was herself.

"And what are you doing in Ghent, madame?" he asked.

She burst into explanations, her shyness vanishing, her eyes fixed on him in frank adoration.

"I could not stay at home; I could not have a whole sea between us. I fretted so much that at last my Uncle Graeme, who is in Imperial service, used his influence to obtain for me the stall of a Canoness at the Noble Chapter here. Some time or other, I thought, my hero would come to Ghent on his travels; oh, they all told me, my family, I mean, that I was a silly romantic miss, but I knew my dreams would come true."

At any other moment in his career, Charles would have been embarrassed, even repelled. But his bitter loneliness, his loss of the friendship of Mlle Luci, his desperate gnawing anxiety about the English business, his fear of his growing dependence on drink—all these played into the hands

113

of the sentimental Clementina. Here again was the same dog-like devotion he had received from his Highlanders, a devotion no separation or misfortune could quench. She, like them, still believed in him, trusted him, regarded him as a hero, though he had failed and was shabby and a fallen star. It was a glimpse into a world he thought he had lost for ever, while his equals shunned him, and his powerful adherents, one after the other, turned the cold shoulder, and even his servants criticised.

The great bell Roland thundered the hour of noon, rousing him from his reverie.

"Are you alone?" he asked.

"We are not permitted to go out alone, but I gave my companions the slip," she said, mischievous as a child. "Oh, it is not really an ordinary convent; it is something between a university and a ladies' club and a finishing school, but still we are supposed to observe the proprieties."

"Which would be outraged, Miss Walkinshaw, if you dined with me at an inn?"

"Outraged!" she echoed delightedly, taking his arm.

He ordered a private room and a dinner he could not afford. Suddenly he was giving himself a holiday from all his troubles. Over dinner he drew her out to tell him her story, and such as it was she related it with a simplicity that charmed him.

"But you will be bored to hear it all over again," she said, happily convinced that he remembered everything about her. "You are only teasing me, I'm sure."

In the year 1716, King James III had sent as his Envoy to Vienna her father, John Walkinshaw of Barrowfield, a gentleman of coat-armour, descendant of the Hereditary Foresters to the High Stewards of Scotland in the Barony of Renfrew. He had been taken prisoner in the ill-fated rising of the previous year, but with the assistance of his wife had contrived to escape from Stirling Castle. At Vienna, a few years later, he played an important part behind the scenes

114

in the escape of Princess Clementina Sobieska to become the bride of his rightful King.

"When her Majesty, your mother, was safe in Rome, my parents came there to kiss her hand, and there was I born, the youngest of ten daughters. Your mother did me the great honour of standing sponsor for me, and gave me her own name, when I was baptised, the only Catholic among our brood of heretics. It was fate! I was destined for you from my cradle!"

He was not really listening. He was absorbed in watching her, so neat and fresh in her sprigged muslin petticoat, her little hoop, and her crisp coif which left most of her dark curls uncovered. He was fascinated, too, by the hint of Scots in her voice.

". . . and so when at last my father's affairs were put in order, and he had built himself a house in Glasgow, my mother, who is a very hard woman, would see us all settled in life, as she termed it, and she forced my father to take my next sister, Catherine, and me to London, to get us into some genteel employment, though I was but ten at the time, while she caught rich husbands for my elder sisters. Och, she's a dour, hard woman!"

"You have very lovely eyes," he said, he who had always found it so difficult to pay compliments to women.

" 'The Black Eye'! I knew you would not forget me, or the vow I made when I nursed you at Bannockburn House, to follow you whithersoever Providence might lead you."

That roused him from the strange dreamy state into which he had fallen, and he was ashamed of himself. He had no right whatever to encourage this poor child's romantic dreams which could have no fulfilment. She must permit him to escort her back to the convent, he said hurriedly; he had remembered that he had an appointment.

But somehow or other, during the walk, he found himself asking Miss Walkinshaw whether he might take her round the fair tomorrow.

When first Charles had returned to France in 1746, his brother Henry had seen in his look something both fated and fatal; and Henry, though ordinarily unperceptive, had his moments of insight.

It was inevitable that Charles, always so intensely attractive to women, one of these days should find himself caught, not by a sophisticated woman like the Princesse de Talmond, but by his own emotional and physical needs. But it was fatal indeed, both for himself and others, that at thirty-two he should fall genuinely in love for the first time with the romantic, sentimental Clementina Walkinshaw.

He scarcely realised he was in love. All he knew was that suddenly the world had become a beautiful place, and Ghent the finest city in it. It was as gay as the gipsy girls who danced at the street corners, in bright bell-shaped skirts and flowers in their hair, twirling and stamping and banging tambourines. He no longer noticed the stench from the canals, no longer fretted when the great bell Roland informed him that time was passing and still there was no news from England. He was under an enchantment, so that even Flanders soup tasted delicious, and there was a picturesqueness in the very dogs which, each carrying its drinking-bowl tied round its neck, solemnly drew handcarts through the streets. It was fun now, where before it had been squalid and humiliating, to have to dodge the duns.

He was writing his letters one evening, letters which lately had become brisk and cheerful and full of renewed hope, when he heard a sudden commotion break out downstairs. Iain Beag's voice, high-pitched and angry, was raised in argument.

"Himself is not to be disturbed whatever. I will not be taking any messages. The burning of your heart towards you, woman! Have you been taken out of yourself that you seek to intrude into a gentleman's lodging——?"

"But he is sick, and I have brought him something to ease him," a familiar voice interrupted.

Charles threw down his pen, tore open the door of his room, and leaning over the banister called sharply to Iain:

"What manners are these? Bring the lady up at once."

Iain obeyed, but he growled beneath his breath as he did so, and even went so far as to make that instinctive gesture of searching for his dirk.

"Your watch-dog does not like me," said Clementina, when the door was shut. "I suppose he thinks it immodest of me to come here. But you had such a cold in the head when we met yesterday that I did not want you to venture out-of-doors. And I have brought you this," she added, smiling, and setting down a bottle on the table, and watching him keenly, like a child, as he pulled the cork and sniffed at the contents.

"What is it?" he asked.

Her pretty mouth drooped, her under-lip trembled just like a disappointed child's.

"Oh! I felt sure you would remember. It is cinnamon. You *must* remember how I dosed you with cinnamon when you were ill at Bannockburn House."

He made haste to assure her that he did; he would have told any lie if it would serve to make her happy again. But then a sudden uneasiness fell upon him. It was the first time she had come to his lodging, and he knew now he was in love, ardently in love, with this adoring, simple, trusting girl.

She was wandering round the mean room, frowning at the dust on the furniture, the torn hangings at the window.

"You who were born in a palace! To live in such squalor, with no one to look after you except that wild Hieland-man!"

"It means nothing to me," he said; but he knew that it did. He was ashamed that she should see how low he had fallen.

She took off her large straw hat with its cherry-coloured

ribbons, drew off her gloves, and began to dust the room with her handkerchief, humming to herself, busy and contented.

"You ought not to have come here, Clementina!" he burst out harshly.

She paused in her housewifery and stared at him, a hurt child again. He came and took the handkerchief from her, retaining her hand, roughly fondling it, tormented by desire.

"No, it was I who was at fault. I should have told you plainly from the beginning that . . . I ought not to have accepted your sweet affection. It was cruel and dishonourable. I did not know that any woman could be so faithful, so devoted, so kind."

"I have no life apart from you. You have never been an hour absent from my thoughts since first I saw you all those years ago. I was born to cherish you. Your mother gave me her name."

Again her utter simplicity and candour moved him, but he fought against his yearning to respond.

"My dear, you must listen to me. You are gently bred, you have lived in comfort, you come of an honourable house, and you are young——"

"I am one and thirty," she interrupted, with the same touching candour.

"Not too old to make a good marriage. Clementina, I say you must listen to me! I am poor, desperately poor—as you see from this mean lodging——"

She would have interrupted again, but he went on urgently, gripping her hands.

"And I have but one aim and object in life: to get back my own. I will allow no man—or woman—to come between me and my purpose. In that I am quite ruthless. I have no home save my rightful country, I wander always from place to place, dodging the spies, visiting my agents, always listening for a call to lead another expedition. What kind of a life is that for a woman to share?" he cried, shaking her, not knowing in that moment whether he loved or hated her, afraid now of he knew not what.

"I could make it a little sweeter," she said softly. "And as for your great aim, it is mine also, since I have no wish but your happiness. I believe in you absolutely, and in my humble little way I would devote my life to serving you."

She released one hand and touched a tear in his coat.

"But if you don't want me, may I please mend your coat before I go?"

He caught her to him then and held her as though he were a dying man holding on to life.

## 3

The whisper spread round Europe: Charles Edward has a mistress. Not just a passing amour like the de Talmond affair; this Miss Walkinshaw goes under the name of his wife.

At the French Court it made a change from Louis's goings-on. Since his break with the Pompadour he had had a succession of young girls scarcely out of their childhood, whom he installed in apartments known as Le Trébuchet, the snare for young birds, taking their babies away from them as soon as they were born, and marrying off the mothers to gentlemen in the provinces.

At Rome King James fell ill with grief, a condition not improved by the conduct of Henry who, having picked a quarrel with the Pope, was behaving very like his mother, flouncing out of the Palazzo Muti and taking himself off to Bologna, where, he wrote the Pope, he intended to live henceforth. His Holiness replied sharply; cardinals must not live outside Rome unless they were legates or bishops, and he positively ordered his Royal Eminence to return. Henry's grudging submission was rewarded by the bestowal of the Commendam of the Basilica of the Holy Apostles; and immersed in such high matters Henry took not the faintest interest in so sordid a thing as his brother's liaison.

Lord Elcho's ears, constantly pricked to hear anything to his former master's discredit, were rejoiced by the tale. That would ruin for ever any chance of the Prince making a good marriage. And, moreover, this Walkinshaw woman had a sister somehow attached to the Court of King George. (Still angling for his pardon, Elcho long ago had ceased to talk about 'the Elector'.)

Earl Marischal heard it with the utmost satisfaction. It gave him a perfect excuse for resigning Charles to his fate and for refusing to mix himself up in any further Jacobite schemes. He even went so far as to warn the English Jacobites against the Prince.

Baron Stosch, principal spy in Rome, who for years had been maintaining that Charles was dead, now suddenly changed his tune. In an interval of pursuing his favourite hobby, the collecting of obscene prints, Stosch wrote in properly shocked accents to St James's that the Young Pretender had debauched a young gentlewoman, a Papist.

His enemies had always called Charles rash, reckless, high-handed; now they were able to call him lecherous as well.

He cared not at all. At thirty-two he was caught up in the rapture of first love. There was something of the cloudy quality of a boy's love in his passion for Clementina. For years he had been starved of affection; suddenly it was lavished upon him by a girl of his own age. He the homeless had a home at last, carrying it about with him in Clementina's heart. No lodging could be squalid when they shared it; together they could make a jest of not having enough to eat.

Thus the summer of that year passed, the happiest he had known since 1745. Then suddenly in October the news he had been waiting for, had almost despaired of hearing, arrived. Lord Elibank and the English Jacobite leaders had come to terms and were ready to put their plans into action. Dr Cameron had organised a simultaneous rising in the

Highlands, and Frederick of Prussia was definite in his promise of a small force of regulars under Marshal Keith.

Charles rushed to Clementina with the wonderful tidings.

"It is time to use the money I have kept in my strong-box; I would not touch a sou of it until I heard definitely from England. They will not have me go over until they are actually in arms, but I must leave at once for the coast where they will send a messenger to me. Clementine!" He ruffled her curls, kissed her repeatedly, a vital, excited boy again. "At last the call has come! I knew it would if only I were patient."

"But you cannot leave me here alone!"

He stared at her, astonished.

"But my darling, I must. Iain Beag will protect you."

"You know how he dislikes me, how rude he has always been to me, calling me a daughter of the little men of the Lowlands." She burst into tears. "I have put up with so much for your sake, flitting like a gipsy from place to place, travelling in the public wagon, creeping out at night to buy stale herrings in the market. And now you would desert me."

Wrought up as he was, a spasm of intense irritation seized him.

"There is no question of my deserting you," he said sharply, "as you know very well. Can't you understand, Clementine, what this means to me? For six weary years I have been listening for this call, straining every nerve to bring it about, and now at last it has come."

"You must take me with you; I can't be left alone."

"You know very well it is impossible for me to take you."

"You are ashamed of me, that's why," she sobbed. "Now that there's a chance of winning back your rights, I'm not good enough for you."

Again he stared at her; and for the first time he noticed how weak was that attractive faun-like face.

"But it's all a silly dream. In your heart of hearts you must know by this time that it's only that. But our love is real. If only you would be sensible, and if you really loved me, we could go to Rome, where your father would maintain us and we could live in style!"

Not daring to trust himself to speak, he turned abruptly and walked out of the room. But he was scarcely outside the door when she was beside him, her arms about him, her tears on his cheek.

"Forgive me—oh please forgive me! I did not know what I was saying . . . the shock of your going away . . . I have a headache . . . I wanted so much to buy a new cloak yesterday when I was wet through and I hadn't any money . . . I'm sorry, so sorry!"

"*I'm* sorry," he echoed, stroking her dark curls, trying to forget the unforgettable thing she had said—'It's just a silly dream.' "I know it's hard for you, Clementine, but if fortune has smiled on me at long last you shall have a coach and six instead of a new cloak, silk gowns and rings and necklaces, and eat off silver plate—my dear and only love."

Entirely alone, wearing a plain cut-wig and a fustian frock like a working man, he put up at a lonely little inn on the coast of Flanders, waiting for the messenger to come and tell him that he had an army again, that once more there was work for his sword.

Absorbed in an old dream, he might never have met Clementina; he was the Bonnie Prince Charlie of the '45. Day after day he paced a yellow beach which stretched for seventy kilometres in an irregular line, unbroken by rocks or cliffs. Above the beach the dunes, changing in a night to new fantastic shapes; and beyond the waste of waters England, the country of his dreams, the kingdom rightfully his. The sea-birds flying low with a clap of wings, and the shrimp-fishers riding their stout little horses into the water, were the only companions of his restless prowling.

Sometimes he thought he heard the bells of the Abbey of the Dunes, completely destroyed at the Reformation, tolling from where the Abbey lay buried under the drifting sand, and he thought:

"Perhaps before I hear that ghostly sound again, the call from England will have reached me."

He came back one evening to the low, white-walled inn among the rustling poplars, with strings of dried fish hanging from its eaves. And in the wretched attic he had hired he found a visitor awaiting him. Colonel Brett. A Colonel Brett in sailor's slops and canvas jacket, looking very ludicrous, but come from England to tell him (oh surely it must be!) that the hour had struck.

"My good friend, welcome, welcome! I've waited for you for what seems years, but here you are at last! Well, are they in arms? What news from the North? Have Frederick's men landed?"

But then he saw, even through the radiance cast by his own rapturous frenzy, the expression on Brett's face. Before the Colonel answered him, he knew beyond all doubting that once again his airy castles had come tumbling about his ears.

"There is a warrant out for the arrest of Dr Cameron. The Guards are doubled at St James's and at the Tower. Elibank's son is in the hands of a Messenger; Hinde-Cotton and his friends have been ordered to their country seats. As for Frederick's troops, there is no word of them." Brett struck his fist upon the table. "I'll tell you this, Sir, there's a traitor somewhere, and one who is within the very heart of our councils."

Charles had wandered to the window and stood looking out to the wide expanse of sea beyond the dunes. He felt sick; he was shivering, and there was a kind of high note in his ears like an aloof fly.

"I've brought you letters from the Oak Society. They urge you to make every effort to discover who this traitor is; they are convinced he must be one of your own agents, and a very trusted one. Young Glengarry thinks the same. They

123

all bid me tell you *they* have been the very soul of discretion——"

"Oh for God's sake!"

He drifted back to the table, staring down into a half-empty ale-mug. Only this morning he had lifted it to drink to the moment when his foot first touched English soil. How many times, in how many places, had he drunk that toast! Scattered about the table were the dispatches from the English Jacobites. He lifted them, glanced at them. Hysterical sentences leapt at him; each man blamed his neighbour, all bleated of treachery, dripped with excuses. With a sudden violent gesture he scrabbled up the whole collection and pitched them into the empty grate, tossing on top of them the remains of his small-beer. Their ink smudged across the paper like weak tears.

'It's just a silly dream.'

Clementina's words stabbed at him, and he saw himself, not now with a reward of thirty thousand pounds upon his head, but just a laughing-stock, begging from door to door, wearying a world that would not take him seriously any longer, England's outcast, Europe's fool.

He had leagued with the Devil, he had sold his soul, and even the Devil had no use for him.

# THREE

## I

HE returned to Clementina, and life slipped back into its old routine, flitting hither and thither to dodge the spies and hide from the duns. Poverty took on a grimmer aspect, for Clementina was pregnant and soon he would have three mouths to feed. Worst of all, the enchantment was over for both of them, and they began to quarrel.

*He* realised belatedly that childishness in a woman of thirty-one can be exceedingly irritating, and that Clementina was essentially emotional and tactless. *She* remembered that though life at the Noble Chapter had been dull, at least it was gracious, comfortable, and secure. Like all romantics, she did not relate words to the things they signified; in her dreams poverty had meant merely not having some of the luxuries to which she was accustomed. She now began both to nag and to whine.

"You didn't really remember about the cinnamon," she exclaimed suddenly one day. "You pretended you did when I brought you some that day at Ghent, but I don't believe you even remembered that I nursed you at Bannockburn House."

This was precisely the truth, and in his present distracted mood it made him angry rather than penitent. He gave her a sharp answer, her own temper flared, and she stormed at him:

"I have made such sacrifices for you, and look what they have brought me! You have a box full of gold under your bed, and you won't even buy me a new gown."

"I have told you that money is never to be touched except for a certain purpose."

"I never thought you were a miser. And I can't even practise my religion because I am living in sin, and with a rank apostate."

"Were you able to practise it among your Presbyterian family?"

"A woman's honour means nothing to you," she raged, evading that question. "You thought nothing of seducing me. I could have made an excellent marriage; both the Duke of Argyll and the Provost of Edinburgh made offers for my hand before I left Scotland, but I would have none of them, though my mother begged me almost on her knees. I chose rather to follow the fortunes of a penniless prince who——"

"Oh stop talking like a bad melodrama! God knows I

warned you of what your life would be like if you joined your lot with mine."

"So you throw that in my teeth! You dare to suggest I forced myself on you!"

They stared at one another in a sort of horror. Then both began simultaneously:

"I'm sorry. . . ."

There were tears, kisses, an impassioned reconciliation. And so it went on. The words, "I'm sorry", became a trifle monotonous, the kisses and reconciliations a little strained.

He was still physically in love with her, and she was doubly dear to him now that she was carrying his child. But apart from her moods and her whining, he was tormented by his adherents' detestation of her, and by their constant hints that she was treacherous. The English Jacobites wrote Colonel Henry Goring a letter which Goring hastened to lay before Charles.

'Sir, your friend's mistress is loudly and publicly talked of, and all friends here look on it as a very dangerous and imprudent step, and conclude reasonably that no correspondence is to be had in that quarter without risk of discovery, for we have no opinion in England of female politicians or of such women's secrecy in general. What we now expect from you is to let us know if our persuasion can prevail to get rid of her.'

He was not going to discard Clementina to please such broken reeds. The English Jacobites had not suffered by the late abortive plot, and he was very well aware that they loved nothing better than to find a good excuse for not honouring their promises. The recent failure he put down to their timidity and indiscretion. But the thought of treachery began to haunt his own mind when Dr Archie Cameron was taken to the Tower and condemned on the old charge of being out in '45.

A condemnation to death on a charge nearly seven years old shocked even that unsqueamish age, especially as Dr Archie was a colonel in French service. But also it convinced

Charles that there must be indeed some very notable traitor who had betrayed the late plot, since it was obvious that the Government, by not trying Dr Archie on a fresh charge, desired to conceal a valuable new channel of communication to Jacobite plans.

In June Young Glengarry visited the Prince, bringing the news that, after months of vainly trying to induce Dr Archie to betray his friends, the Government had put him to death. He had died as he had lived, loyal, true, and brave, paying an eloquent tribute to Prince Charles upon the scaffold.

"I would have given my right arm rather than lose such a friend," cried Charles. "By God, if I could get my hands on the rat who betrayed him!"

Young Glengarry, alias Pickle the Spy, flickered his red-lashed eyes, glancing covertly at the master who so little suspected his treachery. He said in his soft Highland voice:

"Now I would not be saying this whatever, but since you put the obligation upon me, Sir, I must tell you that I am very troubled in my mind about the discretion (I will not say the loyalty) of a lady of whom I would not be speaking ill."

Charles glanced at him sharply, but said nothing.

"For I am wondering, do you know she was attached in her youth to the household of the pretended Princess of Wales, where she has, even now, an elder sister, who is a waiting-woman to that person, and deep in her confidence, they say?"

"Yes, of course I knew it," lied Charles. "I also know there is nothing to be feared from that quarter. The pretended Prince and Princess of Wales hate the Elector as heartily as does the stoutest of my adherents."

He would not, could not, bring himself to suspect Clementina of being the traitor who had disclosed to the Government the details of the late abortive plot. On the other hand he could not refrain from asking her whether what Young Glengarry had told him was true.

"But I told you about it that first day we met in Ghent,"

Clementina replied defensively. "You never have listened to what I say. I told you how my mother insisted on my father taking Catherine, my sister, and me to London when I was only ten, and how he obtained for Catherine a post in the household of the Princess of Wales, and of how when he died my mother compelled me to stay with Catherine, and how when I heard you had landed in Scotland, I rushed home, hoping that somehow I might be of service to you——"

"Yes, yes, of course you told me," he soothed. She was near her time, and he was doing his utmost to prevent her upsetting herself. "I know your true heart, Clementine, but because some of my friends are so jealous and suspicious, I beg you not to correspond with your sister in London."

"Catherine will have nothing to do with me. Nor will any of my family. They say I have disgraced my honourable name," wept Clementina.

She was suffering the full penalties of the romantic. She had always indulged in the dangerous habit of day-dreaming, rehearsing scenes, seeing herself and others in a fairy-tale world. Almost ever since she could remember, she had been emotionally in love with the Prince whose mother had given her her name. One day, of course, they would meet. And so they had, in such romantic circumstances! She never doubted for an instant that Charles had fallen as madly in love with her as she with him when she had nursed him at Bannockburn House. New dreams had taken the place of the old when he was defeated; she would follow him into exile, they would have a son, he would marry her privately, and perhaps one day this son of theirs would become King of Great Britain.

And here she was at Liège, living in two rooms above a chandler's shop, detested and despised by her Prince's friends, snubbed by tradesmen to whom her Prince owed money, never sure of where the next meal or the next week's rent was coming from, obliged to face the fact that when her baby was born she would be expected, like the lower orders, to nurse it herself instead of sending it out to a wet-nurse like the quality.

On October 29th, she gave birth to a daughter, who was baptised in the Church of Our Lady of the Fountains with the name Charlotte.

## 2

In the following year, Admiral Boscawen with four warships attacked and captured two French vessels on the banks of Newfoundland, a preliminary to the Seven Years War. The Pompadour who, though long discarded as a mistress, had made her friendship necessary to Louis XV, and who detested Frederick of Prussia for naming his pug-dog after her, urged his Most Christian Majesty to revenge; while he for his part hoped, by allying himself with his former enemy, the Empire, against Protestant Britain and her ally Prussia, to redeem his personal sins by a 'holy war'. And once again, as so cruelly often in the past, France began to court poor Charles Stuart; he was always good for a threat against England if it suited French policy.

He was living in dire poverty, so Louis learned from Earl Marischal (who was now Governor of Neufchâtel, while badgering King George for his pardon), at Basle in Switzerland. Marischal grunted in disapproval when King Louis actually offered Charles the command of an attack upon Minorca. 'This person's life,' wrote Marischal, 'has been one continued scene of falsehood, ingratitude, and villainy, and his father's' (Marischal's benefactor, from whom he still enjoyed a pension) 'has been little better.'

Nevertheless, as in duty bound, Marischal passed the offer on to Charles, and found that he need not have worried. 'The English will do me justice if they think fit,' Charles wrote in reply, 'but I will no longer serve as a mere bugbear.' This very just appreciation of French policy put an edge on Marischal's old dislike of the Prince; he wrote Charles a long letter of admonition, raking up every old score, and, with a malice extraordinary even for him, added: 'I hear you have threatened to publish the names of your English friends who have pressed you to discard your mistress.'

To this Charles replied in a few lines. 'My heart is broke enough without you should finish it. Anyone whosoever has told you I made such a threat as you mention, has told a damned lie. God forgive them. I would not do the least hurt to my greatest enemy, were he in my power, much less to anyone that professes to be mine.'

'My heart is broke enough.' He might have added his health as well, though his cruel vitality threatened long life. Bombarded from all sides by demands for Clementina's dismissal, especially from the Oak Society who had manu-factured drinking-glasses when he needed their swords, and now sent him smug lectures when he was desperate for a little financial aid, the dreadful suspicion had begun to nag at him that perhaps after all his mistress had betrayed his plans in '52.

For at least it was a very sinister coincidence that a new traitor had made an appearance at the very time when Clementina had joined him, Clementina to whom he had confided all his hopes and plans. That Young Glengarry was, in fact, this traitor, never even entered Charles's head. Young Glengarry was a Highlander.

Meanwhile Clementina's whines had grown worse, and to these she now added deliberate attempts to arouse his jealousy.

"I have friends who would maintain me if I left you," she kept repeating. "Old, tried friends devoted to me."

"You mean that you had lovers before you came to me?" he enquired, flatly, almost indifferently.

"And you had not, I suppose?"

"I have told you about the Princesse de Talmond."

"I'm not speaking of that old harridan. Are you asking me to believe you resisted all the ladies who were so mad in love with you when you came to Scotland in '45? Especially that Flora Macdonald who——"

He struck her then. And observing that she relished the blow, realising that she had deliberately provoked it, he was sickened the more.

But he would not abandon her, because she was the mother of Charlotte.

From the day of her birth she had been a constant marvel and delight to him, this little child who so strikingly resembled himself. She had his straight nose, his long neck and strong physique; her hair was of the true Stuart chestnut. She was intelligent, lively, active, always gurgling with laughter. It was not until she was four years old that she suddenly showed signs of having inherited something else from him—his nightmares.

He was still living at Basle, under the name of Dr Thompson, earning a pittance among the simple Swiss by doctoring them according to the homely methods he had learned during his wanderings after Culloden. But every now and then he would slip off to visit some agent or former supporter on the humiliating business of obtaining a trifling loan, selling one of his few remaining valuables, or getting some news of the great world. In the autumn of 1757 he was absent a whole week. Someone had warned him that he was being hunted by one Grosert who was married to a daughter of the old Elector's tailor, a man who had a genius for all sorts of clockwork and mechanical devices, including bombs. It was just worth discovering the truth about this, though sometimes he wondered why he still cared about the preservation of his life. Beneath all the exasperations and cruel disappointments, something in him remained fixed and undisturbed by any surface wind of adversity: the determination to get back his own. That aim he could relinquish only with his last breath.

The huge red mass of the Cathedral stood up against the sunset and was reflected in the waters of the Rhine, as he walked home to his poor lodging. From a belfry appeared a

131

mechanical man who hit a bell, while carved bears danced the hour of six. Charles frowned. When a Council of the Church had been held at Basle in ancient times, the public clocks had been altered to suit the convenience of the cardinals, and had remained an hour wrong ever since. He could never remember whether they were fast or slow, and he was depressed by the possibility that Charlotte might be asleep. All through the past week he had comforted himself with the thought of his little daughter looking out for his return, pressing her straight nose against the window-pane until, so her mother grumbled, she was making it quite flat at the tip.

There was no round little face at the window when he reached his lodging, but as soon as he opened the door he heard her voice, upraised in an agonised wail. His pulses leapt in alarm as he rushed up the stair; at the top he cannoned into Clementina.

"*La petite! La petite!*" he cried. "Is she sick?"

"She is naughty. She has taken to screaming at night, and all my acquaintances here tell me that I must not go to her, for it will only encourage her in her naughtiness. She is——"

He pushed roughly past her, and wrenched open the door of the small closet where his daughter slept alone. It was dark except for the uncurtained window facing the bed; he could just make out a little white figure cowering in a tumbled heap of blankets, staring at the pale square of window. The wail died to a hiccoughing sob, wild and desolate, on the edge of hysteria. Another moment and he had her close in his arms, tasting the salt of her tears as he kissed her, her sturdy arms clutching him feverishly round the neck.

"My pearl, my little white flower, my angel! What's the matter, Charlotte, my baby?"

"Ghosties!" whimpered Charlotte, pointing to the window.

Patiently he questioned and listened, filling in the gaps in her childish talk. Through the window she could see two chimneys, one taller than the other. That was what they were in the daytime, but at night when Charlotte woke in the darkness they had become two black ghosts in antique costume, who had alighted to hold conference upon the rooftops of men. Each night they seemed to come a little nearer, until one night she knew they would creep in through her window and eat her up. Her mother had told her she was quite safe; her Guardian Angel was hovering over her bed.

"But s'pose he settles?" sobbed Charlotte. "I's fwightened of fings with big wings."

He carried her to the window, opened it, showed her that the 'ghosties' really were only two nice friendly chimneys who could not move even if they wanted to, because they were stuck to the bricks with mortar. And if she didn't like Guardian Angels, why here was Papa to protect her, his darling, his treasure, his little Pouponne.

The silly pet name had jumped into his mind out of nowhere, and he was astonished by the child's instant delight. Her sobs changed into chuckles, and snuggling against him, burrowing her tangled curls into his shoulder, she repeated with a sort of rapture:

"Pouponne! Papa and Pouponne!"

It was his pet name for her from that evening. Clementina, already jealous of the child's adoration of her father, was annoyed.

"Her name is Charlotte. You chose it yourself. She is too old for silly baby names."

"She is not too old to be afraid of being shut up in the dark. She must have a night-light."

"She must not. I won't have her spoiled. I have the care of her when you go flitting off by yourself. And Charles, you must not bid her good-night when you have been drinking. She will smell it on your breath. I am trying to bring her up to have a respect for you——"

"I shall say good-night to my daughter whenever I am

133

home. A smell of wine will do her less harm than letting her scream herself into a fit when she has a nightmare. I know what nightmares are like."

He was angered the more when he discovered that Clementina herself was responsible for one of the child's nightmares. In the vestibule of the Hôtel de Ville at Basle was a Lutheran painting of the Last Judgment; the Devil, in yellow trousers, with a cock's head and duck's feet, was throwing popes, monks, nuns, and cardinals into the flames, watched with approval from above by one enormous eye representing the Deity. Her mother had told Charlotte that if she were naughty that terrible Devil with his grotesque head would throw her into the fire along with his other victims.

"We must move from Basle," said Charles.

Clementina was indignant. At last they had settled down, she cried; she had been able to make some friends, had arranged for Charlotte to be taught her horn-book. And how were they to live? He would sell his jade-handled pistols, Charles replied, and it would be very cheap living in the mountains. They moved to one of the Alpine villages, a charming toy village of wooden houses, their clapboard roofs projecting six feet over the walls, vines climbing over the smoothly dressed pine logs, and the many little windows making them resemble glass villas.

Even the driving purpose of his life was pushed into the background for a summer and a winter while he devoted himself to Pouponne. On the chief festival of the year, the Fête du Mi-Été, they joined the procession that went up into the mountains to spend a week with the herdsmen who, all the short summer, lived up there in low stone huts, tending the village cows and goats which had been driven to find pasture on the fore-alp. While the young men wrestled, watched in silence by their elders who smoked their eternal pipes, Pouponne and the other children searched for wild strawberries, picked edelweiss and Jacob's-ladder with its smell of blackcurrants, chased the great red

134

and blue butterflies, and watched with large wondering eyes the herds of chamois bounding over the crevasses in play or galloping headlong over the snowfields.

Everything here brought back to Charles most vividly the Scottish Highlands, dearest place on earth. The soaring eagles, the steep waterfalls, the blue lakes, the contented poverty, the smell of peat fires, the dark fir woods, the clang of the bell about a cow's neck. And above all the mountains, rank on rank of them, dazzlingly white against the azure sky.

Lying on his back while Pouponne, brown as a berry now, played contentedly beside him, he saw in his mind's eye other mountains, the jagged battlements of great bens baring their black teeth, and near at hand a little loch glinting fitfully like nails upon a targe. The edges of the waterfall close to his latest hiding-place were frozen, and tall grasses had encased themselves in little suits of armour, standing upright like crystalline spears. Between the rocks grew a holly tree, its crimson berries and dark green leaves vivid against the sombre hill. . . .

The vintage was gathered, the lustrous black grapes picked with much laughter and yodelling, the wine was made, the peat was dug, and the long frozen winter set in. Within their nut-brown chalets families clustered round a great stove of green tiles, while the snow slid off the roof with a soft plop, and wolves howled in the forests. And now Pouponne's nightmares began again.

While the men-folk, seldom seen at home, congregated in the *bier-halle* to drink the fiery residuum of the vintage, to discuss the news of the Canton, and the chances of their own team next season in the popular game of *hornussen*, the women, huddled round the stoves with their lace-making, spoke of darker matters.

"Hark!" they whispered, as from far away came a terrible crackling, like subterranean thunder, "the glacier is walking towards us."

Sleigh-bells sounded, muffled by the snow; but they were

not sleigh-bells at all, a woman said fearfully, as she cooked smoked marmot's flesh. It was the fairy goat with icicles instead of hair, who made a fearful jingling when he chased you. There were tales of avalanches, of how the crack of a whip, the barking of a watch-dog, the piercing whistle of a marmot, were sufficient to start a snowy waterfall which, rushing down the vertical face of the mountain, started others, gathering momentum, breaking down trees, dislodging huge boulders, roaring louder and louder and burying whole villages.

Pouponne sprang up screaming in her little bed, babbling about lost souls who pressed against the window-pane with a mysterious humming, holding out piteous frozen hands towards the warmth within.

"I's fwightened of mountains!" sobbed Pouponne.

Her father rigged up a complicated arrangement of strings and little bells between the child's bed and his own. If she had a nightmare she had only to pull this string, and see how it would make the bell ring just above his head. He would be with her in an instant. Pouponne was enchanted, and the bell above his head began to tinkle nearly every night. Bright-eyed she lay there, waiting for him, chubby arms outstretched. Living in a perpetual nightmare himself, these hours when he and Pouponne were snuggled together in his old tartan plaid became oases in the wilderness of his life.

"Mountains are the most wonderful creatures of God, Pouponne, and good friends to the hunted. There was once a prince who was called to a land of mountains by the people who lived in them. Through generations these people had been promised by their seers or wise-men a deliverer, and they knew that this was he, for a new star had appeared in the heavens at his birth. With only seven companions he went to rescue these brave people from those who enslaved them, and to recover his father's lost throne, though everyone said it was impossible."

"What was his name?" enquired Pouponne.

"His name was Teàrlach." (The Gaelic for Charles.)

"That's a *nice* name," decided Pouponne. With a sigh of satisfaction she settled down to listen to a story which had the basis of all true adventure stories—one man pitted against impossible odds.


# FOUR

## I

CLEMENTINA sat biting the end of her pen, immersed in the secret letter writing which, for some time past, she had pursued whenever Charles was absent. At present he was at Brest; once again, now when he was nearly forty, France was tormenting him with cruel hopes, promising him an invasion force, using him as a threat against her ancient foe across the Channel.

Clementina had become really desperate. That she grossly exaggerated her wrongs, loved to appear as the injured party, chose to ignore the fact that she had thrown herself at Charles's head and had sworn to accept all the hard conditions of his life, none of this altered the fact of her desperation. For years she had known that she was obnoxious to all the Prince's friends and adherents, not, indeed, on moral grounds, but because they unjustly suspected her of treachery, and also because her presence with him would prevent him from making a good marriage. Such an atmosphere might have been tolerable if she and Charles had continued to be in harmony, but theirs had proved a tormented, tempestuous love. She could not control her own emotionalism; she knew no way of reawakening his passion save by trying to arouse his jealousy, and by bragging to him of the rich and powerful friends who would support her if she deserted him; poor Clementina who had, in fact, very few friends left.

But she had, she found, those only too willing to be her confederates, now that she had resolved to leave Charles. There was the aged Earl Marischal who, in the midst of a long and sordid squabble with his late brother's mistress over that brother's will, had received the news that at long last King George had pardoned him. Marischal was about to go home to his native Aberdeenshire, and was delighted to find that he could celebrate the end of his long exile by encouraging his Prince's mistress to desert him. In answer to Clementina's appeal he had sent her a handsome sum of money and a letter applauding her resolution.

Lord Elcho also applauded, sent her introductions to various influential people in Paris, and was making secret arrangements for her flight. That she did the cause of Charles incalculable harm was less to Elcho than the knowledge of what the scandal of her flight would do it.

Sitting here in a half-furnished house in Sedan, a house lent to Charles by his friend and cousin, the Duc de Bouillon, Clementina's heart misgave her as she contemplated deserting her hero. But she must be sensible, she told herself; she must remember her duty to her child. She rose and went to the window, whence the sturdy, well-grown figure of Charlotte could be seen very busy about something in the neglected garden.

"It is time to work at your sampler, Charlotte," she called.

The child came obediently. She was a good little girl, thought Clementina, and when she had been given proper schooling in a convent, rescued from this life of roaming and of bitter poverty, she would settle down and become a young lady.

"Oh, look at your hands and your apron, Charlotte! How have you got them so dirty?"

"I've been making a nest for a bird," replied Charlotte, proudly displaying in her small cupped hands a mess of mud and twigs.

"Throw it out of the window directly and come and wash your hands."

"Oh no, Mama! I heard Papa say, 'I am a bird without a nest, I have to flit from bough to bough.' So I've made him a nest, though it's rather small. When is Papa coming home?"

Always Papa. Twenty times a day Charlotte would run to the window, crane out to look up and down the street. And then, when he came, even if he had been absent only an hour, her welcome was as rapturous as a dog's.

Hands washed, apron changed, Charlotte was set down to her sampler.

"When I come back from marketing," said her mother, "I shall expect you to have finished this row of cross-stitch."

As soon as she heard the outer door close, Charlotte ran to the cupboard, climbed on a chair, and fetching down a miscellaneous collection of articles began arranging them on the floor. When her father was absent, that tall, strong, tender man who carried her about on his shoulder and was with her instantly when she woke in the ghost-haunted dark, she took refuge in the story of Prince Teàrlach in which she had now become completely absorbed.

"So Teàrlach crossed the sea in his little boat with his Seven Men," she earnestly explained to a rag moppet given her by some friendly dressmaker, "and he was sick but he wouldn't go to bed, because you feel better if you struggle against it."

She set two spoons, a large one and a small one, side by side.

"This big one's the frigate *Elizabeth*, and the little one's Teàrlach's brig, *Du Teillay*. Woosh! they sail across the sea . . . no, they don't yet. I've forgot to tell you about the letter Teàrlach wrote to his father before he sailed."

She rose and declaimed dramatically:

" 'Let what will happen, the stroke is struck, and I have taken a firm resolve to conquer or die, and to stand my ground as long as I have a man remaining with me.' "

That was a lovely bit. It made little shivers go up and down your spine. Charlotte could never remember the lessons her mother tried to teach her, but she learnt by heart with the greatest of ease every word in the story of Prince Teàrlach.

Now came the sea-fight. From across the hearthrug a kettle, doing duty for H.M.S. *Lion*, hove in sight, while various pots and pans represented other British ships appearing on the horizon. The *Elizabeth* cleared her decks for action, though her opponent had nearly twice her number of guns. "Boom, boom, boom! 'Hoist your jib!' cries the captain of the *Lion*. 'We'll get across her bows.'" The kettle was dragged forward, all her port guns firing a broadside which raked the *Elizabeth* fore and aft.

"Now you see the *Lion* gets between Teàrlach's ships. Bang, bang! She fires her starboard guns, but they pass between the *Du Teillay*'s masts, 'cept for some small-shot which riddles her sails. It's growing dark now"—the spoons were cautiously withdrawn from the vicinity of the kettle—"and Teàrlach's ships can get near enough to talk to one another. 'We must sail back to the safety of the country whence we came,' say the captains. 'You go back,' says Teàrlach to the captain of the *Elizabeth*, 'because you're wounded and your ship's damaged, but I'm going on to Fairyland as I said I would.' 'But the fairy folk will never rise for you if you go alone,' they say. 'You will see! You will see!' cries Prince Teàrlach."

She *became* Teàrlach. She knew exactly how he must have felt as he made that bold decision, as all through the night he paced the battle-scarred deck of his tiny ship, alone in the waste of waters, straining his eyes to catch the first glimpse of the country rightfully his. And she knew what that country looked like. Her father's descriptions had made it more vivid than the real world. She saw now, not the shabby room in which she played, but great towering cliffs loom up through the mist of early morning, breakers crashing

140

whitely against their base. From the cliffs an eagle came soaring, hovering over the little ship.

" 'The king of birds comes to welcome you to Fairyland, Prince Teàrlach,' says one of the Seven Men."

Charlotte bent backwards and forwards on the hearthrug, pulling an imaginary oar. Now she leapt out of the longboat, drenched with cold spray, on to gleaming silver sand; there were rocks the colour of an old blood-stain, and above them a green slope powdered with the gold of lady's-bedstraw. Fishing in the pocket of her apron, Charlotte brought out a handful of imaginary seeds.

"While he was waiting to come over," she explained to her silent audience, "Teàrlach picked some big rosy convolvulus, and now he drops them where he has landed on the shores of Fairyland. And in all the fairy country they don't grow anywhere else——"

"Have you finished your row of cross-stitch, Charlotte?"

The child blinked at her mother. It was always so difficult to come back from Fairyland, and Mama never seemed to understand the importance of that place. Looking at the sampler, Mama administered a sharp slap, and Charlotte howled.

"Papa never smacks me. Oh, *when* is Papa coming home?"

He came home from yet another shattering of his hopes. The great French fleet under Conflans had been almost destroyed by Admiral Hawke in Quiberon Bay. But he tossed Pouponne on to his shoulder as usual, and told her he had brought her a present. It was one of those touching little gifts sent to him from time to time by the faithful ones who had preferred to creep back to their own country and live as best they could, rather than enter foreign service or be a burden on their ruined Prince.

"Shortie-cake, Pouponne," said Charles, taking the box out of its tartan wrapping. "The food of Fairyland."

There were other faithful ones he could no longer main-

141

tain, the starving household at Avignon. Once more he wrote to his father, recommending them to the care of the old King. 'Daniel and Morrison, valets-de-chambre. The first it will be charity to allow him something to live on, for he could not get service anywhere. As to Morrison, your Majesty could not get a better acquisition; he shaves and combs a wig perfectly, and is of the best character. Michel's son is a downright idiot; I gave him 360 livres a year. Mackenzie, Sword, Macdonnell, and Duncan, all footmen. The latter, though no ways fit for service, deserves particular attention; he was a poor shepherd who succoured me when I was skulking in the Highlands.'

Thus he pleaded on the behalf of men scarce poorer than himself.

2

It was not until the following year, the summer of 1760, that King James replied. He wrote a short, touching letter in handwriting almost illegible. His health was altogether broken; he was dragging out the life of an invalid in his bedchamber in the desolate Palazzo Muti. Before he died (and he felt that death was near), he yearned to see his dearest Carluccio again; it was sixteen years since they had met. He enclosed a draft on his banker for 12,000 livres for the expenses of Charles's journey; as for the poor servants sent to him from Avignon, he would make shift to maintain them somehow.

'I endeavoured to persuade your brother to make them an allowance, but though he has just been appointed to the office of Camerlengo, and consecrated Archbishop of Corinth *in partibus infidelium*, he is exceedingly careful over money. If you come, pray don't mention the enclosed draft to him; he looks to have everything at my death.'

So far Charles had kept the vow he had made that day when he had heard how Henry, with their father at least a partial accomplice, had sneaked out of Paris to become a cardinal; he would never, he had sworn, return to the exiled Court in which he had been born. But his father's letter touched him deeply; and after all it would be only a flying visit. He could do it cheaply, as he had learned to do everything; then there would be a good slice of that banker's draft to divide between Clementina and the strong-box he still kept under his bed.

And to comfort Pouponne while he was away she should have the finest wax doll money could buy, to be dressed by Iain Beag, who was clever with his fingers, in full Highland costume.

"So Teàrlach had an awning put up on the deck of the *Du Teillay*, and sat there in his plain black coat and cambric stock to receive the Chiefs of Fairyland."

"What did they look like?" demanded Pouponne, avid for every detail.

They were almost in the room with him as he described the scene, good Bishop Hugh Macdonald, Kinlochmoidart, the Macdonalds of Clanranald and Glenalladale, the first of the faithful ones. And the High Bard, Alastair Mac Mhaisghstir, who had sent him translations of his own Gaelic poems expressing the longing of the Gaels for the leader long promised by their seers. Alastair had sat down beside the fair-haired youth in his black coat under the awning, had explained the advantages of the plaid in war, and had taught him to drink the King's health in Gaelic, '*Deoch slainte Righ*'.

"They all implored Teàrlach to go home, for how could he succeed against such odds? But he said to them, 'I am come home.' There was a young lad standing near him, and on an impulse Teàrlach turned to him with the appeal, 'Will *you* not assist me?' And the boy answered, grasping his broadsword, 'I will! I will! I am ready to die for you though no other man will stand by me.' It made the rest ashamed, Pouponne, to hear a boy speak so bravely. There was another man, a great Chief, the most powerful of them all. He joined in the general chorus begging Teàrlach to go back whence he came. 'In a few days,' Teàrlach told him, 'with the few friends I have, I will set up the Royal Standard, and proclaim to the people of Fairyland that Teàrlach is come over to claim the crown of his ancestors, to win it, or to perish in the attempt. You who, so my father has often told me, were our firmest friend, may stay at home and learn from the newspapers the fate of your Prince.' "

"And did he—oh did he, Papa?"

"No, Pouponne. He cried, 'Not so. I'll share the fortune of my Prince, and so shall every man over whom Nature or fortune has given me any power.' "

That answer of Lochiel rang in his ears, the answer that had decided the issue. If only France had acted then, had kept her sworn word to send him succour!

"So he marched to raised the Standard. He had sent away the *Du Teillay*, so now they could not beg him to go back. Only a few of the Chiefs had come in, but the fiery cross had gone round all Fairyland summoning the rest to the rendezvous. Teàrlach stayed the night in a mean barn, and he could not sleep for anxiety lest there be no response to that summons. Early morning showed him a dim, empty glen, all the mountains round about flushed with the first bloom of the heather. Will they come? he kept asking himself as he dressed——"

"What did he wear, Papa? What did he look like?"

He glanced at the cracked mirror on the wall, and saw himself as he was now, a man of forty, his face ravaged with ill-health and mental strain, his wig ill-dressed, his clothes shabby and flung on anyhow. But behind this reflection he saw another.

"He was tall and strong and upright. He wore a dun-coloured coat, scarlet breeches, and a yellow bob-wig the colour of his own hair. In his blue bonnet he had fastened a white cockade, for that was the emblem of his cause. He had a silver-hilted sword by his side and pistols in his belt, and on his breast was a jewelled Order that sparkled in the sun of that fine summer morning."

"And did the fairy folk keep faith with him?"

"Listen, Pouponne." He imitated pipe-music. "After hours of waiting, when he was nearly in despair, he heard, very faint in the distance, the skirl of the pipes. And then he saw three men upon the skyline of the hills, then three more, and more, and more, marching in two columns, and between them there were the prisoners they had captured in their first brush with their powerful foe. There was one old Chief among them who had been three years bedridden, but, said he, he had felt a kind of new life on the news of Teàrlach's landing. When all had come in there were more than a thousand crowded upon that green level among the heather by the loch. And when the Bishop had blessed the Royal Standard and it was raised on high, you never saw such a flinging of bonnets into the air, nor heard such a shout of acclamation."

He added, half forgetting the child on his knee:

"That was Teàrlach's finest and purest hour of joy; that little gathering of men had no faint-hearts and defeatists among them, no Lowland lairds to sow jealousies, no material motives, no self-interest. In the hearts of all there was nothing but stark love and loyalty."

She did not understand these long words, but, sensitive to her father's moods, she caught some nuance that made her exclaim in sudden anxiety:

"Teàrlach did win in the end, didn't he, Papa? Fairy princes always live happy ever after."

He sat looking down at her, a strange expression on his face. Puzzled by this, and by his silence, she insisted:

"He *was* a fairy prince, wasn't he, Papa?"

Charles had been drinking and was off his guard. His decision to go to Rome, his shrinking from it, his dread of leaving his child who was his only consolation and treasure, all had combined to drive him to one of his old solitary drinking bouts.

145

"No, Pouponne," he answered bitterly, "he is a real prince, God pity him!"

"*Is?*" She wriggled round on his knee to face him, her eyes sparkling with excitement. "Oh, where does he live? What is he doing now? Shall I ever meet him?"

He pressed her curly head against his shoulder, and murmured so low that she could scarcely hear him:

"He lives in what the worldly-wise call cloudland. He is listening for a call that never comes. And will you ever meet him? . . . Perhaps some day when you are older, my darling, and can understand." Then in a sudden frenzy: "Don't leave me, Pouponne! All the rest who loved me are estranged or dead. Promise me *you'll* never leave me, my little Pouponne."

She began to cry.

"I was so longing to hear the end of the story when Teàrlach wins back his father's throne."

He winced at the innocent thrust, but then controlled himself, hating this lapse into self-pity.

"Teàrlach's story isn't ended yet, my treasure. Maybe it will have a happy ending after all, but only if you always love and trust Teàrlach, whatever you hear other people say about him. He can keep his courage and his resolution so long as he has the refuge of your loving, trusting little heart."

## 3

Charlotte was tying the imaginary laces of imaginary brogues.

" 'Before I loose these again,' " she chanted, " 'I'll be up with Mr Cope.' "

She strutted up and down the garden, pausing to explain to her rag moppet, propped against a tree:

"Teàrlach is marching south with only a guinea in his pocket, to give battle to Johnnie Cope. He marches so fast that the nimble fairy folk are glad when the heel of his brogue comes off and slows him down a bit. Now he's marching through some cornlands, and notices that the corn's not been cut. 'I forbade my clansmen to reap,' explains a Chief, 'as a punishment for not coming with me to fight for you.' Teàrlach draws his sword and cuts a few ears. 'Now,' says he, 'they can cut the rest; the ban is lifted.' "

What came next? This part of the story was rather confused in her mind. And also she was vaguely puzzled. Papa had said that Teàrlach was a real prince, and Papa had looked so sad, begging her not to leave him. What could that have to do with Teàrlach, and how could Pouponne leave Papa? . . .

"There's the bit about the Usurper putting a reward of £30,000 on Teàrlach's head, and Teàrlach retorting by putting half a crown on his, but I can't remember where that comes," she told the moppet. "Anyway, Teàrlach is going to try to capture the big town in this part of Fairyland, and on his way there a castle fires at him, and a cannon-ball lands only a few yards from where he's marching. He laughs and cries, 'The dogs bark but dare not bite!' And every night he camps in the open with his men, and they dance reels and sing songs because they're all so happy to have Teàrlach for their leader, and they don't care a bit about the enemy being so powerful——"

Her mother was calling her from the window, but Charlotte pretended not to hear. This was one of the best bits, the capture of Edinburgh and the marching out to give battle to Johnnie Cope and his dragoons.

" 'Gentlemen! I have flung away the scabbard. Mr Cope shall not escape us as he did on our march.' Now there's an awful lot to do here, so you'll have to watch carefully," she admonished the moppet. "You see, I've got to be both Teàrlach and the enemy. Teàrlach's found a guide who can lead his army across a dangerous bog during the night, so that in the morning they can surprise Johnnie Cope (this really comes after the capture of the big town, but I'll have to tell you about that another time); and you mustn't mind if I come dashing right over you, because that's what the fairy folk did. Here I come! throwing off my plaid, drawing my broadsword——"

"Charlotte!" Her mother had come up unobserved. Mama would be angry because Charlotte had torn her gown in the heat of battle. But for some reason Mama seemed more nervous than cross. "Charlotte, we have to go on a journey, and you must be very good and do as I tell you, and not trouble me with questions."

Charlotte was well used to sudden flittings; ever since she could remember she and Papa and Mama had moved from place to place, sometimes in the middle of the night. Mama had a cloak-bag in her hand now, and hurriedly putting on Charlotte's capuchin, urged her towards the gate.

"But where is Papa?" demanded Charlotte, hanging back.

"He is following us. He will be with us quite soon."

"Tomorrow?"

"Perhaps. But now Mama is with you, and you are quite safe, and you are going to ride in a fine coach."

A strange gentleman lifted Charlotte into the coach. He had just set her down when she remembered that she had left her rag moppet under the tree. It was the only toy she had, but when she asked to go back for it, Mama burst into tears and implored the strange gentleman to bid the driver whip up his horses.

Charlotte fell asleep presently, lulled by the rapid motion.

As soon as he came to the part of the street whence he could see the house in Sedan where he was staying, Charles began to look eagerly for someone who was sure to be watching for him. The last thing he saw when he went out, the first when he returned, was that little round face, soft as a rose, framed in curly chestnut hair, straight nose flattened against the window-pane, and as soon as she saw him the ecstatic cry:

"Papa! Papa! Papa! Here's Pouponne!"

Secreted in the deep pocket of his coat today was Pouponne's new doll, but she must not see it until Iain Beag had dressed it in kilt and jacket and plaid made from some bits of tartan, and put a blue bonnet with a white cockade upon its flaxen head. It would be ready, Iain Beag had promised, by the time Charles must start for Rome next week.

He crossed the street the sooner to be able to get his first glimpse of Pouponne at the window, smiling in anticipation of that precious moment.

Pouponne was not there.

Tormented as he was by a dozen problems, he was conscious of a disappointment out of all proportion. Ridiculous, he chided himself; she cannot be for ever at the window. And yet somehow or other, as though where he was concerned she had a sixth sense, Pouponne always had known just when to expect her father. He hurried into the house, calling to her. There was no answer, no bursting open of a door, no sturdy legs racing down the stair. The house seemed oddly quiet, as though it concealed some sinister secret. Then Iain Beag came shambling out from the back.

"The lady has not returned," said Iain. He always referred to Clementina, whom he hated, as 'the lady'.

"Returned from whence?" Charles asked sharply.

"I am not knowing that whatever, Sir. She went out in a hired coach brought here by a gentleman this morning. The knowledge was not on me who the gentleman was. The lady took the bairn with her."

Charles stared at him, a nerve beginning to twitch in his cheek. But it was only because he was in a strained state that the news sounded alarming; Clementina was for ever saying that she had friends he did not know, and presumably one of these friends had taken her and Pouponne out for a drive. Yet how like Clementine, or Clementina as she was now, to go out for the day and not leave him a note of explanation. When she came home she would say that 'my daughter' (she never said 'our') was too tired to have a story told her.

Never mind. At some time during the night, Pouponne would pull the string and the little bell over his head would tinkle, and he would go to her, pretending not to know that naughty Pouponne was only feigning to be frightened; and he would tell her of those halcyon days he had spent in the palace of his ancestors, Holyroodhouse, recruits flocking to his Standard after his brilliant victory over Cope, all his trust in himself and his Highlanders justified, his pipers playing every night, *When the King enjoys his own again.*

Meanwhile there were letters to be written. He must do his utmost to persuade the Pope and the great Powers of Europe to recognise his claim when his father died.

But he could not concentrate this evening. Looking out of the window, he saw something lying under a tree; Pouponne's rag moppet. He went and fetched it in, smiling to himself. Soon Pouponne would have a doll more worthy of her than this; meantime it comforted him absurdly to feel that Pouponne must have gone out only for a few hours, or she would never have left her dear moppet behind.

I'm a plaguey fool, he thought; propped the toy against a bottle of cheap wine on his table, and turned resolutely to his correspondence.

The hours crept by. The house was as quiet as a grave, save for the impatient scratching of his quill over the paper. His mind became full of his father whom he would see at Rome next week among the old familiar surroundings. A sadly wise man even by the time I was born, thought Charles, boyhood memories crowding on him. A man who had been the victim of the most formidable and vile conspiracy while yet unborn; ushered into the world to the clamour of a filthy calumny; his childhood overshadowed by ill health and the melancholy of an exiled Court; bred up in rigid etiquette, yet without any of the advantages of royalty.

And yet, thought Charles, his heart reproaching him for

all these years of estrangement, there was as pure and as patient a life as ever man lived under consistent disappointment and hope deferred, quietly ready for action, gentle with his difficult wife and his squabbling adherents, gay with his children, constantly endeavouring to bring them up to be good Englishmen in a foreign land, clinging heroically to his own father's dying injunction, 'Preserve your faith against all things and all men.'

The Catholic faith, which Charles himself had bartered for the empty promises of the Oak Society.

The Catholic faith, he muttered aloud, desperately justifying that apostasy, which has been the ruin of our House. Which seduced Henry into completing our ruin.

It was strange, he thought irrelevantly, how the two worst blows of his life had struck him unprepared. He had never been happier, nor more sanguine of success, than on that morning after he had entered Derby in 1745. He had never been more confident of Henry's affection and fidelity than on that evening when he had accepted Henry's invitation to supper, and he had found the Hôtel de Sens so brightly lit, with supper ready laid. Henry must be celebrating some good news, he remembered thinking. . . .

Why the devil did such memories come to torment him now?

As he turned once more to his writing, he became aware that it was growing dark. The month was July; therefore it must be . . . as though in answer, the bells of Sedan rang out the hour; it was nine o'clock.

Long past Pouponne's bedtime; and she had not come home.

In ghastly repetition of that other night when he had waited in vain for the return of Henry, his uneasiness turning to apprehension and at last to stark panic, he waited now, hour after hour, for the return of Clementina and Pouponne. He questioned and re-questioned Iain Beag, but that faithful creature could tell him nothing except that 'the lady' seemed to have been in great haste. He made short excursions about the town, enquiring of acquaintances whether they had seen the missing ones. Some had seen the coach drive away, but whither it went they could not tell him.

Each time he came rushing back expectant, only to be met with that sinister silence of the house and the sight of Pouponne's moppet leaning limply against the wine bottle, button eyes staring into space.

In the early hours of the morning, exhausted, almost numb now, while he was pacing up and down the hallway he saw some small white object pushed under the door. He stared at it stupidly, unable to rouse himself to fling the door open, go in pursuit of the someone whose softly running feet he could hear padding away into the darkness. With an enormous effort of will he forced himself at last to pick up the paper; twisting in his heart like a vicious knife was the thought that Pouponne had been kidnapped.

He took the paper to his room, broke the wafer, read what was written there in Clementina's flowing hand. But as with that letter of his father's telling him of Henry's defection long ago, so now his mind refused to take in the sense of what he read.

'Sir, your Royal Highness cannot be surprised at my having parted, when you consider the repeated bad treatment I have met with these 8 years past . . . daily risk of losing my life . . . my health broken . . . pushed me to the greatest extremity . . . no woman in the world would have suffered so long as what I have done . . . I put myself under the care of Providence . . . I will never do a dirty action for the world . . . I quit my Prince with the greatest regret, and shall always be miserable if I don't hear of his happiness and welfare . . . I hope in time coming to merit by my conduct your friendship for me and my child. . . .'

"But *when* is Papa coming?"

"You are quite safe here in Paris with Mama. Papa is cruel, yet you must not think ill of him. Some people get sick in their minds, Charlotte, and then they are dangerous to others."

Charlotte burst into a storm of tears.

"You lied to me! You've kept promising that Papa would be coming, tomorrow, next week. Papa never lied to me, never broke a promise——"

"Charlotte, Mama was forced to lie to you. You are not old enough to understand. See this lovely doll Mama has brought you, darling. Would you like me to call you Pou-ponne——"

"*No!* Only Papa calls me Pouponne. I don't *want* a new doll; I want Papa and my moppet."

They were staying at an auberge, the Hôtel St Louis in the Rue des Grand Augustins. Clementina had taken the name of Madame du Bois, and immediately had applied to the Archbishop of Paris for his protection, telling a pitiful tale. He had promised to get her and her daughter into the guest-house of the Convent of the Visitation in the Rue de Bac; it was very genteel, and very expensive, but Clementina was in hopes of an allowance from Rome. She had written to King James, dilating on her duty to give her daughter a good Christian education, and thus to make her worthy of her royal blood.

"Soon we are going to have a proper home, Charlotte, where you will have good kind nuns to teach you all the things a young lady ought to know, how to play on the harpsichord, and to read and write in French and Latin; and when you are able to write a fair hand, then you shall correspond with your Papa."

It was the bait she was to hold out to Charlotte for years to come.

Lord Elcho was announced. He had written cynically to

his old master, 'Why bother about this woman? There are plenty of others.' He had aided and abetted Clementina in her flight, and since he was writing a Journal, a hymn of hate to Charles, he expected her to provide him with some good material. Encouraging, probing, suggesting, he listened in feigned distress as most willingly she poured out the tale of her wrongs and ill-usage.

"There was a story, madame," he prompted her, "(I scarce like to offend your ears by repeating it), told me by a certain gentleman of my acquaintance, of how, happening to be in a low tavern in Liège, he noticed a man and a woman at a table near him, who quarrelled violently, he calling her '*coquine*', and she replying, 'Although a prince, you are unworthy to be called a gentleman.' My acquaintance actually saw the man strike his companion, and unable to endure so degrading a spectacle, took his departure. Could it have been——?"

"It may have been," replied Clementina, weeping with self-pity. "He often struck me when he was drunk. Fifty times in one day he has beaten me. And he was so madly jealous that he surrounded my bed with chairs perched on tables, and on the chairs he strung little bells on strings, so that he would be awakened if anyone approached me during the night."

"My Papa," observed Charlotte, who had been busy staring at the gentleman's exceedingly tight black breeches exposed by his cut-away coat-skirts, and wondering whether they were going to burst, "my Papa had a little bell above his bed, and when I pulled a string it woke him up, and when I had a nightmare he always——"

"Charlotte, pray remember your manners. You are interrupting our conversation. I intend, my lord, to give this child an education worthy of majesty, if the King will be so kind as to render me assistance."

"Alas, madame, that family has always been distinguished by a lack of generosity, even an indifference to debts of honour. I presented the Prince with £1,500 on my joining

154

him in '45, and have never had a penny of it back, though I have applied to him repeatedly."

"Are you a friend of my Papa?" Charlotte enquired innocently.

He regarded her with distaste. She was extraordinarily like her father.

"I must confess, madame, before I had known him twenty-four hours I heartily repented my folly and rashness in espousing his cause; and most of the people about him were in the same case, cursing the hour they came into his service, which most of them continued in for no other motive but fear to want bread."

King James replied kindly to Clementina's appeal for his protection and aid. She ought, he wrote, to have obtained the Prince's permission before taking this step, but now it was done she must concern herself with bringing up her child in a good Christian atmosphere, and with repenting her own past sins. He, King James, would make her an allowance of 6,000 livres a year, and he had written his son explaining his attitude towards the affair.

With so generous an annuity, Clementina had no difficulty in renting rooms in the guest-house of the Convent of the Visitation, near the Tuileries. It would be a dull but not unpleasant life, and would lend her that aura of respectability for which she pined, especially as she fully intended to give out that she had been secretly married to Charles.

About noon of the day fixed for her taking up residence in the convent, she returned with Charlotte from some shopping to await the coach that was conveying them to the Rue de Bac. As they came into the hallway of the Hôtel St Louis, Clementina noticed a man, his back turned towards her, talking with the *concierge*. The man turned, and it was Iain Beag.

It was too late to avoid him. Charlotte had made a rush at him, clasped him round the legs, and screamed:

"Iain! Iain! Have you brought Papa?"

"Come to my apartments, Mr Stewart," Clementina said coldly, well aware that the *concierge* was watching in avid curiosity. "Though I am afraid I cannot spare you more than a few minutes, for I am just on the point of leaving."

When they reached her rooms and the door was shut, she rounded on Stewart.

"How dare you intrude on me in this manner! I suppose your master has sent you to spy on me. . . . Charlotte, Mama has to speak privately with Mr Stewart; you must go and play in your bedroom. . . . Charlotte, you heard what Mama said."

Chin quivering, large eyes filling with tears, Charlotte climbed down from Iain Beag's knee and went slowly out of the room.

"My master," Iain burst out without preliminaries, "has been altogether taken out of himself; he has a high fever upon him; he cannot eat or sleep, nor will he even permit me to shave him. From morning till night for a whole month now he has kept me and also good Mr John Gordon of the Scots College on our feet, searching and enquiring for the bairn. He will not make his intended journey to Rome; he swears he will burn down every convent in Paris until he finds her. There is a terrible frenzy upon him, and all his cry, day and night, is for '*la petite*'."

"I would rather make away with myself than return to your master. Do you suppose I took this desperate step without cause?"

"He does not wish you to return to him, lady. It is only his bairn he wants, his one comfort in his great misfortunes. I am telling you that you will drive him to some extremity if you keep her from him."

"I would cut the child in pieces with my own hands before I would give her back to one so mad and dangerous!" Clementina cried dramatically.

She went to the door and opened it.

"And now, sir, pray go about your business if you have any. And if you should have a mind to dog me when I leave here, I may tell you, to spare you the pains, that I and my child are now under the protection both of his Majesty and of the Archbishop of Paris."

Peeping round her bedroom door, Charlotte saw Iain Beag leave, but he looked so wild and fierce that she dared not slip out to speak to him. He was muttering to himself in Gaelic, and she caught the familiar name, 'Teàrlach'.

## 5

With a certain bitter deliberation, Charles tore into small fragments two letters he had just received. One was from his father, the other from his mistress.

The King wrote temperately. He had not ordered Miss Walkinshaw to leave his son, but Charles could not doubt the desire he had had of this; and now she had done so and had written to him for his protection and a subsistence for herself and her daughter, 'you cannot but be sensible that I could not do otherwise than grant her request, not only on her own account but even on yours, that her child might have a decent education, which you could not give her in the situation you are, and in reality it would be ruining that poor child if you were to keep her with you in the uncertain and ambulatory life you lead, especially now when she is not of an age capable of being company for you, or of giving you real comfort of any kind. . . .'

Clementina wrote emotionally. Clementina lived in a perpetual melodrama, merely varying her roles. She was now the deeply wronged but forgiving heroine, with a touch of the self-sacrificing mother.

Nothing, she wrote, could be more distressing to her than 'this fatal separation' (which she herself had brought about). His Royal Highness was too good and just not to acknowledge how cruelly he had wronged her, but 'that shall never hinder me from having for your Royal Person all attachment and respect'. By taking her 'desperate step' she had had nothing else in view but his honour and glory and the

157

sacred duty of giving her child a Christian education, her child who was her only comfort in her great affliction. She would rather die ten thousand deaths than let a word slip from her mouth that could do her dearest Prince the smallest hurt or injury. And so on.

He threw the fragments of paper on to the dying fire, and with a sudden vicious gesture pitched after them a battered rag moppet and a new wax doll dressed in Highland costume.

They were gestures of defeat. During the last month of agony he had kept sane only by his resolve to recover Pouponne. He had borrowed money to offer a reward for her, circulated her description everywhere—'Seven years of age, of a fair complexion, round, full face, large eyes, nose straight and a little flat at the tip, very strong for her age.' But since Clementina and Pouponne were now under his father's protection, there was nothing more he could do; the French Court would not act; Principal Gordon of the Scots College, a man whose fidelity to himself it was impossible to suspect (for in his anguish he had suspected everyone of being an accessory to Clementina's flight), and who had worn himself out trying to trace the fugitives, had written finally that since 'the Old Gentleman over the Hills' had intervened, he, Gordon, could do no more, for it would be contrary to the loyalty he owed his Sovereign.

Very well, then. The thing was finished. He had no idea where he was going when he left this house in Sedan today. He was riding away from all human ties, from every treacherous hope, from every memory of what had been. He had been mad to give his heart, first to a woman, and then to a little child, as mad as he had been to give it to a brother.

Clementina had failed him, as Henry had failed him. In each of their flights from him there had been an essentially mean under-handedness. He did not blame either of them; the hurt was too deep for blame. But as he had refused to have Henry's name mentioned in his presence, so now Clementina might write him her whining, self-contradictory, melodramatic screeds until the Judgment Day before he would reply. She had boasted of the powerful friends who would maintain her if she left him; let them do it. She was no longer any concern of his.

He would erase her from his memory. And not only her but the little child she had made her innocent accomplice, whose mind she would poison against him, his own little child whom they would not trust to his custody.

# PART THREE
## 1765 — 1783

### LOUISE

## ONE

*I*

TWENTY years had passed since Europe had been stirred by the tale of how a young prince had set off almost alone to win back three kingdoms, and had come within an ace of achieving the impossible.

Most of the leading characters on both sides in that epic had gone for ever from the stage. King George II, his brutal son, the Duke of Cumberland, Lord George Murray, the famous seven men who had sailed in the *Du Teillay*, all were dead. Dead too, meeting his end in a miserable bothy, half blind from disease, hated by his clan, and neglected by the Government to which he had sold himself, was Young Glengarry, Pickle the Spy.

But old Earl Marischal was very much alive, though nearing eighty. His return to his native land in 1760 had not been a success, for his tenants, stupid, ignorant creatures, had strongly disapproved of his Turkish concubine and his household of True Believers, and also had disseminated the absurd story that on the news of his pardon by King George the bell at Keith Hall, his ancestral seat, immediately had cracked. So he had returned to the comfort of Germany where, though he missed his old friend the sun, he had a fine house built for him by Frederick of Prussia, a garden in which to potter, a fat income, and ample leisure to correspond with the free-thinking gentry whose views he shared.

Late in the year 1765 he was writing one of his sportively blasphemous letters to Hume, whom he had nicknamed, because of Hume's size, '*Verbum caro factum*'.

'. . . I had almost forgot to mention that poor Rousseau, who is in very low water again, has received a donation from —you will never guess it—none other than the Young Pretender, who for years has been quite lost sight of. In Rome they say his father is really dying at last, so we are like to have a new saint and a whole new outcrop of miracles, but since he has been a more unconscionable time about it than even Charles II, his continuing to survive is a miracle in itself. The Pompadour really is dead, having looked like a dead fish for months. By the way, did I ever tell you the story (I admit I had it but at the fourth hand, but can well credit it), that when the Young Pretender was to go to Scotland in '45 they had to bind him hand and foot and carry him on shipboard, so far did his courage fail when it came to the point. . . .'

In Florence, Horace Mann was writing one of his daily screeds to his 'dearest child', as he called Horace Walpole. The former was 'Sir Horace' now; and what with this new honour, the Arms of England displayed over his Legation, his somewhat mythical pedigree conspicuously hung up in the hall, and his coat-of-arms manufactured by the Heralds engraved on his seal and plate, the haughty Florentines at last allowed him the status of a gentleman. But they did not like him any better. He took it for granted that they were as eager to hear as he was to relate minute and loathsome details of the progress of his haemorrhoids; he was exceedingly effeminate; and worst of all in their eyes he had become an Italianised Englishman.

'There is a rumour abroad,' he wrote to Walpole, 'that the Old Pretender is dead at Rome. I wait with the most cruel impatience to have it confirmed. As for the Boy, there is not a spy but is totally ignorant of his whereabouts, and I sometimes wonder if the late Baron Stosch was not correct after all in his assertion that the Boy died years ago. Here is a strange tale they are telling, and one I have only just heard, that in the year '50 he went to England, and abjured Popery at St Martin-in-the-Fields. You will laugh at me perhaps for being solicitous about so pitiful an object as the Boy now is, but he still may be made use of to do mischief. . . .'

In Rome, Henry, Bishop of Frascati, Cardinal-Priest, Duke of York, and Vice-Chancellor of St Peter's, was dictating letters in his magnificent palace of the Cancellaria. As a sign of his most recent dignity the Cancellaria pleased him; but his best beloved home was still his episcopal palace of La Rocca in Frascati, frowning down upon the grey Campagna like a fortress from its steep height.

There amid the barbaric splendour which accorded with his taste, he lived in royal state, unshadowed by the melancholy of exile or by asceticism. There he was busy with his inexhaustible efforts to relieve the poor, with putting up marble inscriptions, collecting from all over the world jewels and rich stuffs for the adornment of his cathedral, and, since the unfortunate accident when he and his guests had been precipitated into the coachhouse by reason of the floor of his dining-room giving way, he was occupied with putting the ancient palace into a thorough state of repair.

In Rome nowadays he was always faintly uneasy, always looking forward to the moment when his forty blood-horses and his costly carriages would carry him and his household at breakneck speed back to Frascati. For not far away from the Cancellaria was the Palazzo Muti, the comfortless, half-furnished palace where he had been born. And in one of those high-ceilinged, marble-floored apartments his frail old father was dragging out a life that had become a living death. In 1762 a stroke had deprived King James of the use of his legs, and his speech had become almost unintelligible; only now and again when Henry visited him, did the Cardinal, not wanting to, catch the name 'Carluccio', and would see the feeble tears run down and the hollowed eyes fixed upon him, dumbly appealing.

"I do not know where my brother is," he would say again and again. "No one knows, Sir."

But he knew, only too well, where his brother's former mistress was. With King James's inability to conduct any business, Henry had the management of his father's affairs, and Henry had been exceedingly affronted to find frequent letters addressed to his father from Clementina Walkinshaw, some with seasonable compliments, others whining for an increase in her allowance. It was one of these letters he was being obliged to answer today; and it was an additional annoyance that he had to answer it through the secretary King James had appointed to succeed old James Edgar. Despite all Henry's exertions at Edgar's death-bed, that faithful servant had died as he had lived, a stout Protestant, and Henry simply could not understand why his father had appointed another heretic, Andrew Lumisden, who once had been in Charles's household, as his successor.

'His Royal Eminence begs to inform Miss Walkinshaw,' he dictated, unconsciously bridling, detesting the necessity to correspond with a loose woman even through a third person, 'that his Majesty being in the most delicate health is quite unable to receive or answer letters. He would further remind Miss Walkinshaw that it is entirely of his Majesty's royal bounty and Christian charity that for so many years past he has allowed her this handsome pension, and that she would be better employed in making sober provision for her livelihood in the event of his Majesty's death, than in demanding an increase.'

"There's the bairn," remarked Lumisden, pausing with uplifted quill.

"What did you say?"

Forgotten every word of your ain native tongue, Lumisden, who had spoken in English, grumbled to himself. Then aloud in Italian: "There is the child, Royal

Eminence. There was a little note enclosed to her grand-father, prettily written; his Majesty would have wanted to pay her some civil compliment on how well she writes in Latin——"

"The letters for my signature, Lumisden," Henry inter-rupted in a glacial voice. "And by the way, if any more letters are addressed to his Majesty from this Miss Walkin-shaw, pray make them up into a bundle and give them to me marked 'X'. I do not wish to have her name mentioned —you understand?"

When Lumisden had gone, Henry sat drumming his fingers upon the satinwood table. He had a great deal of business of his own to conduct, the ecclesiastical business he loved. Yet before summoning his own secretary there was a letter he must write himself, a letter he had put off writing for a long time. What he had told his father was true, that he did not know where Charles was; but he had a shrewd suspicion that Waters, Charles's banker in Paris, knew, or at least had the means to get in contact with the wanderer, and Henry's conscience told him plainly that it was his duty to break the silence of twenty years and write to Charles.

Pulling at his long upper lip, he began to frame sentences. 'His Majesty's death cannot be long delayed . . . he yearns most extremely to see you . . . I shall do what I can to induce the Pope to send you an invitation. . . .'

## 2

From Bracciana on its lake, Charles saw for the first time, a long way off, the dome of St Peter's. He thought he had developed a skin like a rhinoceros, that nothing and no one could ever hurt him again. But this first sight of the city of his birth pierced through his armour. After twenty-two years he was doing that which his enemies had so long and so vainly intrigued to make him do; he, 'the Cardinal's brother', was going to settle in Rome.

His shabby old chaise, accompanied by a few outriders, bumped over the ruts in the Via Cassia, and stopped. Looking out, he saw liveried servants hastily shovelling the snow from the path of a short, stout, swarthy-faced gentleman, very magnificent in a fur-lined cloak thrown over his crimson robes, who had alighted from his equally magnificent carriage drawn by six horses, and was approaching the chaise. For an instant, as long ago when Henry had come to meet him on the road to Paris, he did not recognise his brother. But it was indubitably Henry's voice, pompous, prim, and now just a little shy, that greeted him.

"I offer your Majesty my homage as your subject, and my fraternal love. Welcome home, Sir; this for me is a most happy hour."

Charles prevented him as he bent to kiss hands, kissing Henry's cheek instead, holding him at arm's length for an instant, feeling the old boyhood affection, driven underground but never lost, kindle to warmth.

"My dear Harry! It's good to see you, and that makes the hour happy. But as for home—well. I have a few old friends with me, as you see; Sir John Hay of Restalrig, whom I've just created a baron, Stafford and Mackintosh, and of course Iain Beag. And my 'cello. I hope you won't be ashamed of me; we make such a contrast. Such a very splendid Cardinal, such a very down-at-heels King."

As Henry handed his brother into his own gorgeous carriage, he in his turn was observing the difference nineteen years had made. He was pleasantly surprised. All the spies, who, in fact had lost sight of Charles for years, had asserted that he was a complete wreck, corpulent, pimpled, so stooping that he was almost a hunchback, always fuddled with drink. Actually Henry had never seen his brother look handsomer, though his leanness spoke of years of undernourishment, and the deeply engraved lines on his face made him look older than forty-six. There was, too, an odd, mask-like expression, in striking contrast to the essential openness of his youth, and beneath the pleasant friendly tone there was an edge of cynicism.

"I wish I had better news for your Majesty," Henry said, when they were driving on again, "but in the matter of your recognition I fear His Holiness is not to be moved. Indeed, I have worked as hard as any man could do for it," he hurried on, finding himself unconsciously taking up the old defensive tone, "writing personally to the Kings of France and Spain, interviewing their Ambassadors, and drawing up with my own hand a Memorial I presented to His Holiness. He called a Conclave to discuss the matter, but though Cardinal Albani, always a firm friend to Hanover, was admitted, Cardinal Negroni, once in my service, was disqualified on that very account. All His Holiness is prepared to do is to recognise your Majesty as Prince of Wales."

"How extremely odd. How can there be a Prince of Wales when the King is dead?" And then, abruptly: "Did he suffer much, Harry?"

"He died very peacefully—a most edifying death-bed! I was not present, having retired to the Cancellaria just before the end, for I was quite overcome with grief. He was buried in St Peter's with full royal honours, which makes this refusal of the Pope to recognise your Majesty the more inconsistent. But if your Majesty is patient, and can assure me that——"

"Not quite so many 'Majesties', Harry. It will offend the Pope, and you at least must not quarrel with him. But you were saying?"

Henry shot a covert glance at him. Had there been something faintly mocking in that remark?

"I was about to say, Sir, that I do not despair even yet of gaining our point, if you can assure me that certain horrible rumours are untrue. I mean, of your having apostatised. That, as you will not fail to understand, has shocked the Roman Court."

"So it's raked up that for an excuse for its inconstancy. There's no pleasing everybody. In Rome I am abhorred as a Protestant, and in England detested as a rank Papist. The truth of the matter is, Harry, that like the general run of men, I am entirely indifferent to creeds, but if it will do my business for me, I am very willing to follow the example of our ancestor, Henri le Grand, and to consider an empty title worth the Mass."

And then, before the deeply shocked Henry could remonstrate, he went on seriously:

"In twenty years, Harry, many old aims and dear ambitions have been hewn off me. I'm like the trunk of a lopped tree. But one thing I have kept, and will keep: my just title to the throne of Great Britain. I shall not receive anyone who will not acknowledge that just title; and since it seems I cannot be received in Rome with royal honours, I shall stay for the greater part of the year at our father's old villa at Albano, where at least I can get some shooting."

"I fear you will be very solitary. Roman society will not venture to accord you recognition since the Pope has refused it."

"To be solitary will be no new thing."

"I must also inform your Majesty that though our father has left you all his French investments, there are so many pensions and legacies charged upon them, and moreover several of the pensions he himself received stopped with his death, that I fear you will be somewhat poor."

"I am not precisely unused to poverty either," Charles observed with a dry smile. "At least it will be pleasant to live in a house of my own after so many years of mean lodgings."

They were entering Rome. The streets were crowded, but not by folk eager to get a sight of Charles Stuart, as the streets of Paris had been thronged when he escaped from Scotland in 1746. The Roman populace were making the most of the few days remaining before the Carnival ended on Ash Wednesday, for Easter fell early this year.

It was growing dusk, and all along the Corso the coaches of the quality promenaded as far as the Ponte Molle, playfully endeavouring to blow out one another's flambeaux, ladies pelting their gallants with sugar-plums, all driving slowly to see and be seen. Smart young men wore toupees so huge that they were obliged to take off their hats with the aid of their amber-topped canes; smart young women affected such vast cork rumps under their fashionable polonese gowns that they found it extremely difficult to sit down, and were so overweighted with ships in full sail, baskets of flowers, and marine temples which topped their immense coiffures, that they were all of them suffering from migraine.

"I have always in previous years left Rome before the Carnival," observed Henry, looking with disgust at a stalwart carman disguised as a woman who, clinging to the arm of a very small man, was dancing round a brazier on which a cook was frying *frittata*. "But naturally this year, with his Majesty's lamented death, and your Majesty's return to Rome, it was impossible."

Charles made no comment. For here was the shabby Palazzo Muti, no larger than a modest country manor-house, the Swiss Guards at the gates a witness to the fact that it was Papal property ('a house of my own', he had said), half the apartments shuttered and dust-sheeted, the old billiard-table on which he and Henry had played when they were boys, its cushions flaccid now, the Arms of England recently removed from the roof, the portraits of ancestors, the whisper of frayed hangings sounding like the intrigues of all the old Jacobites dead and gone.

Henry had done his best to make it look welcoming. Henry had killed the fatted calf. But there was the inevitable contrast between Henry (obviously fretting to get back to the important things of life), the white sheep of the family, the boy who had made good, and the prodigal son who had arrived too late to be clasped in his father's arms, who was an embarrassment to a brother who must have hoped he would never come back from the far country.

"That brandy is extremely potent," remarked Henry

when they were alone after supper. "Do you think it wise to drink any more? For I cannot conceal from your Majesty that this unfortunate failing of yours has become very public; and really I am persuaded we should gain ground with His Holiness were it not for the nasty bottle, which certainly must kill you at last. If you could get the better of this nasty habit——"

"You make it sound like a child wetting its bed."

"The singularity and incomprehensibility of your Majesty's temper puts me at a nonplus. I had hoped, Sir, that after all these years of a roaming, and, I fear, a dissolute life——"

"Tell me, Harry," Charles again interrupted, refilling his glass, "what would you have done had you been in my shoes when I escaped from Scotland in '46?"

It was rather an awkward question, and one Henry had not expected. He murmured something about settling down here in Rome, but once more his brother cut him short.

"Settled down to satisfy the gaze of curious tourists. It is strange that I should have to remind you, Harry, that we are a race of soldiers as well as kings. I was the heir to a lost throne; though defeated in one campaign, honour, if nothing else, forbade me to sheathe my sword and let it rust."

"Honour did not prevent you from becoming a renegade from the faith for which our grandfather lost his throne," Henry said tartly. "But one thing I certainly should not have done had I been you, and that was to raise up an enemy for myself in the nasty bottle."

Charles leaned back in his chair with a humorous groan.

"A great Prince of the Church you may be, Harry, but Lord! what a dreadful prig you are!"

"There is no need to be offensive."

"I agree with all my heart. There is no need for you to take it for granted that I am a sot. To you, wine has always been a luxury to be sniffed and sipped and savoured. To me, it has been an opiate. You've never needed opiates, for which you should thank God on your knees." Then impulsively he stretched out his hand. "Damn it all, Harry, don't let's quarrel this first evening when we are together again after nearly twenty years."

The smile that accompanied the words was full of the old irresistible charm, and Henry softened.

"I have been thinking, Sir," he said, changing the subject, "that it is more than time, if I may say so, that your Majesty sought a wife. For I need hardly remind you how vital to our cause it is that you should provide an heir."

"I reminded you of the same thing when I escaped from Scotland," observed Charles dryly. "But as you say, it is my duty to provide an heir, to father a race of beggars."

Henry clicked his tongue in deprecation of the last phrase. Then, taking the plunge, he asked delicately:

"I do trust that your Majesty has no—er—previous commitments?"

His brother stared at him in frank bewilderment.

"Commitments?"

"A person—a woman—has been putting it about that she was privately married to you in Flanders in the year '52."

Charles's face went hard as flint.

"Then this person has told a damned lie," he said deliberately.

Henry nodded, satisfied. He was determined to find a suitable royal bride for his brother, some young, healthy, and religious princess who not only would give Charles children, but make him settle down. Also Henry was pleased by the chance of being able to humiliate this detestable loose woman who still wrote him her whining letters, Clementina Walkinshaw.

## 3

"That was very nicely played, Charlotte," remarked Mère Gabriel, closing the music-book on the harpsichord. "With a little more practice you will have it to perfection for the

Christmas concert. Lulli seems to be your favourite composer, though Rameau is now more fashionable."

"Lulli was Papa's favourite, *ma mère*; he used to play his airs on the 'cello. I hoped that if I learnt them, I might be able to play duets with Papa when he sends for me."

"I see," said Mère Gabriel softly.

She was extraordinarily fond of this child, and had a high opinion of Charlotte's character. It was due as much to that character as to the example set by the Filles de Sainte-Marie that Charlotte, so charming, and of such romantic parentage, had avoided being spoilt. Mère Gabriel had been at the convent in the Rue de Bac when 'Madame du Bois' and her daughter had taken up residence there seven years previously; a hare-eyed little creature, Charlotte had been then, always in tears, screaming in nightmare, finding the convent like a prison after the roaming life to which she was accustomed, asking again and again for her Papa. There had been a long and painful struggle over the question of her Confirmation; Charlotte refused to be confirmed, because she would have to take another name as well as her own. But would she not be happy to take the name of a saint who would be her special patron? they had asked her. They had offered her virgins and martyrs, fiery vigorous saints like Catherine of Sienna, gentle saints like Cecilia. Charlotte had rejected them all. At last she had blurted out the truth.

"I want to have 'Pouponne', and there isn't a St Pouponne. It was Papa's name for me, and it would please him if I could have it sort of officially."

Yes, certainly this very adorable child had been in danger of becoming the victim of an obsession. But although, when she was nearly fourteen, she still clung to the hope of being sent for some day by her father, Mère Gabriel no longer feared for her. The mild and simple rule at the Visitandines, with its strict poverty but without those corporal mortifications at that time general in religious orders, had as its aim complete abandonment to the will of God; and all the in-

172

struction given by the nuns to their pupils was calculated to instil common sense, moderation, and reliance on the Divine. Six years of this education had moulded Charlotte's naturally strong character, without taking from it any of its liveliness and warm affection.

Charlotte hummed the air she had been playing, as she went to the set of rooms she and her mother occupied in the guest-house. As soon as she opened the door of the parlour, her mother said fretfully:

"You are late. Had you forgotten that this is the day when Mr Waters brings our allowance? I am afraid you are very thoughtless, Charlotte. Go and change your mob, pray, and put on a clean apron, the one of flowered lawn with lace. You know Mama likes you to look your best when Mr Waters calls, though you must take care to mention that you are much in need of a new gown, and perhaps that will soften the heart of your royal uncle."

On the death of King James, Henry had cut down Clementina's allowance from six thousand livres to five, a circumstance which had compelled her to move to a cheaper convent of the Visitations at Meaux on the Marne. Not one of Clementina's appeals against this had moved his Royal Eminence, but she was for ever hoping that the reports by Waters of the charm and grace of her daughter would have their effect upon the Cardinal.

"My dear Mr Waters," Clementina greeted the banker as he was shown into her parlour today, "I am most mortified that you should have to take this journey every month, but as I told you before, it was impossible for us to continue to reside in Paris on so short an allowance. Here is my daughter; does she not grow tall? I declare that if my royal brother-in-law could but see her picture, he—my dear sir, is there something amiss? You look so strangely."

"Madame," said the banker, detesting his errand and determined to get it over as quickly as possible, "you must pardon me for any pain I may give you, but I do only what I am commissioned to do. I have received a letter from his

Royal Eminence in which he writes that certain rumours have been put about to the effect that——"

He broke off. He had little sympathy with the mother, but he deeply compassionated the charming, lively child.

"Perhaps it would be better, madame, if Miss Charlotte were not present."

"No!" shrilled Clementina. "This child is my only support and comfort. Charlotte, you will stay with Mama who needs you when she has to receive unkind messages from your royal uncle."

"Yes, of course, Mama," said Charlotte, putting her arms round her mother's waist.

"Very well," sighed the banker. "I repeat that rumours have been put about to the effect that you are King Charles's legal wife. His royal brother, therefore, has sent me the most peremptory orders to obtain your affidavit to the contrary. His Majesty is inclined to consider marriage with some royal princess; you will understand, then, the necessity for this affidavit, distasteful though it must be to you."

Clementina straightway became hysterical, weeping, bewailing her hard fate, and denouncing the cruelty of her royal persecutor. As if it were not enough that he should cut down her allowance to a bare pittance, he who was so rich; now he must put on her this base humiliation! But Waters was watching the child, and was distressed by what he saw. The rosy cheeks had gone quite white with shock; and that she was intelligent enough to have understood what he had said was plain when, after a moment, she asked her mother in a low, strained voice:

"Mama, is it true? That you were never married to Papa?"

Clementina merely continued to sob hysterically. With a touching, grown-up dignity, the child took out her own handkerchief, wiped her mother's eyes, and went on as though their roles were reversed:

"It will not take long to write this paper, Mama, and then

I will help you to bed and bring you a posset to make you sleep. Come to the table now; here is paper and ink."

" 'Whereas I, Clementina Walkinshaw, a native of Scotland,' " Waters dictated rapidly, " 'have heard a report spread about that Charles, now the Third of that name rightfully King of Great Britain, is married to me——' "

"Pray go slower, sir," interrupted Charlotte, still in that calm, grown-up voice. "You see my mother is much distressed."

" '——I, the said Clementina Walkinshaw, do voluntarily and upon my oath before God my Creator, and before the here subscribing witness, Mr John Waters, declare that such a report of marriage is void of all foundation. And I do farther declare, by the most solemn oath here taken, that I will if required do everything, and give whatsoever authentic proofs possible, to confirm this my hearty and voluntary declaration. All which I sign with my own hand.' And now, madame, your signature here, please."

What could he say, he wondered, sanding the ink, by way of comfort to this poor child? He did not like that unnatural control, the quenching of all gaiety in the little white face. But Charlotte gave him no opportunity to say anything at all. Making him a polite curtsy, she assisted her mother from the room.

"The cruel humiliation!" raged Clementina, while her daughter fetched hartshorn, pulled the curtains over the window, turned down the bed. "It will kill me! This will be my death!"

"But you did tell everyone you were married to Papa. You told—me."

"And it was true! I mean, it is true that a Scots marriage took place by the mere fact that I was publicly treated as his wife. And what would you have had me do than say we were married? Would you have expected me to endure hearing people call you a bastard? I did it only for your sake, my poor child; I live only to make you happy and respected."

175

When her mother had dropped off into an exhausted sleep, Charlotte ran out into the woods beyond the convent garden. She could not face anyone yet, not even Mère Gabriel to whom she took all her troubles. Not until she had tried to sort things out in her own mind.

Her mother had lied to her. Not just on one or two occasions, not to quieten her in an emergency, as when she had assured Charlotte that Papa was following them when they left Sedan, but deliberately, daily, in cold blood, for nearly seven years. Then it was more than possible that she had lied when she had dinned into Charlotte that she had been deeply wronged by Papa, who, she insisted, was cruel and even mad.

When, in the years immediately following her flight, Clementina could get no reply to her constant letters to Charles, she had tried the effect of making their daughter write to him, dictating emotional outpourings in which Charlotte was made to say that she was 'languishing in misery and expiring amid opprobrium', while her dear and tender mother, whose eyes were almost blind with weeping, 'desired only to breathe her last sigh in his arms'. Papa had not replied, not even though, to her mother's disapproval, she had insisted on signing herself 'Pouponne'.

"There you are, you see!" her mother had cried. "Did I not tell you that your Papa was cruel?"

But though hurt and puzzled, Charlotte's faith in her father was too deep to be shaken. She *knew* he was not cruel. Engraved for ever upon her little heart was the image of the tall, strong, tender father who had carried her about on his shoulder, had rushed to comfort her when she screamed in nightmare, who had told her the wonderful story of Teàrlach. She had learned that her father and her hero, Prince Teàrlach, were one and the same person; she remembered how, the night before her mother had taken her away from him, he had said that perhaps when she was older and could understand, she would meet Prince Teàrlach, whose story might have a happy ending after all, but only if Pouponne loved and trusted him, whatever she might hear other people say.

"Promise me *you'll* never leave me, my little Pouponne!"

The words had gone on echoing through her mind all through her childhood. Please, God, she prayed every night, make it possible for me to tell Papa that I didn't leave him, that I was carried away. God would answer some day; she was sure of that; but meanwhile, like Prince Teàrlach himself, she was learning the bitter experience of hope deferred.

She was too young to analyse her own emotions, but she was dimly aware that the shock she had received today, of discovering that her mother had deceived her on so grave a matter, made the image of her father the more dear. He was the only human anchor she could cling to now that her faith in her mother was destroyed completely.

# TWO

## *I*

WHILE her younger sisters tried on the dominoes they intended to wear at the evening's assembly, the Princess Louise of Stolberg was writing to one of her numerous correspondents, describing the city of Venice, and the Doge's wedding of the Adriatic which she had witnessed yesterday. Louise was a born chatterbox, and when she was not talking she was writing letters.

'Accompanied by the Papal Nuncio and a numerous train of nobles, the Doge entered the Bucentaur, which is the barge used only for this ceremony, and was rowed towards the Lido, an island two miles distant, where a church and a fort guard the approach to Venice from the sea. Just before arriving at the Lido, the Doge threw into the water a plain gold ring, with the words, "We espouse thee, O Sea, in witness of true and perpetual dominion." It was exceedingly affecting——'

She was interrupted at this point by the entrance of her mother, a sprightly, vivacious widow still a few years on the right side of forty, who immediately exclaimed:

"What do you think, girls! I have it on the most unquestionable authority that the rightful King Charles III of Great Britain is looking around for a wife."

While the two younger girls clamoured for details, the Princess Louise went on busily writing; but her mother was not deceived. Louise was getting on for twenty, she could have no dowry, and the prospect of eternal spinsterhood was grim.

It was hardly less grim for the Princess Mother to imagine having her first-born permanently on her hands. Ever since her husband, Colonel Prince Gustave of Stolberg, had died fighting for the Empire at the Battle of Leuthen in 1757, leaving her with four young daughters, her time had been occupied in trying to arrange good matches for them, so that she might be free to enjoy herself. But if any of them was to remain unmarried, she hoped it would not be Louise, and very much feared that it would be.

The Empress Maria Theresa, that matriarch of Europe, had taken the widow and orphans of the prince who had died in her service under her protection, and had paid for their education at the school attached to the Noble Chapter of Sainte Wandru. When Louise was sixteen, she and her next sister, Caroline-Augusta, had been nominated by the Empress to vacant prebends in the Chapter, and their mother's hopes had soared high. For these well-endowed, semi-ecclesiastical prebends were looked upon as stepping-stones to brilliant marriages.

One of the Princess Mother's hopes had just been realised. The young Marquis of Jamaica, heir of a wealthy nobleman thrice a duke—of Berwick in Britain, Liria in Spain, and Veragua in Portugal—as well as being a Prince of the Empire and a Spanish Grandee, had chosen for his bride the

Princess of Stolberg's second daughter, Caroline-Augusta. It had been a truly gorgeous wedding, and the Princess Mother's only cause for regret was that the bride was Caroline and not Louise.

"Louise, my pet," said the Princess Mother, holding up a hand to stem the eager questions of her other offspring, "it is not the least bit of use in the world to pretend you are not listening to what we are talking about, so pray put down your pen and let us hear what you have to say upon my news."

With an ostentatious little sigh, Louise complied, and remarked with maddening superiority:

"Your information, Madame, that King Charles of Great Britain is looking for a wife has led you into imagining, I suppose, that he will look in our direction."

"And why not, pray? In his unfortunate circumstances he cannot afford to look very high, and dear Caroline-Augusta's husband's uncle is very near him in blood. I shall write immediately to the Duke of Fitzjames; no, on second thoughts it would be better to cut short our stay in Venice and go on to Brussels, or perhaps even to Paris. We must be on the *spot*, you understand."

"I was about to remark, Madame, that I fear you have overlooked the fact that her Imperial Majesty is a very firm ally of King George of Great Britain, and most certainly would not countenance a marriage of any of those under her patronage with his rival."

"H'm," mused the Princess Mother, tapping her fan against her teeth. "I could write her a very humble and pathetic apology after the marriage was accomplished. But really, Louise," she went on fretfully, "I do not know how you are going to catch any husband while you insist on plastering your face with rouge, which makes you look very much older than you are. And you should study your diet; you must remember that we Germans are apt to grow stout directly we are past our first youth unless we take care."

"You need have no fear of my remaining unmarried,

179

Madame," replied Louise with her usual complacency, "when I have found a man who shares my artistic and antiquarian tastes."

The Princess Mother found it unnecessary to move on from Venice, for the very next day there called at the house she was renting in St Mark's Square a Colonel Ryan, who brought letters of introduction from no less a person than the Duke of Modena. Since the latter was closely related to King Charles of Great Britain, the Princess Mother's hopes rose, nor were they disappointed.

Colonel Ryan paid her some very charming compliments, and then got down to business. He had been commissioned by his master, King Charles, to search the Courts of Europe for a suitable bride for his Majesty. It went without saying that he had thought immediately of one of her Highness of Stolberg's charming daughters. (This was Irish blarney; he had inspected several princesses of varying age, fortune, and beauty before he had turned in the direction of Stolberg.)

"For what, Madame la Princesse, could be more suitable? Was not your mother an English lady, daughter of the Earl of Elgin and Ailesbury? And therefore, should his Majesty ever have the happiness of ascending his throne, one of your lovely daughters would be most acceptable to the English people as their Queen."

"The match," sighed the Princess Mother, "would not be acceptable to her Imperial Majesty, sir. And she certainly would not provide a dowry."

"It would be acceptable to France, Madame la Princesse." He lowered his voice. "Smarting from the ignominious Peace of Paris, France desires nothing more than a chance to embarrass her old enemy, Great Britain, and is prepared to make King Charles a handsome settlement if he will marry to please her. As for the question of a dowry, your Highness need not be in the least concerned, for his Majesty already has made up his mind to bestow 3,000 livres a year on his bride for her pin-money. And as for the Empress, why, I have heard that your Highness is the very soul of discretion, a quality one does not usually associate with beautiful ladies, and can so contrive matters that no one will be the wiser until all is concluded."

The Princess Mother, delightfully flattered, delicately enquired whether the Colonel had his eye upon any one in particular among her daughters, and she now felt so kindly disposed towards Charles that she suggested the youngest, Gustavine, who was going to be a beauty. But Colonel Ryan, in the most tactful manner, asked whether she did not think that perhaps a bride of fifteen was a trifle too young for a bridegroom of fifty, and enquired whether she had yet formed any matrimonial projects for her eldest daughter, the Princess Louise.

It was a question the Princess Mother had been yearning to hear ever since Louise was of marriageable age; but now she found herself having some qualms of conscience. If *she* found Louise trying, with her egoism, her hard-headed sophistication, and her self-complacency, how would Charles find her, that poor man who had been so battered by adverse fortune all his life? Moreover she was as certain as any mother can be that Louise was incapable of child-bearing, and if Charles Stuart was seeking a bride so late in life, quite obviously it was because he wanted to provide an heir to his shadowy throne.

But no, she must not be sentimental. She had hawked Louise round Europe in search of a husband for four mortal years, and she could stand no more of Louise's lectures on art and the sciences, Louise's never-ending chatter, Louise's broad German face plastered with rouge.

"You have my permission, Colonel," said she, "to woo my daughter Louise on behalf of your royal master, and I shall pray for your success."

There was no need to pray. Louise was enchanted by the prospect of becoming a queen *in partibus*, and living in royal state in romantic Rome. No longer would Caroline-Augusta be able to crow over her; Caroline-Augusta had married a mere marquis, but when Louise signed her name in the marriage register she would add, 'Queen of Great Britain, France, and Ireland'. So much for Caroline-Augusta! And she who for years had endured the humiliations of genteel poverty was going to receive 3,000 livres a year for her pin-money—a fortune it seemed to her. Moreover she was going to be an old man's darling, spoiled and petted, and given ample opportunities for romantic *affaires*. Or if not given them Louise would make them.

When the formalities of her proxy marriage threatened to be unduly prolonged, it was Louise herself who grappled with the problems of ecclesiastical law involved. Perhaps, after all, thought her mother, her years as a *dame chanoiness* at the Noble Chapter of Sainte-Wandru had not been wasted. On March 28th, 1772, this proxy marriage was carried out in Paris with the greatest secrecy to avoid the opposition of the Empress, Louise kindly instructing the Countess Spada, the wife of one of Charles's gentlemen, on the proper amount of rouge to wear in honour of the occasion.

Under the escort of Colonel Ryan, the bride and her relations travelled to Venice whence they took ship for Ancona; and early in the morning of April 17th, they drove through great cornlands enclosed in whitethorn hedges to Macerata high on a hill overlooking the Adriatic, where Louise's bridegroom awaited her.

The Princess Mother, who had become a prey to fears lest at the eleventh hour some accident should prevent her getting Louise off her hands, had insisted that the marriage be celebrated and consummated on the date of the happy pair's first meeting, and the fact that it was Good Friday was not allowed to interfere with her plans. In the chapel of the family mansion belonging to a cardinal of the House of Compagnoni Marefoschi, placed at Charles's disposal for the occasion, Louise de Stolberg became *de jure* Queen of Great Britain, her bridegroom placing on her finger a turquoise ring engraved with the motto:

'This Crown is due to you by me,
And none can love you more than me.'

They observed each other, this pair of complete strangers, during the bridal feast.

The Princess Mother had had her way for once, and Louise's beautiful complexion was unmarred by rouge, as her plentiful blonde hair was free from powder. Her features were undistinguished, and were somewhat too small for her broad face, but he thought she looked very pretty and girlish in her white satin polonese bunched up behind to expose her silver petticoat, and the Mary, Queen of Scots cap sewn with pearls. He was touched by her youth, though according to the standards of their age she was mature; and he was infinitely relieved to see by her manner that she was no unwilling bride.

Louise on her side thought her bridegroom handsome enough, though because his ulcerated legs had become worse these last few years, preventing him from taking exercise, he had grown somewhat stout. But far more important than his looks was his generosity. Never in her life had she had so many expensive gifts. Best of all, he had made her a queen *in partibus*; henceforth in her letters to her friends she would be able to sign herself, Louise R. Her egoism made Louise de Stolberg a tireless letter-writer.

2

She was entranced by the empty display when on their approach to Rome she and her husband were met by state coaches, with outriders in scarlet liveries and white cockades, sent by the Cardinal Duke. Her delight was enhanced by the ceremonious welcome she received from the Jacobite household in the Palazzo Muti, though this was not at all the palace of her dreams. In place of these cold lofty rooms all leading out of one another, there should be a nest of small boudoirs and cabinets connected by private passages and secret stairs, walls panelled in light woods framed in gold, cherubs twining rosebuds over the doors, Aubusson carpets the patterns of which must be copied in the flower-beds outside. Louise had visited Versailles. Well, she must see what she could get out of her fond and indulgent old husband.

But when, on the morning after their arrival, she was visited by the Cardinal Duke, she realised at once that here was the man to cultivate.

"My dearest sister, welcome!" cried Henry, giving her a chaste kiss. "You cannot imagine how I have longed for this auspicious day. I trust that all the arrangements I have made for your reception meet with your approval; if not, you have but to command me. And now permit me to offer you these little tokens of my fraternal love."

The little tokens turned out to be a magnificent Court gown of gold thread sewn with diamonds, and a small gold box in the lid of which was set Henry's portrait in the same precious stones. Louise appeared so enchanted with the portrait that her brother-in-law had to draw her attention to the draft on his banker for 40,000 crowns inside the box. She was quite overwhelmed, murmured Louise; his Royal Eminence was too, too generous. He begged her to use no titles; they were brother and sister, and he hoped she would treat him with the greatest freedom and confidence.

Dared he ask if she were happy? She was as happy as any bride could be, she assured him; but she managed to insinuate into that assurance a certain little wistfulness that touched his heart. It was really very affecting to think of this innocent, convent-bred young creature married to a man in his fifty-second year, and one who had led so dissolute a life.

"I know, my dearest sister," Henry said after a while, becoming discreetly confidential, "that my brother must have told you how much His Holiness's refusal to grant him royal recognition irks him. I had hoped when his present Holiness was elected in '69 that I might move him to it, but though he is friendly disposed towards our family, he is determined to follow the policy of his predecessor in this regard. Alas that my brother is so obstinate that he will not accept the situation. Yet I am in hopes that the counsels of a young and charming wife may succeed where my own have failed."

Louise, who had lost no time in urging Charles to stand upon his rights, murmured that she would do her best.

"I should fail in my duty as your brother," continued the Cardinal, "if I did not point out to you that if your husband continues to insist upon royal recognition, you will not be able to return the visits of the Roman ladies, nor will the nobility call upon you, since they are explicitly forbidden by the Pope to treat my brother as a king, and he for his part will not receive any who do not so treat him. And therefore I am afraid you will find your life very dull and solitary."

"My dearest brother must not concern himself lest I should be dull," Louise replied demurely. "Young though I am, my tastes are serious. There are the famous antiquities of Rome which I long to visit, the wonderful galleries of pictures, not to speak of the churches and the shrines. I beg you, dear brother, to be my guide and mentor in the matter of which of these marvellous sights I should view first."

Henry was delighted. How fortunate had been his brother's choice of a bride, or rather the choice of his agents, for Charles had shown a distressing lack of interest. Young, healthy, comely, virtuous, and with serious tastes—what could a man ask more in his wife?

"Before I die," said Henry, "(and I must inform my dearest sister that my health has always been delicate), I pray God I may be permitted to see all our family affairs brought to a good conclusion."

On this delicate hint that he looked forward to being an uncle, he took his leave. Stroking the banker's draft for 40,000 crowns with a somewhat predatory hand, Louise rapidly assessed the situation. Her brother-in-law's health was delicate, was it? He was rich and influential; as an ecclesiastic he could have no heirs. He was also guileless, slightly foolish, very easy to deceive. Yes, her aim must be to ingratiate herself most thoroughly with her Royal and Eminent brother-in-law.

## 3

"Mama," pleaded Charlotte, for at least the third time, "do pray let us alight at the next post-house and walk on while the horses are being changed. It will serve to get us a little warmer."

"It is mortifying enough," her mother mumbled peevishly through the collection of cloaks and shawls in which she was huddled, "to have to travel in this open cabriolet because we are so poor. I positively refuse to make myself a spectacle."

Charlotte sighed and said no more. It was December and bitter cold; even the passengers who could afford to travel inside the diligence that was taking them from Paris on the first stage of their journey to Rome, could be heard stamping their frozen feet.

"We shall return in our own post-chaise," observed Clementina, to cheer herself. And then, as Charlotte made no comment: "I know perfectly well you disapprove of this desperate step I am taking, but your Papa has driven me to it. For twelve years past I have endeavoured, God knows, to appeal to his natural feelings by every argument I could think of. But all in vain. Therefore, for your sake, my darling (and you know Mama lives only for your sake), I must shame him into making proper provision for us."

Clementina herself had lost all shame. She believed that if she appeared in Rome, Charles, as a newly married man, would pay her well to be rid of her. Or failing Charles, Henry.

They arrived in the dark at Lyons, and Clementina immediately fell into an argument with the *conducteur*. She wanted her demi-vache containing her night clothes taken from the boot; once loaded, maintained the *conducteur*, he could not take out any luggage until the journey's end. What he was after was a tip, and to Clementina, who had to be careful of every sou, this was a fresh humiliation.

In the Hôtel du Nord, where they stayed for its cheapness, they supped, as was the custom, at the public table, and what little appetite they still possessed was removed by a gentleman, a fellow traveller, who discoursed throughout the meal upon the perils of the journey. He placed on the table a pair of double-barrelled pistols, remarking:

"I am always at pains to reload these once a fortnight for fear the powder is damp, for these roads are infested with brigands, and once in Italy it will be worse. In crossing a bridge it is my invariable habit to alight, for the postilions are frequently drunk, and it was only by this prudence that I escaped with my life when our diligence was overturned into a rushing torrent. I trust, madame," he added, lowering his voice, "you carry with you a travelling chamber padlock, for all landlords are thieves. If you have not one, I strongly recommend you to barricade your door."

Mother and daughter lacked not only a padlock, but the bottles of camphor with which the prudent and experienced travelled, and in the bed they shared were tormented by bugs. Lying sleepless, Charlotte thought with trepidation of the days and nights which separated them from their journey's end; and then, because of the horror she had for their errand, deliberately took refuge in thoughts of these physical hardships.

On the news of her father's marriage, her mother had commanded her to write to him again, and Charlotte, nineteen now, had broken several years' silence by a letter in which her mother had had no hand. Phrases from that letter recurred to her mind on this first night of her journey to Rome. 'The only part I shall have in being your daughter, my August Papa, is despair, since I am utterly without prospects or means. . . . All that is left me is to beseech Heaven as earnestly as I can to cut short my days which are already too full of bitterness. . . .'

She had signed herself, 'your Majesty's very humble, and very obedient, and very unfortunate daughter, Charlotte'; for he had forgotten, it seemed, the little Pouponne whom he had loved.

Lying here now, Charlotte was ashamed of that letter. Not only had it smacked of her mother's love of melodrama, but it had outraged both her instincts and the training she had received by the nuns of the Visitation. There must be some good reason why her father had ignored her existence all these years, and bitterness was alien to her character.

As they drove on to Avignon, and thence to Aix and Antibes, bruised and shaken and frozen in the back of the diligence, Charlotte thought: Perhaps if I could contrive to see Papa before Mama takes some unwise step, I could explain . . . but no, there would be no need to explain. She was convinced that if she saw him she would only have to say, "It is Pouponne, Papa, your Pouponne", and she would be in his arms.

Antibes stank of sardines from the boats unloading in its elegant port, but at least it was growing a little warmer, and Clementina, cheering up, talked of visiting Nice, just become a fashionable resort, on their return journey when, she insisted, they would be rich. She bought a bottle of red wine for only four sous, a basket of pomegranates from which she was to suffer later, and for Charlotte one of the new fantastic hoods called a cabriolet built up on arches of cane, in which Charlotte knew she looked absurd.

"We will hire a felucca and sail to Genoa, which will be cheaper and save us another hundred and eighty-eight miles of road in that dreadful diligence," decided Clementina.

Unfortunately the weather immediately worsened, and the open felucca was obliged to hug the coast. Charlotte's cabriolet was blown into the sea, and Clementina was violently sick. Dosing her mother with drops of vitriolic ether, there came vividly to Charlotte's mind the image of Prince Teàrlach, who during that dreadful night of storm when he sailed to Skye in an open boat, had shielded with his arms the sleeping Flora, and sung Highland songs to encourage the labouring oarsmen.

By the time Genoa was reached, Clementina was in so pitiable a state that she considered going no farther. But a night at an expensive hotel where they had a bed free from vermin made her change her mind; and a week later, travel-stained and exhausted, they entered Rome through the Porta del Popolo, and with scarcely a livre left in their common purse, hired a cheap lodging in the Campo Marzo.

"You may go and enjoy yourself by seeing the sights," Clementina told her daughter, "though indeed you ought to have an escort. *I* shall have no leisure, for I mean to employ every minute of my time in applying to your Papa and to your royal uncle for relief."

Rome was getting ready to celebrate Christmas. Thousands of turkeys with oranges in their bills hung in the shops, between beef and veal masked with silver tissue. In the windows of even the poorest folk were little laurel bushes hung with decorations, and the booths in the dirty narrow streets sold stockings stuffed with fruit and comfits. In the gay bustle, nobody noticed a girl in an unfashionable hooded cloak, who daily made her way to the Piazza Santi Apostoli, and spent hours staring at the dull little Palazzo Muti at one end of it.

There were statues on the roof, but in the centre over the main entrance was an empty space, and somebody had told her that in the old King's days the Royal Arms of England had been there. How deeply that empty space must wound him, her father whose life, she realised now, had been dedicated to the recovery of his rights. Glancing shyly up at the windows, she wondered where he was, which was his room. It was a splendid abode in comparison with the mean lodgings in which they had lived during her childhood, but she knew it could never be home to Prince Teàrlach.

When she returned to the Campo Marzo her mother was always either in the depths of despair or on the heights of optimism. She had written to Charles, she told her daughter, complaining that she ought to have been consulted before he married; she had written both to Henry and the Pope, dunning for money, threatening to make a scandal and refusing to leave Rome until her claims were granted. In an agony of shame Charlotte implored her to let her write these letters, if indeed they must be written, but poor Clementina had a great opinion of her own eloquence, though so far it had brought her no result.

Charlotte was lingering in the Piazza Santi Apostoli one evening, when she heard trumpets sound in the courtyard of the Palazzo Muti. A moment later a carriage with out-riders and footmen carrying flambeaux issued through the gates. There was a press of folk in the narrow street, so that the carriage was obliged to proceed at a foot's pace, and as it passed her, Charlotte saw quite clearly in the light of the flambeaux a man and a woman who sat within. The woman was dressed in the height of fashion, her tight bodice puffed out with a diaphanous buffon, her hands thrust into a muff of Siberian wolf, her fair hair, drawn up over a cushion to a fantastic height, glittering with jewels. But Charlotte scarcely noticed her. Her gaze was fastened upon the man, who was looking straight before him, frowning at his thoughts.

Had it not been for the Orders he wore, and for the Royal Arms of England painted on the panels of the carriage, Charlotte would not have known that this was her father. This man was not middle-aged; he was old. She was close enough to see the deep pouches under his eyes, the sagging muscles of the jaw, the lines deeply etched about the drooping mouth. This *could* not be her Papa, her Prince Teàrlach, the strong and upright, the essentially vigorous and deter-mined hero who, defeated long before she was born, had still, and ever, his eyes fixed upon a star.

But then for a moment the man in the carriage turned his head, and looked, as it seemed, straight at her; and she caught her breath. Only one man in the world had eyes like that, haunted eyes, youthfully and desperately eager in the ravaged face, demanding, appealing, full of an eternal dream, a deathless hope. . . .

"Teàrlach's story isn't ended yet, my treasure. Maybe it will have a happy ending after all, but only if you always love and trust him, whatever you hear other people say about him. He can keep his courage and resolution so long as he has the refuge of your loving, trusting little heart."

Had he found a refuge in the heart of the smart, hard-faced woman who sat beside him now? And if he had not, would he ever remember his little Pouponne? . . . The carriage passed by and was gone. If he had seen her, he had not known her; or if he had known her, she was nothing to him any more.

Charlotte returned to the lodgings to find her mother in hysterics.

"Monsignor Lascaris, Treasurer to your royal uncle, has been here, and has brought me a message from his master, threatening me—*threatening* me, Charlotte!—that if I do not leave Rome immediately he will stop our allowance."

"You know I told you I thought it was a mistake to come, Mama," Charlotte said dully.

"But that is not the worst of it. There is a message sent from your Papa."

The girl froze in the act of taking off her gloves.

"Or rather from your Papa's secretary, Mr Lumisden. (Never a word in his own hand!) Your Papa is willing to take you into his household if you will leave me. *That* is the kind of unnatural father you have, my poor child; for twelve years he has ignored your existence, and now would tear you from the arms of her who has dedicated her whole life to bringing you up to be worthy of your royal blood, who has been content to eat dry bread if you could have your riding-lessons and your music-lessons, and pretty gowns—Charlotte! don't leave me! Promise Mama you will never leave her!"

Oh most poignant echo from her childhood—"Don't

191

leave me, Pouponne! Promise me you'll never leave me!"
Words spoken the very night before her mother had
snatched her from his arms. But now he had a wife; soon,
perhaps, he would have lawful children. Since that day
when Mr Waters had brought the affidavit for her mother
to sign, and she had known that she was illegitimate, all
Charlotte had asked was that her father should acknowledge
her as his natural daughter. Gladly would she go to him as
such, even if it were to be as a servant in his house, despised
by the hard-faced lady whom he had taken to wife.

But not now. The strong sense of duty instilled into her
by the Sisters of the Visitation forbade her acceptance of the
offer, as did her natural compassion for this poor little
mother who was her own worst enemy.

"We shall have to think how we can raise the money for
our fare back to Meaux, Mama," she said practically.

"Your royal uncle did at least send that. Five hundred
crowns—it is an insult!"

"I wish my royal and eminent uncle would send us some
more insults of that nature," remarked Charlotte, who was
blessed with a strong sense of humour. "This one will enable
us to travel inside the diligence and to stay at the best
hotels."


## THREE

### I

"I WAS anxious for you," said Charles, rising to greet his
wife as she came in one evening. "You have been out
all day, and you will tire yourself. We have company
for supper."

"I can never tire of seeing the sights of Rome," replied
Louise, taking off her feather tippet. "And today being All

Souls, I have been to pray in the chapel beneath S. Maria del Orazione. Such a deliciously gruesome place! The altar is made entirely of bones, and the very holy water stoup is a skull."

She rattled on, enjoying in retrospect the assignation she had kept in the subterranean chapel.

When Sir Horace Mann had heard of Charles's marriage, he had written to Walpole that 'his wife will be condemned to live alone, for he is drunk half the day and mad the other half'; but Louise had no intention of living alone. She had lost no time in looking round for lovers, and in this lax Roman society had not looked in vain. But she had to be discreet, for it was of the utmost importance to keep in the good books of her strictly moral brother-in-law.

"I do believe I have made a convert to your Majesty's cause," she continued. "A Mr Coke, a young English Whig, who is making the Grand Tour, waited upon me when I came out from church and begged leave to kiss my hand. He has promised to have his portrait painted by Bartoni in Cavalier costume and wearing a white cockade."

She did not think fit to add that at her command there was to be a statue of Ariadne in the background. Louise considered that she bore a striking resemblance to Ariadne, whose presence in the picture was the nearest she dared go in presenting Coke with her own portrait.

"I say you must have a better care of your health, my dear," insisted Charles. "In your condition you should take more rest."

There was a pause. She came to the fire and held her ringed hands towards the blaze, glancing sideways at her husband. His legs were ulcerating again and were propped upon a stool. He looked old and sick and defenceless, arousing a latent cruel streak in her.

"Oh that!" she said lightly. "I am afraid I was mistaken."

"Again?"

"Again! I must beg to remind your Majesty that our union is not yet two years old. We are still, so to speak, upon our honeymoon. Surely your Majesty can be content with the company of a pretty young wife without distressing yourself in these early days because she has not yet borne you an heir to your throne."

He drew his breath in through his nose, clenching his hands together.

As Louise herself confessed, he treated her with every possible indulgence, playing up to her chosen role of child-wife, encouraging her in her round of pleasure. If she grated on him, with her eternal chatter and her conventional raptures over Rome ("this air of stately repose . . . these antique ruins veiled in wreaths of ivy and eglantine . . . those bosky groves and venerable monuments"), he good-humouredly concealed it. But she had known from the beginning the real reason why he had married so late in life, and her ominous failure to become pregnant, together with her constant assertion that she was when in fact she was not, jangled his nerves and desperately worried him.

She retaliated by twitting him on his age and the 'nasty bottle' as reasons for her barrenness, and he discovered that his child-wife had an indecent and virulent tongue. His relations with women had been singularly unfortunate, yet neither his mother's hysteria, nor de Talmond's possessiveness, nor Clementina's emotionalism had prepared him for feminine cruelty. Or had he after all only imagined a faintly mocking nuance in the words "an heir to your throne" just now? She answered his unspoken question.

"I waited upon my dearest brother the Cardinal this morning. You cannot imagine how hurt he is that your Majesty still refuses to perform your Easter duties. He has had such a great deal to put up with without that, out of pure charity maintaining your Majesty's cast-off mistress and her bastard, valiantly contradicting all the stories about your Majesty's addiction to the nasty bottle, and trying so long and so patiently to induce your Majesty to be content to remain incognito instead of pestering the Pope for recognition of your rights. *I* desire no such recognition. I inscribed myself Queen of Great Britain in the marriage register only in obedience to your Majesty and to indulge your whims.''

She rose.

"Well, I must go and dress. Your Majesty must not dream of staying up for cards after supper; it is natural that at your age you should grow sleepy, and that is so embarrassing for our guests, as I am sure you will understand. And as for this recognition of your royal title, Sir, I am afraid his present Holiness has become a firm friend to Hanover. I hear he has offered King George's brother—I *beg* your Majesty's pardon, of course I should have said the Elector of Hanover's brother—the Duke of Cumberland, one of his own frigates to carry him from Ancona on his forthcoming visit to Rome, and that St Peter's is to be illuminated in his honour.''

He still said nothing. His head was sunk on his breast and she could not see his expression. She sighed elaborately, as though he were a sulky child.

"But there, I fear I am fatiguing your Majesty. I will leave you to take a little repose while I dress and write my letters.''

She tiptoed out of the room.

Charles sat where she had left him, while there echoed through his mind the name, 'the Duke of Cumberland'. It was not Cumberland the Butcher who was coming to Rome to be received with royal honours by the Pope; he was dead. But in Charles's bitter loneliness, his old wounds rubbed raw by his wife's malice, the name invoked the ghost of the Butcher, and he was re-living that day which had given the death-stroke to his great enterprise, which had witnessed the only battle he had lost or Cumberland had won throughout the campaign.

One of the numerous processions of this season of the year passed by outside, keeping the Festa de' Morti, voices reciting in a monotone the *De profundis*, punctuated by a mournful bell; and he saw again the loyal dead lying in their blood-soaked tartan upon Culloden Moor. A gust of hail rattled on the window, and he felt once more the icy snow beating full in his face as he led the rearguard of his army through the night to attack Cumberland's quarters at Nairn.

It was April 15th, 1746.

He had reached Culloden House the previous day, making it his headquarters, and here he had been rejoined by Lochiel and his Camerons who had marched sixty miles in two days in response to their Prince's urgent call. This morning his little army of between five and six thousand clansmen were drawn up for his review upon the moor; they were in good heart, despite their empty stomachs and such bitter cold weather that icicles hung from their shaggy hair and beards. He too was in high spirits, though he had not long recovered from a severe bout of pneumonia.

"We're for battle, my lads! Cumberland has crossed the Spey with nine thousand regulars, and yesterday reached Nairn. We're not much more than five thousand, but we'll meet him here on our own ground and prevent his slipping past and occupying Inverness whence alone we may hope to get provisions."

It had always been his habit to tell his Highlanders the plain facts of the situation, not to buoy them up by making light of the enemy's strength. And now as always they responded. The retreat from Falkirk, forced on them by Lord George Murray, had been a deepening nightmare; many had fallen exhausted by the way, many more had slipped off to their homes. But the hard core remained, and the rest would return when they heard there was the prospect of battle under Teàrlach's leadership.

"I hear," said the Duke of Perth, at a Council meeting later in the day, "that Cumberland is celebrating his birthday. The wine and ale will flow free in his camp at Nairn tonight."

He caught Charles's eye, and the Prince exclaimed eagerly:

"It can't be more than twelve miles as the crow flies. If we could find a guide over some moorland track, we could fall on Cumberland at peep of day, and even if we didn't rout him altogether, our attack would have the advantage of surprise."

He glanced swiftly at Lord George Murray, expecting opposition. But no, Lord George was in favour of the night march and an attack when Cumberland's men would still be sleeping off the effects of the birthday celebrations. They would march in two columns, Lord George leading the van, Charles the rear; a Mackintosh was found who could guide them over an old drove-road.

By two o'clock in the morning three-quarters of the distance had been covered; already the darkness ahead was lit by the twinkling points of light he knew must be Cumberland's camp-fires; when suddenly Charles became aware that the van was marching back on him.

"Where the devil are the men going?" he demanded of their officers.

"Lord George has given orders to retreat, Sir. The main body cannot keep up with him, and it would be, he says, broad day before we could reach Nairn."

"It is scarce two o'clock," snarled Charles, "hours before daybreak on such a foul morning. Good God, what does this mean? We are within a few miles of Cumberland's camp and would have blown him to the devil." He forced down his fury. Once more Lord George had ruined an enterprise which, from its very audacity, had promised success. "There is no help for it, lads," he called as cheerily as he could to his famished and bewildered men. "March back to Culloden House; we'll deal with Butcher Billy in the morning, as we dealt with Johnnie Cope at Prestonpans." And he made himself whistle a tune.

It was six o'clock when they regained their own camp. He sent officers to Inverness to try by any means to obtain provisions for his troops, and, having swallowed a mouthful of oatmeal and whisky, flung himself down in his boots, to be awakened from a dream-haunted sleep by the news that Cumberland was advancing. For the first time throughout his campaign he was in favour of avoiding battle, because of the condition of his men, starving and dead-beat after the abortive night march. But there was no time.

Riding up and down the ranks of his grey-faced Highlanders, he kept turning to look for Cluny's Macphersons, Cromatie's Mackenzies, and other clans who were hastening to join him; but there was no time, no time! From behind the vast, red-coated monster marching up against him loomed a black cloud of sleet driving full in the clansmen's faces. Clanranald and Keppoch came to him, full of wrath; Lord George was denying their Macdonalds the place of honour on the right, the place they had claimed since the days of Bruce.

A traitor. There was little doubt left in his mind now that Lord George had been a traitor from the beginning. He had forced the retreat from Derby, and again after Falkirk; he had supported and then abandoned the night march. And now this fantastically, criminally stupid denial of the rights of the touchy Macdonalds.

"I beg you to let my lord have his way this once," he said hoarsely to Keppoch and Clanranald. "I cannot, in such a crisis, disoblige my second-in-command."

It was all so confused, with the driving sleet, the light-headedness of hunger, the great fatigue, the weakness of convalescence, the nagging, appalling conviction that in Lord George they had a traitor in their very midst. He was riding slowly down the lines, the vicious wind whipping his hair about his face, his back for a moment to that menacing, slow, crablike advance of the red monster, the well-fed red monster with its modern weapons of war. He could not remember what he was going to say to his clansmen, scarcely knew what he did say; his voice was tossed by the gale, as his thoughts were tossed this way and that by mental agony.

But they flung their blue bonnets into the air and acclaimed him as passionately as ever, their high-pitched voices screaming their trust in Teàrlach . . . to be answered by the thunder of Cumberland's heavies.

The shells cut great swathes through the Highland ranks, but they must wait—wait! he implored them, even as Dundee had implored their grandfathers at Killiecrankie, until the foe was near enough for them to be unloosed in their famous charge. But it was bad ground for this, too open, and to keep them inactive was always to cool their ardour. To induce them to stand firm he rode about recklessly, exposed to the furious cannonade, the round-shot striking the ground about him and spattering him with mud. His horse shied with violence, and he saw the head of one of his grooms, shot clean off by a ball, rolling bloody and ghastly at his feet.

He sent message after message to Lord George, who was commanding his Atholl men on the right wing; the centre could not be held in check much longer. But before either wing moved, the untried Mackintoshes in the centre took the initiative into their own hands, charged without orders, swept through two regiments of the enemy, and flung themselves to death upon the bayonets of the second line. Murray's right wing, springing forward after their comrades, broke the Hanoverian left, before themselves being decimated by a flanking fire from the guns.

"*Now*, Macdonalds, now or never!"

They wavered, that great clan, bitter from the insult put upon them. They began to give ground, a fatal sign with the Highlanders. Only old Keppoch rushed into the fray, was hit and fell, struggled up, was hit again, but on he went until a few yards from the enemy he fell to rise no more.

It was a rout. Charles strove to rally them, the sleet and his own tears blinding him. His army, his gallant little army, hitherto undefeated in battle or skirmish, was broken, one half flying towards Inverness, the other across the river Nairn to the hills. He would not leave the field. Deeds of glorious, useless gallantry were all about him; the Stewarts of Appin fell one after another on to a heap of their slain brothers as they wrestled to save their precious flag; Major Gilles Macbean flung himself into a gap in a stone dyke and cut down fourteen of the enemy before he fell.

But no merciful bullet was for Teàrlach. At long last Sullivan caught his horse's bridle and dragged him by force from the field.

Next day Lord George Murray wrote him a letter, blaming him for everything, even for setting up the Royal Standard in the first place, even for the failure of France to keep her promises, bitterly criticising all Charles's most trusted friends and adherents, asking him to receive back his commission of Lieutenant-General, and signing himself, 'your R.H.'s most dutiful and faithful humble servant'.

And on Culloden Moor, Butcher Cumberland had opened his slaughterhouse. . . .

Tapping on the door of Charles's room in the Palazzo Muti, Iain Beag could get no answer, entered anxiously, and found his master slumped in his chair, saliva dripping from his livid lips, his face a high crimson, his breath coming stertorously. It was the first fit he had suffered, and at his age and in his state of health it was ominous enough to encourage his wife to write to her latest lover, a young Swiss dilettante named Victor Bonstetten, who had named her Queen of Hearts:

'I really believe he will die soon, man of iron though he is.'

## 2

Sir Horace Mann, proudly wearing the red ribbon of the Bath with which he had recently been invested (in lieu of the increase in his salary for which he was perpetually pestering his Government), was in his box on the second tier in La Pergola, Florence's principal theatre, entertaining as his guest for the evening the exceedingly eccentric Lady Mary Coke, a daughter of the Duke of Argyll. She was in deep mourning, and wore upon her egg-shaped coiffure the widow's black band with a crêpe veil, for she firmly believed she had been married to the late Duke of York, King George's scapegrace son.

"How I envy your ladyship's fine appetite!" sighed Mann, wistfully watching my lady tuck-in to boar's head, a trussed fowl on a spit, sugar-sprinkled pastykins, and brandy spiced with aniseed, all of which had been sent to his box. "My condition," he went on, coy as a young matron, "prevents me from tasting meat, and as for wine, the most I allow myself is a thimbleful in a glass of water."

He embarked upon a description of his distressing disease, being obliged to raise his voice to a shout because of the din. There was a continual opening and shutting of box doors, a clatter of dishes from the hot suppers being brought in, rowdy laughter from the groundlings in the parterre, a furious argument in progress between two gentlemen who occupied seats on the stage itself, shrill cries from the lemonade women, and the bawling of actors who, by the traditional enormous nodding plumes they wore upon their heads, evidently were acting a tragedy, though not a word of the play could be heard. The *orateur* appeared, begging for a little less noise from the audience.

"God's teeth! Have at you!" roared Lady Mary, falling into one of her famous rages; and she flung at the *orateur* the porcelain dish, gravy and all, which had contained her portion of boar's head.

The audience applauded; Mann sighed. He would have to pay for the broken dish, and would certainly be cheated by the urbane but crafty Florentines. This reminded him, in a roundabout way, of a topic of which he had been full for a twelvemonth, and he embarked upon it, hoping thereby to divert my lady from throwing more crockery.

"I hear a report that when the present Pope suppressed the Society of Jesus, it was discovered that their wealth amounted to——"

"Is that King Charles of Great Britain who has just entered the box opposite?" interrupted Lady Mary, squinting through her lorgnette. She had a perfect passion for Royalty, and cared not whether it was *de jure* or *de facto*.

"The Pretender," corrected Mann, bridling. "He removed to Florence last month out of spite to the Pope, who has refused to grant him the royal tribune in St Peter's during the coming Jubilee Year. But he might as well have stayed in Rome, for I have persuaded the Grand Duke to refuse him all recognition here. As I was saying, it has been discovered that the wealth of the Jesuits amounts to more than ten million pounds in our money, with which they were able to bribe ministers and mistresses in their beastly plots. And what a windfall their wealth will be for Clement XIV, who is the son of a tinker, and has the meanest relations, one a fiddler, another a coachman."

"Who's that flirting with King Charles's wife?" sharply enquired her ladyship, ignoring all this.

Mann raised his quizzing-glass.

"Young Danby, son of a rich Yorkshire squire," said he disgustedly. "I see him with her everywhere nowadays. He even accompanied them to the baths at Pisa, where the Pretender hoped she might be cured of her barrenness." He tittered, and then grew peevish again. "Your ladyship would scarcely credit the pains I have taken to persuade all our English visitors to ignore the Pretender's existence, but with very little success. I was mortified," he added, lowering his voice, "when his Royal Highness, the Duke of Gloucester, upon his recent visit here, actually gave way to the Pretender's carriage in the street, and let down his own glasses to salute him."

"Good manners," pronounced Lady Mary, taking a pipe from her knotting-bag and proceeding to fill it. "My late husband, the Duke of York, would have done the same."

She took a last look at Charles through her lorgnette, and remarked roundly:

"Whoever started the story that his father was smuggled into the palace in a warming-pan as an infant was a God-damned fool. This one's the spit image of his grandfather, except more handsome, and every inch a king. *Breeding*, my friend," she added spitefully to Mann, "something *you* won't understand."

It was a hit below the belt, since everyone knew that Mann's obscure origins were a source of intense mortification to him.

"But he should take care he isn't cuckolded," concluded her ladyship, lighting her pipe. "This cicisbeoship which is so fashionable in Florence must be a godsend to young flighty wives."

In her box opposite, Louise was thinking much the same thing.

At first she had found Florence intolerably dull, especially as the Grand Duke of Tuscany was under strict orders from his mother, the Empress, to ignore the presence of Charles and his wife. And Louise was separated from Victor Bonstetten, who had returned to his native Switzerland, and who alone, she wrote him, had succeeded in touching her heart of stone.

'The vast barrier of the Alps between us serves as my rampart, and I need nothing less for my protection from this dangerous love. The life I am leading here,' she had continued, with her inherent self-complacency, 'would be dreary in the extreme to anyone but myself; I spend the whole morning with my books, am dressed and take a walk, entertain at dinner those few whom I find to have some rudiments of culture, go to the Opera and then to the Casino, which I always leave at nine in order to consecrate the remainder of the evening to my correspondence with my friends.'

But that was before she had discovered the advantage of the old-established Florentine system of cicisbeoship.

It was supposed to have originated from the solitary imprisonment to which husbands subjected their wives; the wives' revolt had taken the form of demanding a male chaperon in whom their husbands had implicit trust. Sometimes the cicisbeo was formally elected, his name inscribed and his duties laid down in the marriage contract. To such a length had it been carried that by this time a lady of fashion was never seen abroad without her cicisbeo, and even devoted married couples dared not flout the custom lest they be laughed at.

So when the play was over this evening, it was young Mr Danby who arranged Louise's mantel round her shoulders, collected her patch-box, fan, back-scratcher, and lap-dog, gave her his arm to her carriage, and escorted her to the Casino, which was near the Arno, and, with its surrounding groves of mulberry trees, was a favourite place for intrigues. Charles had gone home to bed, but Louise's favourite lady-in-waiting, Baroness de Maltzan, was with her, and with the Baroness the latter's own cicisbeo, an adventurer named Scherer.

"She loves him madly," Louise confided to Danby as they lingered in the romantic groves, "and melts into tears at the mention of his name, but then we women have the gift of tears."

Young Danby, who had begun to resent being a mere appendage to a vain young woman who was such a chatter-box, murmured something, inwardly trying to make up his mind whether to propose to a Miss Seymour, his fellow countrywoman, who was staying in Florence with her Mama.

"If," continued Louise, giving him a provocative glance, "I found a man who was wholly original, I should adore him for ever, but until now I have not found one who merited a constant devotion. Yet I believe you may be he, because you would know how to make love only when we are alone. My poor old husband is so madly jealous."

"But I thought, Madame . . . that is, I have heard," stammered the embarrassed young Englishman, "that cicisbeo and cicisbea are supposed to denote platonic admirers of either sex. My Italian, perhaps, is not yet fluent enough to——"

"There are cicisbeos of love as well as of convenience," interrupted Louise. "Do you suppose I have chosen you only to hand me my chocolate, put on my slippers, or teach my macaw to speak English?"

Young Danby remembered his father's warnings about the temptations a young man encountered when making the Grand Tour, and definitely made up his mind to propose to Miss Seymour without delay.

## 3

The Poggio Imperiale, the popular promenade which led from the Roman Gate to a balustrated terrace on the Arno, was crowded as usual this fine June morning, the fashionable having alighted from their carriages at the entrance which bore the figures of a lion and a she-wolf on two pillars, for this was a foot promenade.

Charles walked slowly, leaning on the arm of Iain Beag and supporting himself with his silver-topped cane. The fit he had suffered before leaving Rome had left permanent after-effects; in his mid-fifties he was afflicted with all the ills and humiliations of old age. Above all its loneliness. When he had left Rome, his brother had settled down thankfully to enjoy his splendours and to immerse himself in his ecclesiastical business, and Louise, his barren wife, was becoming ever more openly contemptuous of him, delighting in making a fool of him, twitting him with his slight deafness, his failing memory which made him repeat himself, his tendency to fall asleep during the play, and his occasional recourse to the bottle.

Sometimes it seemed strange to him that Louise and the world in general should think nothing of men drinking themselves under the table at a public dinner, that they should regard open infidelity, poisonous scandal, bribery and corruption, as fashionable habits to be condoned, while they looked with disgust at a man who in his loneliness sometimes drank too much in the solitude of his own room.

But now, as in his youth, he tried to keep up a façade. He would not acknowledge that he was ill and old and beaten. Hard on himself, as on others, he would walk daily here among the modish throng, with his Orders blazing on his coat, brave the rude stares of the 'Nuvulloni', as those who had bought their titles were contemptuously nicknamed, return with grace the salutations of the urbane old nobility who, with their high feeling for rank, risked the Empress's wrath by taking off their hats to the lame old man who was the rightful King of Great Britain.

"Fie on this terrible heat!" exclaimed Louise, mincing along with her arm through that of the Baronesss de Maltzan. "I am sure I shall faint if we continue to walk here in the sun."

To please her, he turned down one of the narrow walks leading out of the main avenue; here there was the shade of ilex, oak, and vine. Almost at once he saw approaching him two gentlemen, strangers to him, but unmistakably English, and his face hardened. He was perfectly aware that Sir Horace Mann made haste to inform every English visitor that to pay the slightest courtesy to the 'Pretender' would be mortally to offend King George, and on several occasions Charles had been made to suffer some studied rudeness from these visitors.

His little party took up the whole of the narrow walk. Someone would be obliged to give way. As he was resolving that it should not be he, he noticed the elder of the two strangers whisper something to his companion, by his look and manner enquiring who Charles was. Immediately afterwards the elder took the younger by the arm, drawing him to one side of the walk; both pulled off their three-cornered hats, and so stood to let Charles and his party pass.

A smile such as few saw on his sad face nowadays, the old smile that had won men's hearts in his youth, lightened Charles's eyes and mouth. As he came level with the strangers he stopped, made them a graceful salutation, and said in English:

"I thank you for your courtesy, gentlemen, and would have the honour of your names, if you please."

"This, sir," replied the younger of the two, "is his Grace, the Duke of Hamilton, and I am Dr Moore, his Grace's physician."

"Your Grace—Dr Moore—I shall remember you with pleasure. I am residing at the Palazzo Corsini, lent to me by my very good friend, the Prince of that name. If there is anything I can do for you during your stay in Florence, I beg you will command me."

He passed on. There was a new elasticity in his step, so that his wife could hardly keep up with him.

"A stout Whig, the Duke of Hamilton," he observed to her, when they were out of earshot, "but a man of honour and breeding, it seems. Thank God there are such left in the world, for I had begun to doubt it. . . ."

He talked on happily. In his bitter mortification the tiny incident had been balm to him. She did not reply. How contemptibly childish he is, she thought, for ever standing on his royal rights, making an exhibition of himself because a stranger salutes him out of pity. She was in a savage mood. She had just heard that Victor Bonstetten, to whom she had been exulting that 'death and disease dance about the head of my lord and master', was about to marry a beautiful Swiss girl; and she had lost her cicisbeo, young Danby having announced his engagement to Miss Seymour.

All the way back to the Corsini Palace this morning, she was composing in her mind a letter she would write to Charles, indulging to the full, without interruption, that streak of cruelty in her nature which now, in her private dealings with her husband, betrayed itself openly.

'Since your Majesty will not listen to reason when one speaks to you, and since you have made up your mind to grumble at me because I dislike walking in the month of June at an hour when the heat is excessive, I humbly represent to your Majesty that my health suffers much from the heat. I know your loyal heart and sensitive soul, and it would be cruel to compel a poor woman to run about the streets in this horrible heat just because your Majesty is bored in your own room. . . .'

"I shall invite the Duke of Hamilton to a musical evening," Charles was saying happily. "I remember to have heard that he has great skill on the violin. Perhaps he would play duets with me."

'. . . You suggest this walk, Sir, in the belief that it will soften your first proposal, which was that I should get up at seven o'clock in the morning, when I do not go to bed till two hours after midnight; but this must have been a joke of your Majesty's. You are not yet of an age for that, Sir, for it would not redound to your honour in the world if it were known that you, who have always passed for a galliard, should have become so degenerate as not to want to spend more than a few hours in bed with a pretty young woman who loves you. But if your Majesty continues to grumble as you have done, I shall feel compelled to justify myself in a public Memorial for being the innocent cause that the Royal face no longer beams with its customary glory, and that its beautiful eyes are clouded. . . .'

## 4

The morning Angelus rang out from Giotto's tower, to be answered by the bells of San Lorenzo, San Michele, Santa Felicita, and from the hills which encircled Florence, grey with olive and dark with cypress, the voices of convent and chapel and parish church joined in the angelical salutation.

Charles heard them with an old pain. Each morning and evening they seemed to reproach him. Though he told himself he no longer believed in the faith for which his fathers had been content to sacrifice their throne, did not believe in the supernatural even, his conscience gave him the lie. But this morning, as he climbed slowly and painfully to the squat belvedere tower on the Palazzo Guadagni, he was hopeful and happy, for this was his first morning in his new home.

It stood on a corner of the old narrow Via San Sebastiano, its main entrance facing the rococo façade of the Capponi Palace. A yellow brick house with shutters; like most of the private palaces of Florence it had been built in the ages of civil strife, and had iron gratings at the windows, huge thick nail-studded doors, and a loggia on the roof beyond the perils of a street fight. Within it was somewhat gloomy, but the courtyard with an open gallery running round each storey was pleasant, and had a fountain in the centre; and from the belvedere there was a beautiful view of Fiesole.

He leaned against the balustrade to recover his breath, looking up at the weather-vane, in the forked iron tail of which he had had his initials and the date cut, 'C.R. 1777.'

It pleased him greatly to have a home of his own at last, he who almost all his fifty-seven years had lived in somebody else's half-furnished palace, in mean inns and squalid lodgings, in the Muti peopled by ghosts and from which the Pope had compelled him to take down the Royal Arms. Here at the Palazzo Guadagni he had put up those Arms, boldly and defiantly, in a stone escutcheon above the archway of the staircase in the entrance, and with them the inscription, *'Carolus Natus 1720 M. Brit. et Hiberniae Rex Fidei Defensor 1766.'*

There was a room he had chosen where he could have his long lonely evenings with his 'cello and his memories, and where, if he drank too much Florence wine, no one would be the wiser except faithful old Iain Beag, who was now his major-domo. It looked out on to the garden which was heavily shaded with ilexes and full of mossy old statues, and he had hung the room throughout with the Royal Stuart tartan. Save for this one apartment, Louise could furnish the house as she pleased, if she kept within his slender means; could entertain her friends, write her interminable letters, give the conversaziones she loved.

But because he had come to have serious doubts of her

fidelity, he had laid down one absolute rule. All the doors leading to her bedchamber, except that which communicated with his own, were to be kept locked at night. She might pose as a martyr to an old man's jealousy, or flay him with her virulent, indecent tongue; he was adamant. It would appear that she was barren, but just in case she was not it was essential for him to guard against the possibility of her providing his enemies with another, and this time a genuine, story of a supposititious heir to his lost throne.

Yet this morning he was so happy to have a home of his own at last that he told himself he was sure she would settle down here. He must try really hard to make allowances; she was still young, and it was hard to be tied to an old sick husband. She did not realise how desperately she hurt him when she twitted him about his insistence on his royal rights; she could not know that all his life he had never lost sight of the goal he had set himself in boyhood.

But now she had a home to furnish and manage as she pleased, she would find interests which would wean her from flirtations and illicit *affaires*. He was spared the foreknowledge that in this home he was to suffer a last and most bitter humiliation at the hands of his wife.

# FOUR

## I

"AH, Florence, Tuscan lily, queen of cities!" apostrophised Count Vittorio Alfieri, flinging one hand, ornamented by an enormous ring, towards the view from the belvedere. "How often have I longed to feast upon thy treasures. Thou who didst lead the advance-guard of the Renaissance, who heard Boccacio tell his stories and saw

Dante wander through thy streets. As soon as I entered within thy gates, I knew I had come home."

"You prefer Tuscany to your native Piedmont, Monsieur le Comte?" Charles enquired, in French, for his visitor had hastened to inform him that he despised the Italian tongue. He was amused by this flamboyant young Piedmontese. In an age when all men wore the wig, Alfieri wore his own natural hair, of a flaming red, which he heavily perfumed. It had a wind-blown appearance from his habit of constantly running his fingers through it. But despite the perfume and the histrionics, there was nothing effeminate about the man. Immense vitality radiated from him; and on the feast of San Giovanni, the patron saint of Florence, Charles had much admired his superb horsemanship when he had taken part in the traditional race in the Square of S. Maria Nuova.

"A prophet, Sir," boomed the Count, in a voice that seemed to come from his shoes, "is not without honour save in his own country, and the same is true of a poet. In my boyhood I was seized with a violent ambition to rescue the classic drama of Italy from the languid and exotic form bestowed upon it, especially by Metastasio. In my mind, which is completely given up to the pursuit of glory, I frequently go over the plan of my life. I determine that until I am forty I shall write tragedies; for five years thereafter, comedies; and for the remainder of my years I shall merely enjoy my fame."

Charles searched in vain for a suitable comment, but his visitor needed none, proceeding at once to self-vivisection. Alfieri had always to impress himself on others, whether favourably or the reverse he scarcely cared.

"I have been from infancy a creature of strong passions. At the age of seven I attempted to kill myself by eating that which I took to be hemlock, but which was, in fact, common grass. At eight I shed tears of rage because one of my schoolfellows received a prize I deemed rightfully mine. At the Academy of Turin, because I would not beg pardon for some misdemeanour, I allowed myself to be confined to my chamber for close on three months, during which time I refused to allow myself to be dressed, combed, or washed. And lately, when my faithful valet Elia inadvertently pulled my hair when he was frizzing it, I cut his head open with a blow from a silver candlestick. The good creature! His only form of reproach is to carry always in his pocket the blood-stained handkerchief with which he bound the wound. In all things I must surpass; in all things have my will. Such is my nature," he added simply.

"To surpass in all things was an ambition of my own youth," Charles said musingly, "though only as a means to an end. An end," he added with a smile, "that would not commend itself to you, Monsieur le Comte, since you have confessed to me that you are a hot republican."

"I hate a hypocrite," cried Alfieri, thrusting one hand into the bosom of his coat. "I cannot dissemble. I would not, Sir, insinuate myself into your house by pretending to be a lover of monarchy. As I have had the honour of informing you, my ambition is to become the greatest tragic poet of our age. But alas, I was too wayward in my boyhood to apply myself to my studies; I was an endless source of trouble to my widowed mother and my tutors. I have no Greek, little Latin, and but small acquaintance with classical Italian."

He sighed elaborately, and ran his fingers through his hair, releasing a wave of perfume.

"Seeking culture in the cities of Tuscany, I came last April to Pisa, and here I first heard the name of your illustrious wife, Sir, famous for her exquisite artistic tastes. Having written my first tragedy, *Cleopatra*, I determined to come hither to Florence, and with your permission to attach myself to your illustrious wife as a recognised *cavaliere servente*, that I may benefit from her criticism of my work."

Since Louise had been complaining, ever since they had settled in Florence, that she had no one with whom she could share her passion for the arts, Charles readily agreed to receive Count Alfieri into his household as an honoured guest.

Alfieri's explanation of the reason why he had desired this was somewhat different when he came to confide it to Louise. He had escorted her to one of those popular entertainments called *cocchiata* in Boboli, part of the gardens of the Grand Ducal Palace, where the walks and alleys were always left dark to please the cicisbeos, and discreetly hidden orchestras serenaded the lovers. In a jasmine arbour Louise and the Count sat side by side in a double Windsor chair much favoured by ladies and their cicisbeos, though some complained that the arm-rest between the two parts hindered love-making.

"Upon my first visit to Florence a year ago," whispered Alfieri, "I was pondering upon the works of art in the Uffizi, when I beheld a lady admiring a portrait of King Charles XII of Sweden. Immediately and without warning, I was struck with a dart of love."

He paused for effect.

"I obtained and clothed myself in garments similar to those in the portrait, and day and night I paraded beneath the windows of the Palazzo Guadagni, hoping that my *donna amata* would read in this the language of my passion. Ah! I did it not of choice. Dreaming and morose by nature, I have been careful to avoid women who seemed agreeable and attractive, lest they distract me from my noble task. At length I conquered myself—or so I thought, and quitted Florence. I am cursed with an ardent nature," he added, rolling his prominent eyes. "On one occasion I ordered my servant to bind me to a chair to restrain me from the pursuit of beauty."

"But what poet has not found in beauty his inspiration?" murmured Louise. She was flattered, intrigued, and excited; Alfieri's egoism did not repel her, for it was complementary to her own. And neither of them possessed the ghost of a sense of humour.

"To the detriment of his art, madonna. I speak from sad

experience. Already I have had three great loves, and for the sake of one I nearly lost my life. Upon my travels in England, whither I went to buy horses, I met and was conquered by a Lady Ligonier, for whose fair sake I was obliged to fight a duel with her husband in the Hyde Park."

He omitted to relate the sequel. He had been vanquished in the duel, Ligonier contenting himself with giving his opponent a mere scratch; and the lady had then broken the news to Alfieri that she infinitely preferred to him her husband's groom.

"Speak not to me of the jealousy of husbands!" implored Louise.

It was now her turn, and in her loud shrill voice she embarked upon her own version of her youth.

"I have experienced misfortunes from my earliest years. I was born the eldest of the children of my mother, who wanted a son and consequently received me ill and treated me with intense hardness all my youth up, placing me in a nunnery, where I learned nothing, in order to save herself expense and have more money for her own amusements; for my mother has never thought of anything else but to play, to enjoy life, and to wear pretty dresses. She wedded me, so as to get rid of me, to the most odious man that ever existed, a man who unites in his own person every imaginable failing, in addition to the lackey's special vice of drunkenness."

"Oh, hor-ri-ble!" moaned Alfieri, burying his red head in his hands. "Beauty chained to a beast!"

"Imagine to yourself, my dear Count," whispered Louise, bending close to him, "the sufferings my delicacy has endured in the marriage-bed, the faintness and the horror which have overwhelmed me at the reek of brandy on his breath, the tipsy caresses, the——"

Alfieri implored her not to distress herself and him, and then asked avidly for more. He was beginning to feel that she was the ideal subject for his muse, this tragic young Queen. On her side Louise was quite certain that here was the lover she wanted; approaching her thirties, she had coarsened, becoming a plain German *hausfrau*, and of late she had begun to despair of having any more amorous adventures.

"You told me, my friend," she said, as they drove home under the stars, "that you quitted Florence last year, believing you had conquered your passion for this—this unknown lady——"

"Ah, why so coy, so diffident?" he interrupted, seizing her hands. "Know you not well that you are she? I came—I saw—I fell! Pure love enchained me for the first time when I saw you in the Uffizi. But I was, as I have told you, deeply disturbed; I galloped on one of my fast horses all the way to Siena and laid my case before my dear friend, Francesco Gori. I begged him to come here to Florence and judge whether your love would hasten or retard my fame, whether you were indeed the one woman in the world who could play the part of Aspasia to my Pericles. Gori assented, came, approved, reported to me, and thus have I returned."

"Let us be content with friendship," simpered Louise. "Love is too dangerous."

He paid no attention. He rarely listened to what other people said.

"I find that at last I have met the woman for whom I have been searching, who instead of being like all the others I have known, an obstacle to literary fame, an impediment to useful occupations, and a detriment to all elevated thoughts, is an incentive and a noble example to every great work. And I, recognising and appreciating so rare a treasure, now give myself up entirely to you, my *donna amata*."

She was, he wrote later that night in his Journal, his Beatrice, his Laura, his Leonora; and he was the young Dionysus to save her from desolation. It was all very classical and romantic; but he was also an extremely virile and ardent Italian of twenty-eight, who had thought nothing of insinuating himself into Charles's house for the express purpose of robbing his host of his wife, so that soon he was inventing more intimate names for the pair of them. She was Psipsia and he Psipsio, names imitating the sound of kisses.

He took care to inflame Louise still further to discontent and to recitals of her wrongs. On the other hand, deeming all to be fair in love and war, he flattered and made himself agreeable to Charles, at the very time when he was busy engineering a final breach between husband and wife and straining every nerve to persuade Louise to run away with him. But none of this detracted from his avidity for literary fame; even when he was making love to Louise he listened to the sound of his own phrases, saving them up and trying them out for his next tragedy.

It fascinated him to watch the old King gradually drop into a doze after supper, when in the husband's very presence he and his willing mistress exchanged intimate caresses.

"How have I offended thee, O Sleep?" he muttered, as, from his deep chair on the other side of the fire, Charles told some story of his youth, repeating himself with the pathetic garrulity of age. "Placid brother of Death, why dost thou not more often shut the eyelids of the worthy spouse? His old blinking orbs are thy meet resting place, yet now thou wilt not alight upon them. . . . Oh joy! it would seem as if the Deity had hearkened to my prayer. There lolls the feeble old head, which tries vainly to keep steady. On the breast sinks the flabby chin; lo, it falls, and falls yet lower. Thus on the arm of Sleep reposeth hoary Age."

He ceased to be the poet and became the lover; or rather he managed to combine the roles. The southern ardour of his embraces did not prevent his sensitive ear from noting when some endearment grated.

"My consuming fire has burnt thy arrows of defence. Oft have I marked thy trembling eyes of sable . . ." (no, 'trembling eyes' was wrong) ". . . thy eyes of sable moist with the nectar of love's silent spell. Thou art a damask rose, pure, fresh, and blooming, crushed in the fingers of a filthy clown. Thou art a trapped dove, but from hands so impious, a cage so drear, I mean to snatch thee. And yet (what strange stratagems must Love assume!), I needs must curb my ire and greet with smiling face thy aged tyrant."

The old King stirred. He was dreaming. In his nostrils was the smell of cut pease; he had slept, wrapped in a plaid, all night in this field on the edge of a bog near Prestonpans. Now the stubble rustled under his feet as, not fifty paces behind the front line, he ran and leapt with his eager Highlanders, shouting to them, "Make haste! Make haste!" In a deep thunder the clan slogans answered him, to be answered in their turn by shouts of alarm from scarlet-clad veterans, Cope's dragoons, riding over their own artillery guard, panic in their spurs, galloping for the nearest refuge, Cope himself going hell-for-leather with the news of his own defeat. . . .

"But alas!" groaned Alfieri, withdrawing his lips from those of his mistress, "what do I see? Just as those fair shining eyes, amorous and ardent, had given me to drink in slow draughts the luscious poison; just as in the silence I already felt that poison course through every vein, nor dared I open my lips, so full was my soul, he is awake, before ever he was sound asleep. To earth I must fix my eyes," he muttered, staring dramatically at the carpet, "burning with love-light. Why dost thou mock my prayers, O Sleep? last of the gods to obey. Malign and envious, thou art the foe of lovers, and carest no more for their sorrows than for their delights."

Had it not been inartistic, he might have expressed his thankfulness that opportunities for illicit love-making were endless since the old husband was so often ill and confined to bed, especially as the lovers had in the Baroness de Maltzan so experienced and willing a pander. Psipsio and Psipsia were, in fact, in the seventh heaven. She presented him with a sketch of the heads of his particular idols, Dante, Petrarch, Ariosto, and Tasso, with a laurel wreath suspended above them and a note beneath—'To one yet more worthy of laurels than they'; and he took for the subject of his new tragedy Mary, Queen of Scots, Louise, of course, posing for the title-role.

But as time went on, Psipsia began to fret for complete freedom to live with her Psipsio without the inconvenience of a husband in the background. From the beginning he had urged her to elope with him; but though as genuinely in love as her egoism allowed her to be, Louise remained her hard-headed self. A diet of bread and kisses could never be to her taste. It was true that Alfieri was a very wealthy man; on the other hand he had confessed that he had deserted, one after the other, his former three great loves. And to run away with him would be to damn herself for ever in the eyes of her rich brother-in-law, whose heir she still hoped to be.

As she had grappled with the problems of ecclesiastical law in her haste to be married to Charles, so now did she turn her coldly realistic mind to the problem of deserting him, while at the same time enjoying the sympathy and esteem of Henry as an innocent and deeply wronged young woman. She consulted the experienced de Maltzan. It would be vital, the Baroness insisted, to obtain the sympathy and protection of the Tuscan Court. As it happened, the Baroness had a friend who might be useful here. This was an Irishwoman, Madame Orlandini, widow of a petty Florentine noble; for several years she had been the mistress of the French Envoy at the Tuscan Court, the Marquis de Barbantine, but recently had transferred her ripe charms to a poverty-stricken, fire-eating fellow-countryman of hers, an adventurer named Geoghegan, whom she kept. But she was still *persona grata* at the Grand Ducal Palace, and was easily persuaded to pour into the ears of the Grand Duchess the woes and wrongs of Louise.

The plot was written, the actors chosen, even the date of the performance selected. It only remained for him who had been cast as the villain of the piece to act his part, though he did not know that he was in the play.

It was St Andrew's Day, 1780.

Ever since Charles could remember, the exiled Court in which he had grown up had kept the feast of Scotland's patron saint with particular honour; and since the rising of 1745 it had been an occasion when he was always emotionally upset. On St Andrew's Day he put on the costume of a Highland gentleman, a costume thirty-five years old now, jacket and kilt ill-fitting, silver lace tarnished. Iain Beag must play the pipes when the traditional Scottish dishes were brought in for supper, and afterwards Charles would play reels and strathspeys on his fiddle while his household danced. On this one day he drank whisky from a little hoard sent him over the years by some old adherent, while the faithful Iain, in a slightly cracked voice, sang the Gaelic songs of the High Bard, Alastair Mac Mhaisghstir, dead long ago like the rest of those who had welcomed a vigorous young Prince on the deck of the *Du Teillay*.

It was, in fact, an occasion exactly suited to Louise's purpose so to provoke her husband that he would give her the excuse she needed for leaving him.

She had been working upon him all day, giving him little digs where it hurt most, making sure he noticed the glances of amused contempt she cast at the Highland costume he loved, affecting little shudders at the music of the pipes, and with marked patience reminding her husband that he had told this or that story many times before. Now, at supper, Alfieri played his part. Gesticulating with his ringed hand, he spoke of the revolt of the American Colonists, expressing his deep admiration for those who had fought and won their freedom.

"I must let you know, Monsieur le Comte," Charles interrupted sharply, "that my sympathy in this quarrel is entirely with England. No nation would part with such possessions without a struggle, and as I told the French Ambassador, the secret treaty France made with the Colonists was a piece of perfidy from which neither she nor they will gain any advantage in the end."

"The English Resident, Sir Horace Mann, is saying much the same thing," remarked Louise. "I am surprised to find your Majesty in agreement with the British Government, your enemy."

A spasm of intense irritation made him flush. Could she not yet understand how passionately he loved England?

"Two years ago certain of the Colonists had the impertinence to send me a Memorial, offering to set up my Standard there. I replied to them in no uncertain terms that England's enemies will always be my enemies also."

Louise tittered.

"I am, of course, a mere woman, and have not your Majesty's great mind, but really it seems to me so quaint a situation. One can only admire, Sir, your Christian spirit of forgiveness towards those who have so often and so con-temptuously rejected your claims."

He moved clumsily, knocking over his glass. Louise immediately was all solicitude.

"Permit me to suggest that your Majesty should retire to bed. The festivities of the day have been too much for you. Stewart can read to you in your chamber the little poems to which you are so greatly attached."

She shook her head discreetly at the servant who was about to refill her husband's glass.

"Some more whisky," Charles said sharply to the man. And then to his wife: "I shall certainly not retire, Madame, until I have observed all the customs of this feast."

Her spiteful sneers and Alfieri's praise of the Colonists had spoilt his evening. Both of them knew with what painful interest he had followed the War of Independence, poring over maps, reading every conflicting report of victory and defeat in the English papers, passionately championing the cause of his rightful country. But Iain Beag now launched into a long Gaelic poem which described Charles's march into England in 1745, and the old King tried to fix

220

his attention on it, to draw comfort from living over again in memory that uninterrupted advance.

Carlisle surrendering on November 20th; he rode in on a white charger with a hundred pipers playing before him. Foot-slogging on again from dawn to dusk, getting into the saddle only to round up stragglers, to Penrith on the 22nd. Next day at Kendal he had his brogues mended, telling an astonished blacksmith, "You are the first of your trade who ever shod the son of a king." Preston on the 25th, the southernmost point reached in the rising of 1715. At Wigan on the 26th he heard how Manchester had surrendered to one of his sergeants and a drummer-boy.

It was in Manchester that he kept that St Andrew's Day, feasting on a perfect banquet of good news. The fiery cross had gone round Stratherrick and the Aird, and seven hundred Frasers were drilling in front of Castle Downie. Eight hundred regulars in French service, commanded by Lord John Drummond, had landed at Stonehaven, surely only the advance-guard of the great army promised him by France. A letter from Henry informed him that the Duke had Louis's sworn word for it that the expeditionary force assembling at Dunkirk would be ready to sail by December 20th. Voltaire had drawn up a Manifesto in his favour, circulating it throughout France. At a Council meeting that night there was no dissentient voice when Charles pressed for an immediate advance on London, Lord George Murray being the most enthusiastic of them all. . . .

"Next day we forded the river near Stockport," he said aloud, not knowing that he interrupted Iain's reading. "I was up to my waist in the water and was like to drown once, and all the while I could see on the opposite bank a very old lady sitting in a chair, watching me and cheering me on. And when I struggled out of the water, she fell on her aged knees, and told me that as an infant she had been held up in her mother's arms to watch Charles II ride into London at the Restoration, and that every year since the Revolution she had sent half her income anonymously to our exiled

Court. Hearing of my advance, she had sold her jewels and now laid the money at my feet, her tears falling on my fingers as she kissed my hand. . . ."

After a pause he added:

"The news of my retreat killed her," but he did not know what he said, for he was watching his wife and Alfieri.

Once when, at a critical moment of his wanderings, he had been hiding in a deserted glen, he had seen, just in time, the evil forked tongue of an adder dart towards him from under a rock. It had seemed for a moment that the very heather, his friend and refuge, concealed treachery. He had something of the same sensation now. In the man who was his honoured guest he had received into his household an adder.

They were in an alcove. A screen concealed them from the rest of the company; but they had not troubled, it seemed, to conceal themselves from Charles. They sat full in his line of vision, and even as he looked their lips met.

He had been heated with alcohol and emotion; now he felt icy cold. He got up from his chair and advanced upon them. Without a word, completely ignoring Alfieri, he took his wife's hand, bowed to her with deadly politeness, drew her to her feet, and walked her towards the door. Her ladies made to follow, but he stayed them with a gesture.

She was just a little frightened. Her provocation of him had been quite deliberate, but with his grip upon her hand, his terrible silence, she wondered belatedly whether she had gone too far. He was old, sick, half drunk, and she was a strong young woman, yet there was that in his eyes which made her fear of him only half feigned when, alone in her bedchamber, he locked the door.

"I think your Majesty must have taken leave of your senses at the same time as you discarded your manners. Your insulting of our guest by saying not one word of good-night——"

"Our guest. Say rather, your lover."

"This is monstrous!" She tried to sound indignant, but

fear shrilled in her voice. "You are heated with drink, Sir; this alone can excuse such villainous behaviour. It is as your brother so often warned me before we left Rome, that the nasty bottle would drive you mad at last. I shall publish among all my friends your brutal treatment of me, as your unfortunate mistress did——"

Her words merged into a stifled scream as his hands came round her throat.

## 3

Much of what had happened was vague to him next morning, horribly vague. He knew, indeed, some moments of stark panic until in answer to his enquiries he was told that his wife was safe and well. He sat down at once and wrote her a formal apology.

He had been, he admitted, heated with wine. He would not refer to the fact that as always on that particular anniversary he had been tormented by memories, for he had learnt by this time that Louise lacked the common charity of feigning any interest in an old man's dreams. It was too late, he supposed, for any real reconciliation between them, but at least there must be decency; and while he on his side deeply regretted losing control of himself, he must insist on her promise that she would not see Count Vittorio Alfieri again. He was writing to the Count, he added, regretting that he could no longer extend to him the hospitality of the Palazzo Guadagni.

When they met at dinner, Louise greeted her husband with a new meekness. She wore a bandage round her throat, but she made no reference to last night's scene, and appearing very subdued and chastened, spared Charles some of her eternal chatter.

A few days later, with the same timid air, she informed Charles that she had invited a friend of hers, Madame Orlandini, to breakfast next morning, having had so little company this past week. She hoped her husband did not

223

object. Anxious to please her, really wondering whether the sordid scene on St Andrew's Day had not cleared the air between them, he set himself to be charming and gracious to Madame Orlandini throughout the meal, though he knew of the lady's reputation and thought her a most undesirable companion for his wife.

"I have promised, Madame," their guest said presently, "to go today to see the needlework of the Little White Nuns in the Via del Mandorlo. They are collecting money for a new bell for their convent, and it would be a charity to help them. Moreover their needlework is extremely fine."

"I would like to accompany you," said Louise, "for I need some new table-linen." She turned to her husband, and asked diffidently: "Dare we hope that your Majesty would consent to escort us?"

He was touched both by her request and the manner in which it was made; for the first time for years she seemed really anxious for his company. As they drove to the convent, he remembered wistfully the first few months of their marriage, when Louise had appeared to be truly happy with him, as he had been with her, ardent and tender and delighted with everything. Could they not, after all, make something of their union, childless though it had proved? He had not made sufficient allowances; he was difficult to live with, often peevish, more often garrulous, obsessed with the past in which she could feel no interest. She was not yet thirty, and he was approaching his sixtieth birthday.

As they alighted at the convent gate, Charles noticed a man hanging about outside. It was that Irish adventurer, Geoghegan, whom Madame Orlandini kept, a stage Irishman, with his exaggerated brogue, his toothy smile, his blarney. The two ladies hurried up the path towards the convent, while Geoghegan remained with Charles whose bad legs prevented him from keeping up with them.

"I've been after wondering, Sir," gushed the Irishman, "would you be remembering a relation of mine who had the good luck to draw the sword for you in '45? A Captain

224

of Grenadiers in Lally's Regiment he was, good soul, and was taken prisoner at the surrender of Carlisle. Sure, he was but a humble follower of your——"

"What a-devil does that mean?" interrupted Charles, pointing with his cane at the convent door which had just been shut behind the two ladies.

"Now glory be to God!" cried Geoghegan, mightily indignant, "if that isn't an unpardonable rudeness of those nuns. Sure, they can't fail to have seen your Majesty approaching. I'll just take the liberty of knocking on this holy door of theirs, Sir, and we'll have 'em all upon their knees begging your Majesty's pardon."

He beat loudly on the door with the head of his cane. For several minutes there was no response; and then, instead of the portal being opened, the judas in it was pulled back and the face of the Mother Superior was visible behind the grille.

"I have to inform you, Sir," she said sternly to Charles, "that the illustrious lady, your wife, has asked sanctuary of us, which was not to be denied. She is now under the protection both of our Holy Mother the Church, and of the Grand Duchess of Tuscany."

She closed the shutter with a decisive snap.


# FIVE

## I

"HAVE no fear, Reverend Mother," Henry whispered, rustling along the cloister of the Ursuline Convent in Rome, "that I shall tire her Majesty. I realise only too well how prostrate my dearest sister must be."

Reverend Mother merely bowed her head in acknowledgement of these remarks. She was a shrewd woman, and she had her doubts about the interesting invalid whom the Cardinal Duke had placed in her care. Conducting Henry upstairs, she tapped on a door; it was opened a crack, and the face of Madame Orlandini, wearing a pious expression, peeped out. She gave a fluttering little cry, opened the door wide, and sank into a curtsy.

The shutters of the room were closed, and it was lit only by a single taper and a little blue lamp burning before a statue of Our Lady on a bracket. Reclining upon a day-bed before the fire, like a fallen lily in her white velvet night-gown and muslin turban, her face deathly white without her rouge, lay Louise. Beside her the Baroness de Maltzan read aloud from a book of devotion.

It was a trifle over-done, but it impressed the simple Henry.

"No, no, my dearest sister!" he exclaimed, as Louise tried feebly to struggle up to greet him. "You must not think of rising." He seated himself in the chair the Baroness had hastened to set for him before she and Madame Orlandini had tiptoed discreetly from the room. Taking one limp hand and touching it with his lips, he murmured, deeply moved: "My poor child, my sweet sister, be assured you are quite safe here. It was in this Convent of St Cecilia that my dearest mother was lodged on her first coming to Rome as a bride, and my father always cherished a particular affection for it."

Louise gave a little sob, and dabbed her eyes with her handkerchief.

"Alas, dear brother, what a sad reunion is this! And yet how blessed I am in having such a brother. May God forgive me that in my dereliction and despair I have reproached you in my heart for having arranged my most unfortunate marriage."

"I assure you," Henry said earnestly, "that I had no hand in it, beyond giving my formal consent. But should you fatigue yourself by talking? I came only to kiss your hand and enquire whether there was anything you lacked."

There was indeed. There was Alfieri. But she was going to have to be extremely circumspect here. It would be necessary to get Henry completely on her side before she tried to obtain for Alfieri an invitation to come to Rome.

"Dearest brother, it will relieve me to unbosom my sorrows, and to justify myself to you for my flight. I have already told you something of my reasons for it in my letters to you from the convent in Florence, yet there were horrors I could not commit to paper. He—he tried to strangle me; I think I shall bear the marks upon my throat to my dying day." She touched the lace cravat about her neck. "And afterwards, disregarding all my prayers for mercy, he ravished me——"

"I beg you not to distress yourself," interrupted Henry, shying away from these intimacies.

"I gave way to panic—I confess it. I could have remained in the care of the good nuns, or taken refuge at the Tuscan Court, whither I was invited by the Grand Duchess—but no! I dared not stay in Florence; I feared what *he* might do. I remembered to have heard how he threatened to burn down every convent in Paris when his mistress (poor creature! how I pity her now!) fled from his mad brutality. I had but one wish: to fly to the arms of my dearest brother. And God raised up friends for His poor handmaid in her necessity. A Count Alfieri, of a most noble Piedmontese House, a very perfect knight, arranged for my escape from Florence. But what a journey was that!"

She shuddered.

"The Count and a good honest Irishman, both fully armed, spirited me away in a coach the Count had hired, and in which I and my two faithful ladies crouched in terror, expecting every moment to be pursued by my husband's ruffians. But such is Count Alfieri's delicacy that he would not enter Rome in my company, lest evil-minded persons should spread abroad reports injurious to my reputation."

"God bless and reward this noble gentleman!"

From Louise's point of view, it was not a very satisfactory remark, but she decided to let it pass. There would be plenty of time to work on the guileless Henry. She clutched his hand and faltered:

"Oh, my dear brother, I am in an anguish lest you and the Pope should counsel me to return to my husband. I would kill myself sooner, and indeed I would be in imminent peril of my life if I returned to that poor madman."

He patted her hand, glancing covertly towards the door through which the Baroness and Madame Orlandini had disappeared. He really did not know how to cope with hysterical ladies. He said loudly and slowly, as though addressing a deaf person:

"My very dear sister, your escape being made with the approval of the Tuscan Court has fully justified your conduct. You may rely on my own kindly sentiments towards you; I have thought of all things essential to your case, and am glad to say that the Holy Father has approved of the measures I have taken for your welfare. This convent is the least restricted in Rome; French is spoken here, and some of its inmates are persons of rank. Do not fear, unless a miracle happens, that His Holiness, or I myself, will ever counsel a return to your husband. But as it is probable that God has permitted what has just occurred in order to move you to the practice of an edifying life, it may be also that Our Lord wishes to effect by the same means the conversion of my brother."

Such comforting words appeared to have struck Louise dumb. Or perhaps he had tired her. He himself felt quite overcome with compassion. This poor forlorn outcast, crushed by her sorrows, and at the season of Christmas too!

"Dearest sister, be anxious about nothing. I am convinced you will be ready to accept the counsel and advice I shall give you for your own good before God and man. I feel deeply for you," he concluded, bending over the limp hand.

The practice of an edifying life was the last thing Louise
desired, and having got into a convent for her own ends, her
main concern now was to get out of it again.

"Is it wise of me," she asked Henry when next he called,
"to remain shut up in a convent? I am apt to brood when I
am alone. You may think me bad-tempered, but I am only
out of spirits, and have such headaches that I can scarcely
speak."

Henry sought the advice of the Pope, and obtained for his
sister-in-law a private audience. His Holiness was easy-going
and indulgent; Louise wept plentifully, was all injured
innocence, and described herself as pining away. Public
propriety would be perfectly satisfied, the Pope told Henry
afterwards, if the Cardinal Duke made over to his sister-in-
law a suite of apartments in the Cancellaria, and he, the
Pope, intended to bestow on her half the pension of 12,000
crowns he had been paying to her husband.

Louise was delighted, as well she might be. Besides the
6,000 crowns from His Holiness, Henry settled on her four
thousand for life, and paid all her household expenses.
Moreover her letters to the French Court, dilating on her
wrongs, had so moved Louis XVI that he had diverted to her
the sixty thousand livres paid to Charles as her marriage
settlement. (She did not think it necessary to acquaint her
brother-in-law with this windfall.) As for the Cancellaria, it
was an ideal place for lovers, since Henry was hardly ever
there, so that all she needed now was her Psipsio.

"My conscience upbraids me because I have not rewarded
the gallant gentleman who rescued me from the cruelties of
my husband," she told Henry. "Dearest brother, pray read
this letter I have received from Count Alfieri. You see how
much he longs to prostrate himself at your feet."

So presently Alfieri was able to write in his Journal:

'As I travelled towards Rome, the approach to her made
my heart beat. I arrived! I saw her!—oh God! the thought

of it still cleaves my heart in twain! —I saw her a prisoner behind a grating!'

This was poetic licence, for Louise had long since left the convent and was queening it at the Cancellaria. She had taken care to discover a suitable present for her Psipsio to give to Henry on being introduced, a beautifully bound copy of Virgil for the Cardinal's library at Frascati; and though as a staunch agnostic Alfieri despised all churchmen, he was convinced by Psipsia of the necessity of keeping in with them while he was in Rome. Once again love made him stoop to expedients he held in horror.

"I will do anything, I will resort to anything," he promised his mistress, "tolerated by these charlatans and aided by their petty priests, who have, or assume, any influence in the affairs of my *donna amata*."

He rented the Villa Strozzi on the Esquiline, and settled down to his writing, installing at the Cancellaria his confidential valet, Elia. The conditions for the resumption of the liaison were ideal; Henry resided for the greater part of his time at Frascati, Pius VI firmly believed in the platonic nature of the friendship, and Roman society was indulgent to lovers. Louise and Alfieri went for long rides together over the Campagna.

'The fifteenth of my horses,' he confided to his Journal, 'is my beautiful roan, Fido, the same that often carries the delightful burden of my lady, and for that reason is dearer to me than all the rest of my stud.'

When the great heat of the summer came on, Henry offered his sister-in-law a house in Frascati for *villeggiatura*, and was very much astonished by her declining the offer.

"What a delightful prospect of staying so near my dearest brother in the coolness and verdure of Frascati! But alas, the heat has made my legs swell, so that I must stay in sweltering Rome."

Even Henry's innocence found something feeble in this excuse; and without giving her notice he sent his secretary, Canon Cesarini, to call on her. The Canon was informed by obviously embarrassed servants that they had orders from their mistress to admit no one today. On the following morning Henry received a note from Louise, and he read it with a puzzled frown.

'I am overwhelmed with distress, my dearest brother, that I was unable to receive your good Secretary when he did me the honour of calling, but I have been so overcome with the heat that, having had no sleep the previous night, I had gone to bed at three in the afternoon.'

Though it did not enter Henry's head that she might not have gone to bed alone, he began to have doubts whether in some respects Louise was quite such an angel as he had deemed her. For clever though she was, she was not quite clever enough to conceal from him her greed. Just before the coming of Alfieri she had approached Henry for his share of his mother's jewels, saying that she wished to wear them only as evidence to the world that her dearest brother believed in her innocence. Her dearest brother had replied that he did not see the necessity for such evidence, and refused. Now she reopened the subject; and because she despised Henry, she did not see fit to use any particular finesse.

"I know you have no desire but to please me, and that is enough for me. Naturally, as your brother's wife, I ought to have these jewels, but I quite understand that circumstances may forbid it, and you have only to say so, dearest brother."

"I am afraid circumstances do forbid it," Henry replied rather tersely.

So Louise was in an ill humour when her mother and her sister, Caroline-Augusta, with the latter's husband, paid a visit to Rome; nor was her mood improved by her mother's outspokenness.

"You need not think, my girl," said that robust lady, "that the trouble I have taken in extracting from his Most Christian Majesty a further settlement of twenty thousand Roman crowns on you for life is because I think you deserve such generosity. It's because I dread having you back on my hands, which you will be, you stupid chit, if you continue to carry on as you are doing with this red-headed poet of yours."

"At the age of thirty, Madame," retorted Louise, "I am old enough, I think, to manage my own affairs."

"You're old enough to know better than to pose as a martyr to the Pope and your foolish brother-in-law, when all Rome knows of your goings-on. One of these fine days the Cardinal's eyes will be opened, and he'll turn you out of here, bag and baggage."

But Louise was complacently certain of being able to manage 'that silly old man', as she referred to Henry when Psipsio and Psipsia were alone. What really infuriated her was her husband's delay in making her a widow.

"That man at Florence must be made of iron to spite us by living, my Psipsio," she sighed. "It is so long since he was ill, and still he lives—may live another couple of years, though on the other hand he may be suffocated at any moment by the humours I hear have arisen in his chest."

"What a cruel thing it is," exclaimed Psipsio, clawing his perfumed locks, "to look for one's happiness to the death of another, yet Love compels one to it. Certainly that man does not seem inclined to depart."

## 3

On the day following the Feast of the Purification, Henry drove in from Frascati to dine with his sister-in-law. The streets of Rome were crowded with people carrying cats, dogs, and birds, and leading mules and horses, to be blessed at the Church of St Anthony, so that the Cardinal's carriage was obliged to move slowly, and this, as always, annoyed him. Alighting in the courtyard of the Cancellaria, he was about to brush past the little crowd of petitioners who immediately approached, when he noticed among them a man whose dress was travel-stained, and who wore the Royal Arms of England embroidered on his sleeve.

The Cardinal halted in his stride, his mouth going dry.

Beckoning the man forward, he snatched a note from his hand, and read it there and then. It was signed, 'John Stewart, Major Domo'; and it informed him that his brother had suffered a seizure and lay at the point of death.

Even at such a moment, Henry's heart sank at the prospect of so long a journey over snow-covered roads, for as he grew older he was more and more attached to his comfort. But he pushed the thought from him. He must travel posthaste to Florence, and perhaps he would have the consolation of reconciling his erring brother to the Church, of persuading him to confess his many sins, and of seeing him die a true penitent.

"Who is with his Majesty?" he demanded of the messenger.

"There is no one with his Majesty except the servants, Royal Eminence," the man replied simply.

"What! It cannot be. Has he not ghostly comfort?"

"Archbishop Martini of Florence calls every day. I beg your Royal Eminence's pardon, but my instructions from Mr Stewart were that I should apply to your Royal Eminence for the expenses of my journey."

Henry repressed a sharp exclamation of annoyance. He would never have thought that Charles included meanness among his many faults, but Louise had impressed on him how, before her flight, her husband had actually grudged her a little mutton-broth in the morning, while his own table was loaded with luxuries.

The Cardinal broke the news to Louise that she must expect to hear the worst, then sent for his secretary. In view of his Majesty's condition, he told Cesarini, it would be necessary to draw up a Memorial to be sent round the European Courts announcing his own accession to the claims of his family to the throne of Great Britain; in future he would use the title of Duke of York for purposes of incognito only. Now that he was likely to succeed to them, he found himself suddenly very much concerned about the royal rights upon the insistence on which he had so often chided his brother.

It was a bitter cold evening in March when Henry, with numerous attendants, arrived in Florence. He was astonished to see how dark was the front of the Palazzo Guadagni; it had the appearance of being deserted. As the thought came to him that perhaps he had arrived too late, his old affection for his brother, overlaid by so many quarrels and by so long a separation, surged up anew, and it was with infinite relief that he noticed that the servant who opened the gates wore no sign of mourning. There was no straw laid down upon the flag-stones; his brother could be neither dead nor very ill.

"His Majesty's sickness does not lie so heavy upon him today," Iain Beag informed him. "Your Royal Eminence is lodging in the town?" he added, glancing at the large entourage.

"I am lodging here, of course," Henry replied sharply. "You had notice of my coming, and ought to have made all fitting preparations."

Iain Beag made no reply to this rebuke, but ushered his Royal Eminence down a long passage, unlit and gloomy. The single candle carried by the major domo flickered over cupboards empty of the plate they were built to display; there was no smell of supper, no bustle of servants. The place was as cold as a vault.

Henry halted suddenly, jerking up his handsome head. From somewhere in this desolate palace came the sound of music, the bass voice of a 'cello speaking meditatively, with frequent pauses. For a moment he was back in the Palazzo Muti, a boy again, playing duets on his flute with Charles, trying to make up by application what he lacked of his brother's natural talent. Then Stewart threw open a door; the music ceased, and Henry, passing round a shabby screen, came into a room hung from ceiling to floor with tartan which billowed out in the draught from the opening door, a draught which bent the flames of a few candles in tarnished silver scounces on the wall.

By the fire, huddled in a faded plaid, with a 'cello between

234

his knees, sat an old man whom Henry could scarcely believe to be his brother. Surely it was something more than serious illness that had wrought such a change, that had bowed the broad shoulders and made so tremulous the hand that held the bow. Of all men Henry had ever known, none had possessed the vitality of his brother. Now of that vitality there remained not a shadow. It was a greater shock to the Cardinal than if he had seen Charles dead.

He sank on his knees, too moved to speak. A tired old voice that had lost all its former resonance, spoke from the chair.

"I am sorry, brother, that you have been fetched on an unnecessary errand. This wretched carcase of mine refuses to die. Sit down near the fire; Iain Beag will fetch you some supper presently. But as for all your chaplains and your secretaries, and so on——"

"They shall put you to no inconvenience, Sir," Henry broke in hastily. "I did not know . . . of course I shall arrange for them to lodge in the town."

"There is plenty of room here, but I can't feed them. I was obliged to dismiss half of my own household when the Pope cut my pension, and to borrow five hundred crowns in order to maintain the rest. You were not embarrassed, I hope, by duns at my gate? They have a tiresome habit of encamping there."

"I did not know . . ." Henry began feebly again, and stopped.

"That I was so poor? No, it's never been a subject of much interest to you, has it? And I should be accustomed to it by this time."

Henry was silent, suddenly and bitterly ashamed. He thought, willy nilly, of his ecclesiastical benefices in Rome, of his abbeys of Anchin and Amand, of his pensions from Spain charged upon the bishoprics of Jaen, Malaga, Segovia, with half a dozen rich prebends, bringing him in a total income of twenty thousand scudi a year; and he was truly, for the moment, abashed. It is never a comfortable feeling,

235

and he made haste to assure himself that his conscience was clear. All his brother's troubles and poverty had been brought on his own head.

Charles had laid aside the 'cello, and was stirring the contents of a saucepan over the fire.

"Remember my quackery?" he asked, with a smile that had in it the ghost of his old radiant charm. "The herbs of the mountains, Iain Beag would tell you, are better than all the doctors' pills and potions. It's good to see you, Harry; I'm a trifle lonely these days. Sometimes the musician, Domenico Corri, is kind enough to come and play duets with me; and before I fell ill I had a visit from King Gustavus of Sweden. There is a great man and a great king. He has written to Louis of France and to Charles of Spain, he tells me, to get me some financial aid. But who would aid an old wretch who tried to strangle his young wife?"

"Did—did you, Sir?" Henry felt compelled to ask.

"I can't remember much about that evening. Yes, yes, Harry, the nasty bottle of which you were kind enough to warn me. But she seems to have survived," he added dryly.

There was a tap on the door.

"Iain Beag has come to fetch me to bed. No nursemaid is more of a tyrant. Tomorrow, brother, I shall be more fit company for you."

As Stewart assisted the invalid to his feet, Henry noticed for the first time a pair of silver-mounted pistols lying on the table. Intercepting his glance, Charles said, with a hint of apology:

"An instinct from my old hunted life. I must have them with me everywhere, like a child with its toys. Though there is no one left to care a button whether I live or die. Even old Marischal has gone at last—did you know? After wishing he were among the Eskimo, for they knock old men on the head. I can understand now how he felt."

That he spoke without a trace of bitterness made what he said the more moving.

The weather changed during the night, and spring came to Florence. The brothers sat together in the sun in the neglected garden; the gentlest of breezes turned the weathervane on the belvedere with Charles's initials cut in the pennon. He had brought down a bundle of papers and showed them to Henry, saying that he had been trying to put his affairs in order before he died.

As the state of his brother's financial affairs was unfolded to the Cardinal, Henry was appalled. Out of his pension from the Pope, cut by half when Louise left him, Charles was still paying her her pin-money; of other resources he had none.

"I have at this moment," he remarked, "not more than six sequins in the house and can obtain no credit. The few servants left are content to serve without wages—God knows why. I have pawned everything except my share of our mother's jewels."

Then, after a pause, he went on with that smile which still had so much charm about it:

"But that is not strictly true. I still keep under my bed a certain strong-box with a hoard of gold never to be touched except for one purpose. You may laugh at me, Harry, but after nearly forty years I am still waiting for a call from England. I cannot cease to wait for it, even if I would."

Henry did not feel inclined to laugh.

"You will inherit my claims to the throne of Great Britain, and that, I am afraid, is all. The money in the box will go to my servants. For my wife I need make no provision, seeing that both the Pope and you yourself have made her so handsome an allowance, and she has, moreover, a pension of sixty thousand livres from France, recently increased, so I hear."

"From France?" echoed Henry, very sharply. "I think you must be mistaken. She has said nothing to me about it."

"And with so rich a lover, who I suppose will marry her when I am dead," went on Charles, ignoring this, "she is most amply provided for."

The Cardinal half rose in his seat, his face turning the colour of his scarlet zucchetta.

"I did not intend, Sir," said he, his voice quivering with indignation, "to trouble your Majesty in your present weak state of health with any reference to your treatment of your wife. But since you add to this treatment so vile a slander, you compel me to open the subject. I am aware that there may have been faults on her side; I have lived these past three years in close contact with the lady, and find her not quite so—er—so angelic as first I deemed her. But to accuse her of betraying your honour, of inferring that even now, in Rome, as my guest, she is leading an immoral life—that, Sir, is intolerable!"

"So Count Alfieri is not in Rome?" Charles enquired mildly.

"Alfieri? Yes . . . no . . . I mean, yes, this brave and honourable gentleman is certainly in Rome, and is very much courted by Roman society. He was received in private audience by His Holiness who, however, declined the dedication of his tragedy, *Saul*; but a perfomance of another tragedy from his pen, *Antigone*, was performed during the Carnival by noble amateurs at the Spanish Embassy, the Count playing the name-part. I did not, of course, attend; you know it has always been my habit to leave Rome before the Carnival in order to be spared having to witness its orgies. But I am told that this tragedy was most elegant, full of the most elevated sentiments——"

He broke off in furious affront. For he had become aware that Charles was shaking with laughter.

"Oh Harry! Harry! Unworldly you have ever been and of so stainless a moral character that you have expected everyone else to be the same. But truly, are you so blind that you could be fooled by Louise regarding her relations with Alfieri? Well, if you have been, I suppose I can't blame you. They fooled me too, until I saw them . . . faugh! you would put it down to the nasty bottle. But I can assure you that he was not the first."

238

Henry was silent, his mind whirling.

"It is not for me to judge her, God knows. And an old man who marries a young wife must expect to be decorated with a pair of horns. But there are decencies.

Still Henry was silent. Tiny incidents recurred to his memory in a new light. He had thought it a little strange (no more than that) when Louise had insisted that Alfieri's valet, Elia, an oily person to whom the Cardinal had taken an instant dislike, should be a member of her household at the Cancellaria. In the summer after her coming to Rome he had been puzzled by her refusal of his offer of a villa at Frascati for the hot months. And then there was that occasion when he had sent his secretary to call on her without warning, and Cesarini had been refused admittance. Her excuse had been lame; he remembered thinking so at the time. But never, never for an instant, had he suspected—this!

He began suddenly to press Charles for proof. Charles referred him to Archbishop Martini, and to the archiepiscopal palace in Florence Henry straightway betook himself. He had always had a morbid horror of the sins of the flesh, but he must know the truth about this matter. And what the Archbishop told him left him no room for doubt.

"All Rome has known of this intrigue for two years, Royal Eminence," Martini said bluntly, "and Florence for three years before that. Unfortunately we regard such amours with too great indulgence here, even, I regret to say, with amusement."

Henry was neither indulgent nor amused. Having paid his brother's debts and assigned him an allowance, he descended upon Rome like a thundercloud.

## 4

Louise was at her interminable letter-writing when she received a note from her brother-in-law requesting a private interview. She thought this a little odd; long ago they had dropped all formalities. Perhaps, she reflected, hope springing up, he had come to break the news that her husband was dead at last.

She composed her features into an expression of grave anxiety when Henry was announced, faltering, as she went forward to receive his embrace:

"My husband?"

He did not embrace her, but made her a stiff bow. She noticed that his swarthy face was flushed and his dark eyes angry.

"My brother is very much better, Madame."

"*Deo gratias!*" She thought quickly; Henry must have seen for himself how poor his brother was, thus catching her out in a lie. "I have been thinking," she ran on, "so much about him while you have been absent, and I am resolved, dearest brother, to make over for his needs a portion of the allowance you have so generously settled upon me. I hope this generosity may ensure my erring husband the peace and comfort of sick old age, and as for me, I am well content to retrench in everything."

"I would suppose, Madame," he answered tartly, "that there would be little need for you to retrench, seeing that my Treasurer has paid all your expenses while you have lived here in my house of the Cancellaria, and that besides the allowances made you by His Holiness and myself, you have a most generous pension from his Most Christian Majesty."

Louise's mouth fell open, but she swiftly recovered herself.

"I did not think it necessary to inform you, dear brother, of a purely private gift which his Most Christian Majesty's compassion for me impelled him to bestow. And I repeat, that I am quite ready to relinquish the allowance you have been generous enough to make me, as a sign to my husband that I have forgiven him—on condition that he agrees to a legal separation between us."

"While no one in the world, Madame," Henry said in an icy tone, "can desire more than I do a settlement between you and your husband, I can never approve of a separation which has no object but interest——"

"Interest!"

"I beg you not to interrupt me, Madame. To bestow money which, in fact, is not yours to apportion, might simplify and hasten this separation which you now seem earnestly to desire, while your consequent poverty might appeal still further to the munificence of friendly Courts. I neither can nor ought to meddle in agreements you make with your husband, but while you are my guest my Treasurer by my order will certainly not pay the allowance I have made you to anyone but yourself."

Louise leaned back on the couch and sighed.

"I confess I do not understand you, brother. I will not believe you are inferring that I am trying to bribe my husband into setting me free. Nothing in my conduct, I hope, can have given you so base an opinion of me."

His hands were trembling with indignation and disgust, and he clenched them together in his scarlet lap.

"Madame," he said abruptly, not replying to any of these remarks, "I must ask you, in order to avoid a public scandal, to prevail on Count Vittorio Alfieri to leave Rome without delay."

Louise drew in her breath with an audible hiss. She was utterly unprepared; for three years she had fooled the unworldly Cardinal to the top of her bent. She did not need to feign the fury that made her voice so shrill.

"I cannot believe that this is my beloved brother who befriended me in my dereliction, and to whom I owe so much! That *he* should outrage my delicacy and insinuate against my reputation——"

"I beg your pardon, Madame," barked the Cardinal, "but I must tell you that while I was in Florence I talked with Archbishop Martini, who undeceived my credulity. Immediately upon my return I sought a private audience with the Pope, and I bring a positive order from His Holiness that Count Alfieri quits Rome—forthwith."

You two silly old men! she thought. Undeceived his credulity! If he and the Pope had proved so gullible in the past, it ought to be possible to bring them back to her side again. She changed her tune.

"Alas, dear brother, you must have pity on my youth and inexperience. I am convent-bred and know little of the world. It never occurred to me that my friendship with Count Alfieri could be misconstrued. That the exchange of lofty sentiments and a mutual love of the arts could be twisted into———" her voice choked in a sob. "Forgive me, I did not know how evil-minded people could be. I thank you, dearest brother, for your good advice which, though perhaps harshly phrased, I am well assured was given only out of your fraternal affection for me."

Henry waited to hear of the departure of Alfieri, but he did not wait in silence. All Rome rang with his indignation, and was alarmed. Such severe treatment of so fashionable a pastime as a liaison must not be made a precedent! On the other hand there were reports that Florentine society had veered round to Charles. If Alfieri had so abused his position as a recognised cicisbeo, the whole convenient system of cicisbeoship was threatened.

Louise did her best. She wrote long screeds to Henry, who was much occupied with his sacred duties, it being Passion-tide. She had always flattered herself on being a good letter-writer; but she moved Henry not at all. She had deceived him; that was the thing that stuck. He had always been quick to take offence, prone to fits of rage followed by days of sullenness. It was his, not her, innocence that had been violated. Alfieri must go.

On May 4th, with a long train carrying his sumptuous belongings, and with his famous stud of horses, Psipsio left for Siena. Psipsia was prostrated, nor was she greatly cheered by the verse sent her by Psipsio on the eve of his departure, verse rather more obscure than usual:

'By life or death will our sharp trial be ended?
Yet since upon a single thread, I know,
Frail as may be, our future is suspended,
Carrying thy life in mine I forward go.'

In a note enclosing the verse he threatened to commit suicide, but considerately added in a postscript that his *donna amata* must trust her lover's unselfish determination to preserve his wretched life for her sake. He was going to make a pilgrimage to places associated with the four great Italian poets who, she had told him, were less worthy of laurels than himself, while working on an ode to 'America Libera'. But from Siena he wrote that he thought of revisiting England, and Psipsia became hysterical. What if there were another Lady Ligonier there to capture his ardent heart! Psipsia must join Psipsio; but meanwhile she must win back Henry, from whom she had such great expectations.

When the injured innocence pose had no effect, she tried bullying. This was a mistake, resulting from her ignorance of Henry's somewhat complex character.

"After the advice you gave me, brother," said she, dropping all customary terms of endearment, "and for which I thanked you at the time, believing it to be private, I made Monsieur le Comte d'Alfieri promise to leave Rome. This he has done."

"A full six weeks after His Holiness's positive order to him."

With difficulty Louise restrained herself from telling Henry just what Alfieri thought of the Pope and of clerics in general.

"I would have tried to persuade him to go earlier, had it not been that after ripe reflection, and taking the advice of the most sensible people, I feared a sudden departure would have looked like compulsion, and confirmed the injurious reports about my conduct which, though groundless, were only too prevalent."

She waited for approval, but none came. For the first time it occurred to her that her husband had some good qualities; *he* never listened to ill-natured gossip or betrayed a secret.

"However that may be, your wish is fulfilled, and your advice followed. The only annoyance is that there should have been any publicity. It hurts my reputation and offends my delicacy. See what trouble you would have spared me if you had not run off to the Pope without the slightest necessity, and thus in the first excitement allowed yourself to hurry to a proceeding which the kindness of your heart must let you see was not very courteous to me."

Henry was staggered. Not a word of repentance, or of apology for the dreadful scandal she had given, for the distress she had caused himself. And her lack of respect for his dignity affronted him almost as much as her brazenness.

She added that the anxiety and mental strain had so undermined her health that she was thinking of going to Baden to take the waters, but of course only if her dear brother approved. Henry not only approved; he was vastly relieved. She had been taught a sharp lesson, and would, he hoped, behave herself in future; while he, by taking instant and determined steps, had cut short a nasty scandal.

He took an affectionate farewell of Louise, treating her as something between an interesting invalid and a sincere penitent; blissfully unaware that she was going not to Baden but to Colmar on the Rhine, where her old confidante, the Baroness de Maltzan, had put her castle of Martinsburg at the disposal of Psipsio and Psipsia. At the same time Henry felt exceedingly annoyed with his brother for not consulting him about a legal separation which, it appeared, was being negotiated between husband and wife.

Perhaps this annoyance had something to do with the fact that when, in the new year, 1784, a courier arrived to inform his Royal Eminence that his brother was again at death's door, Henry neglected to go to Florence. He was exceedingly busy, the roads were very nearly impassable with snow, and in regard to Charles his conscience was clear. He had paid his brother's debts, was making him an allowance, and was aware that the efforts of King Gustavus had resulted in some financial assistance being sent to Charles both from France and Spain.

With Louise gone from the Cancellaria, Henry plunged happily once more into the busy and useful routine she and her sordid affairs had interrupted.

# 5

On the eighth day of Charles's illness, he was pronounced out of danger, and had recovered his speech. He asked instantly for Henry, and was told that his brother, though summoned, had not come. It must be the state of the roads that had prevented his Royal Eminence from making the journey, Iain Beag soothed him, but Charles knew it was not that. There had been no real reconciliation between them during Henry's brief visit to Florence the previous year; Henry could not be expected to keep forsaking the duties of his cardinalate and bishopric to come to a brother for whom he had lost any real sympathy, and whose cruel vitality would not let him die.

He lay alone in his melancholy bedchamber in the Palazzo Guadagni, so desperately weak that he could not without extreme effort lift his hand. Iain Beag tended him, but Iain Beag was getting old too, and was bullied and harassed by his Italian wife. The servants, like all Italian servants, refused to take the smallest responsibility now that their master could not give them orders, and treated themselves to a holiday from work.

Hour after hour, day after day, he lay there; sometimes they even forgot to light his fire.

He was a prey to sick fancies.

"Iain, who is the little child I hear laughing and running up and down the stair? Last night I thought it was in the room with me, came to the bed and put its soft arms round my neck."

"Heart of my heart, there is no little child whatever," Iain Beag tenderly assured him. "Your Majesty was after dreaming."

But the child remained, if not in the house, then in his mind. And presently he knew who she was.

"Papa! Papa!" a loving voice pleaded. A mop of fair chestnut curls brushed his face, chubby arms hugged him. He shrank from the voice and from the embrace. He had no little child; if he still had a daughter she was a grown woman, long since taught to detest and despise him, a daughter he had deliberately cut from his heart nearly twenty-five years ago.

But the phantom would not leave him, and in his extreme weakness of mind and body he had no defence against her. Waking and sleeping he heard sturdy legs racing up the stair, saw a nose squashed flat against the window-pane, felt a soft rounded cheek against his own, while two grubby little hands offered him a mess of mud and twigs, a nest for a bird which otherwise must flit from bough to bough. A spectral bell tinkled urgently above his head, and he struggled to rise and rush to comfort a small somebody tormented by nightmares. No longer did the old dreams of Scotland visit him; instead, he was hurrying home to a succession of mean lodgings, looking for a face that would so eagerly be watching for him; he was buying a doll to be dressed in Highland costume; he was asking endless questions of strangers before running back to a silent house in which a rag moppet leaned limply against a bottle of cheap wine. . . .

There came a day when he was strong enough to send Iain Beag to fetch a notary. Feebly, and with many pauses, he dictated his wishes and a new will, appointing as his executors two brothers, Count Camillo and Canon Tommaso dell Gherardesca, who had always shown him kindness.

It was his pleasure to create Charlotte Stuart, now residing in the Convent of St Marie, Meaux, Duchess of Albany; and by a deed of legitimation to raise her from a natural daughter to the position of a legitimate child, his heir.

# PART FOUR

## 1784 – 1788

## CHARLOTTE

## ONE

### *I*

CHARLOTTE was sitting in the shade of the catalpa tree in the convent garden, reading aloud to Mère Gabriel, who was very old now and blind.

" 'We are always wanting this and that, and yet Jesus is all we can desire. Tell me: you know well that at the birth of Our Saviour, the shepherds heard the angelic hymns of those heavenly spirits; the Scripture says so, yet it is not said that Our Lady and St Joseph, who were the closest to the Child, heard the voice of the angels, or saw that heavenly light. . . .' "

Her eyes strayed from the book to watch a great bee go blundering among the half-opened flowers of the catalpa. It was all so peaceful and familiar. The little severe spire of the chapel rose into the summer sky, with a pigeon or two wheeling about it; a lay sister, a working apron over her black habit, was weeding a bed, watched by a large marmalade cat; and from the town the bell of the cathedral solemnly announced the hour of three. 'We are always wanting this and that.' No, she thought; at thirty, what could one want other than this peace, this gracious poverty, these tranquil, dear surroundings?

" '. . . On the contrary, instead of hearing the angels sing they heard the Child weep, and saw, by a little light borrowed from some wretched lamp, the eyes of this Divine Child all filled with tears and faint with the rigour of the cold. Well, I ask you, in good sooth, would you not have chosen to have been in the stable, dark and filled with the cries of the little Baby, than with the shepherds . . .' "

"Dear child," observed the old nun fretfully, as Charlotte broke off again, "our holy Founder, St Francis of Sales, does not seem able to engage your attention this afternoon. . . . Charlotte, are you not well? Is anything the matter?"

"No, *ma mère*, nothing is the matter," Charlotte replied, oddly breathless. "It is only that I heard my mother talking with a gentleman in the parlour, and I thought . . . I thought his voice seemed familiar . . . but I must have been mistaken."

She went on reading; but now indeed St Francis of Sales could not hold her attention; she was straining her ears to catch again the man's voice through the open window of the parlour. It was so like that of someone she had known long ago that an old dream, never lost, only pushed into the background of her cheerful and sensible mind, rose up to plague her.

She and her mother never spoke of Charles now. After that disastrous visit to Rome in the year after his marriage, Clementina had accepted the situation, and though she still indulged in conventional lamentations over her poverty, she had settled down very comfortably at Meaux, especially since old family friends in high places had got her created Grafin von Alberstrof, a Countess of the Holy Roman Empire. After all, that was better than being the mistress of a King whose claims no one took seriously any longer, perhaps even better than being his wife. He had behaved just as badly to this Princess Louise of Stolberg as he had to herself, it seemed, and this in some odd way greatly cheered Clementina.

As Countess von Alberstrof she was received everywhere

in Meaux, and her past as an exiled prince's mistress only lent her an aura of romance. She had really nothing left to wish for, she was wont to say, if only dear Charlotte would marry; but dear Charlotte was *so* headstrong, *so* self-willed, a real Stuart, taking after her unfortunate Papa in character as well as in looks. She had refused the hand of a most eligible and wealthy English gentleman, introduced to her by good Lord Elcho, simply because he was a Protestant.

"And what will become of you when your Mama, who has sacrificed everything to make you happy, is dead?" Clementina had demanded.

But that was long ago, and Clementina's emotional storms were very rare nowadays. Yet surely there was the old hysterical note in her mother's voice this afternoon, thought Charlotte; and she had just roused herself to go and see what was the matter, when Clementina appeared at the garden door and came hurrying down the path towards the seat under the catalpa, followed by a man. As soon as she was within earshot of her daughter, she began to gasp out disconnected phrases, wildly waving a letter.

"After all these years! ... Duchess of Albany! ... Royal Highness! ... legitimated you! ... go to Florence and live with your Papa! ..."

But Charlotte was not listening. She had risen clumsily, spilling the book on to the grass, shading her eyes against the strong sunlight of July, as she stared at the man, a very little man, with eyes as bright and sharp as a bird's in his old face.

Then she gave a strange cry, and to the scandal of the lay sister who had paused in her weeding, she ran up to this strange man and fairly hugged him.

"Iain! Iain Beag!"

## 2

In the twinkling of an eye Charlotte Stuart was transformed from a nonentity, a bastard hidden away in a convent, into a public figure.

Iain Beag's coming was followed almost immediately by the advent of a messenger in the royal livery of France, who brought her a letter written by Louis XVI's own hand. His Most Christian Majesty wrote in the kindest terms, addressing her as 'my dear cousin'. Her royal father had asked that her legitimation be registered in the Parlement of Paris and be recognised by the French Court. In order to obviate any difficulties on account of his unrecognised claims, her father was content to be styled in this deed, 'Charles Edward Stuart, grandson of James II, King of Great Britain'.

Charlotte caught her breath as she read this. She knew how pertinaciously he had fought all these years for the recognition of his royal rights.

The deed of legitimation, continued King Louis, had been duly registered and recognised. He sent her Royal Highness, the Duchess of Albany, a warm invitation to visit him and his Queen at Fontainebleau, where, he was careful to inform her, she would be accorded the *droit du tabouret*, the supreme privilege of being seated in the presence of the Queen of France. Lastly he begged her to accept the enclosed draft upon his Treasury for 1,000 livres, 'for the immediate expenses of your Royal Highness'.

Life became so full and so hectic that Charlotte felt giddy. There was a whole wardrobe of new clothes to be bought, she who had never had pretty things. Dressmakers and milliners jostled one another for her custom. Poor Sister Porteress was run off her feet answering the door-bell to a succession of visitors, the Bishop of Meaux, the civic dignitaries, the gentry of the neighbourhood with their wives and daughters, all avid for a sight of this new Cinderella. Clementina alternated between fits of weeping at the idea of being separated from her beloved daughter, and boasting to her friends of Charlotte's new honours. "Her Royal Highness, the Duchess of Albany, my daughter," said she, rolling out the titles on every possible occasion.

But Charlotte went through it all in a dream. Only one thing was real to her: the letter Iain Beag had brought her from her father, written in a very shaky hand, the letter breaking a silence of over twenty years, and beginning, '*Chère fille*'. She, like him, had waited all her life for a call, and for her, miraculously, it had sounded.

At Fontainebleau, jealous eyes watched her for gaucheries, and found none. It was not only that she had a natural grace and the instincts of her royal blood; she possessed character. She had escaped all her mother's sentimentality and lack of tact; she had inherited her father's forthrightness and decision; while her convent upbringing had given her patience, fortitude, and cheerfulness. She was new to all the intricate etiquette of the French Court, but there was not the slightest trace of self-consciousness or embarrassment when she made her curtsy to Queen Marie Antoinette before advancing to receive the embrace sacred to Royalty.

Late in September old Lord Nairn, with a Mrs O'Donnel, just created by Charles Countess of Norton, arrived at Meaux to fetch the new Duchess to Florence. They brought Charles's own post-chaise, in which she was to make the journey; and a letter from him which slightly clouded her joy. For though he signed himself her loving father, it was formal, even cold; and, exhausted by the ordeal of taking farewell of her mother, she was plagued throughout the journey by new fears.

What, after all, did she know of this father of hers? she asked herself. She had only childish memories, which no doubt she had romanticised. Why had he suddenly legitimated her, created her a duchess, made her his heir, and sent for her to live with him? Long ago, on an impulse, he had sent for her mother (so Clementina had often told her); and with what disastrous consequences to three lives!

She drove through all the glory of a Tuscan autumn, a succession of golden days and clear, bracing nights; but she saw none of it. Whatever the reason why her father had sent for her, might he not be disappointed, she wondered anxiously, by her lack of beauty, her convent-bred manners, her ignorance of royal etiquette?

As mile after mile brought her nearer to him, she began rehearsing a stilted little speech with which to greet him.

3

For two months past, life at the Palazzo Guadagni had been as hectic and disorganised as life at the Convent of St Marie had become.

Still very frail after his latest illness, Charles wore himself out transforming the melancholy old palace. He had sent to Rome for pictures, furniture, carpets, statuary, left him by his father and stored in the Muti, and to his Paris banker's for his share of his mother's jewels. New servants were engaged, and almost invariably left again; nerves and physical weakness made the old King impossible to please. They were all clumsy fools, he stormed at them; they had chipped this marble table in unpacking it; he had expressly stated that this laquered cabinet was to go in the south bed-chamber and they had gone and put it in the west one. He raged at the sight of moth-eaten hangings, and at the state of furniture stored and neglected for a decade. Iain Beag raged back in Gaelic, and Iain Beag's Italian wife had hysterics every day.

But Charles's peevishness was only on the surface. Under this façade he was as desperately nervous of meeting his daughter as, had he but known it, she was of meeting him.

He had sent for the little child whose phantom had haunted his sick-bed. But the Charlotte who was coming was not a little child; she would be thirty-one in October. And what were her feelings towards him? He had ignored her very existence throughout twenty years, had refused to reply to her many letters, even to have her name mentioned. Certainly she had no reason in the world to love him. It was because he had half regretted legitimating her, directly he had signed the deed, that he had delayed sending for her.

252

He had told himself that he delayed only because he must first be formally separated from Louise. But the Pope had ratified the deed of separation in April, and it was not until July that Charles had sent Iain Beag to Meaux.

He was daunted when he thought of the many explanations which would have to be made to this stranger who was his only child. How could he expect her to believe that all these years he had not thought of her only because he dared not? She was Clementina's daughter; such few letters from her as he had read (for the majority of them he had burnt unopened) had been all too reminiscent of Clementina's emotionalism and sentimentality. But suppose those letters had been dictated to her by her mother, and she had grown up to be hard and calculating like . . . like Louise? Suppose she had answered his summons only to see what she could get, and that, like Louise, she was hoping he would die soon and that she would not have to wait long for her inheritance?

Tormenting himself thus, he felt he could not bear any more from any woman.

Deliberately he shrank from asking Iain Beag for a description of the grown-up Charlotte, sharply bade him hold his tongue when the old Highlander tried to tell him of that meeting in the convent garden, of how Madame Charlotte had known him instantly after all this time, actually had hugged him in the presence of her mother and two scandalised nuns, how very like her father she was, how intensely affectionate and charming.

He was not going to inflict upon himself the exquisite torture of imagining that he, who all his life had been dogged by disappointment and humiliation, could ever know happiness in this world.

But the die was cast. Charlotte, the formidable stranger, was on her way. He who had conversed with popes and kings and poor crofters with the same natural ease, now feverishly rehearsed and discarded a dozen different stilted versions of the speech with which he must welcome his own daughter.

The wise and mellow sunlight of October touched the cypresses and the mossy statues in the garden, as he went feebly up and down the paths, listening for the sounds of her arrival.

He was exhausted by last-minute preparations, tetchy with nervous strain, longing to be in his bed. He had tried so hard to show her without words how much he wanted to make amends for all his past neglect. Accustomed to slop about in an old nightgown, he had bought everything new in her honour, and the hours of dressing this morning had seemed interminable. This frock-coat was too tight, he raged; the essence of style was a good fit, his tailor assured him. The stock, which was stiffened nowadays and of an exaggerated height, choked him, and he was sure he looked ridiculous in the striped waistcoat and breeches which were the present mode. They had wanted him to have the back hair of his wig twisted into a pigtail with the ends frizzed out like a sweep's brush, but he had jibbed at that. He'd wear a bob-wig tied back with a ribbon, as he always had done, and his daughter could think him old-fashioned if she chose.

So here he walked now in his finery, leaning heavily on his tall cane, as nervous as a young bridegroom, feverishly rehearsing. Should he kiss her, or would she resent it? Should he risk her repulsing an endearment? Would he surprise, as soon as she saw him, a look of repulsion, of horror at the change the years had wrought in someone she remembered (if she remembered him at all) as young and strong and handsome? . . . "My dear daughter, it is with very great pleasure that I welcome you to Florence. . . ." No, no! that was too stiff. "Charlotte, my dear child, God bless you for your charity in coming to an old father who has neglected you. . . ." No, that would put them on a wrong footing from the start.

He was filled with a new and ridiculous panic. Suppose she had brought her mother with her? Suppose Clementina had insisted? Charlotte must be completely under her mother's influence. There would be a scene. Clementina would stage one of her famous scenes. He thought of the pricked ears of Sir Horace Mann, of the tittering in fashionable drawing-rooms throughout Europe. No longer a menace, he was still good for a laugh. "What do you think, madame, is the latest about that drunken old madman, the Pretender? Scarcely has his wife left him than he sends for his bastard, and lo and behold his aged concubine comes too!" . . .

He turned in his pacing; and there was a servant hurrying out to inform him that the carriage of her Royal Highness, the Duchess of Albany, had turned the corner of the street.

He was not in the hall to greet her.

His Majesty awaited her Royal Highness, Iain Beag, very much the formal major-domo, told her, in his withdrawing-room. Conscious of the covert glances of strange servants who were consumed with curiosity to see what this new mistress of theirs was like, she followed Iain. She looked very tall and handsome in her great-coat dress with its capes and her little hat tilted over her chestnut curls; she was smiling, seemed quite at her ease. But her heart beat sickeningly and inside her gloves her hands were damp with sweat.

Stewart opened the door of the tartan room, and bowed her in. She found herself face to face across the length of the apartment with the father she had seen but once in twenty-four years, driving in his carriage with his Queen beside him, oblivious of the daughter who watched him from among the Roman crowds.

She sank into a deep curtsy; he bent into a formal bow.

They both began simultaneously:

"Most Gracious Majesty, I am come in obedience to——"

"My dear daughter, I have long looked forward——"

Each faltered into silence. Their glances met and held together, though she could not see him for her tears. Then out of her childhood love for him she whispered impulsively, forgetting all her speeches:

"It is Pouponne who has come to you—Papa. Just your—Pouponne."

He uttered a strange, wild cry.

"Pouponne!" And louder: "Pouponne!"

His cane clattered to the floor as he flung out his arms to catch her to his heart.


# TWO

## I

WHEN Henry received a letter from Charlotte, written the day after her arrival in Florence, he was already seething with anger.

He had always been intolerant of the Walkinshaw affair, and now this offspring of sin had been legitimated and created a duchess. He had only just simmered down from the scandal caused by Louise, and here was the fresh scandal of his brother's taking his natural daughter to live with him. In his wrath he felt almost kindly towards Louise, who still wrote him fulsome letters by every post; perhaps, he thought, he had misjudged his sister-in-law.

It was no use his brother impressing upon him that his recent action did not interfere with his, Henry's, legitimate rights. Trust this young baggage to wheedle her old father into making over to her his hereditary claims to the throne of Great Britain! And then there was her title. It was true that the Albany title had never been officially bestowed on Henry by his father, but it was the hereditary Scottish title of the Duke of York, and there was no excuse whatever for Charles's giving it to his bastard. It was a deliberate insult, nothing less.

But if Henry had been indignant before, his fury when he read Charlotte's letter knew no bounds. That it was exceedingly courteous and respectful did not mollify him. She began, 'My lord, your Royal Eminence', but she went on to call him 'my very dear Uncle'. Uncle, indeed! And what was this?

'Since the moment when I had the misfortune to lose my grandfather, King James . . .'

The veins standing out upon his forehead, he skimmed through the rest of the letter.

'The kindnesses which you have showered upon me up to the present are a sure guarantee that you will partake in the joy and happiness with which I am penetrated today. . . . I am enjoying the honour of belonging very nearly to your Royal Eminence' (he fairly gibbered with indignation) 'and at the same time brought to give all the care necessary for the preservation of a darling father, whose health and strength I shall if possible renew. I would share with him my own, and compensate him for all the troubles fortune has inflicted on him. . . .'

"This woman is a hypocrite," Henry informed a portrait of Pope Pius VI who, with a slightly pained expression, blessed him from the chimney-piece.

'. . . I dare to hope that, since you know the position of the King, my father, the wreck of whose fortune leaves him reduced to a poor competence, you will not refuse to continue the pension you have so kindly allowed my mother since the death of my royal grandfather. . . .'

"Aha! I thought we should come sooner or later to the beggar's whine," muttered Henry, almost winking at Pope Pius. "Like mother, like daughter."

'. . . I desire you, my lord, to understand the sentiments of attachment and respect with which I shall be ever, of your Royal Eminence, my lord, the very humble, very obedient servant and niece, Charlotte Stuart, Duchess of Albany.'

*Niece!* No, that was too much!

He summoned his secretary. He wished to dictate an official Protest. It must be published immediately and sent to all the foreign Courts.

'The Cardinal Duke of York cannot do less than complain strongly of the proceedings of his Royal Brother concerning the irregular and improper action taken in summoning a natural daughter to live with him with so much publicity. . . .'

## 2

"You are not eating, Papa."

"Neither are you, Pouponne."

They laid down their forks and sat looking at each other. Then with a kind of simple awe, he murmured, putting his hand on hers:

"I can't believe it. I still can't believe it's true you're here."

"It is time for your siesta, Papa," she said softly.

He brushed this aside. He could not see enough of her, grudged every moment away from her company. She was like a miracle.

"We must give a ball, Pouponne. Florence shall see what a lovely and gracious daughter I have. God damn the Grand Duke," he cried, with the feeble anger of age, "for refusing to have you presented at Court. But never mind. All Florence has flocked to leave cards, and I insist you claim the royal privilege of not returning their visits. Now let us draw up a list of those we will invite to the ball."

When at last she had persuaded him to take his siesta, she sat thinking. For her too it was like a miracle, this reunion, but there was so much to do, and perhaps so little time. Though by every stratagem she could invent she concealed the fact from her father, she knew that she was ill, had been ill for years. The doctors at Meaux had told her that a fall from her horse when she was a child had caused some slight internal obstruction, and had made light of it. It had not mattered then; now it was vital that she should know the truth.

A physician was announced. She had asked him to call during the hour when her father took his siesta. He examined her in silence.

"I beg you, sir, to tell me honestly the cause of this pain." The doctor cleared his throat.

"Very well, Madame. You have inherited, if I may say so, many royal qualities, including the famous courage of your father. Alas that you should have inherited also the fatal disease of which your paternal grandmother died."

For a moment she did not understand. Then, remembering, she said thoughtfully:

"Queen Mary Beatrice died of cancer of the liver." Before the physician could speak, she asked with desperate anxiety: "Will I live long enough to tend my father to the end?"

Five years was the doctor's prognosis. As for her father . . . the physician shook his head gravely. Already his Majesty had suffered two most dangerous seizures; it was unlikely that he would survive another.

So much to do, she thought, when the doctor had gone, and so little time. It was only ten days since she had come to Florence, but already she had discovered what her main task must be; to reconcile two angry old men. Under all her father's criticisms of her uncle, she had caught a note of yearning which told her clearly of an ancient love between the brothers, a love she must make every effort to bring to the surface again.

There were more mundane tasks as well. Charlotte had learned life in a hard school, and she was not to be imposed on. Her father had made her his unofficial secretary, and one of the first things she had found among his correspondence was a series of dunning letters from Lord Elcho, still pestering for his famous fifteen hundred pounds. She had always detested Elcho, and it gave her considerable pleasure to reply to him. She begged to remind his lordship that in the correspondence he still kept up with her mother he had

259

mentioned that he was living in Rome in splendid style, whereas in his letters to her father he described himself as destitute. She added with hard common sense that as he had admitted that he had no paper to show that he ever had given or lent her father this money, he must please refrain from dunning her royal father for it.

Then there was the household of the Palazzo Guadagni. Under the careless Louise it had done what it pleased, which had included robbing its old master. Charlotte had made up her mind to learn Italian so that she could deal with these Tuscan servants, who were so difficult to manage, so jealous that if one were praised others took offence to the extent of drawing knives, and who, after a tremendous spurt of work for some entertainment, thought it unreasonable to be asked to do a hand's turn for the next three weeks. Their favourite excuse was that today was *festa*; on not one of the innumerable feasts of the Church would they work. Giuseppe, the gardener, was horrified when she told him that the garden must be made to produce plenty of flowers for the house. Flowers in the house were unhealthy, he told her.

But she would get her way in this, because it was all part of her labour of love, of her one supreme object to make the evening of her father's life easy, gracious, and smooth.

When she went to see if Charles had finished his siesta today, she found him sitting up in bed, trembling and muttering with rage.

"I would not have believed it possible!" he burst out, slapping one hand hard against a printed paper which lay on the coverlet. "That he should answer your charming letter with such a blow in the face! That he should dare to question my right to grant you what titles I please——"

"Papa, you will make yourself ill. Please try to be calm. Is this a letter from my royal uncle?"

"Not even a letter; a printed Protest. How Harry has always loved to see himself in print, the pompous fool! I will have no more to do with him after this—no, don't read it, Pouponne; it is too cruel."

But Charlotte did not easily take offence, and she was more interested than hurt when at last she had prevailed on her father to let her read Henry's Protest. A strangely childish man, this Cardinal Duke must be, she thought, if he could work himself into such a state of indignation simply because his sick old brother, all alone in the world, had had his only child legitimated and had sent for her to comfort his few last years. She read carefully, intent on discovering exactly what it was that was enraging Henry.

There were first some very petty sarcasms about 'an indecent uproar that was made some time ago about supposed poverty and destitution', whereas Charles had now 'taken upon himself an expense which will naturally exceed the maintenance of his own Consort'. Henry complained that he had not been informed, nor had his consent been asked; and then got down to what were obviously his real grievances.

'In the third place, he represents the irregularity of this pretended legitimation, which was not necessary to give this person a fair subsistence, which he had already been bound in conscience to do for thirty years past. As he did not do it, the Cardinal Duke, touched by pure compassion, supplied the money privately. . . .'

Yes, thought Charlotte, there was something in that. When she had straightened out her father's financial affairs, she must see whether she could not persuade him to make her mother an allowance, and so remove at least that grievance. Already she had discovered that Charles was not nearly so poor as he imagined he was.

'But it was not necessary to give her those pretended titles, and to place her in a position for which there can be no explanation to the mind of any intelligent person, except the intention of putting a public slight upon the Cardinal Duke and his sister-in-law. . . .'

"Papa," mused Charlotte, "if I could see my royal uncle,

I am sure I could persuade him that there was not the least intention of slighting anyone."

"You will not see him!" cried Charles, sitting bolt upright. "I will never allow you to set eyes on a man so unnatural, so cruel, and one who is no longer any brother of mine."

Charlotte bowed her head as though accepting the prohibition, but she had every intention of writing Henry secretly, hoping to progress step by step to the point when the touchy Cardinal himself should seek a personal meeting with her.

" 'And here,' " she continued, reading the last paragraph of the Protest aloud, " 'is reached the 4th point raised by the Cardinal Duke; that the said legitimation goes very much farther than has been the invariable custom in similar cases, since it reached the very height of presumption to pretend to have this person recognised as of the stem of the Royal House, by granting her titles which would be most justly contended if his Royal Brother were in actual possession of his lawful right. Nor in that case would his Royal Brother, according to the law of the kingdom, have the faculty thus to habilitate a natural child, and place her in succession to the throne; a case utterly without precedent.' "

"Faugh!" exclaimed Charles. "In this Henry merely displays his ignorance. Robert II settled the Crown of Scotland on his eldest illegitimate son, afterwards Robert III, to the exclusion of his son born in wedlock. Moreover, what I have done has been extremely moderate; I've made it clear to Harry that there is no question of interfering with his succession to my claims to the throne, whereas I could have created you Princess of Wales, as Henry VIII created first Mary and then Elizabeth. And now I've a damned good mind to do it!"

He was so angry that she saw it would be tactless to argue the point at present, but she was determined to prevent his doing anything so foolish. He demanded pen and paper, and when they were brought he wrote in his shaky hand, icily brief:

'I have the pleasure of telling you myself that my dearest daughter, being recognised by me, by France, and by the Pope, who has just written to congratulate her on her arrival in Florence, is not "this person" but a Royal Highness to you and everyone. I do not dispute your rights; they are fixed, since you are my brother; but I beg you not to dispute those of my dearest daughter.'

"So much for his Royal Eminence!" snorted Charles, signing his name with a flourish.

## 3

It was St Andrew's Day once more.

Charles had invited a large company to dinner, and there would be dancing afterwards. Determined to make up for the past, he was wearing himself out devising entertainments for Pouponne; he was so immensely proud of her, so eager to lavish upon her all the things she had lacked in her youth. Also he was busy match-making on her behalf.

"There's not a prince in Europe worthy of you, my darling, but I must see you well settled before I die. My good friend, the King of Sweden, has a brother about your age, or there is one of the royal dukes of Ostrogothia whom I might honour with your hand."

She thanked him, pretended interest. When pain twisted itself into a knot inside her, so that she could not eat, she assured her father it was only because she was not used to rich Italian food. Drawn and pale after a night of sleepless agony, she spent hours painting her face so skilfully that he would notice nothing. Secretly she obtained opiates from the physician; pain was an enemy to hold at bay lest it betray her mortal sickness to the father who, for the first time since he was young, was tasting happiness and peace.

This St Andrew's Day, which might be the last both for him and for her, had no cloud to mar it. The old King's chair of estate was set up in his withdrawing-room; he wore his faded, ill-fitting Highland dress; and he invested Charlotte with the Order of the Thistle. She had been most careful to learn her part. She knelt before his chair, and after he had touched her shoulder with his sword, she rose, thanked him, and went round the company formally repeating:

"*Je suis Chevalier.*"

The guests, receiving each a favour made up by Charlotte herself in the form of a thistle, were astonished to hear the King announce his intention of dancing with his daughter. As they paced and bowed and twirled in time with the music, Charlotte remembered vividly the tales he had told her in her childhood, of how Prince Teàrlach had danced at Holyroodhouse during those halcyon days after Prestonpans had been won and Edinburgh captured. But now the strong legs were grown feeble and ulcerated; after one dance he was glad to go back to his chair, his eyes following Pouponne round the room, until presently he drowsed.

They had been invited out to supper by the Duchesse d'Alvi, who had taken a great liking to Charlotte; but as she went to change her dress she was sent for by her father, who told her he was too fatigued to make the effort.

"But you must go, Pouponne."

And when she protested, secretly longing for an excuse to go to bed, he said with the tetchiness of old age:

"Off you go and enjoy yourself, girl." As she reached the door, he recalled her; and the petulance had vanished. "But give me another kiss before you go, my Pouponne. I had forgotten, you know, what it was like to be happy," he added very simply, fondling her hands.

When she returned in the small hours of the morning, she found Iain Beag anxiously awaiting her.

"Himself has the sickness on him," muttered Iain Beag.

She flew to her father's bedchamber. He sat where she had left him, slumped in his chair before the fire, still fully

264

dressed in kilt and velvet coat. He was breathing stertor-ously, muttering to himself, and he took no notice of Char-lotte's entrance.

"Papa! I knew I ought not to have left you——"

"Left me . . . ay, that's what they all do. They all leave me. . . . You only came to see what you could get, and it wasn't enough. . . . Well, go! D'you hear me? Go!"

For a moment she flinched away from this terrible stranger. But then she caught the smell of brandy on his breath, and understood. She knelt beside him.

"Papa, I must venture to disobey you. I am not going to leave you. If you send me away, it must be by force, and then I shall come back."

He muttered unintelligibly.

"Papa, it is Pouponne, just your Pouponne, who loves you."

"Pouponne," he mumbled. "Poisoned my own child's mind against me. Taught her I was cruel and dangerous. Perhaps I was. . . . Never think of her; cut her out of your heart. . . ."

Compassion made havoc of her own heart as she watched and listened. He was like a long ill-treated animal that has lost the habit of trust and is suspicious of kindness. He shrank from her touch, and instantly she withdrew it, but not before her tears had fallen on his hand. He looked at the wetness wonderingly, and with a curiously blind gesture fumbled to find the source of it in her eyes.

"You weep. Why do you weep? Why do you weep for an old reprobate who neglected you for twenty years?"

Then suddenly his mood changed. Terror sprang into his eyes; he seized her by the wrists, digging his fingers into her flesh so that she had all she could do not to cry aloud with pain.

"Pouponne! I thought you had left me. I dream so often that you have left me. But this was no dream. I woke and you were not here. So I went back to my old enemy, the bottle."

She laid her arm lightly round his shoulders; and as he did not repulse her, she said, carefully picking her words:

"Papa, do you remember when I was a little child and had nightmares? About chimney-stacks and devils with ducks' feet? Mama would not let me have a light, nor would she come to me when I screamed because she thought I was being naughty. But you came. You contrived a little bell connected with a string to my bed; and when I pulled the string you were with me almost before the bell had started ringing, and then you told me the most wonderful stories about a place I thought was Fairyland, but it was really Scotland——"

She broke off in dismay, for the terror in his eyes had changed to blind agony.

"Not Scotland—no! Never mention Scotland to me—never!"

"No, Papa, never. I am so very sorry. I did not understand. . . . The day has been too much for you. Will you not let me help you to bed and fetch a posset to make you sleep?"

"I dream," he muttered, not heeding her, staring into the fire. "But the worst dream of all is not of Culloden now, not even of Derby. It is a dream that used to comfort me, for it is of my home."

He bent forward, looking deeper into the red heart of the fire, and with a strangely fey air continued:

"Look how the hand of evening shadows this ben, while this other, which occupies the east like a throne, is all rosy with the sunset, each granite pleat, each gully upon its smocked breast, distinct, without mist. See there where the sun, sinking between a cleft in the hills, strikes a fiery sword across the slate-blue waters of the loch, and here, from every vent-hole in the little clachan, the smoke of peat-fires goes up straight and blue. Can't you smell the bog-myrtle? Can't you hear how the wind of evening rings the million tiny bells of the heather? Listen! there comes the skirl of the pipes. But it is no pibroch they are playing. *Cha till mi*

266

*tuilleadh* is their awful message—'I shall return no more'."

She dared neither move nor speak.

"I stayed on deck that day I left my home, until I could see no longer one shadow of its hills. They merged into a jumble of sad grey shapes; like great bright butterflies the brown fronds of the bracken lay among the green, and the heather made a purple stain on the warm olive of the marsh-grass. But my hills had drained themselves of all colour, standing lifeless under the low grey ceiling of the sky. In their still aloofness there was resignation; they sent their mists after me like airy messengers, bearing benediction."

He was shivering, and very gently she drew the plaid closer round his bent old shoulders.

"I felt my heart leap within me, straining back to them, fighting to escape, though I was escaping from those who hunted me. It seemed to me then that I gave my heart its freedom, content to be mutilated, so one part of me might find shelter for ever within those mighty arms. And the pipes played the lament I have played every night when I sat alone—*Lochaber no more*. Nor I, nor those who fought for me and with me, ever shall return."

"You will at last, my darling father."

Slowly he took his gaze from the fire and looked at her, for a moment without any recognition. Then a small sad smile, which yet had in it something of a child's simple trust, trembled on his mouth. He was indeed the child and she the mother; and as she had depended upon him in nightmare long ago, so now he must depend on her.

When at last he slept that night, she roused Iain Beag. Together they made up a bed for her in her father's dressing-room; she would sleep here in future, she said. She set the communicating door ajar, and by his bed she placed a little silver hand-bell. And now she blessed the pain that made her wakeful; it was her ally in her father's need of her.

# THREE

## I

CHARLOTTE was singing to herself in her small tuneful voice, as she came in from the garden with an armful of purple salvia. The flowers marked her victory in her long battle with Giuseppe, the gardener; and during the months since she had come to Florence she had achieved other triumphs much more important.

She wrote her mother by every post, and one day had suggested to Charles that he should send some kind message. On that occasion he had refused; but not long afterwards had said abruptly:

"You look so like your mother today, Pouponne, as she was when I met her in Ghent. I remember——" He broke off, and sighed. Then: "When next you write to your mother, pray tell her I hope she is well."

After that there was a message from Charles each time she wrote to Clementina; nor was this all. Of his own accord he added a codicil to his will, leaving Clementina an annuity of three thousand scudi. So that old quarrel was healed.

Then there was the Sunday when Charlotte, coming to kiss her father good-bye before going to Mass, found him in one of his difficult moods. He wanted her to play duets with him; it was most unkind of her to leave him.

"I am sorry, but I must go to Mass, Papa," she had replied firmly. And then, on an impulse: "But why don't you come too?"

Charles had shuffled and hedged and raised a dozen objections. She knew very well he didn't believe in 'all that mumbo-jumbo', and had not done so for years. He was not feeling well; the church would be hot; and so on.

"Very well, Papa; but now I must go or I shall be late."

She was just getting into the carriage, when her father appeared on the arm of Iain Beag. Since she was so selfish that she would not stay with him, he would be obliged to come with her, for he would not be left alone, he said very grumpily. But to Charlotte it was the answer to a very special prayer. She guessed that his apostasy in youth had never ceased to torment him, and that in his heart of hearts he yearned to come back to his faith before he died.

Her singing ceased abruptly when, coming into his room this morning, she saw lying on the table a letter addressed to herself and bearing a familiar seal.

"My brother has written to you, it seems," grunted Charles. "If it's another of his insults, I shall . . ." His voice died away in unintelligible mutterings.

Henry wrote in the third person, stiffly, in reply to a letter she had sent, unbeknown to her father, congratulating the Cardinal on his approaching birthday. Dropping the offending title, she had signed herself merely 'Charlotte Stuart'. But the Cardinal Duke was not so easily appeased; he objected to her use of the Stuart name. Yet at least he had written, and that was a step forward in the accomplishment of her main task. She made a mental note to drop the 'Stuart' also in future letters, until she had been able to convince Henry that his recognition of her as his niece meant everything to her father, and that titles meant nothing to herself.

"Papa, my royal uncle writes me concerning Madame." (Thus she always referred to Louise.) "Madame has been sending him assurances of her attachment to him, but he has just discovered that she has deceived him yet again, and is living openly with Count Alfieri. So his Royal Eminence is anxious to combine with you in pressing the French Court to stop her pension if she persists in her misconduct."

Charles moved his shoulders irritably. He had no longer the faintest interest in Louise; he was not vindictive; and he was not going to combine with Henry in anything unless his brother recognised Pouponne. She came and knelt beside his chair.

"Papa, you have given me so much already that you will think me greedy if I ask for more. But I want so much to be allowed to write regularly to my royal uncle. If you will give me this permission I know I can break down these foolish barriers. Please, Papa! "

He looked at her, and smiled. So often lately she reminded him of the Clementina with whom he had fallen in love. It was strange that at last, after so many years, he could think of Clementina with kindness.

"You could charm the bird off the tree," he muttered. "You know very well I can't deny you anything."

She drew up a Memorial to be submitted to de Vergennes, the French Minister, setting forth how 'Madame' had left her husband nearly five years previously for no other reason but to indulge 'an unbridled passion for Monsieur Alfieri'; how Louise had fled to Rome for that purpose, had followed her lover to Colmar, and now was living openly with him in Alsace. She had not brought a penny of dowry to her husband, who had settled on her 3,000 livres for pin-money; in spite of this she had persuaded the French Court that she was in want of the necessities of life, and still enjoyed from his Most Christian Majesty a very handsome pension.

Charlotte sent a copy of this Memorial to Henry, who, highly approving, added his signature to it.

'I am greatly obliged to your daughter for interesting herself so much on my behalf,' he wrote to Charles. 'It proves the kindness of her heart, to which everyone bears witness.'

" 'Your daughter'! Why can't he say 'my niece'?" fumed Charles.

But 'your daughter' was better than 'this person', and Charlotte was encouraged. When she was set upon achieving a goal she was as fixed in purpose as her father had been throughout his sad life. It appeared that the way to win over Henry was to sympathise with his grudge against his sister-in-law, nor had Charlotte the least scruple in doing so. She had her own reasons for disliking Louise. Though her father never spoke to her of his wife, Florence still buzzed with the tales of Louise's goings-on, and worse still in Charlotte's eyes was what she heard from Iain Beag of 'Madame's' vicious tongue and cruel behaviour to her husband before she left him. So Charlotte collected news of Louise's sordid intrigues, and passed it on to Henry.

'Madame' had gone to Versailles to pour her woes into the ears of Queen Marie Antoinette, but had met with a cold reception, for Paris was as full of gossip about her as Florence and Rome had been. She was carrying on an intrigue with Alfieri's own valet, Elia, who had been blackmailing the pair of them, and not getting enough had told all. There was also another lover, a German, Count Proly. Charlotte could not refrain from a maliciously witty comment when writing to her uncle that Alfieri had been thrown by a favourite horse.

'It was thought he was killed, which would have been a great loss for his horses.'

Henry's replies were increasingly friendly. He so far unbent that in his letters to Charles, 'your daughter' became 'my cousin', but still he would not say 'my niece'. Charlotte tried again. Would he not, she asked with gentle pathos, crown her father's joy in her company by acknowledging their real relationship? But this offended the touchy Cardinal. He replied with his former stiffness that he found this correspondence greatly fatiguing, especially as he had to write in French, which he had almost forgotten.

He had underrated Charlotte's pertinacity. In that case, she answered promptly, she would learn to write in Italian, and she would correspond with his Royal Eminence through his secretary, Canon Cesarini, thus saving her uncle all fatigue.

## 2

Charlotte had been in Florence for seven months, when, in May, her father announced that he had a surprise for her. They were going to visit Pisa for the *festa*.

"But not in this great heat, Papa! You know how it will affect your legs."

"I am never affected by any weather," Charles said testily. He still intensely disliked any reference to his health. "I have arranged it all, and I thought you would be delighted," he added, in bitter disappointment.

Hastily assuring him that she was, Charlotte pretended to share his enthusiasm for the visit. The King and Queen of Naples were going to be there, he told her. Ferdinand of Naples was the son of his old friend, Don Carlos, now King of Spain, with whom he had ridden to the siege of Gaeta when he was a boy.

"I was fourteen, Pouponne, and it was my first campaign. Don Carlos, who was in command of the Spanish troops, welcomed me as Prince of Wales, appointed me a General of Artillery, and paid me a thousand crowns a month. They thought that was all I wanted—to play at being a soldier."

Almost he looked a boy again, a mischievous boy.

"My poor cousin, the Duke of Liria, in whose charge I was, told me afterwards that I gave him more uneasy moments than ever he had met with in his life. He was under orders from my father to show me everything that merited my attention, and the first thing that did that, in *my* opinion, was a house where the Duke had been quartered but which had just come under the enemy's fire. I insisted on going into it; I wanted to find out, Pouponne, exactly what it felt like to hear the bullets hiss about my ears, and the great cannon roar when I was in range of them. One of them pierced a wall while I was in the house."

He added, half to himself:

"Some thought it was bravado. It was not. It was all part of my self-training for the day when I would go in quest of my father's lost throne. . . . Strange what trivial things come back to one. When I was coasting along from Gaeta to the Bay of Naples, my hat was blown off into the sea, and I remember as though it were yesterday how I would not let them lower a boat to retrieve it, but cried absurdly to my hat, 'Swim on to England, and I will follow you!' "

Pouponne must have everything new for the visit to Pisa, he said, coming back to the present, and he and she would attend all the festivities, the horse- and chariot-races, the illuminations, the famous Battle of the Bridge. Ever since she had joined him, he had been determined that she should be accepted as their equal by the younger Royalties of Europe, and there would be a whole galaxy of them at Pisa. Above all, the Grand Duke and Duchess of Tuscany would be there, and away from their Florentine palace, where everything was regulated according to the rigorous etiquette of Vienna, they might be persuaded to have Pouponne presented to them.

When, through the good offices of Marie Caroline, Queen of Naples, and sister both of Leopold of Tuscany and Queen Marie Antoinette, an invitation was sent to Charlotte from the Grand Duke and Duchess very soon after she arrived in Pisa, Charles was as happy as though he had won a battle.

"Did they address you as 'Royal Highness', Pouponne? Did they invite you to drink coffee with them? It is not enough to ask you to dinner; only Royalty is accorded the privilege of coffee in their withdrawing-room."

She was able to reassure him on these points. But while she would not have been a very natural young woman had she failed to be flattered by her popularity among Royalties of her own age, Charlotte counted the days till the end of the *festa*. Pisa was notorious for its bad air, and the heat was frightful; her father was impatient of an invalid's diet, would not go to bed until the small hours of the morning, and horrified his daughter by his airy assumption that they would be going on to the *feste* at Lucca and Leghorn.

She was at her wits' end to dissuade him, when Charles's legs became so much worse that suddenly of his own accord he gave up the idea of any further festivities, and said

273

meekly that they would return to Florence whenever she chose.

"My days are numbered, Pouponne," he muttered, gritting his teeth with pain as they jolted along the fertile plain beside the Arno. "Death has been a friend I have courted in vain these last years, and now he will come when you are not provided for."

She tried to soothe him, but he interrupted her with desperate plans for raising the wind. He was a pensioner of Louis of France and of the uncertain Henry; and there would soon be revolution in France, he prophesied. The Monarchy had never recovered from the bad days of the Regency and of Louis XV; besides, what faith was to be placed in the word of France? he added bitterly, remembering her broken promises to himself in his youth.

There remained the jointure of his grandmother, Queen Mary Beatrice, of which not one farthing had ever been paid, though successive British Governments, from that of William of Orange onwards, had solemnly acknowledged it and promised to honour the debt. The Act of Parliament settling this jointure on the wife of James II remained unrepealed, and even without the interest accumulating through the eighty-four years which had elapsed since her widowhood, it amounted to fifty thousand pounds.

"I've written to old Lord Caryll to appeal to King Louis, for France has the right to demand payment of arrears guaranteed by treaties. Since you have this strange objection to marrying, I must provide for you somehow or other, Pouponne."

"I am sure my uncle——" began Charlotte, but he interrupted crossly:

"Who won't acknowledge you as his niece. Is *he* going to be a second father to you when I am gone? Why can't he come and visit us in Florence? He's got nothing to do," said Charles, airily dismissing all the duties of a cardinal and a bishop. "Did he but see you, all his silly prejudices would be swept away."

"You would like my royal uncle to come and see us, Papa?" Charlotte asked eagerly.

"To see *you*. But not unless he acknowledges you as his royal niece."

Victory is in sight, thought Charlotte. She gathered her resources for the final stage in her campaign of reconciling two difficult old brothers. To her it was as vital as ever the winning back of his lost rights had been to Charles.

## 3

The heat in Florence was terrible that summer. But it was less the weather than her tussles with Henry that made Charlotte so pale and drawn. Though professing himself extremely anxious to meet her, for some extraordinary reason the Cardinal positively refused to enter the Duchy of Tuscany. But Charlotte made use of his perversity; it would be far better, she thought, if she could meet him first without her father; and she replied that she would come to meet him at any place he chose to name, only he must not mention this place in his letters, for her father insisted on seeing them, and was far too weak to travel. She would have difficulty enough in persuading him to allow her to be absent even for a day, and he was quite capable of following her.

He was extremely busy, answered Henry; and then, perhaps feeling that this excuse had become somewhat monotonous, added that he was suffering from nervous asthma. He had inherited it from his mother, he supposed, and it was attacking him thus late in life. Charlotte, ill herself, was inexorable; she sent him a prescription for inhalations, and pressed for a decision on the time and place where they would meet.

In October Henry gave in. He sent the Abbé Barbieri to Florence to inform Charlotte by word of mouth that his Royal Eminence would meet his 'cousin' at Perugia on the 25th.

A battle had now to be fought with her father. At first

he took it for granted that he was included in the invitation, and grumbled fiercely about how little his brother considered anyone's convenience except his own. When, gently but firmly, Charlotte insisted that he was far too weak to travel, he was appalled.

"I can't be left alone. If you leave me, you will never come back to me. You promised me you would never leave me, Pouponne."

"It will be only for forty-eight hours, Papa. You have been so anxious that my royal uncle and I should meet, and at last I have persuaded him to it. When I return I shall be able to tell you how he has acknowledged me as his niece," she added, smiling and lifting her chin. She did not look at all like her mother at that moment, but exactly like Charles in his youth.

Her father was possessed by a thousand fears. His new found trust in this one human being was threatened, and he could not rid himself of a superstitious dread that if she left him, she, like the rest, would never return. Somehow she talked him round, but even as he dictated a letter to Henry, agreeing to the proposed meeting at Perugia, his mind wavered. The sacrifice asked of him, he told his brother, was very great; he was so sick that his dearest daughter was absolutely necessary to him. The hours when she was absent would seem like years. But he would let her go, if only that Henry might see how great a sacrifice he was prepared to make in order to be reconciled to his brother.

The Porta Augusta, one of the finest gates in the world, received Charlotte into Perugia, beetling in black magnificence above a whole quarter of the town, its stones still scorched with the fire that had followed in the footsteps of Lucius Antonius as his followers fell back along the steep streets before the soldiers of the young Octavius. Plain letters, as tall as a man, cut round the arch, announced with superb simplicity, 'AUGUSTA PERUGIA'.

Old Lord Nairn, who was escorting her, pointed out historic spots and the view of Assisi between the tall old houses. She answered mechanically, looking so pale that he feared she must be ill. She was in fact sick with apprehension. Everything she had heard about this unknown uncle of hers made her dread that she would fail with him.

He had commandeered the best hotel in Perugia, the Brufani, for his visit; it stood in the Street of Good Changes, and she wondered if this could be a happy omen. His Royal Eminence had not yet arrived but was expected in time for supper, flustered servants informed her. Leaving her French maid, Casimir, to unpack, she took a walk to calm herself, wandering about the town which crouched like a dragon on its rock. The bells of the cathedral rang discordantly, seeming to clang out a tocsin in their wild hammering minor. A storm blew up suddenly; huge sheets of mist swept along the valley from Umbria to Tuscany, and the chain upon chain of mountains echoed the thunder, while the wind shrieked through the passes to Ancona and the sea. The lightning flashed in Tiber, far below her, flowing down to Rome.

She took refuge in the round Roman church of Sant' Angelo, asking St Michael, who presided in a tunic of cloth of silver, to defend her in the day of battle, the private battle that awaited her with an obstinate, haughty, and intolerant old man.

The storm passed as quickly as it had descended, and she returned to the Brufani to find that his Royal Eminence's advance-guard was arriving. He might have been coming for a month by the number of baggage-mules and wagons he brought with him. Watching from a window, Charlotte remembered with dry amusement that hideously uncomfortable journey she and her mother had endured from Paris to Rome long ago, the open cabriolet of the diligence, the verminous inns, the barricading of doors against thieving landlords.

His Royal Eminence arrived in a coach and six, with outriders and a train of chaplains and liveried servants with

277

the cardinal's hat and the ducal coronet embroidered on
their coats. She heard for the first time his voice, accustomed
to command, yet with an edge of petulance, asking some
question in the hall. There was an interval while he went
to refresh himself; then a whisper of silk in the passage, the
door was thrown open, and a monsignor in purple bowed
into the room a very imposing figure.

At sixty, Henry's natural heaviness of build had turned
to stoutness which was emphasised by his robes. His red silk
cassock was buttoned to his feet, with a lengthy train and
close-fitting sleeves; over it he wore a rochet of fine white
linen edged with cut-work, and above that the tabard-
shaped chimere, furred with royal ermine. A hood with a
deep full cape lay on his shoulders, and a scarlet zucchetta
sat upon his own dark, curling hair that showed no trace of
grey.

He extended his hand that she might kiss his ring, and
said in Italian, coldly formal:

"Madame my cousin, I am happy to make your acquaintance. I trust you have had a comfortable journey, and that
you bring me good news of my royal brother."

She answered as formally. The thawing of such ice was
not to be hurried. She still found it difficult to carry on a
conversation in Italian, and this added to the uneasiness of
this uneasy meeting, but Henry was not going to help her
by speaking French. She tried a few words of English, and
was met with a blank stare; evidently his Royal Eminence
had forgotten the language of his rightful country. After a
few courtesies, he begged leave to see whether his baggage
had been arranged according to his orders, and presently
she could hear his voice issuing commands and asking questions.

"The legs of my travelling bed are to be placed in vases
of water; by this means all communication will be cut off
between my person and those insects which infest the bed-
chambers of even the best of inns. . . . Place my jewel casette
here beside the bed. . . . Pour not more than five drops of

the vitriolic acid into this drinking water; it will cause the noxious particles to deposit themselves at the bottom. . . . Has sugar been burnt in every room to clear the air? . . . Cesarini, where is my *sac-de-nuit*? It contains sugar, lemons, and brandy for making punch. A tumbler of hot punch is a necessity in rooms never sufficiently aired. . . ."

At supper he kept interrupting himself in his stilted conversation with Charlotte, to issue some fresh order or to make a reprimand.

"Bring the silver box with my corkscrew; many a bottle of good wine has been spoiled for want of a proper screw. . . . That salad is to be washed and made up under my own eyes. . . . Put these chicken-legs back on the gridiron; they are not done enough. . . . I forgot to bring my marrow-spoon; no, I will not have any of theirs, which will sure to be of pewter. . . . This salt is not as white as it should be; if you scatter some upon a hot shovel, you will find it grows fairer. . . . I said expressly that I desired a cream jelly of chocolate, *not* of coffee, with some burnt almonds. . . ."

She listened and observed; and presently realised that a great deal of this old-maidishness was sheer nerves. And when Charlotte had realised that, all her own nervousness left her.

Alone with her after supper in the room he had chosen for his parlour, his uneasiness became pitiable. He fussed over coffee; he not only brought his own with him but always made it himself, he explained. She saw his hand tremble a little as he spooned it from a silver jar. Suddenly she longed to go to him, put her arms round him, and soothe him as though he were a frightened and difficult child.

"I have to thank you, Madame my cousin," said Henry, "for your services and—er—your dutiful behaviour towards my royal brother, which is the more creditable since he neglected you all your youth. I am afraid that you must find him somewhat trying at times. The old," he added, comfortably referring to Charles's five years' seniority, "are apt to be full of whims."

"I remember," replied Charlotte, "what Sir Thomas More once wrote, Royal Eminence. That old age not only brings sickness, but is a sickness in itself. I thank God that I have been given the privilege of being with my father in this the last of his many trials."

Henry gave her a sharp glance. Was she daring to rebuke him? He said stiffly:

"If my brother would only seek comfort in his religion, the religion he bartered for a mess of pottage. Ah, for how many years have I prayed for his conversion, but all in vain."

"My father performed his Easter duties this year just before we set out for Pisa," Charlotte observed tranquilly.

He dropped his coffee spoon.

"You persuaded him?"

"No, Royal Eminence. He went of his own accord. He was happy, you see, and when we are happy it is natural, isn't it, that we should want to thank God?"

Henry opened his lips to speak, and closed them again. There was silence for a moment. She had bent to pick up the coffee spoon, and as she leaned across to place it on his saucer, she looked full into his eyes.

"He lacks only one thing to set the crown upon his happiness. A reconciliation with your Royal Eminence. He longs for it greatly, I know. Oh!" she cried, clasping her hands in simple supplication, "there isn't *time* now for anything but love!"

"You mean that my royal brother has not long to live?" he asked. His voice was a little hoarse, for he had found himself greatly moved by that last sentence.

She did not answer directly, but continued to look straight at him with her large hazel eyes that were so like her father's.

"There is a secret which I have disclosed to no one. I beg most earnestly that I may speak of it now to your Royal Eminence as under the seal of confession, for my father must not know."

He shied like a nervous horse. To him, women's secrets were always of one nature. But he could not refuse.

"I desire to confide this secret to your Royal Eminence," went on the steady voice, "for two reasons. First, because in your public Protest issued soon after my arrival in Florence, and in many of your letters, you have intimated that in the titles bestowed on me by my royal father there is a denial of your Royal Eminence's just right of succession to his regal claims. This fear my secret will remove."

"It is true there were certain circumstances attending your—er—legitimation that were offensive to me, but . . ."

He broke off. He had spoken hurriedly, almost apologetically. She had thrown all his thoughts into confusion.

"And secondly, Royal Eminence, because you are a priest and my near relation. Even though you will not acknowledge me as your niece, I think you cannot refuse to help your brother's only child to prepare herself for death."

"Death!" he echoed, stunned.

"I have inherited the cancer of the liver which caused the death of your Royal Eminence's grandmother. At the most I have four years to live."

He rose and took a hasty turn or two about the room, murmuring conventional expressions of distress.

He had been deceived by Louise, and because of it he distrusted all women, suspected them of play-acting. His proud and rigid nature had been outraged by the legitimation of this offspring of sin; and his impatience of contradiction, his touchiness on the subject of the royal claims he had forfeited in youth to become a Prince of the Church, and his old jealousy of his brother, all had combined to make him hostile to Charlotte. Even now these things warred with his natural pity, and with his experience as a priest which told him plainly that here was no play-acting, that Charlotte was good and simple with a goodness and simplicity he had seldom encountered.

He halted in front of her, but before he could speak, she continued:

281

"My illness has increased since I came to Florence, though I take great pains to conceal it from my father, and I am sure he suspects nothing. I cannot be sure I shall outlive him. It is principally for this reason that I have troubled your Royal Eminence so often with my pleas for your recognition of me as your niece. If you would grant this request, my father and I could move to Rome, where you yourself would be with him at his end, which cannot be long delayed. But he would not go to Rome, he would not even consent to see you, unless you granted me this. To think of my dying before him, of leaving him in Florence, alone as I found him in that melancholy palace, with only servants to look after him, sitting by himself in his room he has hung with tartan and filled with his sad memories, haunted by nightmares—oh, it breaks my heart!"

She had conquered. The last of his defences were swept away. He went to her, and stooping put his arm about her. She looked up and smiled through her tears, and begged his pardon for distressing him with her distress; and in that smile and in that voice he saw and heard the brother he had always loved, even against his will.

"My poor dear child," he murmured. And then, in deliberate surrender: "My dear niece."

# FOUR

## *I*

VERY slowly, by easy stages, Charles Edward Stuart progressed on what he knew would be his last journey. Strange irony of fate that it should be to Rome.

It was December. Immediately on Charlotte's return from Perugia he had suffered another seizure, and had been obliged to keep to his bed for six weeks. Pain and weakness made him difficult. He wanted to go to Rome, in fact could talk of nothing else; he yearned to be with his brother, now that Henry had recognised Charlotte. But there was the old question of the Pope's refusal to admit his regal rights. Charlotte's loving tact had prevailed in the end. He wrote in an almost illegible hand to Henry that he had decided to preserve a strict incognito when he came to Rome, and to be known as the Count of Albany. Thus he would preserve his dignity as a free Sovereign.

He did not talk much on that slow journey. The last time he had driven along these roads Louise, his young bride, had been beside him, and his hopes had been fixed on an heir. Those hopes had gone the way of all the others; he had nothing left now but the love of brother and child. Charlotte too was lost in her thoughts. It was strange indeed to be travelling with her father to Rome as a royal princess, to the city where, thirteen years before, she had suffered such bitter humiliation with her mother, and which she had left with the threats of a furious Henry ringing in her ears.

And here at Viterbo was Henry himself to meet the travellers, to assure his brother that he himself had super-intended the proper refurnishing of the Palazzo Muti, to greet Charlotte with real warmth, embracing her as his royal niece.

"Oh how much cause we have for rejoicing!" he whispered to her. "The Prodigal has turned his back upon the swine and comes home after, alas, so many years of riotous living."

She smiled rather dryly. The stay-at-home brother in the parable had always seemed to her so second-rate, but no doubt he had had his point of view. There was no time to judge others; no time for anything but love.

Charles himself had the same thought. Ignorant of the mortal illness she so gallantly concealed, he concentrated all his remaining strength on giving parties and entertain-ments in honour of Pouponne, insisting on accompanying her to the theatre, though he was so weak that he had to have two boxes thrown into one so that he could recline on a couch. Neglected and humiliated, he for forty years and she for more than twenty, suddenly no one could do enough for them. Pius VI granted Charles the use of the Royal Tribune in St Peter's, repainted and refurnished the Palazzo Savelli at Albano close to His Holiness's own country palace of Castelgandolfo, to accommodate the old King and his daughter during the summer months, and made no protest when Charles exercised the kingly office of touching for the Evil there. Distinguished visitors called every day at the Muti, and Roman society jostled for the honour of being presented.

It was all very pleasant; yet there were wounds in Charles's heart it was plain had never healed. A certain Comte de Vaudreuil asked to kiss his hand; the name meant nothing to Charles, but when he saw this gentleman, who bore so striking a resemblance to the elder Vaudreuil, he who had been in charge of that disgraceful arrest at the Paris Opera House forty years previously, the old King fell down in a fit.

Pouponne was there to comfort and tend him. She was there to rush to his aid when another visitor, an Englishman, tactlessly drew him on to speak of the Forty-Five; and the vivid memories of Derby and Culloden, of the butcheries of Cumberland, brought on fresh convulsions. Hope, too, attacked him like an enemy, and forgetting that his brother would inherit his shadowy throne, he would talk to Pouponne as though she were his Heir Apparent.

"This Lowland poet, Robert Burns, has written verses in your honour, Pouponne. '*The Bonnie Lass of Albany.*' Scotland, Highland and Lowland, will recognise you as their Queen when I am dead. You must distribute medals; I have drawn up some designs, and like this one the best."

And he showed her a sketch which depicted her pointing to the Royal Arms, with her eyes on an empty throne; on the reverse a ship drew near to the coast of England in a storm, with the motto, *'Pendet Salus Spe Exigua et Extrema'*—'Salvation depends upon one small last hope.'

But as 1787 drew towards its close, she noticed a change in him.

He had always taken an intense interest in world events. Now when she read to him the English and French newspapers, he commented absently or not at all. Ireland, encouraged by the success of the American Colonists, was threatening insurrection; England's Royal Family, in the persons of Farmer George, his rapacious wife, and a wildly extravagant Prince of Wales said to be married to the Papist Mrs Fitzherbert, had never been more unpopular. The impeachment of Warren Hastings, scapegoat for the Government's misdeeds in India, echoed across the Channel, as did rumours of the King's madness. In France a national madness was boiling up to revolution.

But to Charles Stuart, approaching his sixty-seventh birthday, it all meant as little now as the cheerful din of the Carnival outside the windows of his quiet little palace in the heart of Rome.

One of the most precious comforts Pouponne had given him was her intense interest in the superb adventure of the Forty-Five. Snubbed for so many years, it had been a miracle to him that she was as avid to hear as he was to tell that old story. But now Pouponne herself had grown shadowy, less real sometimes than the ghosts who mingled with the visitors in his crowded drawing-rooms. Often he would speak aloud to them, muttering of old plans and enterprises, warning dead adherents against dead spies.

Once again he was listening for a call. Each day he inspected his pistols, each night made sure that his strong-box containing the money to transport him home was safe beneath his bed. Noticing how often he smiled in his sleep, Charlotte realised that his dreams were happy at last. He smiled as though he smelt the heather, or heard the music and the poetry of that race in whose hearts he would reign until the end of time.

The new year came in. It was the centenary of the Revolution that had driven Charles's grandfather from the throne. A more awful anniversary was approaching, January 30th, the date of his great-grandfather's execution. And as the bitter cold days passed, the shadow of death darkened over the Palazzo Muti.

Henry became busy with solemn preparations. He was determined that his brother should be buried with full royal honours, and this could be done in his own cathedral at Frascati, where he had a free hand. And now that he was soon to become Henry IX, he was a prey to superstitious fears lest Charles should die on the 30th, that date of ill omen; it would dishearten all those who were prepared to acknowledge his own claim.

Just after Christmas, Charlotte had been stricken down with smallpox, and her recovery was retarded by her grief in being unable to tend her sinking father. A dozen times a day she sent to enquire after him; always the message came back that he would do very well so long as he knew that she was being patient and doing what her doctors told her.

Very early in the morning of January 30th, she could bear it no more. All night long she had felt his need of her like a living presence in the room. She summoned her women; they must assist her to her father's bedchamber. In the anteroom, luminous with the snowlight from the unshuttered window, she turned faint with fear, as a figure, hooded and habited, came gliding soundlessly on bare feet towards her. Then she saw it was the Irish Franciscan, Michael McCormick, her father's confessor.

"No, Madame," whispered the priest, in answer to her unspoken question, "his Majesty still lives. He has received Viaticum with every testimony of faith. . . . But I think there is still something he desires."

There were figures kneeling round the great bed. Iain Beag's voice lamented in Gaelic. The eyes of the dying man opened as she flung herself on her knees beside him; those eyes were glazing, but there was full recognition in them, and something of the old vitality in his voice as he spoke for the last time.

"I was waiting for you, my darling. I wanted to tell you that I think Teàrlach's story has a happy ending after all."

The bed in which he lay had changed into a ship, a gallant little ship with all her canvas spread; and where the canopy had been just now was only sky, iridescent as the inside of a shell, a-gleam with soft colour. The horizon was bounded by familiar hills, over which drifted slate-blue clouds as though the mountains smoked; and smudged over all, infernal in its beauty, brooded one dark cloud-feather lined with flame.

His soul was wrapped in utter peace. He remembered one thing only: the goal which had tormented him all his life, always just out of reach. But now it was greater than the goal for which he had striven; it was the pearl of great price, and it contained in its great white heart all he had ever loved and hoped and suffered for. It was the Cause, it was Scotland, it was Pouponne . . . it was God. . . .

Across the immensity of the sky above him a single bird came flying strongly. An eagle, he thought, groping after memories bitter-sweet. Steady and purposeful it flew towards those distant hills; it was homeward bound, and knew its way. He too must go homeward, but the ship which had been bearing him had vanished. He was alone except for the winged creature, his guide.

All his remaining strength was concentrated in one supreme last effort. With a wrench that tore him free from earth, his soul leaped upwards, found wings, and was free.

# AUTHOR'S NOTE

All the characters in this story were once living persons, and wherever possible I have allowed them to speak for themselves by the use I have made of their letters, memoirs, journals, and in the case of Alfieri, of his autobiography.

On the invasion of Italy by Napoleon in 1798, Henry was obliged to flee from Rome, where the Cancellaria, and also his palace at Frascati, were sacked by Berthier's troops. After many weary wanderings, the old Cardinal returned to Rome in 1801, and died at his beloved Frascati six years later.

Of Clementina's last days very little is known. She died at Fribourg in Switzerland in 1802, in extreme poverty despite the fact that she had been left an annuity by Charles and 15,000 lire a year by their daughter. All she herself had to leave were twelve pounds, six silver spoons, and a geographical dictionary. She bequeathed a louis apiece to her relatives in Scotland 'should any of them still remain', but no one came forward to claim this pathetic bequest.

Psipsio and Psipsia never married. The French pension Louise enjoyed as the widow of the King *de jure* would hardly have been continued to the wife of a Piedmontese count. On the death of Alfieri in 1803, she lived openly with the artist Fabre, of whom Psipsio had long been jealous and who was fourteen years her junior, until her own death in 1823.

Charlotte Stuart, Duchess of Albany, survived her father only twenty-two months. After an unsuccessful operation for cancer, she died at Bologna on November 17th, 1789, and was buried in the church of San Biagio there. In 1797 this church was destroyed by the French, and it is not known for certain whether the remains of Pouponne were ever reinterred.